First there was *Jurassic Park*

Then came *Cretaceous Stones*

Followed by *Dragons of the Great Divide*

And now both humans and dinosaurs have become *Endangered Species* . . .

For fans of Michael Crichton, Andy Weir, and James Rollins

Endangered Species: The electrifying Book 3 conclusion of the Cretaceous Chronicles trilogy.

Praise for the Cretaceous Chronicles series

In his Cretaceous Chronicles trilogy, Jeff Dennis displays a talent for deftly juggling a large cast of characters—each one sharply drawn—whilst keeping the narrative charging ahead like a herd of frightened brontosaurs. His work is so impeccably researched, you'll wonder if he's been everything from a helicopter pilot to a paleontologist, though the fine details and immersive setting never get in the way of the thoroughly engaging plot.

Highly recommended.

— Jeffrey Thomas, author of *Punktown*

What readers are saying about *Cretaceous Stones* (Book 1)

Like Weir + Crichton

"I love sci fi. I've read every one I can get my hands on. I'm a Crichton fan going back to A Case of Need. I love this book! It was like a mixture of Weir and Crichton. I don't want to give too many details because it's a fun ride, but the mix of space and dino thriller is awesome. I'm definitely going to read more of this author. Highly recommend!" . . . **eBook reader**

"I picked up *Cretaceous Stones* on a whim and ended up losing sleep over it in a good way. The whole meteorites carrying dinosaur eggs idea sounds crazy, but Jeff Dennis sells it. Once things start going wrong, they really go wrong. It's tense, chaotic, and honestly kind of addictive." . . . **Alba Wolfgang**

Dinosaurs, Meteorites, and One Heck of a Family

"What would you do if a meteorite landed on your ranch — and something hatched from it? That's the wild ride Jeff Dennis drops you into right from page one of *Cretaceous Stones*, and I have to tell you, I was hooked before the first chapter was done. The story follows a Montana ranching family, the Gilliams, whose lives get turned completely upside down when prehistoric creatures start showing up on their property. What I loved is that Dennis doesn't just write a monster story. He writes a story about people under pressure — a husband and wife trying to protect their kids, hold their marriage together, and survive a situation nobody could have prepared for. It felt real. The kind of real that keeps you reading at midnight when you swore you'd stop two chapters ago. The pacing is tight, the characters have actual depth, and the Montana setting is so vivid you can practically smell the pine. If you like thrillers with a sci-fi twist and characters you genuinely root for, this one delivers. Highly recommend.". . . **Barbara R**

Sci fi masterpiece!

"I am a huge Michael Crichton fan and I was a bit skeptical when I started this book. But man oh man I was wrong . . . The characters and world building are excellent, there's action and drama and even a tiny bit of romance! Overall 10/10 read! Can't wait to read everything this author has ever written!" . . . **Jacob Ray**

A suspenseful sci-fi thriller

"Think of a thriller on par with *Jurassic Park* - the science with the latest in dinosaur knowledge coupled with scenes of prehistoric terror and you have something akin to this book. A non-stop thrill ride where beasts from the distant past become a very real nightmare in the present." . . . **Nero Phillips**

Everyone must read *Cretaceous Stones*

"I loved *Cretaceous Stones* and highly recommend it. I was captivated by the story from the first page, and much of the story will stick with me for a while. The book is a reminder of how fragile life is. The author, Jeff Dennis, must have spent hundreds (if not thousands) of hours researching dinosaur behavior, basic human behavior, and wormholes in interstellar space to write something as mind-boggling as *Cretaceous Stones*. This powerful story of fear, science, and opportunity that turns to greed mostly revolves around the reactions of a family, the Gilliams, who experience the reintroduction of dinosaurs from the Cretaceous period (60 million years ago) onto their property through meteor strikes along the Continental Divide. Fantastic job!" . . . **David Shockley**

Futuristic Thrill and Adventure!

"*Cretaceous Stones* is the first book of The Cretaceous Chronicles, a futuristic sci-fi thriller series about dinosaur's return to Earth. To be really honest I thought this was going to be "another Jurassic Park" but I was pleasantly surprised by the author's twist! We know they went out by meteors, but in this book, they come back by meteor. The meteors contain the dinosaurs nests and eggs from the Cretaceous Period. Wow! It takes place along the Continental Divide, in Montana. I enjoyed reading this and would recommend it!". . . **Victoria Fulenwider**

A great thriller!

"If you liked *Jurassic Park*, you should really enjoy this book. The author had my attention in the first chapter. His ability to build the story and activate the imagination is excellent. I could imagine the smells, the noises, the excitement and terror as the story developed! Can't wait to read the next 2 books of the trilogy!". . . **Jos**

Jurassic Park without the park

"Dinosaurs are loose in the wilds of Montana and Idaho. This book has all the excitement and adventure you'd expect, coupled with great characters. The first dinosaur encounter comes quickly in the first couple of chapters, making the reader want to keep turning the pages. The characters are well done. It's the kind of story that has you thinking about the characters when you go to sleep at night, and leaves you wondering what you'll do without these people in your life when the book is finished. A great balance of their personal lives and background and the excitement of the adventure scenes. I definitely want to go back and read the first book in the series and am waiting with bated breath for the next one." . . . **Ina Castillo**

A thrilling prehistoric adventure packed with mystery and danger

"*Cretaceous Stones* is an exciting and imaginative adventure that transports readers into a world where the past feels alive and unpredictable. Jeff Dennis blends prehistoric elements with mystery and action, creating a story that is both engaging and suspenseful. The concept is unique, and the stakes feel high as the characters navigate a dangerous environment filled with ancient secrets.

What's the most enjoyable part of the book is the sense of discovery woven through it. The setting is vivid, and the author does a great job building tension as the story unfolds. The characters are easy to follow, and their journey keeps the momentum going with plenty of twists and challenges along the way.

Recommended for readers who enjoy adventure stories, prehistoric themes, and fast paced plots with a mix of science and imagination. This book is a fun and gripping read that combines mystery and prehistoric intrigue—*Cretaceous Stones* is a great start, or addition, to an exciting series. " . . . **Jade**

What readers are saying about *Dragons of the Great Divide* (Book 2)

Dinosaurs, Danger, and Heart

"A thrilling ride from start to finish. *Dragons of the Great Divide* blends pulse-pounding dinosaur encounters with real human emotion—love, fear, ambition, and sacrifice. The characters feel genuine, and the wilderness setting makes the danger feel immediate and raw. It's exciting, immersive, and hard to put down. A fantastic sequel that keeps the adventure roaring." . . . **Michael M.**

Loved it

"Book two was just as good as the first! The action and adventure was fun and exciting. Love it." . . . **Jessie Bradford**

Check out if you love dinosaurs

"*Dragons of the Great Divide* was such a fun, wild ride. It's basically like a modern-day *Jurassic Park* set right in the American West. The story picks up after the first book with these paleontologists, Hayden and Nora, trying to survive a Montana landscape that is literally crawling with dinosaurs hatched from meteorites. I really liked how it wasn't just straight action. It has a bit of everything, from romance to this quirky wildlife videographer named Jackson who adds a lot of personality to the chaos. What's impressive is how much is actually going on. It's not just people running away from T-Rexes in the woods. It touches on some darker stuff like human trafficking and greed, which makes the stakes feel way higher. The setting in the River of No Return Wilderness is super intense. If you're into sci-fi thrillers that aren't afraid to get a little gritty and complicated, you should definitely give this one a look." . . . **Emily**

Great Read

"The story throws you back into a modern West stalked by T. rex and other Cretaceous predators, while authors Hayden and Nora chase new material, a daring pilot risks everything, and a ruthless trafficker turns dinosaurs into deadly business. Especially liked how the book balances high stakes action with very human problems: marriage stress, family worries, missing Indigenous women, and the price of greed and fame. It is a quick, engaging read that feels like a movie, but still cares deeply about friendship, love, and courage in the face of danger." . . . **Cass Spooner**

Dragons of the Great Divide

"*Dragons of the Great Divide* by Jeff Dennis delivers an exciting prehistoric adventure that blends science with imagination, bringing the age of dinosaurs vividly to life. With fast-paced action and richly described creatures, the story pulls readers into a thrilling world where survival, discovery, and wonder collide." ... **Ronnie Lee**

A Dinosaur Adventure with Heart and High Stakes

"*Dragons of the Great Divide* (The Cretaceous Chronicles) is a fast-paced adventure that imagines a modern world suddenly sharing space with dinosaurs. The story mixes thrilling encounters with plenty of human drama, following researchers, pilots, and explorers who are drawn into the danger for different reasons. The characters feel real, with relationships, fears, and ambitions that add depth beyond the action. Between helicopter missions, mysterious disappearances, and close calls with massive prehistoric creatures, the tension rarely lets up. In the end, it's an exciting, imaginative read that blends sci-fi thrills with stories about courage, loyalty, and the risks people take when curiosity and ambition collide." . . . **Melanie Pendleton**

Not just a science fiction thriller

"Wow, what an insane ride start to finish. *Dragons of the Great Divide* is more than just a science fiction thriller. It has a complexity of human nature/condition that gets you quickly invested into the characters leaving you rooting for them in the face of adversity. From greed, vanity, deception, love and obligation leaves you reeling. It's a fast paced adventure with just the right amount of danger, mystery, twists and turns great for your imagination." . . . **Mary W.S.**

Now I'm Going to Have to Read the First One

"I picked up this book not realizing it was the second in a series. Dinosaurs come to Earth in a hail of meteorites - got to love that, since it has long been theorized that a great meteor was what caused their extinction event in the first place. :-) This book follows Jackson Lattimer, an adrenaline-loving videographer as he heads into the mountains to film the resurrected T-Rexs. What could go wrong; right? This one was a page turner, with the feel of Crichton's *Jurassic Park*. Even though it's second in the series, it's an easy standalone read. But it definitely made me want to read the first one now." . . . **Beaches and Reads**

ENDANGERED SPECIES

Jeff Dennis

Nightbird Publishing

By Jeff Dennis:

Cretaceous Chronicles:

Cretaceous Stones (2022)
Dragons of the Great Divide (2024)
Endangered Species (2026)

Hobo Duology:

King of the Hobos (2012)
Hobo Jingo (2017)

Standalone Fiction:

The Wisdom of Loons (2009)
Daydreams and Night Screams (2013)
To Touch Infinity (2015)

ENDANGERED SPECIES

Book 3 of the Cretaceous Chronicles

JEFF DENNIS

This is a work of fiction. The events described are imaginary. The characters and settings are fictitious. Any references to real persons or places are included only to lend authenticity to the story.

ENDANGERED SPECIES

FIRST EDITION

Cover illustration: Raúl Martin
Cover & title page design: Carole Maugé-Lewis

Print: 978-0-9911871-9-5
eBook: 979-8-2332504-6-0

Loganville, Georgia

jeffdennisauthor.com
jeff@jeffdennisauthor.com

First Printing: May 19, 2026

10 9 8 7 6 5 4 3 2 1

Endangered Species is dedicated to my loyal readers who have supported me through the first two books of the Cretaceous Chronicles trilogy. Thank you, fellow dino lovers.

"Look closely at nature. Every species is a masterpiece, exquisitely adapted to the particular environment in which it has survived. Who are we to destroy or even diminish biodiversity?"

– EO Wilson, world renowned biologist and multiple Pulitzer Prize winner

---

Grief is not a failure of belief;
it is the price we pay for love.

– The Reverend Thomas Caldwell

Heads Up

May 28: Gilliam's Guidepost

Heart Butte, Montana

Two years after the meteorites came down . . .

DEATH ARRIVED IN A STYROFOAM COFFIN.

A severed Tyrannosaurus Rex head sat in the Styrofoam chest on a bed of dry ice. Ribbons of misty vapor swirled from the container like ghostly snakes. FedEx had delivered the alarming package five minutes ago.

Bryan Gilliam circled the dining room table, his eyes riveted on the prehistoric head as he viewed the atrocity from different angles. The beast's marbled eyes set beneath bony ridges seemed to follow him as he moved. The powerful jaws made him shudder. The banana-shaped, serrated teeth reminded him of curved knives. Sticky rust-colored blood glistened in a metallic sheen where the head had been cleaved from the body.

The detached head was horrific enough, but the spread of five mangled photographs spiked on the beast's teeth almost made him lose his lunch.

Five snapshots—one for each member of the Gilliam family.

The familiar photos pegged on those wicked teeth froze Bryan's soul.

His eyes drifted to the pic of himself, leaning on his walking cane, posing in front of one of the barns on their ranch here on the southern edge of the Blackfeet Indian reservation. Another shot of wife Loretta with her hand in a bowl of popcorn during a Gilliam family movie night. A print of nine-year-old daughter Lianne holding her two most precious dolls from her younger years—Lyle the stuffed lion and Patches, her Cabbage Patch doll. Pictures of his two teenage sons: Ethan, decked out in his baseball uniform and Paul playing guitar and singing into a microphone onstage at a high school dance.

Bryan and Loretta had taken these photographs recently. They resided on the family photo album site, a highly secure private network braced by impenetrable firewall security and accessible only by family.

Someone has breached our digital platform.

He was furious. Also rattled. The invasion of privacy brought back old fears that had only just begun to dissipate.

Over the past two years the Gilliams had found themselves obtaining a level of celebrity that attracted the kooks and crazies of the world. The stalker types who wanted to rub shoulders with luminaries, the desperate souls who wanted to grab a little fame of their own. Outsiders who wanted to be on the inside. The national spotlight had shone on the Gilliam family, and the glare got to be too much. So they had circled the wagons and closed down communications with the outside world. Kept everything on their 1,285-acre homestead as best they could. They were not to talk to the press or share their cell phone numbers with anyone they didn't know. All members of the Gilliam clan were aware of the situation and respected their need for privacy.

Even his teenage boys, Paul and Ethan, with their frequent activity on social media, understood.

But is it possible one of them slipped up?

Well, oldest son, eighteen-year-old Paul, had recently been leveraging the Gilliam fame to promote his rock band, Moonrise. But the boy knew where to draw the line between personal and business when doing media events. No, Bryan really couldn't see any reason why Paul or Ethan would put these particular pics out there for the world to see. Logical thinking held that someone had hacked into the Gilliam online scrapbook.

He checked the sender label on the lid: Western Adventures, with a PO box. Missoula, Montana 59802.

Western Adventures, my ass! he thought, flinging the Styrofoam lid to the floor.

He shuddered as he perused Lianne's photo. Whoever had done this had positioned his daughter's photo so that a pair of T-Rex teeth punctured her neck. Likewise a jagged tooth pierced Ethan's eye in his pic.

Those placements have to be deliberate. Bryan felt a hot anger rise in his throat. Threats against him and Loretta were one thing, but going after his children was an abomination.

Here we go again, he thought. Their lives had been under threat much of the time since that cursed meteorite struck their east pasture two years ago to the day. That immense charred extraterrestrial boulder hatched out those damned Dromaeosaurs and had altered their way of life forever.

We've paid the ultimate price for being the first humans to come in contact with dinosaurs.

Bryan often reflected on how much different their lives would be if that meteorite hadn't hit their property.

But his thoughts were now focused on who might be behind this decapitation debacle.

He cycled through possible perpetrators. The prime suspect was Leonard Sheridan, leader of the Animal Emancipation Faction (AEF), a powerful radical animal rights group known to be a domestic terrorist organization. Bryan and Loretta had recently brought a criminal lawsuit against Sheridan for his part in the complete destruction of Gilliam's Guidepost two summers ago. The Gilliams had already won a settlement of ten million dollars from the organization in their civil suit. Now, at the urging of their attorney—Atlee Pinnaker—they were going after Sheridan personally. Sheridan was currently incarcerated at Montana State Prison in Deer Lodge, but Bryan knew full well that inmates could still run their crime syndicates from their cells.

Another prime possibility was Thomas "Hoops" Terrell, a ranch hand whom Bryan—and private investigator Mike Mathews—had tracked down and helped convict in last year's kidnapping/murder of Indigenous women that involved the Blackfoot wife of one of

Bryan's longtime hired hands. Terrell was also serving time in Montana State Prison without bail awaiting his first trial date, which had been postponed twice since last August.

A third suspect was Kelton Rendaya, disgraced equine veterinarian who was convicted of illegal animal trafficking last year. Bryan had worked with PI Mathews to locate Rendaya's dinosaur habitats and lead authorities to the dino holding pens, sealing the conviction. Rendaya had been hit with just a slap-on-the-wrist fine and two years' probation on multiple trafficking charges, but the FBI later nailed him for the murders of two North Dakota state troopers. He was also doing hard time at Montana State Prison and would definitely have an ax to grind with the Gilliams.

There were also any number of AEF sympathizers who could have sent this ominous package. Many staunch animal rights activists sided with the AEF after the deadly shootout at Gilliam's Guidepost two summers ago where several AEF stormtrooper gunmen were killed. An outpouring of sympathy went to AEF even though they invaded Gilliam's Guidepost, setting free the dinosaurs, murdering partygoers, nearly killing Bryan, and burning all buildings on the Gilliam ranch to the ground. The sympathetic response was due largely to the misdirected and erroneous notion that Bryan and family tortured and abused the dinosaurs at their government sponsored research sanctuary.

Why are so many people influenced by misinformation and propaganda? Ah, the ills of social media.

It was a question Bryan had grappled with for years, ever since he'd naively bought the patriotic line of bullshit the government had slung that resulted in him doing two tours of duty in Afghanistan.

"Oh my god! What is this?"

Bryan turned to see Loretta standing behind him. She gawked in disbelief, her face tense as her eyes scanned the gruesome display in the Styrofoam container.

"It's a housewarming gift from one of our deranged fans."

"Not funny, Bry," she said, wrapping her arms around his waist from behind. "That is some serious shit, right there."

"Indeed it is," he sighed, turning and pulling her close.

Loretta took a step back and looked at him, worry tightening her face. "This is a police matter, hon. We've got to call this in right away."

"For sure," he said, thinking. "But first I'm gonna give Mike Mathews a call. Mike's more thorough than the police. He performed a miracle in finding Kanti last summer."

"He did, but you helped him a great deal."

"True. And I'll do what I can to help him this time, Lor." Bryan tilted his chin at the Styrofoam container with its bizarre cargo. "Mike and I will find whoever sent this. We make a great team."

Loretta stared at the impaled photos of their family. "There is a very implicit threat here, Bryan. I worry about you getting involved in this. I don't want you playing detective again," she said, referring to his assisting authorities with Kanti Lyttle's abduction case last summer.

Bryan kissed her on the cheek. "No worries, babe. Mathews will do the up-close work. I'll just provide him the leads."

They stood there, arms around each other, eyes on the bloody spectacle sitting atop the dry ice. Long moments passed in silence.

Finally Loretta said. "The kids can't see this, dear."

He nodded. "I know. Help me lug this mess out to the barn."

"You don't wanna pull the pictures and bury the head in the woods?"

"No. It's evidence. Like you said, it's a police matter. And we shouldn't touch the photos. There are probably fingerprints all over them."

"You're a regular Sherlock Holmes, aren't you, dear hubby of mine."

"It's all elementary, my dear Watson."

Loretta gave him a weak smile, but it vanished quickly. "I'm scared, Bryan."

"Me, too, Lor. Me, too. But we'll get to the bottom of this."

Nessie Lives

May 28: Tally Lake

Flathead National Forest, Montana

HAYDEN FOWLER EYED THE NARROW pebbled beach below.

Midafternoon and still no visitors.

No action whatsoever.

He and Idaho federal wildlife biologist Bill Carlton had been perched high up in the branches of this towering western larch for three hours watching, waiting, observing the bait pile below. Hayden figured the ten pounds of raw prime rib and five pounds of fresh pig shank should be enough of a delectable meal to entice a hungry Tyrannosaur.

"I'm beginning to think this is a huge waste of time," he heard Carlton say.

Hayden looked through the crosshatched tangle of limbs at Carlton. "Oh, ye of little faith."

"Let's face it, Hayden. We haven't even seen a squirrel or a rabbit, let alone a carnivore."

Hayden wasn't about to give up. He just *knew* there were T-Rexes nearby. He could feel it, could smell them in the mossy-pine-scented air. After all, he was the *dinosaur diviner*, a title Nora had bestowed on him. She'd told him he had a special talent for knowing where the beasts roamed, calling what he did *dowsing for dinosaurs*. At first it had been a tongue-in-cheek witticism, an intimate joke they shared. But after two years of successfully rooting out the dinos, Hayden and Nora both acknowledged that maybe Hayden did possess a dinosaur-locating superpower.

"Just be patient, Bill. They're here, I'm telling you. I'm rarely wrong. You'll see."

Carlton sighed and checked his tranquilizer rifle for the umpteenth time. "Oh, I'm not doubting you," he said, "I just don't put much faith in tips from hunters. I can't begin to count the number of times huntsmen have led me on wild goose chases."

Hayden thought about what had brought them to this scenic, remote lake in the heart of the Flathead National Forest, twenty miles west of Whitefish. He had received several calls from big-game hunters who reported spotting Tyrannosaurs drinking from Tally Lake shallows a few days ago. It was the first reported sightings of the spring and he had been excited by the news. He'd called Carlton and invited him on this T-Rex tagging session, which was a restart of Hayden's dinosaur migration study he'd begun last year.

This getaway was a welcome relief for him after a long frigid winter suffering through cabin fever at home in Eden Prairie, Minnesota. These wide open Montana spaces, big sky, and warm weather worked on him like a liberating balm. This is what he needed, to be out doing fieldwork again.

He'd spent the harsh winter months working with Nora on their second co-authored book, cooped up in their Minnesota home. There was immense pressure on them to repeat the huge bestselling success of their first book, *Cretaceous Stones: The Return of Prehistoric Life to Earth*, which documented their critical part in tracking dinosaurs that had hatched out of the cluster of meteorites that peppered eastern Idaho and western Montana along the Continental Divide just two short years ago. While both he and Nora Lemoyne were well known for their paleontology credentials, the book escalated them into the stratosphere of international celebrity.

This work went on while he recuperated from serious injuries incurred after last August's helicopter crash in Idaho's River of No Return wilderness area. The crash had left Hayden clinging to life. He'd lost a kidney and suffered cracked ribs, serious liver damage, head trauma, and nearly fatal internal hemorrhaging that put him in a coma for four days. Bill Carlton had been on that doomed flight and had also survived, as had Peter Lacroix, the pilot. Three others died, including Hayden's good friend, Jackson Lattimer, celebrated wildlife videographer/documentarian. Hayden and Carlton both knew how lucky they were to still be walking, talking, and breathing.

Hayden did his best not to relive that disastrous crash. But it was always there in the back of his mind, taunting him. And having to recreate the experience in written form didn't help his frame of mind.

But being back out here doing his thing, searching for T-Rexes and other prehistoric carnivores, made it a lot easier to dim those nightmarish memories.

But just where are those Tyrannosaurs?

A sliver of doubt began to creep in. Three hours jammed into this fork of rough-barked branches in a treetop overlooking the deserted lake and no results?

The experience also brought back visions of tagging T-Rexes with Jackson Lattimer at Willow Pond in Wyoming last summer, a much more successful trip than this outing was proving to be. He remembered watching Jackson run helter-skelter through the woods with Tyrannosaur hatchlings chasing him. That pond had been a popular T-Rex gathering place/watering hole. Not so, apparently, this lake that stretched out below them, a tannin-hued mirror reflecting the majestic Salish Mountains and Canyon Creek Ridge. To the southeast loomed the snow-capped peaks of Ashley Mountain.

Hayden's six-foot-four frame wasn't taking to this treetop perch very well. His lower back hurt. His legs stung and burned, like they were pierced with hot acupuncture needles. The sun's glare off the lake had given him a splitting headache and he felt queasy. He didn't have near the strength or stamina he had a year ago. The crash had depleted him.

Nora didn't want him to make this trip due to his health issues but he insisted on it, telling her it would work wonders for his mental and emotional state. And Nora, tired of his moping about the house and worried about his obvious depression, finally gave in, making him promise that he would call her daily. She didn't want to suffer again like she did last year when he went incommunicado in Idaho post helicopter crash. Nora hadn't known for more than a week if he was dead or alive.

A vision of Nora floated through his mind's eye. Hayden wondered what she was doing at this moment. He'd been gone less than 24 hours and he already missed her. He considered Nora Lemoyne to be his better half, something he could never claim about any of his three ex-wives. Nora was his lover, best friend and confidant, fellow paleontologist and dinosaur tracker, co-author of two books with him.

He smiled thinking about her and wanted to hear her voice. Just as he reached for his satellite phone in his belt holster, it buzzed, startling him. He pulled it out, checked the display.

"It's Gilliam," he told Carlton.

He connected. "Hey, Bryan. Problems at headquarters?" he said, referring to the helicopter air strip built on Gilliam's Guidepost last year as home base for his and Nora's company, Fowler-Lemoyne Aviation.

"Nothing wrong at the heliport, Hayden. Things are going swimmingly here. Contractors finished installing the underground fuel pumps. The two new helicopters were delivered three weeks ago. You should see them, Hayden. They're real beauties. Also Pete just hired two pilots. We'll be back in business real soon. Hopefully next week."

Hayden knew Gilliam would deliver, that he would make an excellent general manager. "That's great to hear, Gill."

"Yeah, things are proceeding nicely. Where are you? Still in Minnesota?"

"No. I'm in your neck of the woods. Sitting in a tree on Tally Lake in the Flathead wilderness area."

"Where is that?"

"Probably a hundred and fifty miles west of you. It's beautiful out here. Deserted. A real ghost lake. No people around. Just the way I like it."

"What're you doin' there?"

"Tracking Rexes."

"Back at it, huh. Any luck?"

"Not yet. This is our first day out."

"Is Nora with you?"

"No. She stayed home this trip. She's handling the final edits on our new book. The publisher isn't real happy with us since we were four months late delivering the manuscript. I'm here with Carlton."

"Bill?"

"Yeah, the one and only."

"How's he been?"

Hayden looked at Carlton, caught him yawning. "Bored out of his gourd."

Carlton rolled his eyes at him.

"Give him my best, would ya?" Bryan said.

"Will do. Uh, why'd you call me, Gilliam? Surely it wasn't just to shoot the shit."

"No . . . I have, um—I mean *we* have a situation here you should know about. I think you'll be interested."

Hayden didn't like the sound of it. "Try me."

Bryan Gilliam proceeded to fill Hayden in on the details of the severed T-Rex head and the threat against his family.

"Did you call the police?" Hayden asked, thinking about the new helicopters and the expensive aviation gear sitting in the hangar at Gilliam's Guidepost.

"No. I've got a call in to a private investigator. Mike Mathews, the PI who helped us find Kanti Lyttle and Ahwee Red Crow last year. The crazies are back and I intend to find them."

"I'm sorry you're being targeted again, Gill. It's a clusterfuck world for sure. But I think you should contact the authorities. If nothing else to protect our assets there, our hefty investment. And for your own protection. You don't want another invasion of the cuckoos. Of course it's entirely your decision. I'm just saying—"

"Thanks, but we already have 24/7 security in place. The best money can buy—round-the-clock human guards, motion sensor cameras inside and outside the hangar, trail cameras in the woods surrounding the heliport. Rest assured, everything is safe here at the Guidepost. But that's not the reason for my call. I thought you'd be interested in the Tyrannosaur head. It's a fresh kill. It means they're out and about. They're appearing again. Where, I don't know, but I thought you'd like to know, maybe get a jump on them for your tracking study."

"You sure it's a fresh kill?"

"Yeah. The blood is sticky wet. The scales are moist and the hide is elastic."

"That could just be from dry ice condensation."

"I don't think so, Hayden. I'm pretty sure this thing was killed in the last twenty-four hours. At any rate, Loretta and I are keeping it in our walk-in freezer—for evidence and for you to come take a look at it if and when you want to."

"I appreciate it. I definitely want to examine it. But it'll be a few days until I can get out to your place."

"No problem. It'll be here for you. Lor and I look forward to seeing you."

Suddenly the thrashing of a large animal crashing through the woods to their right echoed across the lake.

Carlton jerked to attention.

Hayden said to Bryan, "Gotta run. We've got a development here."

Excitement spiked his pulse. He disconnected and shoved the sat phone back in the holster.

A huge grizzly bear burst out of the woods about a hundred yards down the shoreline and trundled onto the narrow beach. Hayden grabbed his videocam from the fanny pack and focused in on the approaching bruin. The grizzly bounded along the shoreline in a loping sprint, headed for the bait mound. The bear pounced on the meat pile, ripping it apart with its sharp, four-inch foreclaws and dug into the delicious treat.

"Wow! That's one big bastard!" he heard Carlton exclaim.

Hayden zoomed in with the camcorder, using a technique Lattimer had taught him to reduce blurring.

The bear sat on its haunches, hunched over, devouring the strips of beef, its dark eyes hyperalert, scanning the surrounding area. Its large black snout glistened wetly in the afternoon sun, sniffing the air for danger, its small rounded ears pivoting independently, listening for sounds of potential trouble.

"Not what we expected but that is one beautiful scary animal," he whisper-spoke to Carlton.

"Yeah, an exquisite creature," Carlton replied quietly, "This is special. You don't see many of 'em in the wild anymore."

Hayden continued to film. "Yeah, quite a rare sighting. Grizzlies are as primordial as dinosaurs in a lot of ways."

And then, quick as a lightning strike, a scaled reptilian creature exploded from out of the lake and attacked the grizzly. Its massive hinged jaws latched onto the bear's hindleg in a vise grip. The bear roared in pain, swiping its rapier claws at the attacker, but the lake creature was too low slung for the distressed bear to land a slash.

"Jesus!" Carlton bellowed. "Is that an alligator?"

"There're no gators in Montana," Hayden said, concentrating on his videotaping. He recognized the heavily armored plates running along the high ridge of its back and the wide mouth filled with large conical, striated teeth. A different build from alligators though similar. "I think this guy might be a great, great, great ancestor of our modern crocodile," he yelled to Carlton over the noise of the attack. "More specifically, the late great Deinosuchus, translated from the Greek to mean *terrible crocodile.*"

They watched in terrified fascination as the aquatic animal Hayden thought to be Deinosuchus clamped onto the bear's mid-section. Blood stained the rocky beach a dark shade of crimson. The grizzly roared one last time before Deinosuchus dragged it down into the water. The crocodilian rolled over, once, twice, three times, clutching its immense meal in its powerful jaws, blood inking the water. The bear screeched out in desperate moans that lessened in volume with each roll to the surface.

And then the Deinosuchus took its prey down into the depths.

Hayden and Carlton stared slack jawed at the bloody whirlpool swirling in ever widening circles, fifteen yards off shore.

Hayden stopped filming and lowered the videocam. "Good Christ almighty! Our crocodilian made mincemeat out of that seven-hundred-pound grizzly. What kind of monster patrols these waters, Bill?"

"Nothing of this day and age, that's for sure."

Hayden was almost certain it was a Deinosuchus, a genus of giant crocodyliform that went extinct 73 million years ago, which was six or seven million years before the Cretaceous-Paleogene extinction event that ended all dinosaurs. He knew they populated riverine and aquatic environments in what is now Montana, Wyoming, and South Dakota.

He felt charged up. Excited. His paleozoological mind racing. This crocodile on steroids wasn't from the same time period as the other dinosaurs they had seen thus far.

Did this mean one or more meteorites hit Tally Lake?

And if this *is* a Deinosuchus, how did that affect the current theories of where the dinosaurs came from?

Are there more than one patrolling these waters?

He said to Bill Carlton, "I believe Tally Lake has its own Loch Ness Monster."

"You might be right," Carlton responded from his perch. "Only this Nessie is much more deadly."

The 12-Step Shuffle

May 29: Narcotics Anonymous Meeting
The Alano Club
Kalispell, Montana

"HI, MY NAME IS PETER AND I'M addicted to oxycodone."

"Hello, Peter," came the boisterous response from the group.

A full house today. A dozen fellow addicts grouped around him, sitting on folding chairs, another half dozen standing along the wall.

Peter Lacroix scanned faces and returned a nervous smile.

He squirmed in his seat, his hands slick with sweat. This was his third meeting and he felt the same jitters he'd experienced his first two weeks.

The meeting facilitator, Barney, an older white-haired man with a snowy goatee and sad eyes added, "We're very glad you're here, Peter. What do you wish to share with us today?"

"Well, I just want to say I made some progress last week."

"Excellent. Tell us about it."

Peter hesitated, fondling his plastic Narcotics Anonymous welcome chip, the blue and black logo shining brightly under the fluorescent lighting. After a long pause he raised his head and spoke to Barney. "Okay, well, I know it doesn't sound like much, but I cut my oxy intake down from 300 milligrams a day to 150."

"Outstanding!" Barney said, nodding enthusiastically. "Good work. That's a pretty drastic reduction. Have you experienced any side effects?"

"Yeah. Some sweating and nausea. Insomnia. Itchy skin."

"Are you working with your doctor on your recovery?"

"No. My doctor is the pill pusher who got me into this mess."

Peter glanced around the circle, at the faces staring at him, then changed his tone. "Well, that's really not a fair assessment. I definitely needed pain medication after my accident. I was in a bad way the first couple of months. But I'm lying to myself thinking I still need the oxy." He looked back at Barney. "To answer your question, no I'm not consulting with my doctor on this. I'm doing it all on my own." He shook his head. "Um, that's not entirely true. My wife is giving me tremendous support as well."

Barney smiled. "That's great. This is a wonderful first step, Peter. Self-deception is the first hurdle we must clear in our battle against addiction. Just be careful you don't come down too fast. Serious withdrawal symptoms can be as bad as the addiction itself. We must be patient and understand that healing doesn't happen overnight. You have taken a step in the right direction and we commend you for that. Don't we, people?"

An affirming chorus of "Yes we do!" and "Absolutely!" arose from the gathering, which gave Peter more confidence.

He said, "I know the stuff is toxic. That I'm poisoning myself. I know I'm distancing myself from my wife and children when I'm under the influence. I want to get out from under it once and for all, but it's so damned hard."

Barney nodded. "We understand, Peter. All of us here can relate. You're on a spiritual journey. The awakening takes time."

Barney continued with his spiritual message, and Peter looked around the circle of attendees, aware that most of them knew who he was. These NA meetings were designed to be anonymous. First name basis only. But that didn't apply here. Peter's recent personal history was splashed all over social media and the internet. They knew he was Peter Lacroix, the helicopter pilot who survived last year's tragic crash in the wilds of Idaho. They knew about the prehistoric flying reptiles, the Quetzalcoatlus, that had brought down the aircraft. They knew he was associated with bestselling author and renowned paleontologist/dinosaur tracker, Hayden Fowler, who had also survived the crash. They were aware that Jackson Lattimer, internationally famous wildlife filmmaker, had died on that ill-fated trip along with two others. Peter's fame had followed him here, and he noticed attendance at this Power of Choice NA meeting had swelled the past two weeks as word had leaked out that a national celebrity was attending.

He had mixed feelings about their familiarity with him. He appreciated their support and, once he got going, felt liberated by unburdening himself at these weekly meetings. Yet, at the same time, he felt naked and vulnerable by the loss of his personal privacy. He was uncomfortable with the way many of them looked at him, with starstruck reverence shining in their eyes. Like he was somebody special. He didn't feel special. Peter just felt like another flawed addict trying to get straight.

He continued. "I told you last week a little about those giant birds that attacked my chopper. They still haunt me. I see them in my nightmares, which come more often as I withdraw from the oxy. The things I love most are suffering due to my using—my wife, my two children, *flying*. My employer has grounded me until I get clean. I feel like a bird with broken wings, seeing the big, open sky above that once was my domain and having to remain earthbound. My family and my desire to get back in the cockpit give me the incentive to conquer this poison that's killing me. I know I have to quit the junk and I'm determined to do it. And you all are helping me do that."

He heard a few shouts of "Right on!" and "We're here for you, Peter," over enthusiastic applause. These people—some of whom had much bigger drug problems than him—were behind him. Peter blushed in embarrassed appreciation.

This wasn't easy for him. He'd long seen himself as a private person, a strong independent type who had always been able to take care of his own problems. Brin strongly urged him to attend these meetings and he had pushed back, refusing to admit he had a problem. But she had kept on him and finally *demanded* he go. His wife of six years finally convinced him that he was ignoring her and their two kids—three-year-old Kimi and newborn Jacob—while he languished in physical pain and self-pity under the fog of his opioid addiction. The quality of the Lacroix domestic life had gradually deteriorated in direct proportion to Peter's using. It took him many long months to see the negative effect his drug use had on his beautiful family. Brin was right. He needed the help that a Narcotics Anonymous support group could give him.

He sat back and listened as others shared their tales of woe. A man named Brett told of losing everything—job, marriage, lifelong savings—to his crystal meth addiction. An emaciated redhead, Stephanie, related her two experiences of overdosing on heroin and being revived by Narcan injections. A Blackfoot Indian, Virgil, talked about waking up naked in a rat infested back alley twenty-four hours after leaving a party on the reservation where he had indulged heavily in his crack cocaine habit. Unfortunately the crack was laced with fentanyl. Virgil was quite sure he had died during the blackout, recalling a face-to-face conversation with the Great Spirit who told Virgil he would let him live if he promised to get some help. Virgil said it was the defining moment that brought him to Kalispell and the Power of Choice Narcotics Anonymous group.

As Virgil related his tale of communing with the Great Spirit, Peter thought about his own personal relationship with God. These NA meetings were all about faith: Faith in God. Faith in spirit. Faith in *self.* He had rediscovered his long absent belief in a supreme deity after eleven harrowing days and nights atop that desolate Idaho cliff overlooking the Salmon River. After the crash, he felt certain that God had abandoned them. He'd prayed daily even though he thought it to be a hopeless exercise. But then, on the eleventh day, he, Hayden Fowler, and Bill Carlton were rescued in what Peter considered to be divine intervention. God had been listening after all. God—or in Virgil's terminology, the Great Spirit—had delivered. Peter's long AWOL faith had been restored. He'd even attended Mass last Sunday at St. Francis Xavier Parish in Missoula, his first time inside a house of worship in years. Brin had been shocked but willingly accompanied him, a big smile on her face, caressing Peter's arm throughout Father Patrick's liturgy.

Peter tuned out as the drug confessions continued, thinking about his own situation. He hadn't flown since the accident. Eight months grounded, which was an unnatural state of being for him. Losing the sole company helicopter in the Idaho crash, Fowler-Lemoyne Aviation had basically closed down operations over the fall and winter months while Hayden Fowler and Peter recovered from their injuries. As Peter regained his health, Hayden and Nora promoted him to Chief Operations Officer, giving him full authority to build a helicopter fleet, oversee aircraft maintenance, and hire pilots. He was also tasked with drawing up plans for a new, second heliport in Missoula. Peter was grateful for the promotion and pay raise, which allowed him and Brin to sell their shoebox starter home and buy their sprawling new house on six wooded acres in Florence, twenty miles south of Missoula.

As his body healed, his obsession with flying returned. And now, almost nine hard months later, he felt ready to take to the skies once again. But his oxy addiction was a showstopper. Bryan Gilliam, general manager of the company, refused to let him pilot a chopper until Peter proved his sobriety. Thankfully, proof was left to the honor system. No peeing in a cup or blood tests or other indignities. There was no need for it as Bryan and he had shared a close trusting friendship for the past two years. Peter could lie to himself all he wanted but he could never lie to Bryan. His friend would pick up on it immediately. Bryan told him that when Peter said he was clean he would take his word for it. The situation forced Peter to start examining himself with brutal honesty. Caused him to finally stop lying to himself. It's what ultimately led him to the NA meetings.

I have to kick this oxy thing, even if it kills me.

It was a refrain that ran through his mind daily.

He'd spent the past month interviewing pilot candidates, all the time wishing he'd been the interviewee rather than the interviewer. He was envious of the two he had hired, knowing they, and not he, would be piloting the two new metallic blue Bell 407s he had special ordered three months ago, the choppers that were now sitting in the Gilliam's Guidepost Heliport hangar. He had made the trip to Heart Butte on the day of delivery and climbed into the cockpit of one, sitting snugly in the pilot's seat, fondling the cyclic pitch stick and fantasizing about lifting off into the wild blue yonder.

This can be you again, Lacroix, he'd told himself as he perused the instrument panel and dreamed of soaring with the eagles once again. *You have got to stop feeding yourself that junk. If you don't, you'll be forever anchored to a desk.*

He came out of his reverie with the scrape of chairs and the padding of feet. Bodies moved around him. The meeting was breaking up.

He heard a female voice beckon him. "Have you selected your sponsor yet, Peter?"

He glanced up to see the thin redhead, Stephanie, lurking before him with a dazed, awestruck smile, a look Peter had seen all too often since his story of survival had made him famous. His skin prickled in discomfort.

"Uh, no, I haven't," he said, standing to face her.

"Well I hope you'll consider me," she said, crowding him. "No one here knows more about you than me. I've read all about you online. I'd love to hear more about those dinosaurs you faced off against on that cliff in Idaho. Must've been scary as hell. I have also read Hayden Fowler and Nora Lemoyne's book three times, the chapters that feature you probably more." She brushed her hair with her fingers, tilted her head as if examining him. "Gosh, I can't believe it's actually *you* attending our meetings here in Kalispell. So how about it, Peter? Will you let me be your sponsor? I could be a big help to you. We could support each other, be good for each other. Whaddaya say?"

He felt trapped. Peter looked away from the woman's stalker-like stare, watching people file out of the room. Members looked at them as they passed, several giving him expressions of sympathy.

He thought: *Two heroin overdoses? How is this woman going to help me? And I certainly don't need a dino groupie in my life.*

Peter looked at her. Her slender face conveyed desperation. He felt sorry for her. How to tell this poor woman he had no intention of choosing a sponsor? Not her or anyone else here. Brin was the only support he needed.

"I really haven't decided on a sponsor yet, Stephanie." He sidestepped her and moved toward the exit.

"Well please keep me in mind, Peter," he heard her say. "Will I see you next week?"

He shouted over his shoulder, "I don't know."

And with that he walked out of the Alano Club into the late spring sunshine of Kalispell.

Publish Or Perish

May 29: Eden Prairie, Minnesota

NORA SIGNED OFF THE ZOOM CALL with Penguin Random House executives in New York. Members of the editorial staff had also participated.

She let out a frustrated breath, feeling drained and disappointed. The hour-long meeting had sapped her strength and resolve.

Nora had failed in her quest to buy more time on the final manuscript turnover of their second book. She was having second thoughts about the book as a whole and wanted to make some sweeping changes.

But she didn't want to tell them that.

Instead Nora told them about yesterday's exciting discovery of another new dinosaur species at Montana's Tally Lake. She thought the powers-that-be would be swayed by the event, that they would allow her and Hayden more time to work the new material into the book. They certainly seemed intrigued by the video clips Nora showed them of the Deinosuchus attacking and killing a mature grizzly bear. She was sure Hayden's impressive videos would win them over.

She had been wrong.

They were tired of waiting.

The suits remained unyielding.

One of the executive bigwigs—Chief Operating Officer Lawrence Goldmeyer—had arrogantly talked down to her. She had listened to him drone on in a patronizing tone about how she was new to the big publishing process and therefore did not—*could* not—understand the complexities of the business. According to Goldmeyer, she couldn't possibly comprehend how delays by authors upset the finely-tuned balance of a book's successful launch. Goldmeyer had even threatened her, suggesting Nora's requested delay would amount to a contractual violation subject to legal prosecution.

"If we give you another few weeks to add a chapter about this prehistoric crocodile," Goldmeyer said, "then sure enough about that time you and Mr. Fowler will make another discovery that you'll want in this book as well, and we slip another couple of months out. The answer is no, Ms. Lemoyne. We can't have any more delays."

Henry Wycliff—her and Hayden's literary agent—spoke up in Nora's defense. But in the end, it wasn't enough. A contract was a legal document and they had already tested its limits more than a few times.

The greatly anticipated follow-up to Hayden and Nora's huge bestselling book of last year—*Cretaceous Stones: The Return of Prehistoric Life to Earth*—was behind schedule due to their slow output. Of course, the aftermath of the Idaho helicopter crash and Hayden's excruciating rehabilitation was to blame for much of it. The folks at Penguin Random House had been understanding and extremely accommodating about those early delays.

But there had been more recent delays caused by burnout and crushing pressure to deliver another blockbuster bestseller.

She and Hayden had worked around the clock to deliver last year's book on time while also burning the midnight oil to establish their new aviation company. Then suddenly, like a thunderbolt from hell, Nora had to deal with the chopper accident that left three dead and Hayden in a coma. He was a broken man lying in a hospital bed. She was exhausted and drained emotionally. And yet many critical deadlines loomed. Nora wrote the early chapters while Hayden recuperated and somehow she managed to meet the first few scheduled turnovers.

Lately, however, proofreading the manuscript front to back, Nora came to the disappointing conclusion that their work was rushed and sloppy. She wasn't happy with what she delivered to their editor, Molly Barnes, feeling it wasn't good enough, that it didn't measure up to the high standards of their debut, which prompted her to completely rework several long chapters.

And now she realized with dismay there were other chapters that needed restructuring.

Hayden didn't seem to give much of a care, but she was a perfectionist who fretted over every word. One question kept dogging her: How do you follow up the overwhelming success of a book that sold millions of copies in hardcover, a book that still held its place in the top ten on all the critical bestseller lists 16 months after publication? Nora felt the intense gravity of their first book bearing down on her during writing sessions. She found herself second-guessing every word and sentence, every paragraph and page, knowing that millions of people would soon be reading it.

How do you explain that kind of pressure to corporate stuffed suits whose only interest is the bottom line?

Their new book, *Dragons of the Great Divide: Running with the Beasts*, was supposed to be released this week, with a month-long author tour to follow. Nora and Hayden's missed deadlines had pushed the publication date out at least four months.

Four months in the book publishing business is an eternity. Lawrence Goldmeyer had pounded that into her head, ad nauseum.

*Face it, girl. Goldmeyer is an asshole! We made the man plenty of money and he treats me like I'm some empty-headed teenager. Maybe his name should be Gold-*digger*!*

She smiled at the thought.

But as angry as she was at Goldmeyer, after listening to the team's presentation on how big corporate book publishing rolled, Nora came to a reluctant acceptance.

Goldmeyer explained: "I want you to understand, Ms. Lemoyne, that book publishing is a well-oiled machine consisting of hundreds—*thousands*—of people working on each release. It's an assembly line production, a confluence of specialists operating in synchronous unity to put books into the hands of interested readers. If one section of the assembly line breaks down, other sections downline must adjust on the fly. Section breakdowns are costly and throw off established timelines."

A well-rehearsed spiel she was sure Goldmeyer had made many times before.

After Lawrence Goldmeyer left the meeting various members of the publishing team explained their parts in the process.

Kelly Bradwell, Director of Marketing, went first.

"Hi, Nora. First of all, congratulations on the success of *Cretaceous Stones*. Everyone in my department loved the book and we all thank you and Hayden for giving us a great book to work with. It's been a titanic journalistic achievement. That campaign went flawlessly and we are all being rewarded by its success."

"Thank you, Kelly," Nora said. "Hayden and I both appreciate the hard work your team put in to make it happen."

"How is Hayden doing these days?"

"He's getting his strength back, not to mention his old sense of orneriness."

That brought a few laughs from those on the call.

Kelly Bradwell said, "I see he is back out in the field. The video footage he shot of that crocodile on steroids is sensational. Your co-author seems to have a talent for finding these creatures."

"Yes, he does. It's a gift but he denies it. Says it's just blind luck coupled with zoological logic. He calls it *paleo zoo logic*. Three words."

A few snickers.

"Well, it'll be fascinating material for your next book. Now let's talk about your current book, shall we?"

Nora braced herself.

"I have to be honest with you, Nora. My advertising people are frustrated. Because of recent delays we have no advance reading copies to send to key reviewers. My publicity people are griping about not having copies to include in their press kits. Granted your forthcoming book already has a lot of pre-pub buzz, but we could be making an even bigger splash if we had a good supply of ARCs. Advance reader copies supply the fuel that ignites preorder sales, and preorder sales determine our starting position on the bestseller lists."

Nora tried to remain calm and not take the beatdown personally.

Next up was Mary Chatsworth, V.P. of Strategy and Finance. "With every day that goes by without a finished book, we lose precious revenue we had worked into our detailed budgets. Not to mention the costs in time and money of rescheduling with our printers, book binders, and distributors. Head buyers at bookstores and library purchasing agents are overwhelming us with questions about release dates. Readers are getting impatient. Look, I know writing a book is difficult and we here at PRH are sympathetic to what you and Hayden have been through, but we need to get your next book out there. We need to strike while the proverbial iron is hot."

The message was clear. Their late manuscript was creating a logjam in the book publishing flow. And a scheduled initial print run of 400,000 hardcovers represented a monumental logjam.

No more delays, they'd stated emphatically. The discovery of the Deinosuchus was great source material, they all agreed. But another month or longer delay was just not possible. Deinosuchus would have to wait until their next book. Nora had argued that it would be old news by then and would lack the punch it would have now. She and Hayden could not sit on it and keep it secret for another year or two. The world would soon find out about it. Other publishers would come out with the extraordinary discovery long before Penguin Random House. But in the end, her arguments landed on deaf ears.

They were only giving her until Friday to finalize the entire book. She glanced at the stack of paper sitting on her desktop—526 manuscript pages, many tagged with different colored tabs for the edits she wanted to incorporate. The pile was daunting.

She sighed. *I left my paleontology career for this?*

She grabbed her mug and went to the kitchen to make more coffee. While waiting for it to brew her cell phone chimed.

Hayden again, his fourth call since he'd been gone. She smiled. He was keeping his promise about staying in touch.

"Hey, Hayden," she said dully.

"You okay, baby? You sound down."

"I just got off a call with our publishing team. Lots of heavy hitters showed up. It didn't go well."

"They weren't excited about the Deinosuchus?"

"They were, yes. But they said it would have to wait until our next book. They kind of read me the riot act about all the delays."

"Jesus. Sorry you had to go through that, love. I should have been there to back you."

"Yes, you should have," she said, more bitchy than she intended. "They're only giving us three days to finalize the manuscript."

"Shit. Wasn't Henry able to get us more time?"

"Wycliff was on the call and he gave it his best shot, but it wasn't enough to persuade them. They want our book out in the world. They're tired of tinkering with it. Truth be known, I'm tired of it, too."

"Well, will you be able to handle the final edits?"

"There's a ton of work to be done, Hayden. You're not coming home tomorrow?"

"I can't leave now. These Deinosuchus sightings are the biggest news since those Quetzalcoatlus brought down our copter."

Nora listened as Hayden told her about seeing the Deinosuchus again this morning, this time feeding at their bait mound. He and Carlton had tried to sedate the animal with tranquilizer darts but their shots missed. They were planning to stay camped out at Tally Lake a few more days to film the beast and hopefully marking it with a satellite tracking tag.

"It's incredible to see this creature up close, Nora," he said, excitement brightening his voice. "It made a quick meal out of that grizzly as you saw. That bear had to weigh seven- to eight-hundred pounds, all claws and muscle and fur, and that Deinosuchus took it down like it was a puppy.

"Since then I've been thinking. Its appearance creates new questions. According to fossil carbon dating records, Deinosuchus died out seven million years before later Cretaceous carnivores we've seen—T-Rex and Dromaeosaurs and Quetzalcoatlus. If we're assuming that all fifteen meteorites contained Late Cretaceous dino eggs like we've seen thus far, then this animal is an anomaly. That begs the question of whether the meteorites that have yet to be found contained forms of prehistoric life that died out long before the Cretaceous-Paleogene extinction event. And if so, how that would dovetail with the Mallory-Rayburn-Britton Theory of Terrestrial Cretaceous Rebirth. Would it invalidate the MRB concept? And since this is the first aquatic creature we've seen, are there more of them? Did several meteorites hit lakes and ponds? Did maybe a few hit the oceans? Is that why they haven't been located yet? I'll have to check with Lacroix, but I think he said five meteorites were still unaccounted for. Or were there more than the fifteen meteorites the astronomers originally reported? It wouldn't be the first time the government has intentionally misled the public."

"Yeah, all that is fascinating to ponder, Hayden," she said, hearing the exhilaration in his voice. He sounded happy for the first time in a long while, enthusiastic about his work again. "It's a lot to unpack. I have to ask. Is Tally Lake a resort area? Is there a swimming area there? A beach?"

"There's a beach here, but it's a glacier-fed lake so the water is too cold to attract swimmers this early in the summer. Plus much of the lake has a brownish tinge to it and looks polluted, but it's not. The lake is surrounded by dense forest and heavy foliage that generates a good bit of organic decay, which stains the water. And though there is a campground and a boat launch, we haven't seen anybody else here in two days. Tally Lake is hidden away in the middle of nowhere. I call it a ghost lake."

Nora asked, "So remind me again. How did you and Carlton find it?"

"A couple of big game hunters—Marcus Stanley and Jerry Manoogian—were in these parts hunting black bear and wild turkey last week. I've known Marcus for a few years and he called to tell me they were tracking a bear that led them to the lake where they saw a couple of Tyrannosaurs at the water's edge drinking. Said I might want to check it out."

"They didn't try to take one of the Rexes?"

"No. The penalties are too great for that now. All dinosaur hunting licenses have been suspended in Montana. The game wardens and wildlife rangers are keeping a close eye."

"So what are you planning, Hayden?"

"Oh, I'll be coming back. And you'll be coming with me, *ma cherie*."

"Says who?"

"Says *me*. You have just *got* to see this marvelous creature up close, Nora. It'll suck the air right out of your lungs."

"I prefer to keep my lungs inflated, thank you very much."

She heard Hayden's hoarse laugh. "Anyway," he continued, "I've got calls in to a couple of divers who worked with Jackson Lattimer. I want to get some underwater footage of the beast in its natural habitat. I also want to see if we can find the meteorite it hatched out of."

"You think there is a meteorite at the bottom of that lake?"

"I do, yes. So will you accompany me to Tally Lake?"

"I guess, yeah," Nora replied, happy that Hayden was sounding more like his old self, but annoyed that he was dumping all the final book edits on her. "The more immediate issue, Hayden, is if you're not home by Friday you won't be able to check my manuscript changes and sign off on the final book before I submit it."

"That's all right, *mon amour*. I'm sure any edits you make will greatly improve the book. We both know you are a much better writer than me."

"You know, I'm pretty tired of hearing that every time you want to get out of some work, Hayden."

"Hey, I'm just saying that—"

"I know exactly what you're saying," she said, exasperated. "But I have to ask. What am I supposed to do? Forge your name on the signoff sheets?"

"No. I have to stop off at the Guidepost to see Bryan Gilliam about that T-Rex head that was delivered to him. You can email a copy of the final signoff sheets to Loretta and I'll sign them when I get there, then email them back to you."

"Without seeing any of the content?"

"Yeah. I trust your writing skills implicitly, sweets."

"I'm tired of hearing that, too."

"Sorry about that. I love you and miss you, Nora. I really mean that. Wish you were here with us."

"Be careful, hon. With that beard of yours I'd hate for that Deinosuchus to mistake you for a grizzly bear."

She heard him laugh then smack a goodbye smooch before signing off.

Nora smiled and disconnected. Filled her mug with piping hot coffee and returned to her bedroom office. Sat at the desk and began digging into the stack of manuscript pages.

So much work ahead while Hayden is off playing dinosaur spotter.

I must be crazy to love this man the way I do.

The T-Rex Headache

May 30: Gilliam's Guidepost

Heart Butte, Montana

"WOW, THAT IS ONE UGLY CUSS!" Mike Mathews said, gawking at the severed Tyrannosaur head in the oversized Styrofoam chest. "Who'd you piss off this time, Bryan?"

"Don't even go there," Bryan Gilliam said as they moved the unwieldly container out of the walk-in freezer to a worktable in the utility barn. "I nearly swallowed my tongue when I opened this."

"Understandable," Mathews said, eyeing the Gilliam family photos spiked on the beast's lower teeth. Drops of dried T-Rex blood spotted the snapshots like dark brown freckles.

"You can imagine what this has done to Loretta and me."

"Absolutely. It would shake me up, too." Mathews inspected the cooler from different angles. "You say this came in dry ice?"

"Yeah, but it evaporated yesterday. We kept the head in the freezer to preserve it."

"Well," Mathews said, scratching his chin, "freezing it might have preserved the head but the dry ice evaporation and low temps have degraded the photos." He snapped on a pair of nitrile gloves. "The photos are our best shot at getting clean fingerprints. Did you or your wife handle any of these?"

"No, we knew better than to touch them."

"Good."

Mathews dipped a small fiberglass brush into a jar of black powder and lightly dusted the surfaces of the pics. Bryan watched him work. Gradually, a smear of fingerprints became visible.

"We're in luck. I see two well defined prints on your wife's pic and another on your younger son's photo."

Bryan watched Mathews press a strip of tape over the powdered area and gently lift, then affix it to a light gray fingerprint card.

Bryan pointed at the card. "You think this will lead us to whoever did this?"

"No guarantees." Mathews held the card up to the light, examining the captured prints. "You told me your top three suspects are doing hard time at Montana State, correct?"

"Yeah, last I heard."

"They might not have anything to do with this, but all three certainly have clear-cut motives for harming you and your family. Because they're convicted felons, their prints are registered on AFIS and any accomplices working for them on the outside would probably exist on AFIS, too. Then again, it might be someone after a big chunk of your newly-acquired fortune. If so, it's probable they would have criminal records and could be found on AFIS as well."

"What is AFIS?"

"It's an acronym for Automated Fingerprint Identification System, a digitized database containing prints of those who have been arrested or convicted of crimes. It also contains prints of anyone who has undergone thorough background checks—you know, people working in the government or military who need high-level security clearances. The AFIS algorithms can give us a match in seconds. Unfortunately, fingerprints aren't as surefire as DNA, but it will give us a good starting point. Hopefully it'll generate a few good leads. I always like to start with fingerprints and see where they take me."

"So you just hand over that card to AFIS and we get answers right away?"

"Not that simple, Bryan. I'm a private investigator, and as such, I don't have access. Even though I'm licensed in the state of Montana, AFIS is restricted to official law enforcement, the FBI, and other authorized government criminal investigation agencies. I received thorough fingerprint training during my days working for the Billings PD and I still have connections there. They'll run this card for me."

Bryan nodded. “What about DNA?”

“What about it?”

“You said fingerprinting isn’t as surefire as DNA. You think we can find any DNA on this package?”

“Maybe. But, again, as a private investigator I don’t have the wherewithal or tools to collect and analyze DNA samples.” Mathews nodded at the T-Rex head. “Have your kids seen this mess yet?”

“No. Lor and I decided it best to keep it from them.”

“Bad idea. You want to keep them safe, Bryan. You want to keep them informed. They need to be on the alert. You should talk to them. Don’t show them the bloodied head but let them know there’s a reason to be extra cautious. Your two boys are out in public a lot and they especially need to be on their toes.” Mathews surveyed the T-Rex head and debased family photos. “This is some serious shit.”

“Tell me something I don’t know, Mike. You think we need to get bodyguards for my boys?”

“Wouldn’t hurt. You can afford that level of protection, right?”

“Well yeah, but . . .” Bryan looked at Mathews. “Jesus this is one insane asylum world we live in, huh.”

“I can help you with the personal protection for your sons. You should also contact the authorities. I know you have stellar security here on the ranch and I’ll certainly do all I can to track down the culprits, but the police and maybe even the FBI need to be aware of this threat. Especially considering what’s gone down here the past two years.”

“Yeah, Hayden Fowler told me the same thing, almost verbatim.”

“It’s sound advice, Bryan.”

Bryan groaned. “I know it is, but if the police get involved it becomes public. We become nightly news sensationalism all over again. Tabloid content for all the social media morons. We’ve done our time in that yellow journalism shitstorm. Loretta and I have no desire to go back to being the center ring attraction in a three-ring media circus. The spotlight on us is just now starting to dim and we don't want to relight it. It's why we've been so secretive about our settlement with the AEF. Surely you can understand our desire for privacy."

"Of course I can. But what good is privacy if you're dead?"

Bryan worked with Mike Mathews last year on the missing and murdered Indigenous women's cases and he had appreciated the PI's directness through it all. He wasn't so sure he appreciated it now.

Mathews picked up on it. "Look, Bryan, I'm sorry to be so candid, but we know from past experience your enemies mean business. I don't have to remind you they tried to kill you and burned your ranch to the ground, do I?"

"No, but—"

"And last year they went after Kanti Lyttle and Ahwee Red Crow, close Blackfoot friends of yours. Your enemies play hardball, Bryan, and they won't hesitate to do bodily harm to your family. I've seen this kind of thing more times than I care to admit. This T-Rex head sends a message that the authorities need to know about."

Bryan turned to the PI. "You're right. Lor and I need to talk with our kids and I need to take this to the police. But it's such a hassle." He pointed at the insulated cooler. "This whole thing is a huge clusterfuck."

Mathews nodded. "I know, I know. But you have done so much good work for the Blackfeet Nation. You and your family have blended with their culture. I think if you went to the tribal police and explained the situation, they would keep it under wraps while they investigate. They would respect your privacy."

"Maybe," Bryan said. "But you remember how hesitant Blackfeet Law Enforcement Services were last year to help us find Kanti and Ahwee. They kept putting me and Apisi off, saying they didn't have the staffing."

"Trust me. This is different. Contact them and show them this T-Rex head eating your family photos. It'll move them to action, I'm sure. They don't want any more trouble on the rez than they've already got."

Mathews reached for the Styrofoam lid and read the sender label. "Western Adventures in Missoula?"

"Yeah. I checked them out. It's a bogus company. I couldn't find a website or any online chatter about them. No Yelp or Google reviews. Nothing with the Better Business Bureau. They don't exist."

"Of course they don't. The PO box is probably fiction, too, but there's enough damning evidence here to get a warrant on the FedEx shipping records. I can work with Atlee Pinnaker to get that done."

Mathews leaned over the cooler, flipping up each of the photographs, examining the reverse sides. "You say these pics were hacked from your private family server?"

"Yeah, it's the only place these snapshots exist. What are you looking for?"

"Sometimes prints of digital photos contain residual metadata on their backsides, but I don't see any here."

Mathews straightened and removed his gloves. Pulled out his cellphone and took pictures of the T-Rex head and Styrofoam container, including the 12-digit tracking number. "You checked the tracking on this package, right?"

Bryan nodded. "That's the first thing I did."

"What was the origin of shipment?"

"West Glacier, Montana, which I thought was weird, since it's a Missoula address on the sender label. West Glacier is a long-ass way from Missoula."

"That doesn't matter. We already know the company is bogus. They can put any address they want on the sender label. FedEx only checks the validity of the destination address. What's important is that it was shipped from West Glacier. It's a starting point, but no guarantee that the people behind this live anywhere near there. We might have better luck in narrowing our search if I can find something in your VPN logs. I'd like to take a look at your family photo server. It might give us a clue about who has been mucking around in your private network. The logs will indicate when file downloads occurred and who initiated them. Can you take me to them?"

"Sure," Bryan said, "but I must warn you, I'm a complete neophyte when it comes to computers. My boys handle all that cyber stuff. Ethan and Paul designed our company website and they maintain our server. I won't be much help there."

"All I need is login credentials. Give me that and I can do the rest."

"You know how to check server data?"

"Nothing to it," Mathews said with a confident grin. "I received thorough cybersecurity and computer forensics training during my years with the Billings PD."

Bryan led the way out of the barn that had been repurposed as rehearsal space for son Paul's band. They passed by the makeshift stage that held a drum kit, amplifiers, and electric guitars propped up on stands. Two big PA speakers loomed on either side of the stage like giant black eyes.

"How's your oldest doing with his music?" Mathews asked, eyeing the instruments lining the stage.

"Quite well, actually. His band Moonrise has a four-song EP that's getting a lot college radio play and they've been in the studio working on a full album of original songs. They're all still in school so it's a slow process."

"I took guitar lessons when I was a kid but quit when my fingers started bleeding," Mathews said with a chuckle. "I was a real wuss as a kid."

"Somehow I doubt that," Bryan said, knowing the PI was a veteran of the Second Gulf War in Iraq and had spent 15 years with the Billings Police Department as a patrol officer and detective. Mike Mathews, with his crooked nose and unyielding narrow face, wore his street cred toughness on his wiry frame like a well-tailored suit.

"Oh, believe it," Mathews said. "I didn't toughen up until I went through Basic Training."

"My Basic was hell on earth," Bryan said. "But then we were shipped off to Afghanistan, and that turned out to be an even hotter hell in a sandbox."

"No doubt," Mathews replied. "Iraq was no picnic either."

They stepped out of the barn into the afternoon sunlight. Bryan pulled the big steel doors shut behind them and led the way across the quadrangle to the house. Bryan strolled slowly, cautiously. He'd left his cane in the house. His legs were getting stronger and he was trying a few hours each day to get along without the walking stick.

They crossed the concrete slab of the heliport pad. Bryan glanced into the open hangar, seeing their fleet mechanic, Carl Lacey, with an array of tools spread out on a blanket next to the landing struts, working on the blade assembly of one of the new Bell 407s. Bryan shouted a greeting to Lacey who gave them a nod and a smile in return.

Seeing the shiny, bright blue aircraft lifted Bryan's spirits. Soon there would be helicopters flying in and out of Gilliam's Guidepost Heliport again. The quad and landing pad had been silent since the crash. Fowler Lemoyne Aviation was shut down for eight long months. During that dark period, Bryan handled mountains of paperwork and red tape, lots of back-and-forths with the FAA and NTSB concerning accident details. He'd met with insurance adjusters and negotiated with chopper manufacturers. He'd worked with contractors who were building company offices in the back of the hangar. And through it all, there had been no incoming or outgoing flights. There had been no revenue stream to feed the company coffers.

During this time, Bryan also dealt with the fragile and uncertain health of his business partners. Hayden Fowler and Peter Lacroix had survived the crash and eleven eternal days stranded in the River of No Return wastelands of central Idaho, clashing with carnivorous dinosaurs and fighting to survive. Both had healed over the long winter months, but both still displayed infirmities. Neither were all the way back to form. It remained to be seen how both men would handle going back up in a helicopter.

Hayden was driving in from Tally Lake the day after tomorrow to look at the T-Rex head. Peter Lacroix was due in from Missoula this weekend to begin working with the new pilots. Bryan thought it would do everyone good to get back in the air again and getting Fowler-Lemoyne Aviation firing on all cylinders once more.

He wondered how Peter was doing with his drug rehab stint. Bryan had been the one to inform Peter that he was grounded until he kicked the opioids. The act was one of the most difficult things he'd ever had to do. It was tough seeing the man broken like that and having to give him bad news. But it was his responsibility as general manager. The hurt, the look of crushing disappointment and strains of anger on Peter's face had saddened him. Peter Lacroix was an excellent pilot and the Idaho crash had not been his fault. But Bryan knew they couldn't chance another air catastrophe, especially if it was proved the pilot manning the controls was high on oxycodone. As much as he liked Peter, Bryan knew they couldn't risk putting their paying passengers in that kind of jeopardy.

They arrived at the back entrance to the house, which went through the sunporch. He held the door open for Mathews.

As Mathews entered the house he said, "Lead me to your VPN server. Let's find these rude assholes who dare to send you bloody dinosaur heads!"

Bryan smiled. Things were looking up.

He knew he had the right man on the job.

Dino Snares and Sweet Eclairs

May 31: Sawtooth National Forest
Custer County Idaho

JUST AFTER DAWN.

Haze clung to the pond like a gauze shroud. The sun played peekaboo behind the jagged peaks of the Sawtooth Mountains. Bluebirds and chickadees screeched their morning wakeup songs. Chipmunks and pikas chittered as they scampered through the underbrush.

They'd been out here since one AM hoping to snare a Tyrant Lizard King, better known as Tyrannosaurus Rex.

Mick and Claire Prescott sat in the cab of their Polaris Ranger UTV. Max Baker and Ray Yount camped out in the transport truck in a stand of lodgepole pine behind the drop net on the far side of the pond. The two teams had been in contact throughout the night via walkie-talkies but there hadn't been much to chat about.

They'd found this spring-fed lagoon on a scouting trip two days ago. A scattering of tridactyl (three-toed) footprints embedded in the moist clay loam and mounds of fresh dung near the waterline alerted them to the recent presence of T-Rex. The prints were deep and wide with large, blunt claw impressions. No doubt they belonged to Tyrannosaurs and not the smaller, more mobile Dromaeosaurs.

A T-Rex watering hole.

Judging by the volume of tracks and scat, it was a popular gathering place for the Tyrant Lizards.

So where are they? Mick Prescott wondered.

The Prescotts ran a successful, albeit illegal, trapping business that supplied traffickers with exotic animals, sometimes venomous and nearly always dangerous. They did some legal trapping, too, but the big money came from illicit activities.

And it didn't get much more illicit than trapping Tyrannosaurs.

With nothing much to do but wait and watch, Mick Prescott sat behind the wheel, peering out at the pond, musing about the beautiful woman sitting next to him, his wife Claire.

Mick met Claire Wilson fifteen years ago when both were employed at the Denver Zoo. He was a Carnivore Habitat Specialist working the Predator Ridge exhibit, which included spotted hyenas, tigers, polar bears, and African lions. Claire was a Zoological Nutritionist who collaborated with zoo veterinarians and animal care specialists to establish balanced diets for all the zoo's animals. It wasn't love at first sight but more of a slow burn romance, time and mutual interests eventually cementing their relationship. Marriage followed thirteen years ago, in the chapel of a small church in Centennial, Colorado.

Mick reached over and caressed his wife's wrist. "You okay? You're awfully quiet, my sweet e-Claire."

She smiled at him. "I'm fine, Mickey. Just bored is all."

Mick's pet name always brought a smile from Claire. He'd first called her e-Claire back when he was trying to get her attention. There were a couple of other guys at the zoo who had their eyes on Claire Wilson—she of the long blonde tresses and arresting amber eyes—and he wanted to do something that would set him apart. One afternoon he showed up at the end of her lunch break with a half-dozen éclairs and a greeting card. On the card he'd written:

The confections in this box are nowhere near as sweet as you, my sweet e-Claire. Thinking of you, Mickey Prescott.

At the time he thought the whole idea of it was hokey, a clumsy attempt at getting her to notice him. He'd been embarrassed giving her the sticky carton of pastries and the card with his ridiculous attempt at romantic prose. But she surprised him. Her face lit up with a wide grin and she kissed him, knocking over the box of éclairs in her excitement. She told him it was the loveliest notion any man had ever shown her, and embraced him in a warm hug.

Mick was shocked that his cheesy ploy had worked. And it kept on working. Every year on the date of that momentous lunch they celebrated with a candlelight dinner at a fancy restaurant topped off with a delectable dessert of éclairs and champagne. And now, nearly fifteen years on, she remained his precious sweet e-Claire. She never tired of the pet name he had given her.

Mick leaned across the seats and kissed her cheek, which led to a short make-out session.

Claire cut the heated grope session short, sitting back in her seat and saying, "As much as I'd like to, we can't get carried away, Mickey. We have to stay vigilant."

"Yeah, you're right," he said, grabbing his pack of Lucky Strikes from the dash and lighting up.

As he smoked, he thought about the early days of their business partnership...

Sharing an entrepreneurial spirit, nearly a year after their wedding, they left their jobs at the Denver Zoo to strike out on their own. They purchased a couple of vehicles, an assortment of trapping gear, updated their passports, and rented warehouse space in Montbello, setting up their animal procurement operation. Their business was legal in those early days, traveling the globe acquiring animals for U.S. zoos. But as time went on, they saw that the real money was on the other side of the law.

Seduced by the dark side, the Prescotts abandoned their once solid ethics and began their unlawful activities.

Mick and his wife spent much of their time in Africa and South America, trapping venomous reptiles and dangerous mammals for a growing list of illegal animal trafficking clients. But then the Great Dinosaur Rebirth happened two years ago and they returned home to Denver. The last two years saw them working the Continental Divide in eastern Idaho and northwestern Montana, trapping Late Cretaceous Period dinosaurs. The demand for exotic prehistoric animals was high, especially the meat eaters. A healthy T-Rex netted them a hundred grand, a Dromaeosaur got them forty K minimum. A much better hourly rate than trapping for zoos.

However, the work did present many potential hazards. Dino

trapping was a dangerous way to make a living. In addition to the unpredictability of the beasts the Prescotts hunted, the chance of getting nabbed by Fish and Wildlife agents loomed large. The fines for trapping/trafficking dinosaurs were significant. And most illicit animal trafficking charges brought substantial prison time.

Politicians—who Mick thought of as self-serving sycophants—only muddied the already murky waters of legality. It really chapped Mick's ass, the way the politicos were so wishy-washy about the dinosaur invasion. When the dinos first started hatching out, the public went into a mass hysteria and the feds set up bounty programs that rewarded game hunters with big money for kills. Then the scientific communities and animal rights groups applied immense pressure to stop the killings. The movement switched to preserving the species. But did that stop state Fish, Wildlife, and Parks agents from monitoring and arresting trappers? Hell no! If anything, the investigative web tightened.

Then, just as quickly, farmers and ranchers pushed back, and the legal pendulum swung the other way. They were losing their crops and livestock to the invasive species. The politicos changed their tune again. Once again it was open season on dinos. Back and forth it went: bounty killing then preservation. Then back to kill rewards. State and federal politicians blew in the breeze, leaning whichever way they thought would win them favor and keep them in power. And all through the back and forth, trappers, and the traffickers they supplied, were viewed as Public Enemy #1.

And now in the late spring, the preservationists had won out, at least in Montana; it was now illegal to hunt and kill dinosaurs once again. It was a dizzying turn of laws and regulations made more confusing by mealy-mouthed politicians.

This world would be so much better off without those pointy-headed power-mongering pinheads!

Claire's voice brought Mick out of his musing. "I can tell you're stewing again, Mickey. What's up?"

He unscrewed the top off his thermos and gulped a slug of coffee. "Just the same ol', same old. Wondering why we're always targeted." He glanced at the drop net rigging strung under the forest canopy, the way they had so painstakingly concealed it to prevent detection by Montana Fish, Wildlife, and Parks aircraft. "All this subterfuge. Jesus! We're not killing these animals. We handle them with care. We treat them with respect." Mick lit up another smoke and took a deep drag. "Our work doesn't hurt anyone," he said on the exhale.

Claire touched his arm. "In case you forgot, Kelton Rendaya did. He hurt a lot of people."

She was referring to one of their former top clients, the Montana veterinarian-turned-animal-trafficker whose Tyrannosaur got loose and killed two North Dakota state troopers last year during transport to a customer.

"Yeah, well Rendaya is a greedy fool."

"You still worried about him ratting us out?"

"No," Mick said. "The time for that has long passed. If he was going to turn us in, he'd have done it before sentencing, when he had a chance to cop a plea deal. Kel's a hot mess, but he's not a snitch. I respect him for that."

"I don't trust him, Mickey. He's still a problem, even behind bars." Claire turned and glanced out the side window. "I don't want to end up in a Deer Lodge prison cell next to him. He worries me."

Mick took another swig of coffee. "The only thing that worries me is how we're gonna make up for all the business we lost with Rendaya bein' locked up. The man was a gold mine for us last year, you have to admit."

"Yeah, he maintained a pretty wealthy client list, for sure. But I don't know..." She peered out her passenger side window again, leaving the comment hanging.

Mick regarded his wife. "What's the matter, Claire? You seem stressed."

"I am. This life on the lam, this constant dodging the authorities is getting old. I'm not feeling the thrill of the chase anymore. The buzz is gone." She turned to him. "You ever feel that way, Mickey?"

"No. Can't say that I have. This work still excites me. Even with all the problems."

"Well look, I'm more worried than ever about getting busted," she said. "Kelton Rendaya wasn't the only trafficker who got popped last year. Don't forget Trapper Charlie. He was arrested and convicted, too." She turned to look at him. "Have you ever thought about going back to a fulltime job, Mickey?"

He frowned. "You mean zoo work?"

"Yeah, legit 1099 work with job security and benefits."

"Wow, you've got the heebie-jeebies bad, my darling." He considered her, studying her in the faint morning light. "I thought we were a team here. I thought we were the dynamic duo of wild animal trappers, baby."

"We *are*, Mickey, we are," she said, rubbing his arm.

He said, "We're making ten times the income we could ever hope to make with zoo work."

"I know that and I appreciate it. It's just that I'm having visions lately about following Kelton Rendaya and Trapper Charlie into a Montana State prison cell. The money doesn't do us much good if we're behind bars."

Mick snuffed out his cigarette in the dash ashtray. "I can't go back to designing and maintaining habitats, my love. That work is pure boredom. This is my life...*our* life, out here communing with nature, chasin' down ferocious beasts. It still gives me a rush."

Their conversation was interrupted by squawking static on the walkie-talkie. Ray Yount's voice cut through it. "We've got action, folks. We're picking up what sounds like a solitary bipedal creature trampling through the thicket behind us. Sounds huge. Too big for a Drome. Could be a bear but its movement says otherwise. I believe we've got a Rex comin' our way."

Mick plucked the handset from the dash mount and pressed the Talk button. "Excellent! All set with your tranq guns?"

"Rifles are loaded and ready, Mick."

"Be on your toes and use extreme caution, guys," he said, excitement coloring his words. "Direct him into the drop net area and be aware of your angles. There's nothing more dangerous than a cornered Rex. Give him room to run."

"This ain't our first dino rodeo, Mick," Yount said.

"I know, but it never hurts to be reminded."

"Roger that."

"It's showtime, baby," Mick said to Claire.

He opened his door and hopped out. The damp morning air felt cool against his face; a soft breeze carried an earthy mossy scent. Claire came around the vehicle and stood by his side, listening, training her binoculars on the capture area.

They heard thrashing deep in the woods on the far side of the pond, the desperate sounds of a large panicked animal on the run.

Shouts—Baker and Yount's voices—muffled by the thick vegetation.

"The animal is in distress," Claire said, scoping the far side of the pond with the binocs. "Their tranq darts must have landed."

"Yeah," Mick said, hoping and praying they had the right mixture of ketamine and xylazine in those dart syringes. A dead T-Rex did them no good.

He pulled the drop net remote transmitter from his belt and nervously rubbed his thumb over the trigger button. This was a precision operation requiring exact timing and teamwork. He and Claire had performed this dance dozens of times. She was the eyes on the prize, ensuring the animal was within the confines of the rigging. He was the triggerman who had to activate the net at precisely the right moment. But their roles depended on Max Baker and Ray Yount doing their jobs in anesthetizing and herding the Rex under the net. No matter how many times they'd pulled this procedure off, Mick's nerves still spoke to him at this point.

More crashing through the brush, tree branches snapping.

Closer now.

Shouts from Baker and Yount.

Frightened wails from the creature, a cross between a trumpeting elephant and a braying donkey.

"That sound always gets to me," Claire said.

"Me, too. You picking up anything yet?"

"No." Claire swept the field glasses across the far side of the pond, checking the edge of the forest.

They had started using the drop net last year on their aquatic captures after they'd lost a Dromaeosaur to drowning in a Montana lake. Once sedated, they'd learned these creatures tended to head for water, where it was difficult to extract them. Hence the net, which if executed properly, would prevent the Rex from going into the pond.

"I see it!" Claire exclaimed. "Now, Mickey, NOW!"

Mick pressed the trigger. With a sharp *whoosh*, the drop net ripped away from the canopy and plunged into the forest below.

"You got it, Mickey!" Claire shouted.

The Rex burst out of the woods and onto the mossy bank entangled in the net, the creature fighting the mesh of its captivity, enraged, squealing, snapping its big jaws, trying to bite its way out of the Kevlar-reinforced netting with those large, serrated teeth.

"It looks healthy," Mick said. "Big, too. I estimate he's a twelve-footer. Probably weighs in at eight-hundred pounds or more."

The animal quickly wound down, losing energy as it fought against the net and the drug took effect.

Mick saw two sedation darts entrenched in the animal's side, the syringes bouncing as it struggled to escape.

"Our guys' aim was true," Mick said, working the remote to tighten the net around their quarry.

"Our buyer will be thrilled," Claire said, peering through the binoculars.

Baker and Yount stepped out of the woods dressed in camouflage fatigues, whooping and hollering, waving their tranq rifles around like they were a conquering army. They moved in on the netted Rex, which had dropped on its side on the lichen-covered bank, drawing in labored breaths that lessened with each exhale.

"Good work as usual, gents," Mick hollered across the pond.

Ray Yount gave them a thumbs-up.

Mick slid the drop net remote in his belt holster and looked at Claire. "Our buyer awaits. Let's go get our prize."

Max Baker backed the transport truck out of the woods to the edge of the pond, next to the downed Rex. Baker and Yount lifted the lid off the large heavy-duty aluminum crate that sat on the flatbed trailer, then set up the portable gantry crane that extended over the animal and crate. The steel crane and hoist assembly was capable of lifting up to five tons; an 800-pound Rex would present no problem for this rig.

Mick and Claire moved in, cautiously checking the health of the sedated animal. Satisfied that the Rex was properly dosed, they began stripping away the netting and prepping the canvas slings. Most of the weight was in the Rex's broad chest, so the four of them worked at slipping blanket-padded slings under the hind legs and head, careful to stay clear of the bite zone.

Yount activated the hoist from a wireless remote control pad. He worked the toggle, a loud screeching whine carrying across the pond as the winch pulley lifted the sleeping creature. When the Rex was a few feet off the ground, Yount stopped the crane, and they all moved in to secure two more slings under the creature's midsection. This heavy duty webbing protected the Rex's torso and ensured the animal was fully supported on the lift up into the truck.

Up, up, up the anaesthetized animal went, until it hung suspended twelve feet up, swinging in the stiff breeze.

"Careful, Ray," Mick yelled to Yount.

"No worries, Mick," Yount shouted back, concentrating on the swaying animal as he punched buttons on the controller.

He then activated the trolley that ran along the gantry's top beam. The winch groaned as the swaddled beast was pulled horizontally until it hung over the top of the open crate. Yount worked the toggle, deftly lowering the animal, setting the beast down gently on the floor of the crate.

It took Baker and Yount less than fifteen minutes to seal up the crate and break down the gantry crane rigging. The beast would sleep for another four hours, just long enough to deliver it to their customer in Montana.

Mick and Claire walked around the pond to their Polaris.

Mick Prescott was a happy man. They had just made a hundred grand for a few hours work.

Taxidermists, Meteorites and Magnetometers

June 1: Gilliam's Guidepost

Heart Butte, Montana

"HAVE THE POLICE SEEN THIS YET, Gilliam?"

Hayden Fowler glanced at Bryan over the severed T-Rex head as he used a scalpel to scrape flakes of dried blood from the neck.

"Yeah, two officers from the tribal police were here yesterday."

"*Tribal* cops?" Hayden said with a huff. "I'd say this calls for *real* police."

"Blackfeet Law Enforcement Services *are* real police, Hayden. This is their jurisdiction. One of them was a senior detective from the Criminal Investigations Division, so I know they're taking this seriously."

"As well they should." Hayden rubbed the blood samples into a plastic baggie. "So what did they have to say about it?"

"Well, they agreed it was a serious matter, especially in light of past history here on the Guidepost."

"No shit! Was this officer's name Captain Obvious?"

"Ha-ha, Hayden. I'll have you know these guys impressed me. They dusted the container and the head for prints, same as Mathews. Collected a couple of DNA samples. Took a bunch of pictures, then left. Said they'd be in touch soon but that they would increase patrols around my property in the meantime."

"This Mathews fella? He's the PI you told me about?"

Bryan nodded.

"He find anything?"

"Mike's tracking down a few leads. This morning he got two

court-ordered search warrants to get into FedEx and the postal service, though he isn't real high on the postal service avenue panning out. He says USPS doesn't maintain records of private PO box renters and that the box number is probably bogus anyway. But he *does* think getting into FedEx records will be worthwhile. And Mathews is excited about a script he found on our private server."

"That's where they hacked these photos?" Hayden said, pointing at the five Gilliam family snapshots, smiling faces punctuated by drops of blood.

"Yeah. He found two unknown IP addresses. Mike thinks the IP addresses are most likely proxies but he says he has ways of uncovering their source."

Hayden used the scalpel to peel away a strip of scaly Tyrannosaur hide and dropped it into a second baggie. "This beheading was done by a professional, Bryan. I'm quite sure of that."

"A pro? Whaddaya mean?"

"This is the work of an experienced taxidermist. See how precise the cut line is? Very carefully done. Not torn and ragged the way an amateur would separate the head. This was done by someone with a good working knowledge of organic anatomy and top-of-the-line tools. It's no easy chore taking the head off an animal this size. The clean and precise way it was done suggests an expert. I suggest your investigators check out taxidermists in the area."

Bryan leaned over the table and took a close look at the smooth, straight slash through the neck. "I didn't notice that before. Neither did Mathews or the Blackfoot detectives."

"That's because they're trained to look at criminal forensics whereas I'm focused on zoological morphology."

Hayden wiped off the scalpel with a cloth and placed the blade in his tackle box along with the baggies containing blood and hide samples. "The best taxidermists care about preserving the integrity of the hide so that there's minimal visible damage when they mount their specimens. I've seen a lot of their work in my travels." He pointed at the head. "I'm pretty sure someone with taxidermist training did this. It might not pan out, but then again, it might."

"Thanks, I'll pass that along to Mathews and the Blackfeet police."

"Please do. You need to get to the bottom of this soon. Have you talked to your kids yet?"

"No. Paul will be back from his Bozeman gig Sunday. Loretta and I wanted to have the entire family together for our talk."

Hayden looked across the way at the stage on the other side of the barn, absent now of the clutter of music instruments that had been there his last visit. "How's Paul's band doing?"

"Damned good considering they're four high school students."

"Four? I thought they were a power trio," Hayden said.

"Yeah, Paul's girlfriend Sin has worked her way into the lineup, and she's quite a good singer and percussionist."

"Sin?"

"Yeah. Sinopa Harwood. Sin for short. She's a Blackfoot, just like Paul's rhythm section, Kit and Ox. Seems the boys are having a bit of heartburn over Paul bringing Sin into the band."

Hayden grinned. "So Paul's girlfriend is the Yoko Ono of the band?"

Bryan laughed. "Well, Moonrise aren't—*isn't?*—the Beatles, so no. Sin is a nice girl. Very polite. A beautiful young lady. She's no Yoko Ono but Loretta and I do worry about her breaking our son's heart."

"I hope your oldest avoids the mistakes I made with women when I was his age," Hayden said with a hint of regret. He grabbed a caliper and a small, spiralbound notebook from the tackle box. Began measuring the Rex's teeth. "So how is Moonrise doing these days under the superb management of Sir Bryan Gilliam?"

Bryan smiled at Hayden's playfulness. "They're getting regular weekend gigs, building their fan base and trying to get into the studio when time permits to record their album."

"I hope they get their album out soon," Hayden said, using a cloth tape measure to get the circumference of the skull. "I've about worn the digits off their EP disc. Your boy is one talented son of a buck, Gilliam."

"Thanks. We're proud of him."

"You get him any personal security yet?"

"Yeah. Detective Mathews is hooking us up with bodyguards for both Paul and Ethan. For Loretta and me as well." Bryan shook his head, his salty brown locks brushing his shoulders. "I guess we're all gonna have to suck it up and say goodbye to our privacy for a while."

"It's the smart thing to do right now, Gill," Hayden said, packing up his tools and closing his tackle box. He pointed at the Rex head. "This is a very serious threat."

"Don't I know it."

The two men stared at the severed head in silence. Hayden wondered whether this had been one of his tagged Rexes he'd been tracking.

"What're you gonna do with it, Gilliam?"

"The police told us to keep it in our freezer. It's evidence."

"They didn't want to take it?"

"No. They told us they didn't have a proper place to keep it."

Hayden continued to stare at the head, taking in the elongated snout and rows of blade-like teeth. The haunting golden-crimson eyes that, even in death, seemed to be watching him with predatory insolence. A prolonged shiver moved through him as he thought back to the pair of Rexes that had attacked their Idaho survival camp last August. In his mind he relived the grisly scene of the Rex plucking his friend Jackson Lattimer from the campsite and taking him over the cliff, plunging a thousand feet into the Salmon River below.

"Are you okay, Hayden? You look a little shaky."

Bryan's voice pulled him out of the disturbing daydream. "Yeah, I'm fine, Gilliam!" he snapped, perturbed at being questioned. He nodded at the head. "Have you seen any of these bad boys around your ranch lately?"

"Not any Tyrannosaurs, no. But Loretta and I saw a couple of Dromaeosaurs last week on a horseback ride through the western pastures. First ones we'd seen this spring. They were at the edge of the woods feasting on a freshly killed deer. We only glimpsed them for a minute or two; they dragged their prey into the forest and disappeared when they saw us coming."

"They're gonna to be coming out in bigger numbers after the long winter," Hayden said.

Bryan shook his head in disgust. "Yeah, here we go again."

Their conversation was halted by the loud screeching of the barn doors opening. They turned to see Loretta Gilliam enter.

"What're you two aging hippies goin' on about out here?"

Hayden hadn't seen Loretta in a few months and she looked different—*fantastic* in fact. Younger and thinner, dressed in a bright floral top and snug-fitting jeans tucked inside knee-high snakeskin cowgirl boots. Her auburn hair was cut short and wrapped behind her ears.

"I didn't see you when you came in earlier, Hayden," she said, walking up to them. "My hubby isn't the greatest host."

Bryan rolled his eyes and threw up his hands in a *What're you gonna do?* gesture.

"Hey, Loretta. Great to see you, my dear," Hayden said, pulling her in for a hug. When they separated, his eyes took in the whole of her lithe body. "You look mighty fetching today."

"Thanks. You look great yourself. Much better than the last time I saw you. When was that? Four months ago? Three?"

"Yeah, February. At the Lacroix housewarming party."

"How're you feeling?"

"Fit as a fiddle," he lied; he rarely felt like his old pre-crash self these days. "I'm out and about again. Just finished up my first fieldwork in what feels like forever. Bill Carlton, the Idaho wildlife biologist, you remember him, right?"

Loretta nodded. "Yes, a fellow survivor."

"He accompanied me to Tally Lake in the Flathead National Forest, a good ways west of here. We stumbled on a new dinosaur species, at least one we haven't seen yet. Deinosuchus, an aquatic carnivore. Huge crocodilian animal. We saw it take down a mature grizzly. I've got some amazing video to show you folks."

Even Jackson would be impressed, he thought, lamenting his late friend, the internationally renowned nature videographer Jackson Lattimer.

"It killed a grizzly bear? Was Nora with you?"

"No, she's back in Minnesota putting the finishing touches on our next book. Nora's the responsible one," he said with a self-deprecating grin. "But, hey, enough about me. How's your iridium business doing?"

"It's dead in the water." Loretta frowned. "We ran through the last of our meteorite stock two months ago. The iridium was great while it lasted. We made a small fortune off the tech industry. If I had another one of those space rocks we'd be sitting in clover, as they say. We're still selling the meteorite jewelry, however. That's going well."

Hayden gave her a look of mock surprise. "From what I hear you Gilliams are already sitting in clover with that settlement money you got from AEF. Double-digit millions is what Nora told me."

Loretta blushed, then said, "Damn, I knew I shouldn't have told Nora. But I must say, you're a fine one to talk, Mr. Moneybags Bestselling Author! How many millions have you pulled in from your book, Hayden?"

"Busted," he said, laughing.

Hayden had long appreciated Loretta Gilliam's moxie. Beautiful and tough, she didn't back down from anyone or any*thing*. He recalled that she had wounded a Dromaeosaur in the Gilliam Guidepost quadrangle last year and chased it off into the woods.

"Anyway," Hayden said, tugging at his beard. "I might have a line on another meteorite."

"Really?" Bryan said, interested now. "Where?"

"I'm just speculating at this point but Carlton and I both believe there might be a large meteorite sitting on the bottom of Tally Lake. Maybe more than one. We're assuming the Deinosuchus we saw taking down the grizzly hatched out of a meteorite, same as the Rexes and Dromes and Triceratops. I sent copies of the videos I shot to the Smithsonian folks and they're excited about this new discovery. They've agreed to cover the cost of boat rental and divers to film the creature in its natural habitat. I've already put in calls to a couple of guys who worked for Jackson Lattimer. They're experienced in filming dangerous aquatic animals—saltwater crocodiles, great white sharks, orca whales. I'm also looking into renting a marine magnetometer that we can drag behind the boat that'll detect the presence of extraterrestrial boulders."

Bryan, eyes wide, said, "Meteorites?"

"Yes."

"How does a magnetometer find meteorites? Does it look for iridium or something else?"

"Iridium isn't magnetic, but the meteorites we've seen thus far are loaded with iron-nickel alloys, which *are* magnetic. Regular stones and rocks have different compositions from meteorites. The kind of magnetometer I'm talking about will zero in on those meteorites, if there are any. That said, Tally Lake covers a large area—more than thirteen-hundred acres. It reaches depths of three-hundred feet or more. The depths aren't the problem but the acreage is. Also, the water is tea colored so the visibility in some areas is limited. It could be problematic for filming."

"Would we be able to lift a meteorite out of the lake?" Bryan asked. "Could we use our choppers with a dropline basket?"

"No. This isn't a job for helicopters. I'm not gonna lie. It would be a tough extraction. Divers would have to chisel out small sections and bring them up to the boat. Quite laborious and very dangerous with our Cretaceous carnivore cruising the lake. These divers I'm talking about specialize in underwater photography, but they're interested in wildlife, not meteorites. It might be difficult to get people to do the kind of underwater work we need done. But, hell, it's all just conjecture at this point. We have to locate a meteorite first."

"How populated is this lake, Hayden?" Loretta asked. "Are there swimmers? Boaters?"

"It's quite remote. There are campsites with a boat launch but Bill and I didn't see anyone the three days we were there. And the water is so cold I doubt there are ever any swimmers in Tally Lake, unless it's the Polar Bear Club or something."

Loretta let out a soft chuckle, then said, "What about boating and diving restrictions? Do you need a license to operate a boat or for dragging the lake with a magnetometer? For scuba diving?"

"We checked on that. You don't need a boating license or a diving permit. They're moot points anyway since we aren't likely to see another soul when we're doing our thing there."

"Just the Deino—what did you call it?"

"Deino*suchus*. It's quite the beast. A fully-grown grizzly bear was no match for it. Carlton and I call it Tally Lake's Loch Ness Monster. Nessie 2.0. And who knows, there could be more than one of them. I'm betting there is."

Hayden observed Bryan and Loretta looking at each other, some silent marital communication passing between them.

Finally Loretta said, "Why don't we go to the house and get comfortable, have something to drink. You can show us your videos, Hayden, and we can talk about this.

She turned and led them out of the barn. "Wow! Possibly another meteorite and a new dino species? I don't know if we should feel excited or frightened."

Hayden grinned, following in Loretta's footsteps. "Probably a lot of both," he said, his grin melting away as they walked across the quad to the house.

Clipped Wings

June 2: Gilliam's Guidepost Heliport Hangar

Heart Butte, Montana

PETER LACROIX SAT IN THE COCKPIT of the FRASCA Bell 407 flight simulator working the controls. He flew over a digital landscape of forested wilderness.

His right hand felt clammy on the cyclic stick.

His left hand trembled on the collective lever.

His feet were uncoordinated on the anti-torque pedals.

His pulse raced.

Rivulets of sweat ran down his sides and back, his shirt plastered to the back of the seat.

His armpits were soaked.

Peter wanted this first simulated flight to go well.

It wasn't.

Frightful memories of the Idaho crash stormed through him.

It's been so long.

My piloting confidence is gone, he thought, shaken.

Bryan Gilliam bought the simulator as a pilot training tool. The cockpit was an exact replica of the two new 407s Peter had purchased for Fowler-Lemoyne Aviation. The massive 30 x 30 foot simulator took up most of one corner of the building, rising 20 feet up into the rafters. Enormously heavy, Bryan had hired a few of his Blackfeet friends to reinforce the concrete flooring.

The FRASCA simulator promised to deliver authentic Bell 407 full-flight piloting scenarios. The training module offered state of the art integrated Garmin avionics, full motion chassis roll and pitch mobility, realistic in-flight vibration, true-to-life overhead rotor blade hum, and high fidelity flight modeling (convincing panoramic high-definition bubble window landscape displays).

This training device came close to duplicating the in-air piloting experience.

Too close, maybe?

Peter flew over a ridge of Engelmann spruce and subalpine fir. The view opened up to an impossibly high cliff on his right with a sheer drop down to a wide river snaking through the canyon far below. Freaky how alarmingly close the scene represented the Idaho crash site.

A dark dèjá vu feeling overwhelmed him.

Paranoia stabbed him in the chest as he conjured up those prehistoric flying reptiles that had caused the accident. In his mind's eye he saw a swarm of Quetzalcoatlus darkening the digital skies.

It all came rushing back in a demented daydream.

Their enormous wingspans.

Their long beaks.

The easy way they glided on the thermals like large black albatrosses.

The way they came at his chopper in a thick, black cloud.

Terrible sounds of the flyers being sliced and diced by the rotor blades.

Dashboard LED readouts and digital displays going haywire as the chopper spiraled out of control.

He could feel the aircraft skidding through the treetops, tumbling, plunging, the landing skids ripping out large swaths of foliage.

His breathing quickened and he gasped for air, on the verge of hyperventilating.

Bad mistake taking that oxy this morning, buddy boy.

You're certainly not helping your cause.

And this is just a simulator. What happens when you're up in the air for real?

Get a grip, man!

He cut his simulated flight short, shut down the unit and removed his headphones. His arms shook. He felt dizzy, couldn't catch his breath. The rugged backcountry display disappeared, the bubble windows now clear. He stared through the windshield at the interior of the hangar, seeing fleet mechanic Carl Lacey working on the fuselage of one of the 407s across the way.

Peter thought he would be sick but he held it back, taking long, deep breaths, trying to resettle himself, to regain his equilibrium.

He climbed out of the simulator and bent over, hands on knees, the queasiness squeezing him. He shook his head, trying to chase the nausea and terrifying visions.

"You okay over there, Lacroix?"

Peter looked up from his crouched position to catch a glimpse of Hayden Fowler approaching. *What is Hayden doing here?* He straightened and leaned against the simulator frame. Hayden was the last person he wanted to see in this wrecked state.

"Hey, Hayden," he said, his voice a weak croak. "I thought you'd be back in Minnesota."

"I stuck around an extra day knowing you were coming."

Hayden wore jeans, muddy hiking boots, and a green sweatshirt bearing the words WAR IS THE ONLY TRUE PORN. His hair and beard were much longer since Peter had last seen him at their house-warming party in February. Fowler had the look of a scruffy feral mountain man, like one of those ZZ Top rockers or a *Duck Dynasty* dude. The shaggy change coupled with Hayden's six-foot-four frame made him a truly imposing figure, and Peter swallowed hard at his approach.

"How're you doing, my friend?" Hayden said, his words laced with pity, his bearing suggesting sympathy.

"Good," Peter said, not liking the way Hayden looked at him, as if he was roadkill he just ran over with his car.

An awkward silence ensued, Hayden checking him out with a judgmental stare. Peter shifted his feet and looked away, uncomfortable with the examination.

"You look like shit, Lacroix," Hayden said finally.

The barb hurt. "Really? *That's* what you have to say to me after all this time?"

"Well, I was hoping to find you in better shape, to be honest. You still on the pain meds?"

Peter looked at him, held his stare. "I'm okay, really, Hayden. I just had a, um . . . a bad experience with this simulator. It's unbelievably realistic, which is good, but it was my first time at the controls since the crash and, um, it brought back some bad shit. Surely you of all people can understand that."

"I do, yes," Hayden said, softening, a more empathetic light in his eyes. "I'm still dealing with a few demons myself. A few aches and pains." He laughed then, surprising Peter. Hayden's moods had always quickly fluctuated. "Maybe we should rename the company the Fowler-Lemoyne *Infirmary*. You with your bad shoulder and cranky back. Gilliam with his bum leg and gunshot wounds. Me down to one kidney and recovering from a head injury. All three of us with residual nightmares. Jesus, Lacroix, our women seem to be the only ones who are doing well."

Peter nodded. "Yeah, maybe that's because they aren't burdened with testosterone. It tends to make us susceptible to doing crazy stunts. Makes us want to play hero all the time."

"You might have a point there, partner."

"I mean, look at Jackson Lattimer. He—"

"I'd really rather not, Lacroix."

"Jesus, you're right. Too soon. Sorry, Hayden. My bad."

"It'll *always* be too soon," Hayden said, his eyes heavy with tears. "So you never answered my question. You still on the junk?"

"I'm almost completely clean."

"What does *almost* mean?"

Peter hated this kind of interrogation. He'd been through it with Bryan Gilliam a couple of times and he had no patience for it. "Look, Hayden. This grounding is killing me. I wasn't meant to live with clipped wings. I wasn't meant to be an office worker. I *know* I'm capable of flying a bird again. I'm ready to be your and Nora's personal pilot again. I'm—"

"The man I'm looking at right now is *not* ready to pilot our aircraft," Hayden said, giving him that hypercritical look again. "I know I wouldn't go up in a chopper with you at the controls right now."

"Wow!" The comment crushed Peter. "Could you be any more

direct?"

"I came out of the womb *direct*," Hayden said with a sneer. "The way you keep avoiding my question tells me all I need to know, Lacroix."

Peter sensed he was losing ground here. "C'mon, Hayden. You know I really appreciate all you and Nora have done for me, giving me a job and keeping me on the payroll during the company downtime the way you have. Giving me that big promotion. But I'm lost being earthbound. *Please* let me fly again."

Hayden ran a hand through his beard, seeming to give it some thought. "It's not up to me. It's Gilliam's decision."

"Whaddaya mean? The company is in your name, isn't it? I mean, it's Fowler-Lemoyne Aviation. Not *Gilliam*-Lemoyne."

"No, but it *is* Gilliam's Guidepost Heliport. Bryan's the general manager. He oversees all aspects of the heliport. You know that, Peter. We discussed this when we set up the company."

"And yet, I'm the one hiring and training the pilots. Shouldn't I be the one making decisions about pilot readiness?"

Hayden shot him an irritated look. "When Gilliam says you're ready, that's when you'll be back in the cockpit. Full stop. He's the one you need to convince. Not me." He laid a hand on Peter's shoulder. "I know you've been through a lot. We've been through a lot together. You're one hell of a helicopter pilot, Peter. I doubt there are many other pilots that could have saved us during that Idaho crash. The way you brought our crippled aircraft down in those treetops saved most of us. You performed a miracle over the Salmon River, but we must consider the safety of our passengers when we put pilots behind the controls. I know it's hard, but get yourself clean, Lacroix. That's your golden key back into the pilot's seat. Convince Gilliam and we'll get you back in the air where you belong. Now if you'll excuse me, I've got a plane to catch. I've been away from Nora for way too long."

Peter watched Hayden walk away, his boots slapping against the polished concrete floor.

The big man had spoken in true Fowleresque fashion.

Millionaires and Bodyguards

June 3: Gilliam's Guidepost

Heart Butte, Montana

"YOUR FATHER AND I WOULD LIKE TO DISCUSS a couple of things with you kids," Loretta said, scanning the faces of the three young Gilliams gathered in the den.

Ethan, two months shy of sixteen, muttered, "Uh-oh, That always means trouble."

Sister Lianne, nine, glanced at her mother with a worried expression. Just-turned-eighteen Paul lounged on one end of the sofa, not engaged whatsoever. He yawned and stretched out his long arms, rubbed his eyes. He had come in at three AM from his weekend band gig in Bozeman and looked exhausted.

Bryan shook his head. "No. Not trouble, Ethan. But important."

Loretta started it off. "First, we want you to know about something we feel you're entitled to know. Something we've been keeping from you and we realize now we've been wrong to do so. We um, well . . ." She looked to Bryan for support and he nodded, telling her with his eyes to continue. "We came into a good bit of money last year. From a legal settlement. That lawsuit we brought against those AEF people who set our dinosaurs loose and bull-dozed our property. Those people who torched our home and shot your father."

"You mean the *animals* who shot Dad," Ethan stated bitterly. "They aren't people. They're *monsters.*"

Bryan said, "That may be true, Eeth, but—"

"How much money did you and Mom get?" Paul croaked, his voice hoarse from singing the past two nights.

Bryan looked at Loretta, then said simply, "Millions."

"*Millions*?" Ethan shouted in surprise. "Plural?"

"Yes, millions. With an 'S' on the end."

Paul sat up on the sofa, more alert now. "How many millions exactly, Pops?"

"*Ten* million. That's how much it was worth to, um, those *monsters,* to avoid a public trial. But because of taxes we only—"

"I *knew* it!" Paul cut him off. "I had a hunch. I wondered where you got the cash to buy the band new instruments and book us all those hours of studio time. Where you got the money to buy us the new tour bus. I suspected you were lying when you said it came from our meteorite jewelry and iridium sales."

Bryan struck a defensive tone. "I wasn't lying. Some of the money *did* come from the jewelry. More from our iridium sales."

"*You* bought Paul that bus, Dad?" Ethan turned to face his older brother. "You told me *you* bought it with your gig money. What a lyin' sack of shit you are, Pauley puke."

"And you believed it, Ethan! You're so frigging gullible. Maybe if you were doing somethin' important like me Pops would throw some cash your way, too."

Ethan's face flushed scarlet. He clenched his fists and stood. Took a step toward Paul. "You're a self-centered asshole, you wanker!"

Bryan quickly moved in between his two boys, arms out, keeping them separated. "All right, let's settle down, guys," he said, turning to Paul. "You have no right to say that to your brother, Pauley. Ethan's accomplishments on the baseball diamond are no less impressive than your musical exploits. And Ethan, your brother doesn't own the bus. Your mother and I do. We're the management team for Moonrise and the vehicle is registered in our names. One more thing. Both of you need to watch your language around your sister. She's very impressionable."

"I'm *not* im…impwessible," Lianne spluttered.

"It's okay, Lee," Loretta said, patting her hand. She cast a cautioning eye at both sons. "Let's keep the peace, shall we, boys?" "Now, as far as the money goes, our lawyer, Mr. Pinnaker, advised us to put the money in a trust, which we did. It's a tax shelter and earns interest. Each of you will get your shares when you turn twenty five."

"Twenty-*five*? What the hell," Ethan whined. "That's it? What about right now? You're buyin' all this music shit for puke face here," he said, pointing at Paul, "but you haven't gotten me a goddamned thing."

"Watch your tongue, Ethan Joseph Gilliam," Loretta warned.

"Yeah, you didn't get me anything either," Lianne yowled. "It's. Not. Fair!" she screeched, pounding the sofa cushions to emphasize each word. "I won't be twenty-five for a hundred years!"

"Quiet down, Lee," Loretta looked over her children, thinking: *I love all three of you dearly but you are so spoiled.* To Lianne she said, "Your father and I haven't forgotten about you and Ethan, baby girl. You wanna tell them, Bry?"

"Sure," he said, maintaining his position between Ethan and Paul. "We've got a beautiful monogrammed saddle on order for you, Lee, with a matching riding vest, cowgirl hat, and Western boots. You're gonna love the saddle. It's got a silhouette of Beauregard hand tooled into the leather."

"Sill-oh . . . *what*?"

"Yes. A silhouette—a picture of your horse. Engraved into the saddle. It'll make Beau feel special."

Lianne smiled. "Beau *is* special."

"Of course he is, honey," Loretta told her. "But that's not all we got you, Lee. We got you a GoPro videocam so you can film your rides."

"My own camera? Thanks, Mama."

"That was your dad's idea."

"Thank you, too, Daddy."

"So what about me?" Ethan said.

Bryan said, "For you, Eeth, we've contracted a company to build out batting cages with automated pitching machines and overhead LED lights for night practice. You can invite your teammates over for batting practice. Whaddaya think of that?"

Ethan beamed. "Awesome! Really cool, Dad. Thanks."

"You're welcome, son."

Loretta exchanged looks with Bryan. She wondered if he was thinking the same thing she was: *Are we giving our kids too much? Is this the right thing to do? Should we have kept the money secret from them?* She looked from Lianne to Ethan and finally to Paul. *They've been through so much the past couple of years. They deserve this and more.*

"Are we done here?" Paul said. "I'm whipped. I need to crash."

"Your father has one more piece of business to discuss with you."

She knew this would be a much more difficult conversation.

"Yeah. Take a load off, boys."

Paul retreated to his end of the sofa. Ethan returned to his spot in the recliner.

"A few days ago an incident occurred here that has us, well…I won't pretty this up…it has us a bit concerned," Bryan began.

"What kind of incident?" Ethan asked.

"The details aren't important, Eeth. What *is* important is to know that all of us need to exercise extreme caution each and every day. We've gotten a bit lax lately. We've let our guard down through the long winter. We all know our history. It's no secret that we have been targeted by some unbalanced people in the past . . ."

Loretta observed her daughter listening to Bryan's words of caution. Lianne focused on him with wide-eyed innocence, hanging on his every word. She looked so young and fragile—so *vulnerable*—sitting there with her hands folded primly across the lap of her jeans, dressed in her favorite pink t-shirt with the words JUST A GIRL WHO LOVES HORSES stenciled over a sketch of a galloping stallion. She was Loretta's precious little darling.

". . . I don't think it will amount to anything," Bryan continued, "but just to be safe we've decided to take some more precautions in the form of extra security."

"More security?" Paul said. "Christ almighty, we've already got enough security guards roaming the ranch to cover Fort Knox. Can't hardly take a dump without some peeping eyes on me."

Lianne giggled and Ethan let out a muffled snort.

"I think you're embellishing things just a little," Bryan said to Paul. "But you're right to a certain degree. We have enough professional security here at the Guidepost. It's when you and Eeth are out and about in the outside world that has us concerned."

"What's that mean in plain English, Pops?"

"It means when you're out playing your music you're unprotected. You're an open target."

"Jesus, I pack my Glock every time I leave the ranch."

"I know, Paul, and I appreciate that you followed my instructions. But a gun doesn't do you much good when you're up on stage singing and playing. That's when you're most exposed."

"All the venues we play at have security watching our backs."

"They're rent-a-cops, Pauley. Most of them lack professional training."

"What exactly are you saying, Pops?"

"You know that private investigator I've worked with? Detective Mathews?"

"Yeah."

"Well, he set us up with bodyguards for you and Ethan. He assures me they are real pros."

"A *bodyguard*?" Paul shrieked. "No! No way I'm letting some cop ride with us in the tour bus."

"They're not cops. They have Secret Service backgrounds."

"Even worse. Kit and Ox won't stand for it. I don't either."

"You *will* have a bodyguard. At least until we get to the bottom of this new threat."

"No I won't," Paul said, voice rising. "I'm eighteen now and an adult. You can't tell me what to do anymore."

"I've got news for you, son. The legal age in Montana is twenty-one. Three more years to adulthood for you, buddy boy."

Ethan jumped in. "Why do *I* need a bodyguard? I just play baseball. What, is this Secret Service guy gonna stand on second base and watch over me?"

Bryan let out a quiet groan. "You guys need to learn that the world can be harsh. There are some bad people out there who—"

"You think we don't know that?" Paul said. "After what went

down here at our picnic? You think we're stupid, Pops?"

"No, I don't think you're stupid. Just a little naïve about the ways of the world. You're going to get a bodyguard whether you like it or not."

"I refuse!" Paul stood, flicked his hair away from his face petulantly and went to Bryan, poked him in the chest. "And you can't make me, old man."

Loretta listened to them jawing and came to Bryan's defense. "If you don't agree to this bodyguard protection, your father and I will have no choice but to take the band bus away."

"*What?*" Paul said, turning to her, astonished. "You wouldn't *dare*. You can't do that."

"Oh, but we can. And we will if you don't cooperate."

Paul looked at his parents. "Jesus, you two treat me like I'm a child. I get no respect from you at all."

Loretta felt the back of her throat burning in anger. She wanted to tell him that respect had to be earned. But that would only pour fuel on the fire. She recalled the argument they'd had last week, when Paul skipped his high school graduation, saying he was done with education and had no interest in college. That he was going to be a famous rock star. Loretta loved her oldest son more than life itself, but his immaturity and selfishness was wearing thin. His rock music thing was short term at best. She knew it and Bryan knew it. Unfortunately Paul did not.

"I can't believe this shit," Paul said, turning and walking away. "I gotta get some shuteye. We've got another gig tomorrow night."

Loretta watched Paul leave the den, heard him clomping up the stairs to his bedroom then slam his door shut. "So does this mean he's accepting the bodyguard treatment?" she said to Bryan.

Bryan hunched his shoulders. "Your guess is as good as mine."

Lianne raised her voice. "Hey, how come I don't get a body-guard? I'm important, too, ya know."

"Yes you are, Lee," Loretta said, sharing a laugh with Bryan. "That's why you have the best bodyguards on the planet."

"Who, Mama, who?"

"Your daddy and me."

Kootenai Wildflowers

June 4: Gilliam's Guidepost

The Cellar Suites

Heart Butte, Montana

BRINSHOU STOOD BY THE FREIGHT ELEVATOR, waiting for the cage to rise that would take her down to Peter's suite in The Cellar. She held a bouquet of sweet smelling flowers in one hand and a small travel bag in the other.

Her eyes were heavy and gritty. Her legs were stiff. Her back hurt. She'd gotten very little sleep last night and the four-hour drive across the night-cloaked mountains and dark plains east of the Rockies had drained her.

Brin tapped her foot nervously. Peter had no idea she was coming and she prayed she made the right decision. She hoped he would see her visit as a sign of her enduring love for him and not as an attack.

She would have driven across the continent in a snowstorm for her beloved husband if she had to.

She tried to gather up her courage.

He needs me right now. More than ever.

She kept telling herself that.

Peter left their home in suburban Missoula three days ago to begin his work training newly-hired pilots at Gilliam's Guidepost. Brin suggested he wasn't ready to be away for a week. As expected, Peter had disagreed vehemently. He reminded her that he had been doing well battling his opioid addiction and was weening himself off the drugs. He'd been attending NA meetings and maintaining a positive attitude, he told her. She couldn't refute any of that. That was all well and good, but it still didn't make him fit for a week away on his own. And after their FaceTime call last night, Brin knew without question she shouldn't have let him leave home.

She was convinced he was in trouble.

During the call Brin tried to convince him to come back home. But Peter had been insistent, saying he owed it to his business partners—Hayden, Nora, and Bryan. He explained that he was contractually obligated to hire and train pilots and that he had to do that at Gilliam's Guidepost. It wasn't something he could do from their Florence home like the deskwork he'd been doing the past few months. The pilots he managed were a critical piece in getting Fowler-Lemoyne Aviation back operating again, he'd said.

Brin stared into the deep dark mouth of the elevator shaft that Bryan Gilliam called a cage hoist system. Last summer the entire Lacroix family—Brin, Peter, Kimi, and Brin's mother Kachina—lived in this subterranean living space built by Bryan Gilliam and his late brother-in-law, Jimmy Enright. Bryan told them the freight elevator was a holdover from the days when zinc was mined out of these depths. Bryan and Jimmy Enright, both Afghanistan veterans, had converted the mines into underground apartments as a luxurious survival bunker for the Gilliam and Enright families. She could hear Bryan's gruff voice in her mind's ear:

"This is where we will live when the power hungry morons who rule the world decide to finally launch their missiles of doom."

The comment had ratcheted up Brin's anxiety and she recalled having trouble sleeping the first few nights they spent in their Cellar suites. It had been difficult for her to adapt to living underground. The apartments, however, were plush and comfortable, with all the modern living conveniences one could possibly want. But this pitch black shaft and rickety elevator still made her uneasy.

The cables groaned. A cool, damp breeze washed over her as the cage lifted up through the deep shaft.

Still slower than a drunken snail, she thought, impatient.

Brin's thoughts revolved around last night's FaceTime call. Despite his efforts to show himself as happy and confident, Peter looked and sounded beat down and defeated. A three-day growth of stubble fuzzed his face. Shadowy bags hung under glassy eyes. He seemed dazed, confused at times. She saw it in his mannerisms, could hear the doubt creeping into his voice. His speech was slurred as he went on at length about Hayden Fowler tearing into him, telling him he wasn't ready to pilot a chopper.

"Hayden read me the riot act and it really got to me," he'd said in a weepy, whiny tone. She found his victim stance embarrassing.

Peter used to be the strong one. Now I'm the caregiver.

It wasn't lost on her how their roles had reversed since the crash. Before Peter's chopper had gone down in the Idaho wilderness he had supported her and held her up through her battles with serious anxiety. Now Brin was the pillar of strength in the marriage.

She feared Peter had backslid being on his own these few days.

Would he really have loaded up with oxy knowing we would be FaceTiming?

There were times during the call she thought Peter might even be suicidal so Brin thought it best not to let daughter Kimi see her father this way. Of course, their three-year-old protested loudly. She wanted to say hi to Daddy. She missed Daddy so much. Kimi carried on like the toddler she was but Brin held her ground.

It was their first time apart since the helicopter crash nine months ago. This trip was critical. For their marriage. For their growing family. For her husband's health. Brin *had* to see Peter up close and personal. She needed to deal with him face-to-face.

The cage arrived, jerking to a stop in front of her. The scissor gates slid open and Brin entered. She set her bag down and punched the button for level 2. The gates clattered shut and she felt her stomach lurch as the cage bounced once, twice, before descending.

She clung to a support bar and peered through the iron latticework as the cage lowered. The low-wattage bulb dangling overhead cast faint light on the chalky shaft walls. A dusty, moldy metallic odor mingled with the stench of grease and crankcase oil. The warped wooden slats of the platform vibrated beneath her feet. This clanging, rattling drop always made her uncomfortable.

I absolutely needed to make this trip, she thought, trying to take her mind off the bumpy ride down.

Petey needs me.

She passed the level 1 landing, the interior of the cage brightening as the well-lighted hallway opened up. A series of doors lined either side.

Level 1 slowly rolled past and she was plunged back into semi-darkness. The thick mildewy air brought on a sneeze.

Another few squeaky bounces and level 2 opened up in front of her. The cage jerked to a stop. Bright fluorescent light streamed in. The gates scraped open. Brin grabbed her travel bag and stepped out, the light hurting her eyes. She walked down the narrow hallway to Peter's suite. Stopped, put an ear to the door. Listened. Heard a sitcom laugh track playing in a distant part of the suite.

She took a deep breath and knocked.

She waited. No activity. She knocked again, harder this time.

Feet shuffling, quiet and slow, then getting louder.

The peephole darkened.

Brin stood there, feeling naked and on display, wondering what must be going through his mind as he peered out at her through the tiny eyehole.

"Brin?" Peter said, surprised, his voice muted behind the door.

The door opened and he stood before her, shirtless and barefoot, wearing a pair of Toronto Maple Leaf sweatpants, his short dark hair tangled.

"Um, wow! This is certainly a surprise," he said. "What are you doing here, Brin?"

"I came to see you. To *be* with you."

He stepped out into the hallway, looked at her travel bag, then behind her. "Just you?"

"Aren't I enough?"

"Uh, yeah. Of course. But where are Kimi and the baby?"

"I came alone. Kimi and Jacob are in good hands with Mother."

"You drove all that way through the night alone? That could have been dangerous, honey. If you had broken down—"

"But I didn't. I was really worried about you after our call last night. Aren't you glad to see me?"

"Of course I am," he said, leaning in and kissing her cheek.

He looked even more tired than he had on the call. "I hope I didn't come too late," she said. "I didn't wake you did I?"

"No. I was just watching TV in bed."

"Alone, I hope."

"Brin!" he said with a wounded look. "That's not even—"

"I'm kidding, Mr. Mopey." She grabbed his hand and stroked his wrist. "Don't be so sensitive. I brought some flowers to cheer you up. A little something to brighten your bachelor pad."

"It's not a bachelor . . ." he started, then glanced at the bouquet. "Thank you, honey. They're beautiful."

She extended the flowers to him, explaining, "It's an arrangement of Kootenai wildflowers. The purple flowers are a mix of camas and bush sage. The white ones with the little cones are beargrass, and the gold-colored ones are yarrow. These particular wildflowers have deep spiritual significance for my people."

"Oh? How so?" Peter said, taking the bouquet and taking a deep sniff.

"They represent renewal and endurance. They provide spiritual balance and are known to us Kootenai as living symbols of survival."

"They smell fantastic." He looked at her, then down at her bag. "This looks like more than an overnight stay."

"It is. I'm staying the rest of the week."

"What about the store? Your work?"

"Luana and Nuna can handle it, just like they did when I was here last year working for Bryan."

Peter seemed in a daze as he stared at the floral arrangement.

She slid her hand up his arm. "You don't seem very happy to see me, Peter. Don't you want me here?"

"Sure I do," he said, snapping out of his stupor. "You just caught me by surprise is all. Here, let me take that for you." He grabbed her travel bag. "Come on inside. It's chilly out here."

She followed him into the suite and he shut the door behind them.

"Let's get your flowers in some water," he said, going to a

cupboard in the kitchenette and pulling out a vase. "They're really beautiful." He set the vase on the counter and turned to her, his face pinched, like he smelled something bad. "But I really don't think I'm in need of any—what did you call it?—renewal and endurance? Spiritual balance? There isn't any reason why you needed to come all this way just for me. I'm fine, really."

Self-deception is a particularly damaging lie. Brin had been there herself, many times and it had never served up a positive outcome. He needed to hear the blunt truth. "No, you're not fine," she told him, pained at seeing him wince at her frankness. "Far from it. The drugs are killing you, Peter. They're unraveling you and pulling us apart. Pulling our family apart." She went to him and put her hand on his bare chest. "It's been going on too long, dear, and it needs to stop."

He removed her hand and stepped back. "So this is an intervention, then."

"If that's the way you want to see it, then yes. It's a long *overdue* intervention," she said, her voice shaky, tears pooling in her eyes. "Kimi has asked me a couple of times lately, 'Is Daddy okay, Mommy?' It breaks my heart when I hear those words from her. It's devastating when I have to lie to her."

She saw him slouching against the counter, shoulders slumped. A tear trickled down his cheek. His words were a strained whisper. "The last thing in the world I want is to hurt our little girl. Or you."

Brin went to him, wrapped her arms around him and brushed a tuft of hair up off his forehead. "I know that, baby. I love you so much, Petey. *That's* why I'm here. I'm not judging you." Her tears were flowing freely now. "I just want things to be the way they were before those damned meteorites came down and delivered those hellish beasts."

"That's what I want, too, Brin. But you have to understand, I almost died on top of that cliff in Idaho. In fact there were a couple of times I thought I *had* died. You don't get over something like that quickly. I'm having a really difficult time coming back to reality. Getting off the oxy is the hardest thing I've ever tried to do."

"Harder than learning to fly a helicopter?"

"Absolutely. Piloting a chopper has always felt second nature to me. Kicking opioids on the other hand, well, it just seems impossible at times."

"I understand. I really do. I'm here to help. But you have to *let* me help. You have to let me back inside your head and your heart. Can you do that for me? For yourself?"

He gave her a weak nod.

She locked her hands behind his neck and pulled him close, leaned her forehead against his. She looked him directly in his bloodshot eyes, her cheeks wet with tears, her arms shaking. "I almost lost you after the crash and now I feel like I'm losing you to drugs. Can't you see my pain here? Can't you *feel* it?"

"I *can*. I feel your pain and I'm so, so sorry."

He sobbed along with her. They stood in the kitchenette holding each other, weeping and sniffling.

After several long tearful, wordless minutes, Peter broke the embrace and wiped at his eyes. "Look at us," he said between snuffles, red-faced with embarrassment. "We're bawling like a couple of newborn babies."

She reached out and dabbed a tear off his cheek. "Crying is nothing to be ashamed of," she said, trying to get control of her runaway emotions. She ruffled his hair and smiled. "It shows me how much you love me. How much you care."

"I *do* love you, honey," he said, coming out of his slouch and standing taller. "I knew you were the only woman for me the first time you waited on me at the Smokehouse all those years ago. That hasn't changed. I care about you more than anything else in this crazy world. And god, I would *never* do anything intentionally to hurt you or our kids. But this addiction thing is kicking my ass. I'm really struggling, Brin. And being grounded isn't helping matters."

"I know that, and I'm always here for you."

He pushed away from the counter with a look of determination. "It's time for me to man up once and for all and do the right thing."

"What, uh . . . What do you mean?" she said, watching him leave the kitchenette.

"I'll be right back," he said, disappearing into the back

bedroom.

She heard him opening and closing the medicine cabinet door in the master bathroom, then rifling through drawers in the bedroom dresser before returning to the kitchenette. He entered holding two large prescription pill bottles.

"I should have done this months ago," he said, holding the bottles out for her to see. "This, my dearest Kootercake, is the absolute end of my stash." He handed the pills to her. "Take this to a pharmacy and get rid of them. I never want to see another oxy capsule in my life."

Brin shook the bottles, shocked at the volume—forty or fifty white oxycodone pills, if not more!

Brin felt a joyous buoyancy lift her heart. He hadn't called her Kootercake since before Kimi was born. She'd forgotten how much she liked what was once his go-to pet name for her.

She went to him and kissed him. "You called me Kootercake."

He smiled. "I did. And I'm sure if you look the word up in your Kootenai book of terminology you'll see that it means *The most beautiful woman on the planet.*"

He sounded like the Peter Lacroix of old.

"Oh, Petey, I love you so much," she said, hoping and wishing this would be the start of a new beginning.

Sookie's Lair

June 9: Tally Lake

Flathead National Forest, Montana

NORA BREATHED IN THE SWEET PINE SCENT and leaned back to let the afternoon sun warm her face. The 70-degree day and cloudless sky elevated her spirits.

She sat next to Hayden on the aft deck of 30-foot charter boat, *Deep Descent*. Three hired divers lounged on a padded bench facing them. A gentle breeze rippled the lake's surface. An osprey soared high overhead, gliding, circling, searching for fish.

Dive boat captain Clyde McAllister, mid-forties, stood at the helm decked out in a wide-brim booney hat, Carhartt cargo shorts, and deck shoes. His polo shirt had an anchor embroidered on the breast. He scanned the lake from behind blue-mirrored aviator sunglasses, steering the boat with bulging Popeye forearms. They slowly cruised the deep water, searching for submerged meteorites in a tight back-and-forth configuration the captain called a lawnmower pattern. A G-882 magnetometer trailed the boat on a Kevlar-reinforced electronics tow cable that unspooled from a large hydraulic winch. They had spent the past two hours trolling the lake, searching for magnetite, nickel-iron alloys, and ferrous deposits that could indicate a meteorite.

Nora and Hayden had learned that extraterrestrial boulders bearing dinosaur eggs were different from standard stony meteorites. They were loaded with iridium, a rare earth heavy metal that had no magnetic qualities. But the dinosaur meteorites they'd seen had enough ferromagnetic material to register on their G-882 cesium vapor magnetometer, a precise and highly sensitive device that could detect ferrous metals several hundred feet deep.

Hayden scrutinized the colorful display on his laptop, checking readings on the MagLog app.

So far, no hits.

And no appearance by the Deinosuchus, which Hayden had taken to calling Sookie.

Nora soaked up the sun, listening to the hum of the twin outboard motors and sporadic beeps coming from Hayden's computer. She pulled in a deep breath and her entire being expanded. This pastoral lake in the Montana wilderness revitalized her. After months of steady writing and editing, her Minnesota home office had become a confining prison cell. This getaway cleared her head and lifted her soul. She was back out in the natural world, doing fieldwork with Hayden again.

It felt familiar, comfortable, like old times.

Last week she had put the finishing touches on the book that had become pure drudgery. It wasn't her best work. But she cut herself some slack knowing it was the best she could do given the tight timeframe and Hayden's lack of help during the stressful final week of rewrites (she was still a bit miffed at him for that). The book was with their publishing team now, for better or worse. She feared *Dragons of the Great Divide: Running with the Beasts* wouldn't sell anywhere close to the number of copies their first book had.

If only there had been more time.

It could have been so much better if the powers that be had let us include a chapter or two on Hayden's discovery of the Deinosuchus.

Save it for the next book, publishing executives told her.

As if there will be another book.

No contracts had been offered for a third Nora Lemoyne-Hayden Fowler book yet, and she wasn't sure she would sign one if it came to be.

Truth be told, Nora had been thinking about returning to paleontology, her first love. Some of the best days of her career had been leading the Smithsonian Expedition in Choteau, Montana.

Back before the meteorites struck with their clutches of Cretaceous eggs. Back before her life had taken a bizarre turn.

Hayden's voice pulled her out of her musings. "We're over one of the deepest pockets in the lake. Three-hundred-fifty-seven feet."

"That's my reading as well," Captain McAllister yelled through the open pilothouse window. "This is the deepest lake in Montana."

One of the divers spoke. "Yeah, that water's colder than a nun's nasty." Nora looked at the Australian dive team leader, Caleb Campbell, whom everyone called CC. "Bloody dinkum, that'll be sure to wake us up. But this searchin' for a drowned space rock is goin' slower than a week of Mondays."

The other two divers smiled. Americans Milo Harper and Lana Kim were accustomed to Campbell's colorful Aussie jargon. They had worked together on a number of dives. All three had gone on dives with the late, internationally renowned wildlife videographer Jackson Lattimer. Caleb Campbell had last worked a video shoot with Lattimer filming saltwater crocodiles in the Adelaide River in Australia's Northern Territory, just weeks before Lattimer's death in Idaho. Harper and Kim had done high-risk dives with CC, in the U.S. and Europe, the most recent being photoshoot dives with humpback whales in Resurrection Bay, Alaska three weeks ago.

The three divers didn't hide their boredom and exasperation at having to wait. They were eager to get in the water and do their thing. But Hayden had cooled their jets. He'd explained that Tally Lake was big—1,200 acres or more—and finding a meteorite before committing to the dives would be the most practical way of going about finding Sookie. It would be a difficult task, yes. But without a meteorite as a base marker, they would be diving willy nilly with no clear plan. When pressed, Hayden explained his theory:

"These Cretaceous creatures tend to stay close to the meteorite from whence they hatched. They often return to their hatchout stone. I've seen this homing instinct many times. Sookie will be in close proximity to its mother meteorite, I guarantee it."

Nora scanned the impressive array of dive equipment and submersible cameras spread out on the rubber-coated deck: blue neoprene dry suits and accompanying fleece undergarments for cold water diving. Face-plated helmets equipped with wireless comm units. Fins, black neoprene gloves and hoods, weight belts, scuba tanks, regulators, gauges, videocams in waterproof cases, dive computers, LED video spotlights, dive torches. And there were wicked-looking knives and spearguns that reminded her of the danger that lurked beneath the surface.

Nora asked about the sophisticated spearguns and Caleb Campbell filled her in:

"They're specially configured powerhead spearguns with .44 magnum cartridges that fire bang sticks mounted on the shafts. These things have saved our asses many times over the years. Great for keeping pesky sharks and barracudas at bay."

Nora wondered if they would be a match for Sookie.

Campbell addressed Hayden. "I'm surprised we haven't gotten a gander at this Sookie critter yet, matey."

Hayden looked up from his laptop. "Me too. Sookie made an appearance the first two days Carlton and I were here. It was a no-show on day three, however. Probably because it got a plentiful meal out of that grizzly. And now it's been ten days since we were last here, so, who knows. He could have left the area, but I doubt it. I have a lot of confidence in my natal homing theory. If we could find a meteorite we could zero in on Sookie. I'm sure of it."

Milo Harper yawned and checked his watch. "More than two hours out here, going back and forth, and nothing is registering on your fancy high-tech equipment. It's a wild goose chase, Fowler. I don't think there's any meteorite out here and I'm quite sure your Sookie monster is long gone. Dumb nickname, by the way—*Sookie*. I mean, really, why the hell do we have to sit here while you search for that stupid rock? Why couldn't you have looked for meteorites on a separate charter and then called us in?"

Campbell slapped him on the arm. "Shut your cakehole, lad. You're being paid by the hour whether you're in the water or out. And show Mr. Fowler the respect he's earned. Hayden's ability to find these prehistoric beasts is legendary. He's been called the Dino

Diviner, don't you know."

That made Nora laugh. The moniker she had given Hayden now lived on in the public's consciousness thanks to several mentions in their bestselling book.

"I don't know about being a diviner," Hayden said. "I was wrong about finding Tyrannosaurs here. Rexes are the reason Carlton and I came here in the first place. We were out here three days and we didn't spot a single Rex."

"That's not your miss, big guy," Campbell said. "You told me a couple of hunters gave you the lead. That's on them, not you, mate. Your dino divining reputation is intact."

"Well, we did find fresh T-Rex tracks in the mud along the shoreline. So my hunter friends weren't wrong."

Lana Kim spoke, her slight Korean accent pleasing. "Maybe the Rexes were scared away by Sookie. Whaddaya think?"

Hayden nodded. "It's possible. But it would take a lot to spook a Tyrannosaur." He tugged on his beard. "That said, last year Nora and I saw a trio of Ankylosaurs savagely beat down a pair of mature Rexes using their clubbed tails. They nearly killed one of them."

"Yeah, I read about that in your book," Lana said. "I believe you referred to them as 'huge otherworldly armadillos.' Really cool. It's the perfect name for them."

Nora touched Hayden's arm and spoke. "Yes. *Ankylosaurus Magniventris* is a species all their own, with their armored plates and those wrecking ball tails. They're known in paleontology circles as 'the stiffened lizard.' It was something to see, three herbivores getting the best of a pair of T-Rexes, the most fearsome predator of the Late Cretaceous."

"Yeah," Hayden agreed, taking Nora's hand. "It might be the most amazing thing we've seen in our dino chasing travels."

"And that's certainly saying a lot," Campbell said, his adoration for Hayden and Nora evident in the inflection of his words and the shine in his eyes. "Jesus, mates, I feel like I'm in the presence of royalty here—the royal couple of paleozoology. I've watched your interviews on social media. I've read your book. Several times in fact. I've even read your earlier books, Hayden."

"Where in the hell did you dig up those pieces of shit?"

"You can find almost anything on eBay, me lad. And they're *not* pieces of shit." Campbell looked out across the lake. "Jackson used to talk about you and Nora like you were gods."

"Oh, for Christ sakes, stop it, Caleb," Hayden said, waving him off. "We're anything but gods."

Nora said, "And I seriously doubt Jackson Lattimer ever saw me as anything close to a deity. Some of the names he called me were—"

"Please, don't go there, dearest," Hayden said, cutting her off.

She flinched. She should have known better than to say anything negative about Jackson Lattimer. Nora doubted Hayden would ever get over his friend's death.

Campbell said, "The point being, I'm sitting on a skiff with two of the world's most famous hotshot scientists. When I got your call I couldn't pack me gear and hop a plane out of Sydney fast enough. And I was lucky enough to get these two onboard, two of the finest underwater videographers in the business," he said, throwing his arms over his dive partners' shoulders.

Nora's thoughts went back to last week, when they had shown the divers video Hayden had shot of the Deinosuchus taking down the grizzly bear. The three of them had been excited about the opportunity to video this crocodilian throwback in its natural habitat. They couldn't wait to hit Tally Lake and get Sookie on film. Caleb Campbell in particular seemed to possess the same reckless, thrill-seeking gene as the late Jackson Lattimer.

Hayden had asked them, "Are you sure you guys don't wanna use shark cages?"

"Shark cages?" Campbell said. "Where's the fun in that, matey? Bugger that! Cage dives are for the tourists."

All three of them signed their release waivers eagerly and without hesitation. Nora thought it would be difficult to get them to sign the documents that released her and Hayden from any liability on the dive should something go wrong, but she had been wrong.

She spoke to Campbell. "Our work pales in comparison to what you folks do, CC. I could never put my life on the line the way you all do to film dangerous animals. That takes a certain kind of chutzpah and courage I don't have."

"Oh, you've got it in spades, Nora. You just don't lean into it the way we do. You wouldn't be out here on this charter rig if you didn't have courage. Ours is the living on the edge kind of courage that's necessary for our type of work. Your courage is more self-contained."

Damn right it is, she thought. *These thrill seekers are cuckoo beans crazy. They're attracted to danger the way our magnetometer is attracted to iron.*

Hayden addressed the divers. "Well, whatever you want to call your kind of courage, I'm glad you were available on short notice."

"I wouldn't miss this for anything," Lana Kim said. "We're so excited to be here. This will be a history-making dive for sure."

"You might not be saying that after Sookie shows up," Hayden said with a grim smile.

"You mean *if* Sookie shows," Milo Harper said.

Campbell gave Harper the stink eye, then turned to Hayden and Nora. "Anyhow, since you were talking about that battle between Ankylosaurs and T-Rex, I must ask the experts. Which do you think would win in a head-to-head death match? A T-Rex or Sookie?"

"In the water I would go with Sookie, ten times out of ten," Hayden said. "But on land I'd put my money on Rex."

Nora chipped in with, "I'll second that. But I'll say that in shallow water it might be a draw. Rexes have very powerful legs when they can maintain their footing. They get much of their forward thrust and jaw crushing force through their legs."

Suddenly Hayden's laptop erupted in rapid beeping. The beeps quickly coalesced into a constant buzz. A large red bloom flashed on the display like an explosion, alarming Nora.

"What's happening, Hayden?"

He studied the readout. "Our nanoteslas just spiked into the thousands."

"*Nanoteslas*? What are they?"

"Units of measure that show the size and relative density of magnetic objects. There's a good chance we're going over a very large meteorite. But it could also be a sunken boat or maybe a buried pipeline. We won't know until we get eyes on it."

"I'm picking up something large, too," Captain McAllister shouted from up in the pilothouse.

Just then a loud crack from the tow winch captured everyone's attention. The drum whined as it began unspooling long lengths of cable. Nora watched the magnetometer cable stretch out far behind the wake of the boat, the drum continuing to spin out cable line with a continuous *whirrrrr*. It reminded her of a game fishing trip she had been on in the Caribbean with her father, when they'd hooked a big marlin that ran with the line as the reel spun madly.

"What the bloody hell is that?" Campbell shouted.

All heads turned to the back of the boat, eyeing the winch assembly, the drum continuing to spin out of control.

Hayden yelled, "Could that be Sookie toying with us?"

The boat suddenly jerked to a stop, dead in the water.

The drum had released all 650 feet of cable.

Bodies banged and bumped.

Two of the air tanks rolled across the deck and clanged against the far gunwale.

Hayden clutched his laptop to keep it from tumbling to the deck.

The cable screeched as it stretched.

The twin outboards roared.

The air filled with the sooty exhaust of an overworked engine.

"Holy mother of god!" Lana Kim exclaimed, looking out to where the tow line shuddered. "Is Sookie strong enough to anchor a boat this size?"

Nora's fear deepened. *Can this really be happening? Is a Cretaceous crocodilian on the end of our magnetometer cable?*

Hayden's laptop screen went dark, his MagLog app no longer registering. The buzzing sound went silent. "Sookie or whatever just ate our mag device," he called out.

"That's our cue, mates," Campbell yelled to his fellow divers as he stood. "Time to gear up and hit the water. It's deep here so we'll need the dual trimix tanks."

The three divers quickly donned their dry suits, tanks, weight belts, fins, and gloves. They grabbed their cameras and spearguns. "Manage your buoyancy carefully," Campbell barked. "Find the best spot to set up the light rigs; it's gonna be dark down there and we'll need substantial lighting to get clean footage. And watch each other's backs. Launch your spears if necessary. Let's be on our toes, mates. Maintain circular visibility at all times."

They slipped on their helmets and entered the water off the dive platform near the stalled winch. Campbell went in first followed by Kim and then Harper.

"What's going on back there?" Clyde McAllister yelled from the pilothouse as he revved the outboards and twisted the wheel. "I can't budge my boat. It's like we're hard aground."

"Don't worry about the boat, skipper," Hayden returned. "We're where we need to be. Shut it down. You're wasting fuel."

McAllister shut down the engines. The boat rolled in the lapping waves. "I'm responsible for this craft and the safety of all aboard," he said with worry.

"Everything's cool," Hayden said, powering up the OTS Aquacom Combox sitting on the bench between him and Nora. "We'll pay for any damages to your boat."

"But how're we going to get out of this?"

"You worry too much, skipper."

"Someone needs to."

With shaky hands, Nora logged into her laptop and accessed the Open Broadcaster Studio app, which would receive real-time wireless video feeds from the divers. The Combox that Hayden controlled allowed two-way audio communications with Campbell.

Hayden pressed the PTT button and held it down as he spoke. "How goes it, Caleb?"

"We're following the mag line down to whatever awaits us." Campbell's voice was strong and clear albeit tinny coming through the small speaker labeled on the unit as 'silver bullet.' "It's colder than a penguin's bath down here. Might freeze our bits off before all is said and done, mate. It's murky, too."

Nora pressed the comm button. “So we see,” she said, checking out the split screen on her laptop: three panels of shadowy coffee-colored water, clouds of bubbles, and a faint impression of the magnetometer towline.

Campbell came back with, “We’ll get more light on things when we’re a bit deeper.”

Minutes passed in silence on the divers’ descent. The video panels on Nora’s laptop became darker the deeper they went.

Captain McAllister joined them on the aft deck. “I can’t believe we’re stalled like this. Never seen anything like it. I’m worried about your dive team. Are they going to be all right?”

“They’re pros, skipper,” Hayden said. “They’ve swum with great whites, orcas, barracudas, saltwater crocs. You name the predator, they’ve filmed it. This should be a breeze for them.”

All three panels on Nora’s laptop display suddenly lit up. She and Hayden stared at three different angles of a crocodilian creature with its jaws clamped onto the end of their tow cable. They were dim, distant images, but it was definitely a Deinosuchus.

Campbell’s words came through a blizzard of static. “We’ve got our high-wattage spots working. Are you getting a clear picture of this up on deck?”

“Clear enough, yes,” Nora responded.

“We’re keeping our distance with maximum zoom. What a magnificent animal. Terrifying, even from this far away.”

Hayden said, “It looks like it’s just lying there on the bottom.”

“Yeah, I think it’s tangled up in the cable. Looks like he might have confused the magnetometer for a big fish, with the mag’s tail fin and all. He’s definitely big enough to rock the boat.”

“Ten-four, that,” Hayden said.

“Maybe thirty meters from here is what I think might be your meteorite. Lana and Milo are scoping it out now. Are you picking it up on your viewscreen?”

The second panel on Nora’s display showed a videocam approaching an immense black boulder covered in fuzzy green algae deeply embedded in the mud. “Yes, I’m seeing it now through Milo’s camera,” she answered.

As Harper moved around to the backside of the rock Nora saw a deep fissure with ragged edges. Milo videoed the crevice for several long minutes, focusing on the green fernlike vegetation growing in the interior that seemed to be thriving in the lake's cold water. Milo then swept his camera low, to the lake floor, where Lana Kim picked what looked like shards of eggshells out of the mud, the colors faded with age. She smiled from behind the faceplate and gave an enthusiastic thumbs-up.

"That's one of our meteorites for sure," Hayden said.

And then everything went wrong in the blink of an eye.

A greenish-brown blur rocketed in from the gloomy depths.

Lana Kim never saw the Deinosuchus coming.

The creature snatched her up in its powerful jaws. Lana's camera tumbled through a storm of bubbles, then went dark on Nora's laptop.

Nora and Hayden watched the horrific attack unfold through Milo Harper's videocam. A shocking amount of blood inked the water a brilliant crimson. One of Lana's air tanks flipped end over end. A severed arm drifted through the gore and blue shreds of her neoprene drysuit floated in the frothy wake. Harper struggled to get his speargun bang stick in position to fire, but the Deinosuchus was too quick. All Milo could do was watch helplessly as the creature dove with Lana Kim's mangled body into deeper water.

Nora gasped and stared slack-jawed at the screen.

A second Deinosuchus, bigger than the first, swooped in frighteningly fast and made quick work of Milo Harper. The view turned opaque with blood, then Harper's videocam blinked out.

"Holy motherfucker, we're under attack!" Campbell's voice was frantic coming through the comm unit. "There're at least three of 'em! Jesus fucking Christ!"

Nora watched her laptop helplessly as Campbell moved in and got off a bang stick shot that stunned the second Deinosuchus. The jolt to the creature's snout caused the beast to let go of what was left of Milo Harper before swimming off into the dark depths. Squiggly ribbons of blood trailed Harper's mutilated torso to the lake floor.

"I can't believe it. Me two dive mates are gone," Campbell

lamented over the comm system. "I'm trying not to heave in my helmet. I'm coming up. It's a death trap down here. Jesus, I've never seen anything that big move like that in the water. I'm spooked. It's almost supernatural the way they move!"

With the other two Deinosuchus disappeared into the depths, Campbell kept his videocam trained on the one tangled in the cable as he slowly made his way to the surface.

"It'll take me twenty-five minutes to get back topside," they heard Campbell say. "We were deep, around sixty meters— that's 197 feet for you Yanks—and I'm at my first decompression stop of four. But if one of the Sookies comes after me I'll be up there in a flash, the bends be damned. I'm keeping a close eye on the one below me. Looks like he swallowed the magnetometer and the cable is stuck in his throat. I've got my cam on him. Can you see him?"

Hayden acknowledged they could see the beast, mired in the mucky bottom. Shock had paralyzed Nora's voice.

"Good. All this chatter is using up my air so I'll sign off now, but I'll keep the line open."

"Godspeed, Caleb," Hayden said.

"Thanks, mates. See you soon."

Eternal minutes clicked by. Nora and Hayden's eyes remained glued to the top window on her laptop.

Fifteen excruciating minutes later, between Campbell's second and third decomp stops on his ascent, the Deinosuchus started tracking him, dragging the mag cable with it.

"Uh, CC," Hayden said, "it looks like you've got a stalker."

They heard Campbell's breaths coming fast. The camera swerved and they lost focus on the hooked beast, their view lost in a swirl of bubbles.

"You still with us, Caleb?" Nora said, finally finding her voice.

"Yeah, just loading another shaft in case that bastard gets too close. Here we go. Can you see Sookie now?"

"Yes," she said, observing the creature moving rapidly along the lake bottom, kicking up clouds of mud, furiously shaking its massive head and biting at the cable lodged deep in its throat, but unable to get its teeth on it. "Looks like it's passing beneath you and veering off, CC."

"Yeah. It's doing everything it can to lose that mag cable. Might be my saving grace. Look, its heading into deeper water. On your starboard side. It's straightening out the tow line, taking it to where the force might yank it out of its throat."

Hayden said to Nora off mic, "Damn, these Sookies are smart."

How smart can they be if they mistake a magnetometer for a fish? she wondered.

Abruptly, the boat shifted, the stern swinging around to starboard. The cable hummed with the tension. The winch assembly groaned, as if it was about to throw a few rivets.

"Unbelievable the strength of these creatures," Hayden crowed. "CC is right. They *are* supernatural."

Suddenly, the stern took a dramatic dip, a violent downward tug that sent water flooding over the dive platform and aft deck. Nora held on to her laptop with one hand and grabbed onto Hayden with the other. The aft bilge pump kicked into action, working furiously, whining and gurgling, trying to keep up with the intake of water.

Caleb Campbell's voice was drowned out as the Combox washed overboard.

Another powerful tug on the tow line and the boat's back end sunk deeper.

Captain McAllister lost his hat and sunglasses. He cried out, "Oh my god! My boat!" maintaining a desperate hold on the railing.

The boat perched at a precarious angle, the bow raised skyward. Nora clung to Hayden as the water rushed across the aft deck, up to their knees now.

Panic overcame her. *If we sink we're all dead.*

And then, a sharp crack and a boom like a bazooka shot, as the magnetometer cable snapped. The *Deep Descent* righted itself with a booming splash.

The three of them sat, drenched, gasping, stunned.

Tally Lake was quiet once more.

After a long silence, Nora said, "What in the hell have we done, Hayden?"

Hide and Seek

June 12: Gilliam's Guidepost

Heart Butte, Montana

"ENJOY YOUR VISIT, DETECTIVE." The front gate security officer handed Mike Mathews' his driver's license and private investigator ID card through the gatehouse window. Mathews slipped his identification into his wallet and glanced at the Glock 40 MOS pistol tucked in the guard's shoulder holster. A second guard standing nearby also wore a Glock strapped to his chest. The Gilliams had a professional security team monitoring their property, which he found reassuring.

The gate swung open. He drove his Jeep Grand Cherokee up the long, loose-gravel driveway to the farmhouse at the top of the hill.

Mathews was excited about what he planned to share with Bryan and Loretta Gilliam. He had zeroed in on at least one of the perpetrators behind the decapitated T-Rex head. It had been a long, frustrating wait of nearly two weeks for things to pop. Going through legal channels always took time. The process was painfully slow. He knew this, but it didn't make it any easier.

The wait was frustrating, yes, but at least it enabled him to work his other half-dozen cases that took him all over western Montana. Thankfully there had been no follow-up threats to the Gilliams. He liked Bryan and his charming wife Loretta. They were good salt of the earth folks who hadn't let their fame and fortune corrupt them. They had endured much hardship and Mathews felt a driving obligation to help them.

For twelve agonizingly long days, he'd had nothing substantive to take to the Gilliams. But then, yesterday afternoon, he'd received critical information as a result of the subpoena he'd ordered. And today, he felt all was right in his world of law and order.

Mathews had traced the two proxy IP addresses he'd found in the Gilliams' Virtual Private Network (VPN) server logs to the Internet Service Provider host, MontanaLink Networks. This led him to the Autonomous System Number (ASN) and the approximate geographic location of the perpetrator(s) who had hacked into the Gilliams' online family photo albums. The hosting area was Columbia Falls, a rural town of 6,000 residents, situated along the Flathead River, 19 miles southwest of West Glacier, the shipping origin of the T-Rex head.

That was solid, critical information that greatly narrowed the search, but it was only a surface dive into the data. It wasn't specific enough. The culprits were still hidden behind two anonymous proxy IP addresses, and the only way to get those identities was through the legal system.

His work often had him waiting on the legal wheels to roll, wading through bureaucracy and authorization delays. It pained him, but he had no other recourse if he wanted airtight, by-the-book evidence that would hold up in court.

With assistance from his attorney friend, Atlee Pinnaker (who was also the Gilliams' personal lawyer), he had obtained a court-ordered subpoena for internet service provider MontanaLink Networks in Columbia Falls. The criminals who swiped the photos off the private Gilliam server—the pics that ended up spiked on the teeth of the severed T-Rex head—were hiding behind a digital wall, and Mathews wanted to find them in the worst way.

Twelve long, exasperating days waiting for a response from the MontanaLink Networks' legal department.

The Gilliams could all be murdered and buried in the time it takes for things to go through the legal quagmire.

Finally, yesterday afternoon, on day twelve, MontanaLink Networks came through, cooperating fully.

Mathews now had the identities of the perps in hand—two names with street addresses and phone numbers, both in the Columbia Falls area—and he couldn't wait to share the information with the Gilliams.

And last night it got even better. He made another startling discovery that tied things together nicely. Hayden Fowler—who Mathews knew from last summer's investigation of an equine veterinarian turned convicted exotic animal trafficker—suggested that the perp could possibly be a professional taxidermist. Mathews put little stock in the idea at first, but the more he thought about it, the more he believed it had some merit. So he checked taxidermy businesses in the Columbia Falls area and came up with three. He checked out two of them that had websites. The bigger of the two, Vista Hills Custom Taxidermy, specialized in big game mounts. That was intriguing enough, but when he searched through the site he found an *ABOUT* page that gave a short history of the business (family-run trade in their 27th year of operation) along with brief profiles and pictures of the three onsite taxidermists. The senior of the three, Kyle Birnham, was the longtime owner of the business. And thank the digital gods, Kyle Birnham matched the name of one of the two anonymous proxy IP registrants. Mathews couldn't believe his good luck. They had somebody to go after! Last night Mathews sat on his bed in his Great Falls hotel room, staring at the photo of Kyle Birnham, pointing a finger at him and cursing loudly. "I'm coming to get you, ya spineless motherfucker!" Mathews regarded taxidermists with the same contempt as he held for big-game trophy hunters.

He pulled into the paved circle in front of the Gilliam house and parked, shut off the engine. Got out and stretched his legs. The two-hour trip from Great Falls had left him groggy and stiff.

"Hello, Mike. How was your drive?"

He turned and saw Loretta Gilliam coming down the front steps, moving with the purposeful, lithe grace he had come to associate with her.

"Scenic," he said. He had forgotten how tall Loretta Gilliam was, almost as tall as her husband.

"You're smiling," she said coming up to him. "You've got a great big grin on your face."

"It's automatic when I'm approached by a pretty lady."

"Aww," she said, giving him a lighthearted slap on the shoulder. "You're too kind to this old worn-out rancher mom, Detective. Sweet flattery and smiles. I'm not used to seeing you like this. What gives with the good mood?"

Mathews laughed. "Cherish it while you can, Loretta. Smiles are few and far between in my line of work. But today, I smile. I've got some good news for you and your hubby."

"We could certainly use a little of that. What is it?"

"I tracked down the people who sent you the dinosaur head."

"Really? That's wonderful, Mike! Come on inside. Bryan will be glad to see you. He's in the den watching TV."

They moved to the den and Loretta served coffee. The TV was on at low volume, some game show featuring washed-up, has-been celebrities trying to outwit each other. Mathews spoke over the audio, laying out what he had done to identify the two people behind the severed T-Rex head.

When he finished, Bryan said, "I don't get a lot of that techy mumbo-jumbo, Mike, but it's great news however you did it. So are we gonna sick the law on them now?"

"Not yet. Unfortunately I have to file for two search warrants. One to get inside the taxidermy shop where the decapitation most likely took place, and the second to search Kyle Birnham's home. Those warrants will allow me to check the business computers and all of Vista Hills Custom Taxidermy's work areas as well as all business and personal phones and accounting records. I need to see if there were any transactions with outside parties concerning this crime. These warrants require a lot of specificity. I started writing them last night. If I get them right, they'll go a long way in determining motive."

Bryan shook his head in frustration. "That'll take too long, won't it?"

Mathews didn't disagree, but he knew they had to handle this by the book. "We want a stand-up conviction, Bryan. This is a blatant threat to kill, which according to Montana Code 45-5-203 is considered, and I quote, 'making a threat to commit a criminal offense involving violence, which can be classified as assault with a weapon.' It's a felony, carrying a maximum sentence of twenty years and/or a $50,000 fine. But we have to jump through legal hoops to get solid evidence that will hang this Kyle Birnham."

"Couldn't you just turn over what you have to the tribal police?" Loretta asked. "Wouldn't that be quicker?"

"No. Blackfeet Law Enforcement doesn't have jurisdiction in Columbia Falls. The Flathead County Sheriff's Office does. We've got a history with them. You remember working with them last year in the Terrell kidnapping case, right, Bryan?"

"Sure. The deputy, Stuart Fenski and the detective, Tal Boone."

Mathews nodded. "That's right. So they will expedite anything I bring them quickly. They'll take action right away when I get them the warrants. I guarantee it won't take another two weeks. It'll just be days—long enough for me to get the requests written and submitted to Atlee, and then for Judge Adamson in Kalispell to give them his blessing. Seeing as how Atlee is your personal family lawyer, he'll hop right on it. And the judge is already familiar with the details of this case since he approved the subpoena for the internet provider. I've known Judge Adamson for years and he's always quick when dealing with search warrants. In the meantime we just have to pray this Birnham tool doesn't stage a second act."

Falconry for Pterosaurs

June 13: Bitterroot Mountains

Darby, Montana

MICK AND CLAIRE PRESCOTT cruised along Highway 93 in their F-150 pickup, towing a Polaris Ranger on a flatbed trailer. They were south of Darby, close to where they would park the truck and take their off-road Polaris up the mountain.

The east fork of the Bitterroot River meandered off to their left. Towering black cottonwoods and bushy willows hugged the river-banks amongst sprays of wild roses and purple lupine. Kelly Clarkson's power anthem "Stronger" thumped from the speakers. Claire slapped her knees in time with the music and sang along with the choruses. Mick concentrated on the twisty roadway, his mind buzzing with anticipation. Today they were on their way to check into a claim that couldn't possibly be true.

A man calling himself 'The Quetzal Whisperer' had contacted Mick through the exotic animal trafficking network on the dark web, telling him he had eight Quetzalcoatlus—flying reptiles of the Late Cretaceous—trained to hunt wild game. The Whisperer said he was an accredited and licensed master falconer who had used falconry training techniques to mold the pterosaurs into disciplined hunters. He'd found the pterosaurs when they were newborn hatchlings, back when the meteorites first came down along the Continental Divide. For the right price, he'd turn a couple of them over to the Prescotts.

Outrageous? Preposterous?

Yes and yes.

Mick and Claire were intrigued but dubious.

The husband and wife animal trappers shared an immense curiosity of exotic wildlife that began when they met as employees at the Denver Zoo, fifteen years ago. They knew that Quetzalcoatlus were the pterosaurs that had legendarily brought down that helicopter in Idaho last summer, the doomed flight that nearly killed the famous dinosaur chaser author and ended the life of the celebrity wildlife videographer, Jackson Lattimer. As far as Mick knew, there had been no other sightings of the pterosaurs since. So a man with the strange handle claiming he had raised eight of them from hatchlings and trained them to hunt was too tempting to resist.

They arrived at the switching point, a turnoff at the base of the mountain shaded by a stand of ponderosa pine. Mick parked the truck and they unlatched the Polaris from the trailer. The interior was cramped compared to the truck cab, but the smaller off-road vehicle would serve them better on the rutted Forest Service road.

The path swept upward, the Polaris shifting into a lower gear on the steep incline. The forest thickened, with pine trees and Engelmann spruce soaring to lofty heights on both sides, blocking out the sunlight. Mick turned on the headlights as they rode the winding trail through the dark tunnel of trees. To say the Quetzal Whisperer lived off the grid was a huge understatement.

Claire shut off the music. "You think this whisperer dude is on the up and up, Mickey?"

"I'm trying to keep an open mind," he responded, concentrating on the twisting dark trail.

"There's no way you can train a wild pterosaur," she said. "It's just not possible. It would be like trying to work with cassowaries."

"Wow, there's a reference from out of the distant past." He glanced at her. "You just can't let that go, can you? That cassowary that attacked you in the Down Under habitat? That was what? A dozen years ago?"

"More like fourteen. But who's counting."

"What was its name? I forget."

"Demetrious. There were two of them. The other one was Flo."

"Yeah. They were hugely territorial and unpredictable. And as you learned, aggressive."

"You got that right. Demetrious came at me that day, ticked off about me being in his space. I was shocked at how quick he was. He gouged my arm, deep. His claws were sharp as razor blades. It bled quite a bit and hurt like the dickens. Took forever to heal. I still have a small scar."

Mick reached over and patted her arm near the old wound. "My brave, sweet éclair."

"Stop it, Mickey," she said, laughing, pulling her arm away.

"Old Demetrious had to have outweighed you by fifty pounds. We both know Cassowaries have been known to leap at threats and gut them with those claws. You were quite fearless—*are* quite fearless—my dear. I've seen your nerve and pluck at work many times during our dino trapping runs."

"Well, what can I say, Mickey. This plucky gal never backs down from a good challenge," she said in a self-mocking tone. "Just call me Wonder Woman!"

Mick grinned, appreciating his wife's playfulness. "It must be those rugged North Carolina genes. I hear they grow 'em tough in the Outer Banks."

"I think it has more to do with my older brothers picking on me. Robby and Sam were both accomplished bullies. But getting back to those cassowaries, they remind me a lot of the dinos we've been trapping, especially their beaked facial structures and those three-toed feet with the deadly inner claws. They move with that hopping bipedal locomotion just like the Rexes and Dromes. And those casques on the tops of their heads give them a primeval look. Strange species, they are."

"Yeah, they're definitely a throwback to the prehistoric age," Mick said. "Cassowaries and all ratites—flightless birds—are considered to be close living relatives of avian dinosaurs. I've even read that cassowaries *are* the contemporary dinosaurs of the rainforest."

"You read that right," Claire said. "I learned in my AZA certification training that cassowaries fall into a primitive bird group known as *paleognaths*, which includes ostriches, emus, and kiwis. All very primordial and dinosaur-like. And I know from hard learned experience that cassowaries in particular are *absolutely* not trainable. They are large intelligent birds with an independent streak and anger issues. Quetzalcoatlus would be even more impossible to train. They can fly. They're much more mobile than cassowaries. Stronger pound for pound, too. Makes me wonder about this Quetzal Whisperer's claims. I hope we're not walking into a scam. Or even worse, a trap."

Mick thought about the loaded Remington 12-gauge shotgun secured under his seat and the Sig P320 handgun in the glovebox. He also had two canisters of Griz Guard bear spray in the driver's side pocket with enough firepower to stop a mature grizzly from 35 feet. "We're prepared if it's a trap," he said.

"I know, but we don't really know what we're walking into."

"We'll approach this guy with caution, Claire. It's just too intriguing to pass up. Can you imagine how much we could make on a domesticated Quetzalcoatlus?"

"He said they were *trained*, not domesticated. Big difference. And it's hard to say how much profit would be in it since we don't know his asking price."

"I tried talking price with him on the dark web but he wasn't having it. He was being cautious, which I respect."

"If there is any truth to his claim, this won't be cheap, Mickey."

"No, it won't. But something as rare and unique as this, we could name our own price."

"True," she said, "but I still say we could make a lot more coin if we sold directly to end buyers. Cut out the middle man."

"No," he said adamantly. "We've covered this many times, Claire. It's too risky dealing directly with the end clientele. The collectors. The traffickers are our safety net. They take the risks. They're the ones the Fish, Wildlife, and Parks agents and game wardens go after, not us. It's safer to trap than to traffic."

She waved her arm dismissively. "Trapping or trafficking. It's all just semantics when you come right down to it."

He side-eyed her. "How many wholesale animal trappers have you heard about getting busted?"

"Well, none."

"And how many traffickers?"

"Yeah, I know, but—"

"How *many*, Claire?"

"Three that I know of."

"I rest my case, madame éclair. I'd say we're doing all right for ourselves. We've already raked in a couple-hundred grand."

Just two weeks into June and the couple had already bagged and sold a Tyrannosaur, a pair of Dromaeosaurs, and a Triceratops.

"Not bad for three weeks' work," Mick continued. "We've stayed out of prison and no one has gotten hurt or killed."

She flubbed her lips in frustration. "You're right, Mickey. I should know by now not to get greedy. Self-indulgence usually brings misery. We need look no further than Kelton Rendaya as an example."

"Yes indeed. Oh, how I miss our best customer."

"Me, too. He was easy to work with and he always paid up front."

They climbed higher into the Bitterroot Mountains. The evergreen forest thickened. The temperature dropped. Occasionally the road swung out wide where there was a break in the trees with clearings that overlooked breathtaking vistas with steep slopes descending into the valley. They saw signs for Trapper Peak and Lost Trail Pass. Forest Service road markers appeared along the route. A logging skidder and a loader were parked off the shoulder, backed halfway into the woods, their huge tires coated with mud.

"What's the road marker we're looking for, Claire?"

"Um, one-forty-two." She squinted, peering through the windshield. "Looks like we're coming up on one-thirty-eight."

"Four more miles to the turnoff. Does this guy even have a zip code?"

"Who needs a zip code when you've got trained flying reptiles."

Mick let out a hardy laugh.

Claire smiled, then became serious. "The dinos have started coming out in big numbers again the past couple of weeks."

"Without question," Mick said, hunching over the wheel and concentrating on the dark service road. "Good for business, bad for humanity. The body count is high. *Too* high."

"Yeah. I wouldn't wish what happened to those divers at Tally Lake on my worst enemy. The news footage was frightening. I can't imagine being attacked in the water by huge prehistoric crocodiles. What was that creature called? Deinuh-something?"

"Deino*suchus*," he said, sounding it out: *Dine-uh-syoo-kuhs*. "That Australian diver who survived said there were three of them, twelve to fifteen feet. Still considered to be juveniles. Told that interviewer they'll be thirty-five feet and weigh close to four tons when fully grown. He called them Sookie monsters. He wasn't trying to be cute. I'd say the Forest Service has a big problem on their hands there."

"It gives me the shivers, Mickey."

"It was certainly a horrendous way for those divers to die. And then there was the attack three T-Rexes laid on those hikers in Glacier National Park the week before. Seven hikers and two park rangers. Not much left but scattered skeletons and mounds of bloody entrails. I think the politicians are gonna have to change their tune about protecting these animals."

Claire said, "You know, I've been thinking about how weird it is that these new species are showing up—the Quetzalcoatlus last year and now this Deinosuchus. One avian, the other aquatic. What do you attribute that to? I mean, where have they been hiding?"

"Well, both have shown up in extremely remote locations. It took unlucky accidents for humans to run into them. But even more to the point, I think a lot more egg-bearing meteorites came down than the government told the public."

Claire mulled this over, then said, "Do you ever think about how strange these times are? How weird our lives have become?"

"Every waking second, my sweet éclair. To steal a lyric from the Grateful Dead, the past couple of years have been a long strange trip."

"Yeah, we've been truckin' through a magical mystery tour."

Mick smiled. "Good one, honey."

They rode in silence for several minutes before coming to Forest Service road marker 142. Mick rode the brake pedal and made the turn, tires crunching on the coarse gravel. They passed knobby stumps and slash piles, evidence of recent lumber harvesting. Pine saplings and wild grasses crowded the narrow lane, raking the sides of the Polaris. A large mule deer observed them from the underbrush.

The gravel road ended, giving way to an uneven dirt path, crowned in the middle with twin ruts from heavy logging equipment. The woods became more congested. Old growth Douglas fir and western larch created a domed canopy high overhead. The air was heavier here, dampish. They bounced and juddered over the washboard surface, passing a trailhead sign dappled with moss.

They were in the heart of Montana's rugged backcountry.

A couple of bumpy miles along they came to an ancient wooden gate, flanked by tall stone pillars etched with crude avian forms and strange symbols.

The gate was open, as the Whisperer promised it would be. Mick pulled to a stop. "Can you make any sense of the drawings?"

Claire snapped photos with her phone. "The winged silhouettes have an Ancestral Puebloan vibe to them. The humanoid figure with outstretched arms and the giant winged beast shadowing it overhead is a bit off-putting."

Mick felt a distinct pressure in the air, an ominous weight, as if they were being watched. "Any idea what those symbols mean?"

"Not a clue."

Suddenly, a piercing shriek and loud fluttering came from the trees above. Mick looked up in time to catch a large bird with an impossibly long neck and protracted beak take flight. The creature's wingspan had to be fifteen feet.

Claire flinched, dropping her phone. "Holy shit! Is that—?"

"Yes, I believe it is," he said, startled. They both watched in stunned fascination as the flying reptile cleared the treetops. "Crazy, but I think it was a Quetzal sentry going to report our arrival to his master."

"What? Really? How weird is *that*, Mickey?"

"Get the Sig out of the glovebox, Claire."

She fumbled at opening the box, pulled out the holstered pistol. "You think we're going to need it?"

"You never know." He switched his foot from the brake to the accelerator. The Polaris lurched forward. "Let's go see what this Whisperer dude is all about."

They proceeded slowly, jouncing over the rough trail, twisting through thick woods. A half-mile in, they broke into a wide glade, the sunlight blinding after the ride through gloomy forest.

The Quetzal Whisperer's compound came into view, a weather-worn lodge built of old timber and river stones, the back half buried into the hillside. A small dilapidated shed stood to the left, surrounded by ladders, bow saws, and a collection of aged cedar crates. A battered black Ford Ranger sat near the shed. The pickup had bulky off-road tires, padded perches and wire cargo cages in the rear bed, and enormous animal bone bumpers. Attached was a repurposed horse trailer with the legend *THE WINGMASTER* painted across a side panel in stylized calligraphy script.

As they got closer, Mick spied a heavyweight falconer's perch, thick as a telephone pole, with a claw-scarred base and old blood-stains tinting the wood. He could tell by the wide, deep grooves in the base that animals much larger than falcons or hawks had roosted there. Next to it stood a rack of leather hoods and armor-plated harnesses.

He parked next to the pickup and shut off the engine. A wind-chime clinked in the distance. Otherwise the place was eerily quiet. He instructed Claire to holster up as he retrieved the shotgun from under his seat. They got out and moved cautiously across the weed-choked yard, Mick in the lead. A brisk crosswind slapped him in the face, the air much colder and thinner up here in the higher elevation.

As they got closer to the lodge, he could see the front door was a heavy slab of dark reddish-brown Douglas fir engraved with looping hieroglyphics and bird feather patterns. The front stoop was constructed of uneven granite blocks, lined on either side by crude stone sculptures resembling large birds in flight.

This guy goes all out to live up to his freaky rep, Mick thought, glancing back to make sure Claire was still with him. She nodded at him, holding the pistol out in front of her with both hands.

The front door opened and a tall wiry man in his late fifties stepped out. He had sun-coppered skin and shoulder-length salt-and-pepper hair. His eyes were mismatched, the right a steely blue, the left a milky white without a pupil. A scar started just below his sightless eye and ran across his left cheek, like he had shed a thin silvery tear. The scar caused his face to sag to that side. He wore falconer leathers, dyed in faded green and ocher, reinforced with scaled ceramic plating. A black cape stitched with eagle feathers covered his shoulders. A carved bone whistle hung from his neck on a strip of rawhide.

He leaned against one of the bird monuments. "The Prescotts I presume," he said, his voice as gruff as his visage.

Mick drew to a halt. "You presume correctly."

"Welcome to Quetzal Villa. I'm Whisperer. Any problems findin' the place?"

"No, your instructions were on point."

Whisperer turned his cloudy eye toward them. "And I trust you kept this location to yourselves."

"Of course. We're discreet. Secrecy is the law in our business."

"I agree. But one of your former top clients is now doing prison time. You can imagine how that might make me a little nervous dealing with you."

Mick was tired and in no mood for this, but he knew he had to keep the conversation civil. "I see you do your homework."

"Indeed I do. I've had to tighten up my operation since I started raising Quetzals. And when I say Quetzals I'm not talkin' about those pathetic little things that are Guatemala's national bird. I'm talkin' about Quetzalcoatlus, the big winged creatures from the Late Cretaceous. My flying reptiles."

"So how do you know about us?" Claire asked, stepping beside Mick.

"Word gets around on the dark web. I wouldn't have invited

you here if I didn't think I could trust you. That said, your former big-money client, Kelton Rendaya, is serving time in Montana State. That makes me uncomfortable."

Mick and Claire had faced the same question of their reliability from several of their buyers. "We had nothing to do with Doctor Rendaya's incarceration," he said. "It was his own greed and carelessness that landed him in a jail cell."

The Whisperer stared at them for a long, awkward moment before saying, "Nonetheless, I must insist you return your firearms to your vehicle. Guns have a way of scaring my kids, and trust me on this, you do *not* want to upset my kids. You do and there'll be hell to pay."

"Uh, by *kids* you mean—?"

"Yes. My Quetzals. You met one of 'em on your way in. His name is Thrall. He's very protective of my land. Thrall is a natural gatekeeper."

"We saw that," Mick said. "He's a most impressive specimen."

"Thrall is the biggest of the bunch. Wingspan of seventeen feet and he's still a growing boy."

"How'd you acquire your Quetzals?" Mick asked.

"I found a nest containing six large eggs down at Trapper Creek two years ago. I didn't know what they were, just that they weren't like any eggs I'd ever seen before. They certainly weren't terrestrial. I didn't want to disturb the nest, and so I decided to camp out and keep watch. The mother Quetzal never returned. Over the course of a few days, all six hatched out. They immediately started feeding on trout and sculpin. From birth, my Quetzals were skilled fishermen."

Claire said, "How long until they were flying?"

"Took ten long months for their wings to develop enough to take to the skies. Gave me plenty of time to train 'em right. Then, last September, that first group produced three more hatchlings. The young'uns still need more work but they're super intelligent. They're quick studies."

As Whisperer talked, Mick did the math in his head. "I thought you said you had eight Quetzals."

"That's true. I do."

"But you just told us you have nine—a half-dozen two-year-olds and three younger ones."

"I *had* nine. Now I have eight. I sold one a couple weeks back."

"Who was the buyer?" Claire asked.

The falconer wagged his index finger in admonishment. "That's none of your concern, little lady. It's my business, not yours. I always protect my buyers. If we do business here today you wouldn't want me making the sale public. After all, we're dealing in highly illegal reptiles here. As you so elegantly stated, Mr. Prescott, secrecy is the law in our business."

Mick said, "So you're willing to part with one or two of your Quetzal *kids*?"

The Whisperer grinned, an unsettling look. "For the right price, absolutely. Now put those goddamned guns away. Your cell phones as well."

"Our phones? Why?" Claire protested.

The Whisperer moved down off the stoop. "I can't take any chances of being photographed or having my voice recorded. I can't have what we do here leaked out to the public. My conditions are no guns and no phones. You're not willing to do that then you can just get in your car and head back down the mountain. If you comply with my wishes, I'll give you the grand tour and introduce you to the kids. I'm sure you'll be quite impressed with what they can do."

FIVE MINUTES LATER, firearms and phones reluctantly stashed in the Polaris, Whisperer led them through his lodge. They entered a great room with a vaulted ceiling supported by A-frame beams of dark tamarack and larch. Glyphs of avian wings and talons were burned into the beams. A model of a Quetzalcoatlus hung above a wide stone hearth, positioned as if in midflight. The bones were a lacquered, burnished ivory held together with bronze wire and hemp cord. The wingspan stretched nearly twenty feet across the room. Its spearheaded skull was tilted slightly down, as if watching over the room from above. The walls were covered with maps on parchment skins that were medieval in appearance.

They passed an alcove where Mick saw harnesses hanging like dead snakes, drones with beaks and wings, and leatherbound field journals. A desktop computer and a pair of large monitors sat on a stone credenza. A corkboard bolted to the wall showed a topographical map with red string and feathers pinned in crisscross patterns that could have been Quetzal flight paths.

They moved on, Mick surprised at how much larger the interior of the lodge was than it looked from the outside. They passed through living quarters, three spacious rooms, each with low beds covered with furs and woven blankets. Water basins and toilets. Polished obsidian slates set into the walls in lieu of mirrors. Mick could see his reflection as they passed but he thought it strange. *Why not real mirrors?*

They reached the back of the house, coming to a set of heavy oak doors with iron pull rings. Whisperer stopped in front of the doors, turned and said, "I'm sure you are quite curious about my blind eye. Most people are. And no, it wasn't caused by one of my Quetzals. I had a tussle with one of my rebellious falcons five years ago. His name was Fernando. A very surly and independent bird. Refused to be trained. One day he'd had enough of me trying to bend him to my will. He went for my face. It wasn't pretty. Had to put him down. In my twenty-plus years of working with raptors, Fernando was the only bird I haven't been able to train."

"You still working with falcons now that you have Quetzals?" Mick asked.

"Oh yeah. I've got five falcons and a couple of Harris's hawks. They're good birds."

Claire said, "Do you make your living entirely off of falconry?"

"I'm proud to say I do. Falconry is my passion. Most of my revenue comes from guided hunts and aviation bird abatement programs."

Mick was curious. "Bird abatement programs?"

"I've got several long-running contracts with airports, farmers, and vineyards to use my raptors to scare off nuisance birds like crows and pigeons and starlings. You'd be surprised. Those contracts are quite lucrative. And it's all legal and above board."

"As opposed to raising and selling pterosaurs," Claire said.

Whisperer sighed and shot her a perturbed glance. "Yes, as opposed to *that*."

He turned and pulled the doors open. Mick and Claire followed him through a long dark tunnel of obsidian-black stone. Hunching over to negotiate the low-ceilinged passage, they arrived at another set of doors. Whisperer led them out into an expansive canyon, a vast hollow maybe a half mile long and surrounded by cliff walls hundreds of feet high.

"This is the Aerie," the falconer said. "It's where my pterosaurs and raptors get their education."

It was warmer here, the afternoon heat radiating off the canyon's stone floor. Mick breathed in the stench of bird guano and the putrid odor of dead things. A chorus of screeching started up. He scanned the cliff walls, trying to pinpoint the eerie shrieks, spotting two Quetzals roosting in natural perches embedded high up in the granite. At the base of the cliff, a partially devoured elk carcass hung from a steel rack, blood painting the bedrock a rusty brown.

Mick surveyed the area. What caught his eye first was an ultralight gyrocopter, stripped down and skeletal, looking half bird, half war relic. *THE WHISPERING WINDJACK* was emblazoned across the fuselage.

"Interesting flying machine you've got there," Mick said.

"Yeah, the Windjack is my pride and joy. Me and my crew use it in conjunction with our bird drones for flight-pattern training and scouting."

"Oh, so you have a crew?" Claire said. "You're not a solo operator?"

Whisperer turned his chalky eye on her. "My, my, my, but aren't you an inquisitive little lady. I may be a world-class falconer, but even I cannot do it alone. I have very capable help in my two fulltime employees, Rooster and Joan of Arc. They're very accomplished raptor handlers in their own right, and that's only because I taught them everything I know."

"Where are they?" Claire asked. "Why haven't we met them?"

"You're testing my patience, Ms. Prescott. I thought you were smart enough to know that too many questions in our business can bring negative consequences."

"Are you threatening me?"

"No. Just reminding you of business protocol. But since you asked, Rooster and Joan are working with the juvenile Quetzals at our indoor facility. The young pterosaurs are just learning to fly and they need daily TLC. They're not disciplined yet. We can't keep them out here in the Aerie. Now, no more questions, please."

Whisperer led them to a grouping of what appeared to be base training platforms, constructed of larch beams lashed together with hide and bolted down with rebar pipes. Volcanic sand, shredded leather, and braided rope mats covered the surface of each. To the left were smaller, vertical roosts wrapped in astroturf that Mick supposed were for the falcons and hawks.

Tufts of loose feathers fluttered across the sunbaked floor.

The pterosaur shrieks increased in volume, as though the Quetzals were excited by their appearance.

Whisperer raised an arm high in the air and blew his carved bone whistle, a single, warbling note. Low. Echoing. Guttural.

Five Quetzals launched from their cliffside perches. It was an impressive sight, these giant pterosaurs with great wingspans gliding high above. Lower and lower they descended in a coordinated, tight circle, their flight creating moving shadows below. One by one, they came in fast and hard, squawking as their talons dug into the sand and rope mats. As they landed, they tucked in their wings and looked to Whisperer for further instructions. Mick observed them, the respect they showed their master through their ethereal, iridescent amber eyes.

"I'd like to introduce you to my Quetzal kids," Whisperer croaked. "You've already met the big guy in front here, Thrall."

Incredibly, the pterosaur named Thrall focused on Mick and lifted his right wing as if in greeting.

Mick glanced at Claire, who gave him a surprised, if not wary, look.

Whisperer continued. "And behind Thrall are Talgarin, Crayth, Ashara, and Novera."

As each was introduced, they followed Thrall's lead, dipping their long, slender beaks in a courtly gesture and giving Mick and Claire a wing wave.

"Your training is most impressive," Mick said, thinking: *How can wild animals be taught to do this? Animal handlers have had success with lions and bears and even orca whales. But these are a prehistoric avian species. Unbelievable!*

"Thank you. I have worked diligently with these guys," Whisperer said, taking a dramatic bow. "And now I've got a special treat for you, a presentation to show you just how intelligent these guys are. If this doesn't convince you to make a purchase, nothing will."

He pointed at Thrall. The pterosaur straightened, hyperalert, staring at his master with those predatory amber eyes. "Thrall, fetch me a rabbit."

Thrall spread his powerful wings. Flapped them, once, twice, three times, lifting off, up, up, up, emitting a strange, low-pitched honking sound as he ascended, quickly disappearing over the canyon rim.

Whisperer continued instructing his Quetzals. "Talgarin, fetch me a squirrel. Crayth, fetch me a possum. Ashara and Novera, surprise me. Bring me gifts of your own choosing."

Each of the pterosaurs flew up and out of the Aerie, honking like deep-throated geese on their way out. Mick and Claire watched the noisy departure in open-mouthed wonder.

After Ashara and Novera cleared the Aerie, Mick said, "Fascinating. They understand English commands."

"Of course, they're very bright animals." Whisperer beamed like a proud parent. "They understand a vocabulary of a couple hundred words."

Claire said, "Your Quetzals are carnivores. Won't they eat their prey?"

"No. They know to bring me what I ask for. They know they will be rewarded for doing so. Just wait, you'll see. It won't be long."

Fifteen minutes later, Thrall winged back into the Aerie, clutching a plump rabbit in his elongated beak. He landed on his platform and dropped the bloody hare at Whisperer's boots.

"Good boy, Thrall. You have earned a big feast."

The pterosaur then went through a meticulous grooming process. Thrall pecked at his hide with his pointed beak, then stood on one foot while scratching at his sides and under his wings with the claw of his other foot.

"What is he doing?" Claire asked.

"Getting rid of debris and parasites he might have picked up in the outside world. These creatures are fastidious about cleanliness."

A few minutes later Talgarin flew in with a ravaged squirrel, the rodent's bushy tail hanging from the side of his beak. Talgarin dropped his catch at Whisperer's feet and began cleaning himself as Thrall had.

Crayth was next, bringing in a bloated possum.

Mick could not believe what he was seeing. These prehistoric flying reptiles that ruled the skies 66 million years ago were carrying out human commands.

How is it that these ancient carnivores are subservient to man?

A long pause followed the return of the first three Quetzals, and Mick noticed Whisperer getting anxious. After twenty minutes of the falconer's fidgeting and mumbling to himself while walking in circles, Ashara and Novera flew in over the ridge in tandem.

Ashara delivered a human hand.

Novera dropped a human forearm at Whisperer's feet, the flesh ragged and oozing fresh blood at the elbow.

"That's my girls," Whisperer said, complimenting them, his cloudy eye glowing a luminous platinum.

He's actually excited about these gifts of human body parts, Mick thought with revulsion.

He looked at Claire, who wore a horrified expression.

They both turned to the Quetzal trainer.

"Hey, I never said my kids were perfect," Whisperer said in a deadpan voice. "Shall we head back to the lodge to talk business?"

He's treating this outrageous act like it's routine, Mick thought.

Did Ashara and Novera actually take a human life?

Was there a hidden message in the Whisperer's command that instructed them to commit murder?

Should we report this to the authorities?

They followed Whisperer back to the lodge, Mick's mind in turmoil. He was sure of just one thing: the man leading them was a maniacal genius.

The Paleontology Impasse

June 15: Eden Prairie, Minnesota

HAYDEN AND NORA SAT AT THE KITCHEN TABLE eating Vesuvio pizza delivered from their favorite takeout place, Pizza Lucé. The Italian meatballs were extra spicy today, just the way they liked them.

Today marked the fifth day they'd been back home after the tragic events on Tally Lake. Five long days of trying to regain their equilibrium. Five days of attempting to patch their shattered souls. Five days of trying to make sense of what happened.

They had been detained the first 24 hours by U.S. Forest Service officials and Flathead County Sheriff's deputies, who bombarded them with ceaseless questions. Hayden didn't care for their interrogation techniques, thinking the questioning was pointed and accusatory. He lost his patience several times with their "Why didn't you report the Deinosuchus inhabiting the lake sooner?" and "Why were you dragging the lake with a magnetometer without securing a permit?" and "Why did you hire divers when you knew of the dangers that lurked beneath the surface?"

Why, why, why?

And the repeated question that really irritated him: "Do you feel responsible for the deaths of the two divers and the destruction of the charter boat?"

Explain yourselves. Defend your actions.

So many questions. It was exhausting and debilitating.

Finally, citing the Montana Lakeshore Protection Act, officials fined them $500 for the unauthorized use of the magnetometer, then released them.

"Are you fucking kidding me!" Hayden had railed when

informed of the misdemeanor. "Two people lose their lives and you give us a fine for using a metal detector? Jesus fucking Christ, what a scam! Anything to generate revenue for Flathead County, am I right?"

The issuing officer told him, "Mr. Fowler, sir, if you don't calm down we'll have no choice but to lock you up. Being a celebrity doesn't give you the right to ignore our laws."

The threat of jail had shut him up. But he remained irate.

They had witnessed two human beings devoured by enormous aquatic beasts. They had nearly gone down with the capsizing boat. They had nearly lost their lives along with the divers. The catastrophe had been soul crushing enough, physically and spiritually, but the constant questioning and the misdemeanor fine only rubbed truckloads of salt into their gaping emotional wounds.

The Smithsonian Institution, the underwriters of their doomed outing, used their significant powers to run interference for them, handling the national media and doing damage control through the Smithsonian's social media platforms.

Hayden and Nora's cell phones had buzzed nonstop the first few days they were home. Hayden—stressed and still in shock—made calls to the two dead divers' families, sending his and Nora's condolences. They were two of the most difficult phone calls he'd ever had to make. Lana was only 28 years old, Milo Harper, 33 with a wife and two young children. Such a waste. After the second call, a heartbreaking conversation with Lana Kim's fiancé, Hayden turned his phone off. He felt the twin clinch of tragic loss and personal guilt. Everybody involved knew the risks going in, and Hayden leaned on that understanding to help ease his guilt.

"I heard from Molly at Random House this morning," Nora said after taking a sip of Diet Coke.

Hayden groaned. "And what did our esteemed editor want?"

"She asked if we could get a short chapter on our Tally Lake experience written in a week. If we can, they'll get it in the first edition."

"Unbelievable!" he spat. "So it takes the horrific deaths of two young divers to get their interest? They didn't want anything to do with the first sighting of Sookie as I recall. Damned New York liberal elitists! I told you to keep your phone turned off, Nora."

"We can't continue to shut out the world, Hayden. We have a business to run and a book in production. And the truth of it is, *we* are the ones who put those poor divers in the water. Their deaths are on us and we need to be transparent about it."

"I didn't see you rushing to call Kim's and Harper's families."

"Don't go there, dearest. I'm just say—"

"What'd you tell her?"

"Who?"

"Molly. What did you tell her about the chapter they want?"

"That we could do it."

"What? You gave in? Just like *that*?"

"Relax. I'm well aware of your allergy to writing."

"Cute, Nora. I *do not* have an allergy to writing or anything else," he said, anger tightening his words. "It's just—"

"I started on it after breakfast," she said. "Got around five-hundred words written. I wanted to get my thoughts down while the experience was still fresh. It's actually kind of therapeutic."

Hayden shook his head in disbelief. "You just let them yank you around like that? You let them walk all over you."

"One thing you've never learned, Hayden, is the value of knowing which battles to fight and which ones to let go. You always want to rush in with your sword drawn. You want to start slicing and dicing immediately. If I had done that when they turned down my request for extension, we probably wouldn't be getting this chance now. Our publisher has been pretty good to us, dearest. *You* were the one who was so desperate to get your Deinosuchus encounter in the book. Now that's going to happen, thanks to me handling things professionally. Don't worry. You won't have to lift a finger. I'll do the work."

He looked across the table at her. Nora's luminous green eyes shone behind the lenses of her jade-colored designer frames in a determined stare he knew all too well. Her brunette bob brushed her cheekbones as she leaned in to pull another slice from the pizza pie.

God how he loved this woman, even when she was being difficult.

"Are you trying to lay a guilt trip on me, *mon amour*?" he said.

"Yes."

"Well, you can't make me feel any more guilty than I already do. But Listen, I'll help you with the writing. I'll start working on a piece about my first sighting of Sookie."

"A little late but thank you. I appreciate it."

"Better late than never, right?" he said with a hopeful grin.

"And in case you have forgotten about Fowler-Lemoyne Aviation, I'll bring you up to date. I spoke with Bryan."

"I *haven't* forgotten our company," he said irritably. "Wow, talk about slicing and dicing, woman!"

"Cool it, big guy. I'm just saying you've had things on your mind other than our company."

"I was just at the heliport two weeks ago," he protested. "When was the last time *you* visited the Guidepost?"

Nora gave him a look that said, *Don't you dare go there, mister!*

"Okay, okay. I'll back off. So tell me, what did you discuss with Gilliam?"

"He and Loretta are worried about you—about *us*."

"Did you tell him everything is hunky dory with us?"

"No. Because they're not. I told him the truth."

"The truth? What's that?"

"That we're hurting. That we're dazed and confused."

"You tell Gilliam about the meteorite at the bottom of the lake? That there's no way we can retrieve it?"

"There's no need to tell him, Hayden. I would think it's pretty much a foregone conclusion now."

"Yep. Silly me." He plucked a napkin from the holder and wiped pizza sauce from his beard. "Did Gilliam say whether they've received any more threats since the decapitated T-Rex head?"

"He said things have been quiet, fortunately."

"That's good. Did he give you any updates on our new choppers and pilots?"

She leaned across the table and tore off another wedge of pizza, took a bite, chewed and swallowed. "He did. Bryan filmed a new commercial announcing that Fowler-Lemoyne Aviation is back in business. It ran on several local TV stations last week and the response has been enthusiastic. He's signed up a mining company for weekly prospecting excursions and a couple of real estate developers for aerial land surveys. Weyerhaeuser also signed a contract for regularly scheduled timber studies."

"Weyerhaeuser? Don't they have their own choppers?"

"They do have a helicopter fleet, yes, but they're dedicated to forestry fertilization and pesticide application in their tree farms."

"So the negative publicity from our crash isn't hurting us?"

"Apparently not. People tend to have short memories."

"So what about our new pilots? Are they making progress?"

"Yes. Two of the new-hire pilots began making flights out on Monday. A third is going through training with Peter."

"And how is our favorite drug addict doing? Has Lacroix kicked his habit yet? He was a complete wreck when I saw him two weeks ago."

Nora gave him a salty stare. "That's rich coming from you, dearest. If you recall, when I met you, you were living inside a whiskey bottle. I would think if anyone should have some empathy and compassion for Peter it would be you."

He waved his meaty hands in surrender. "Okay, okay. I hear you loud and clear. I'm being crass and insensitive, and that should have died with the old drunken me. So how is *Monsieur* Lacroix?"

"Bryan said Peter has been doing much better, especially since Brinshou came to stay with him in Heart Butte. He did an excellent job training the new pilots, and yesterday, Peter did an hour test flight on the simulator. He passed easily and is cleared to return to the cockpit next week."

"That's great news. Lacroix is an outstanding chopper jockey and we're gonna need him. And just so you know, I never blamed him or Larry Bing for the crash."

Nora offered a weak smile. "I know you didn't." She got up from the table and went to the sink.

He watched her back as she rinsed off her dish and put it in the dishwasher. Her movements were sluggish, unfocused, as though her mind was on something else.

"What's going on with you, Nora?"

Nora stopped moving. "What do you mean?"

"You've been all over my case today. And since we've been back home you've been distant, preoccupied with something."

"Well, there *is* something we need to talk about, Hayden," she said, keeping her back to him.

"Uh-oh, that sounds a lot like I've been summoned to the principal's office."

She stood at the dishwasher, reluctant to turn around. "When I finish writing this Deinosuchus chapter for our book, I'm calling it quits."

"What? Writing books?"

Nora turned to face him, wringing her hands. Tension creased her forehead. She appeared to be tightly wound. "Yes, I'm through being an author. I'm also finished with our dinosaur fieldwork. Tally Lake was the final blow for me. I'm just not wired for the violence and danger, honey. I still haven't gotten over the Livingston Rodeo slaughter from two years ago. I miss the paleontology world—digging up fossils. That's my passion and has been ever since I was a young girl digging in the Wisconsin dirt. I never should have left it. I spoke with Marvin Huebert at the Smithsonian. I told him of my desires, and he was all for me leading another expedition this summer. Marv said he would support me all the way."

"You *what*? Another paleontology dig? Where?"

"Northern Alberta . . . Canada."

Hayden flinched as if he'd been slapped. "I *know* where Alberta is, Nora," he snapped. "When?"

"The caravan rolls in three weeks, the second week of July. It's scheduled to run into early September."

"And you've already signed on?"

She hesitated, then came to him where he sat. Stood before him and draped her arms across his shoulders. "No. I wanted to talk with you about it first."

"Well aren't you thoughtful," he said, turning his head away.

He couldn't look at her after hearing this news. "What about me? What about *us*?"

She gently stroked his beard, forcing him to look at her. "I think our relationship can, and will, withstand a two-month separation."

"So you've already made up your mind, then?"

"Yes. This can't come as a shock to you, hon. We've talked about this before."

He looked deeply into her eyes. The forthright honesty there was too much for him and he looked away again. "This couldn't have just happened, Nora. When did you approach Huebner?"

"A month ago. The middle of May."

"So, well before Tally Lake, then."

"Yes."

Hayden felt the flush of anger heat his face. "And you've kept it from me all this time. Why?"

"I needed time to think it through. It's a big change."

"I'll say it's a big change! And you didn't think enough of me to consult with me about it?"

"It's not that, Hayden."

"Then what is it?"

"I've already told you what it is. Were you not listening?"

"Oh, I was listening all right. Just didn't care for what I heard. What about our company? You just said we have a company to run and you blasted me for being checked out."

"Fowler-Lemoyne Aviation will prosper without me. Without you, too, if I'm being honest. Face it Hayden, we have mostly been absentee investors. Bryan and Loretta Gilliam are pretty much running the show. They've done a great job building the heliport and managing the day-to-day business. And Peter has been super, hiring and training qualified pilots, mechanics, dispatchers. Peter's been a godsend, developing plans for the Missoula heliport and taking charge of all the insurance red tape after the crash. It's our names on the company stationery and we've been the financial conduit, but our partners are keeping the company going."

Hayden scratched at his neck. "So you're leaving, then." A statement, not a question.

"I thought I already established that."

"Jesus, Nora. When did our relationship become transactional?"

"Oh, I don't know. Maybe when you dragged me into dinosaur scouting? Maybe when you talked me into writing two books with you? Or maybe when you maneuvered me into starting up an aviation company with you? All of it has been against my will. Against what I want."

"Don't you *dare* play the victim card with me, woman! You came along with me willingly, every step of the way, and we're both better off for it."

"Are we?"

Hayden was furious. His chest burned with a scorching bitterness and he wanted to lash out, but he held his anger in check.

An awkward stretch of silence ensued.

His mind wandered, searching for reasons why Nora wanted to put distance between them. *It has to be the erectile dysfunction,* he deduced. Since the crash that took a kidney and nearly his life, he'd experienced increasing bouts of ED. Nora told him it was okay, that she understood. The times he was unable to please her physically she would say she was happy for the intimacy. She told him she was content. But now he wondered.

"I've gotta ask, Nora, are you leaving me because I haven't been able to—uh, y'know—*perform* lately?"

Nora let out a low snicker. "Are you kidding me, Hayden? You must think I'm pretty shallow. Why is it men always think their cocks are the center of everything?"

"That's a little harsh, don't you think? Nothing like kicking a man when he's down."

"Okay, maybe that was a little too much. Look," she said, taking a knee and kissing him tenderly on the mouth, "I love you more than I've ever loved another man. You have to believe that, my big cuddly teddy bear. I'm saying our love is strong enough to survive two months apart. Don't you believe that?"

"I'm not sure *I* could survive it, no."

It was her turn to look away. "Maybe there's a way to avoid a separation."

"How so?"

"You could come with me. We could use your expertise on the dig. Remember how much fun we had together in Choteau? Unearthing that magnificent Maiasaura skeleton and her nest of fossilized eggs? Remember that thrill of discovery?"

Hayden felt his already bludgeoned soul being battered further. "I can't go with you, Nora, and I think you know that."

"You could travel with us and then do your own thing, your dino tracking and paleozoology studies."

He shook his head. "There hasn't been any live dinosaur sightings in northern Alberta. My work is in Montana and Idaho."

"So we're at an impasse then," she said.

"If that's what you want to call it," he said regretfully as he gently pushed Nora away and stood. "I need some fresh air. I'm going out for a while." He brushed past her and grabbed his keys from the hook by the door.

HAYDEN HEADED NORTH ON I-494 in his Porshe Macan, Pearl Jam blasting through the surround sound speakers. He knew he was driving too fast, especially at dusk, weaving in and out of traffic. He didn't give a shit. He was worked up, strangling the steering wheel and screaming curses over Eddie Vedder's vocals, spewing his anger at the world.

Nora was slipping away from him. She was leaving him and hightailing it to Canada to play in the dirt. She had been condescending and disrespectful. She had belittled him and he had just sat there taking it. He burned with resentment.

He seethed over the arrogant Montana Fish, Wildlife, and Parks officer who'd written him up, putting a ridiculous misdemeanor on his permanent record and hitting him with a fine.

He mourned the loss of the two young scuba divers who had been slaughtered in horrific fashion. He fumed over being blamed for it.

He was angry at the charter dive boat company insisting he pay for the extensive damage to the vessel. And the captain, Clyde McAllister, was even threatening to sue for physical injuries he claims he suffered. *How in the hell is any of that my fault?*

Hayden raged. The walls of the world were closing in on him.

The T-Rex-shaped air freshener dangling from the rearview mirror seemed to mock him. Furiously, he yanked it off and threw it out the window, damaging the mirror in the process.

Hayden stewed. He was glad he left the house when he did. No telling what might have happened had he stayed much longer. He would never think of hurting Nora, but he just wasn't in control of his emotions today, so better safe than sorry.

He knew he couldn't go back to paleontology work. Not even for Nora. Not when live Cretaceous creatures roamed Montana and Idaho. He had to keep going with his migratory tracking studies. He had to keep studying the marvelous beasts that had returned to Earth.

There would probably be another book to write. Would he be able to do it alone? Would it be another bestseller without Nora's input? Probably not.

Christ, Nora, how could you do this to me? To us?

As he hit Maple Grove and the I-94 junction, he thought he might keep driving all the way to International Falls.

He did his best thinking behind the wheel of his Porsche.

A Taxing Encounter

June 16: Vista Hills Custom Taxidermy

Columbia Falls, Montana

DETECTIVE MIKE MATHEWS WAS INCENSED. His request for a search warrant for Vista Hills Custom Taxidermy was denied by district court judge Franklin Adamson.

Attorney Atlee Pinnaker called him this morning with the bad news. The judge noted that though there had obviously been a menacing threat leveled against the Gilliam family, there was not enough evidence to support probable cause. There had been no bodily harm and no financial loss or property damage. No extortion or blackmail attempt. There had been no additional threats since the severed T-Rex head delivery. And the two crimes at the center of the threat—cyber hacking and dinosaur taxidermy as a violation of the Endangered Species Act—were misdemeanors at best.

So Judge Adamson had quashed the warrant.

Mathews was irate. After all, Judge Adamson issued the subpoena that uncovered the hidden computer IP address leading to the proprietor of Vista Hills Custom Taxidermy. The IP address was a smoking gun pointing right at Kyle Birnham. The warrant should have been a no-brainer. Yet for some reason, the judge denied it.

Mathews was not to be deterred. He had a hunch that Birnham was behind the T-Rex head, and his hunches were usually on target.

But what is the motive?

He decided to make the three-hour drive to Columbia Falls to check out the taxidermy business in person. Maybe get an up-close look at Birnham. He didn't need a warrant for that.

The shop sat on a few acres of heavily wooded land on the outskirts of Columbia Falls. A hand-painted sign with a depiction of a snarling grizzly greeted him as he entered the gravel lot:

VISTA HILLS CUSTOM TAXIDERMY
PRESERVING THE WILD

The building was a capacious wooden A-frame structure with warped siding and dark, dusty windows. A grove of old-growth pine surrounded it, providing a canopy of shade.

Mathews parked his Jeep Grand Cherokee between two battered pickups and shut off the ignition. He donned his Moroccan leather Indiana Jones fedora with its special sheepskin headband. Straightened his bolo tie and got out, walked over the crushed gravel to the entrance. He noticed a side yard heaped with twisted wire cages and mounds of bloodstained sawdust. A corrugated steel shed sat behind the building with a KEEP OUT sign spray-painted in red.

He walked up the front steps, eyeing a rusted tin moose head bolted above the doorway. He entered the shop, a soft buzzer sounding. The air was heavy with pine disinfectant, varnish, and something musky, like decayed flesh half-smothered by chemicals. Dim overhead fluorescents cast a sickly hue over the displays of taxidermied animals—a full grizzly rearing up in mid-roar, a mountain lion, a wolf, three coyotes, and two black bears, all in unnervingly lifelike poses.

Nobody was around. The place was deserted, populated only by the stuffed beasts. It gave him a moment's pause, all the glassy eyes staring at him as if the still-life predators were sizing him up. He walked along a glass counter cluttered with bones of all shapes and sizes. Molds, surgical scalpels, and tubes of epoxy. Knives, forceps, a bone saw. Several labeled jars containing formalin and tannin compound. Oily rags.

He heard a gravelly voice call out. "What can I help you with?"

Mathews turned to see a large man enter through a beaded curtain, wiping his hands on a bloody apron, recognizing Kyle Birnham from the website headshot photos. He was a strapping hulk of a man, well over six feet with broad shoulders. Long, wiry black hair shot through with ash gray, pulled back into a greasy ponytail. Leathery face. Forearms crisscrossed with pale scars. Huge square hands, like catchers mitts. Penetrating muddy hazel eyes that were every bit as unsettling as the acrylic orbs of his animal mounts.

Mathews noticed the index finger on his left hand was missing at the knuckle. "Hello," he said, holding Birnham's stare. "I'm from Missoula and I'm Interested in your price for mounting a full-body black bear. I've heard you're one of the best at preserving bears."

"Oh yeah?" the taxidermist said, scrutinizing Mathews with his hooded eyes. "Where'd you hear that?"

"Hunter friends of mine."

Birnham's look said he didn't buy it. He moved around behind the counter. "You don't look like a big game hunter to me, pardner."

"I didn't know there was a big game hunter *type*."

Birnham tapped a fingernail against the glass countertop, thinking. "Yeah, there is a type. Rough and tumble. Backwoods machismo. You look more like a city slicker. A wannabe cowboy. An urban rat."

"Rat?" Mathews said, thinking *Why the hostile attitude? Is it possible he's onto me?* "With all due respect, sir, is that any way to treat a potential customer?"

The taxidermist gave him a long stare, then the hard lines in his face softened and melted into a lopsided grin. "You're right. Sorry about that. I had a fight with the missus this morning and it's carried through my day. Bitch doesn't know when to shut her yap."

"Sure. Understood. The world would be a much better place if women kept their thoughts to themselves," Mathews said, playing along with the man's obvious misogynist leanings.

"You damn well got that right, stranger."

Mathews pointed to the pair of taxidermied black bears on the showroom floor. "You did an outstanding job on those two. What's something like that cost?"

"Depends on how big the bear and what shape it's in when you deliver it. Whether it's dressed out and field prepped or still full-bodied. But the average price for a full body mount is somewhere between four and five grand. Does that fit your budget?"

"Yeah, I could handle that. Do you do animal pickups?"

"We can. But it's expensive. I didn't catch your name, pardner."

Mathews had come prepared with fake ID. "Alex Sandusky."

Birnham sighed and planted his elbows on the counter. He glanced up at a wall calendar, then turned to Mathews. "Listen, Mr. Sandusky, I'll have you know bear season ended yesterday."

"No worries. I obey all Montana hunting laws. I've got a field prepped black bear in cold storage back home. I took it last week. A male. Weighed in at two-hundred-seventy-six pounds. Five-and-a-half feet when standing erect."

Birnham smirked. "Nice fairytale," he said, squinting at him suspiciously. "Why come all the way here? We're more than two hours from Missoula. Makes me wonder why someone would come into my shop out of the blue so late in the season. Most of my bear customers hired me back in April. And for that matter, there are several good taxidermists smack dab in the middle of Missoula. A good buddy of mine runs a decent mount shop on South Garfield Street. Much easier to deal with him than come all the way up here. That is if you're really a hunter, which I doubt. So why don't you come clean and tell me the true purpose of your visit, Mr. Alex Sandusky, if that's your real name."

Mathews had learned through the years that an overtly defensive arrogance was often a cover for guilt. If only he had that search warrant now. *Damn you, Judge Adamson!*

"Are you this antagonistic with all your customers, Mr.—?"

"Birnham," he said harshly. "And no, my customers all love me and the work I do. I've known most of 'em ten years or more. I even hunt with a lot of 'em. But you come waltzing in here giving me a line of cockamamie bullshit about bein' a trophy hunter. You're no more a hunter than I'm a ballerina, Mr. Sandusky. Now I'm a busy man so you'd best get to the point. Why are you here?"

Mathews knew the time had come for his prepared speech. "Okay, okay. You win, Mr. Birnham." He made a show of looking around the shop and the front door, checking that they were alone. "What I'm really interested in is the side hustle you're known to be running."

"Side hustle? What the hell are you talkin' about?"

"I've heard from more than one source that you're a specialist in dinosaur taxidermy."

"You're a cop! I knew it! You have that self-righteous swagger. That police *pig* stink."

"I'm most definitely *not* a cop. I'm an exotic animal trapper with a list of very wealthy clients." Mathews had prepared this script in his hotel room and practiced it on the drive from Great Falls. "And dinosaurs are at the top of every one of their want lists. Especially the carnivores—the Tyrannosaurs, Dromaeosaurs, and Quetzalcoatlus. The Triceratops are in demand, too, for their horns, but they're not as prestigious as the flesh eaters. For a while my clientele were happy with live specimens. But now, two-plus years after the return of the dinosaurs, they have become much too large and unruly. The hassle of housing and feeding these aggressive creatures is too much for most. Too much trouble keeping them hidden from the authorities. So taxidermy is suddenly the new craze amongst the elite rich. But you already know that, don't you?"

"You've got a lot of nerve coming—"

"They're a competitive bunch, my customers," Mathews continued, talking over Birnham. "They all desire safe versions of these ferocious beasts. They all want a stationary T-Rex standing tall in their trophy den. Many want a couple of taxidermied Dromaeosaurs adorning their back lot. And the pterosaurs with the impressive wingspans—the Quetzalcoatlus—are much better petrified since it's almost impossible to keep them contained when they're alive. I'm here to cut a deal with you, Mr. Birnham. I can bring you a lot of dino business. You say you make four-to-five grand on a bear? You could make twenty times that on a full bodied T-Rex. Hell, you could make ten times that on just the head. That's petty cash to my clients. What I can bring you will jump you up three to four tax brackets. That's how lucrative my deal is. So whaddaya say? You wanna do some business?"

"You're a lyin' bastard sonofabitch!" Kyle Birnham yelled, pulling a sawed-off shotgun from behind the counter and pumping it with a metallic *clack . . . ka-chunk.* He took aim, the twin barrels trained on Mathews. Wildfires flared in Birnham's dark eyes. "You know what I say? I say get the fuck out of my shop and don't ever darken my doorway again."

Mathews held up his hands and backpedaled to the exit, never taking his eyes off the crazed taxidermist. "You'll change your mind after you think it over, Kyle. I'll see you soon."

Outside, he rushed down the front steps to his vehicle and hopped in, tore out of the parking lot in a spray of gravel, turning left on River Road. He cruised along the Flathead River until he came to a turnoff where he could pull over.

Leaving the motor running he took a look at his cell phone, reviewing the videos he'd recorded in the shop. His SpyFocus minicams had performed flawlessly, one embedded in his hat band, the other disguised as the ornamental clasp in his bolo tie. It had been a big risk going in wearing the miniature cameras but it had worked. Birnham had been so focused on tearing down Mathews and covering up his illicit activities that he was oblivious to the possibility of being recorded.

He watched several minutes of footage, pleased with the video quality and sound reproduction. It captured all of Birnham's narcissistic behavior and crazed reaction. He knew this evidence would not be admissible in a court of law, but it would certainly get him his search warrant. And it would give law enforcement a clear idea of the kind of individual they were dealing with. Mathews was one-hundred percent sure Kyle Birnham was their man. Or at least one of them.

If nothing else, the footage of Birnham wielding an illegal short-barreled scattergun would get him a fine and a few weeks in jail.

Mathews pulled out of the clearing and back onto River Road. The recordings would certainly be of interest to the Flathead County Sheriff's Department and district court judge Franklin Adamson.

No doubt about it, Kyle Birnham is hiding something.

Two Heads Are Better Than One

June 16: Gilliam's Guidepost

Heart Butte, Montana

TIME ILLUSTRATES ITS SWIFT PASSAGE through our children.

Bryan thought about that as he observed daughter Lianne snapping Lego pieces together, her tongue stuck out the side of her mouth in concentration. They were in her bedroom seated at a folding card table, assembling the 1,257-piece Fantastical Tree House Lego set Lianne got as a birthday gift from her Aunt Olivia. Lianne did most of the construction while Bryan provided company and encouragement. He watched her sort through the spread of pieces with intense focus, a celebratory smile blooming on her face when she came up with a fit. He hated to admit it but his nine-year-old daughter possessed more of a knack for building Lego sets than he did. His patience and mechanical aptitude began and ended with work on cars and farm equipment.

The only thing she loves more than Legos are horses—specifically her horse Beauregard.

My little Lee-lee. She's growing up so fast.

My how time flies!

It felt like only yesterday that Bryan read her bedtime stories to help her drift off to sleep. Mostly lighthearted fairy tales like *Room on the Broom* and *Princess Smartypants*, the two books she requested over and over. He remembered working with her on her reading and writing lessons. And there were the days of teaching his little Lee-lee how to ride a bike, running alongside her as she pedaled, cheering her on, then celebrating with her on her first successful ride without training wheels. After conquering the bicycle, she'd graduated to horseback. Didn't matter that Lianne was knee-high to a stirrup, she rode horses like she had been born in the saddle, proving to be a true equestrian prodigy. And when she lost her first baby teeth she would smile like a pigtailed jack-o-lantern. The vision of his gap-toothed sweet little Lee-lee always produced a smile if not a full-throated chuckle.

Memory lane took Bryan back a few more years. Times when eldest son Paul would crawl under pickup trucks and tractors out in the barn with dear old dad and watch with a fixated fascination as Bryan tinkered with broken-down engines and leaky transmissions. Pauley had been an inquisitive little tyke back then, wearing out Bryan with endless questions. And then there were the days of tossing the ball with Ethan in the quadrangle in his first year of organized baseball, playing T-ball at age five. And taking the boys out trick-or-treating on the reservation when they were around Lianne's age. Pauley fancied himself as Blackbeard, so his costume was always a pirate getup, replete with long-tailed waistcoat, striped clamdigger pants, tricorn hat with Jolly Roger emblem, eyepatch, fake sword, and hooked hand. Ethan's Halloween go-to was usually Batman. Bryan's musings also took him back to teaching both boys how to shoot, out in the western grasslands, firing at burlap targets pinned to bales of hay. He still could hear their yelps of joy when one of them hit the bullseye.

Yes, my kids remind me every day how fast it's all flying by.

And then he hit on his most precious memory of all—his and Loretta's first kiss. It happened under the vast star-studded Montana night sky, twenty-three years ago, next to a big green John Deere hay baler on Loretta's family's wheat farm in Shelby. He remembered every luscious detail of it, like an indelible supercharged erotic dream. The soft texture of her lips, the slick sweetness of her searching tongue. The heat of their bodies pressed together, the musky jasmine fragrance of her perfume mixing with the grassy-sweet scent of freshly harvested wheat. All these years later he could still hear her whispered sighs as they locked lips, her warm breath in his mouth. Could feel her hands raking the small of his back, pulling him in tight. He recalled every beautiful second of that lengthy first kiss, every touch, taste, and scent of that special night that made him believe that anything was possible. It was the kiss that led to where they were today—twenty-one years of marriage and three children.

The sentimental recollections cycled through his mind like a speeded-up film loop. As he reflected on The Sublime Kiss, he was hit with a wave of melancholy, a profound and penetrating sadness. Those simpler happy days were well behind him, never to be experienced again except in the recall of his nostalgic daydreams. He cherished his kids more than ever, but there were times now when he looked at them and wondered who they were, pondered to where their small, innocent selves had disappeared. Bryan had resolved to spend more quality time with Lianne this summer. The speed with which the calendar pages were turning, it wouldn't be long before his little Lee-lee would be joining her brothers in wanting little to do with him and Loretta. And Loretta was still the love of his life. But the love they shared possessed a whole different vibe now than it had during the heady and exciting early days of their relationship.

The passage of time. It's a bitch!

"Where does this piece go, Daddy?"

Lianne's voice pulled him out of his reflections. She held up a bright green brick.

"Um, that looks like a sidewall on the lookout tower, baby girl."

She gave him an exasperated look. "I'm *not* a baby, Daddy."

"That's just a figure of speech, darling" he said. Seeing she wasn't having it, he relented. "Okay, got it. Can I still call you peanut?"

"Sure, peanut's okay. So is Lee or Lee-lee. And I like *princess*, too. Just not baby girl. I'm not a baby anymore, you know."

"Message received," Bryan said, smiling. "Is it still okay to call you *sweetie*?"

"Sure. I'll always be your sweetie, Daddy."

A surge of heat spread across his chest. She could melt his heart with just a look and a few words. "Your mother told me you two went horseback riding this morning and that you rode in your new saddle. How was it?"

"It was super fun! I love riding with Mama. I love my new saddle, too."

"Did Beauregard like it?"

Lianne snapped two more tiles in place. "Beau *loved* it. I think he liked having his name on the saddle. His picture, too. He sure seemed extra happy when we rode."

"Did Mommy show you how to use your new videocam?"

"Yeah. We made silly faces and took some selfies. But Mama didn't want me using it while we rode. She wanted me to keep both hands on the reins."

"That's smart advice."

"Mama is *very* smart."

"Yes, she is, Lee."

He watched her complete the main trunk of the treehouse. "I'm sorry I was busy this morning, baby—er, um, I mean *peanut*. I really wanted to see you in your new cowgirl outfit."

"That's okay, Daddy. We took lots of pictures. I'll show them to you later."

"I'm looking forward to it."

She looked at him. "Can I ask you something?"

"Sure. Anything. Ask away."

"Why won't you and Mama let me have a dog? All the horse ranches in my books have cute dogs running around. We're a horse ranch and we're rich now but we still don't have a dog. Marnie even has two dogs but I don't. Why, Daddy?"

Bryan smiled. *Ah, the roundabout logic of young girls.*

"Because our ranch has a problem with Dromaeosaurs, Lee. Did you see any Dromes on your ride this morning?"

"No. And Mama and me were keeping our eyes open."

"That's good, Lee. However, I'm afraid a dog wouldn't, um—well, it wouldn't last too long with Dromes around. It's hard enough keeping our horses safe. Your cousin lives on a wheat farm where there aren't any Dromes. Marnie's dogs are safe."

“But Aunt Livvy and Marnie have those big three-horned things, right?”

“Yes. Triceratops. But they’re plant eaters, princess. They don’t bother dogs and other animals. They just eat lots of wheat.”

She gave him that exaggerated little pout he found so endearing. “That’s not *fair*,” she said, before resuming work on her Lego treehouse.

Bryan was about to get into the realities of fairness when his cell phone buzzed. It was the front gate security. He picked up. “Something goin’ on out there, fellas?”

“This is Harvey. Sorry to disturb you, Mr. Gilliam, but you have a FedEx delivery that needs your signature. Should I reject it?”

All members of the Gilliam’s Guidepost security detail had been briefed on the severed T-Rex head that the Gilliams received two weeks ago. A stab of worry hit Bryan between the eyes. *Another FedEx package?* “What does it look like, Harvey?” he said, standing, pushing his chair into the table.

“Unfortunately it’s another Styrofoam cooler.”

The words hit Bryan like an EF5 tornado. “Who is it from?”

“Uh, hold on, Mr. Gilliam . . .” Bryan heard the muffled sounds of Harvey talking with the delivery driver, then, “the sender is Western Adventures in Missoula. Same as last time. Should I decline it?”

Bryan felt something snakelike slither up into his throat. He was having trouble breathing. He did his best to hide his panic from Lianne but she picked up on it. She looked at him worriedly.

“Mr. Gilliam, you still there?” Harvey said into his ear.

“Yeah, I’m still here, Harv.”

“So do you want to reject the delivery?”

Lianne watched him closely. He tried to keep his expression neutral, but it was difficult. He wanted to turn his back to her but knew that would only make things worse. He thought about the situation. If it was another threat, he and Loretta needed to be aware. Law enforcement would need to know about it. And it could give Detective Mathews more incriminating evidence to take to the judge to obtain the needed search warrant. “No,” he said finally.

"Send the driver up to the house and I'll sign for it."

"Okay, will do, Mr. Gilliam," he heard Harvey say, his tone implying he thought it might not be such a great decision.

Bryan clicked off the call. "I have to go downstairs and meet the FedEx guy, Lee," he said, patting her on the arm. "Just keep working on the treehouse. You're doing a great job. I'll be back in a flash."

She looked up at him, her brown eyes wide. "This is part of that thing you and Mama were scared of, isn't it?"

"No, princess. Everything is fine," he said, knowing by the look in her eyes that she didn't believe him for a second. His daughter might be young but she was no fool.

Bryan met the FedEx driver on the front porch and accepted the package, signing for it with a shaky hand. He brought the Styrofoam cooler into the den and set it on the coffee table and regarded it for a good long while, hesitant to open it.

The container seemed to pulse with an electric pearlescent glow, as if it might be radioactive.

That's ridiculous, Bryan old buddy.

Just your fears creating illusions.

Get a grip for Christ sakes!

He approached the package cautiously, his legs weak and trembling.

Removed the sealing tape.

Pulled the top off with a Styrofoam squeak.

He stared at another decapitated head mounted on a bloody base, this one human.

The shock knocked him back a step.

He felt lightheaded, nauseated.

His skin prickled, as though a million worms were traversing his flesh.

The walls rotated and swirled, like he was on a wobbly merry-go-round.

He knew that face very well—Chogan Stimson, the Gilliams' longtime ranch hand. The Blackfoot's dusky skin was mottled and two shades darker than it had been in life. His face was stretched in a petrified expression of surprise. A note laser-printed on an index card hung from his mouth.

TWO HEADS ARE BETTER THAN ONE!
YOU WILL FIND THE REST OF MR. STIMSON
IN YOUR NORTHERN WOODLANDS

Bryan felt his legs buckle just before he hit the floor.

The last thing he heard before he fainted was Lianne's worried voice.

"Daddy? Are you okay?"

The Spirits of Ninastoko

June 19: Chief Mountain (Ninastoko)

Blackfeet Indian Reservation

Glacier County, Montana

LORETTA GILLIAM HATED FUNERALS.

This one touched her almost as much as the memorial service they'd held for her brother Jimmy.

She stood with Bryan and her three children on what was hallowed ground to the Blackfeet Nation—a wide limestone slab midway up Chief Mountain on the eastern edge of the reservation. The Blackfeet called this area *Ninastoko*, a revered place where Native souls passed through to the next life. The ridge offered a breathtaking view of the eastern plains—a vast flatland of sweeping golds and browns that seemed to go on forever. The late morning sun sparkled on the mirrored surface of Duck Lake. A warm breeze blew across her face.

It's a far too beautiful day for such a solemn event, she thought.

Bryan stood to her right, clutching her hand. Her kids—Paul, Ethan, and Lianne—were on her left. A small group of Blackfoot friends and family were gathered around them to pay their respects to Chogan Stimson, a quiet man who was brutally taken long before his time. Loretta looked around at the small crowd. As per tribal funeral custom, the mourners wore long-sleeve white shirts and white pants. Most had slathered white kaolin clay on their faces and hands, and many had removed their shoes. Loretta knew the Blackfeet regarded the color white as a symbol of purity, peace, and a connection to the spirit world. White was a sign of respect for the recently departed as was the removal of shoes.

Chogan Stimson worked for the Gilliams on the Guidepost ranch for fourteen years. He was as close to family as a person could be without sharing the name. Chogan wasn't just an employee of the family, he *was* family.

Bryan found Chogan's headless body strung up in the top of a hundred-foot black cottonwood tree in the Guidepost's northern woods. Bryan had needed assistance from Blackfeet Law Enforcement officers to get him down. The medical examiner estimated from rigor mortis and lividity that Chogan had been killed and beheaded 24 hours before his head was delivered. That put the time of death at somewhere around 10 AM June 15, four days ago. The tribal police figured his body had been hung high up in the trees to prevent hungry Dromaeosaurs from getting at it. After all, a threat was only a threat if there was something there to be seen.

Mighty considerate of the assholes, Loretta thought, her anger intensifying again. Since learning of the murder three days ago, her moods had fluctuated between fury and sorrow.

Chogan's death had also hit Bryan hard. He'd gone ballistic about the lapse in security on the Guidepost, grilling Chief Security Officer Toby Flanagan about it: "How could this possibly have taken place with the small army of security officers you have posted around the clock?" Not finished there, he'd torn into the guards who had been on duty during the time it was estimated the body had been strung up in the trees. "Why the hell am I paying you fuckups? Are you clowns sleeping on the job? Drinking? Drugging?" Bryan's hostile anger brought results: three junior watchmen were booted off the Gilliam security detail and replaced by senior guards.

Chogan had been a hardworking, soft spoken man who pledged his loyalty to the Gilliams every day for fourteen years. He had even risked his life to help Bryan defend the ranch against the marauding AEF murderers two summers ago.

Loretta's eyes were misty, her heart torn and tattered.

Her thoughts were glum. *What kind of deranged monster could lop off a man's head and leave the remainder of his body dangling in the trees? Especially a kindhearted man like Chogan?*

Loretta stole a glance at Chogan's body, lying between the ceremonial fire and freshly dug grave, wrapped in a buffalo hide stitched shut with animal tendons. There would be no coffin in this semi-traditional Blackfoot earth-and-sky funeral. No embalming. The Blackfeet believed that all living things came from the earth, and therefore, bodies should be returned to the earth unencumbered after death. They saw coffins as prison walls that hampered a soul's passing to the next life and embalming to be in direct conflict with traditional Blackfeet spiritual and cultural beliefs.

Poor, unlucky Chogan. They had no suspects or motive, though the private detective, Mike Mathews, was convinced the Columbia Falls taxidermist he'd been investigating was involved. Two detached heads delivered to the Gilliams in Styrofoam coolers in the past two weeks, both sent from the same fake company. Identical clean and precise cutlines and professional separation of the heads from the bodies. The same MO in both gruesome events. The connection was obvious. The detective's logic was sound. Mathews had provided the tribal police with copies of the video he'd recorded during his visit to Vista Hills Taxidermy. After viewing the footage of the owner's meltdown, the Blackfeet police agreed with the detective, as did the Flathead County sheriff. And now they waited for a judge to issue search warrants for the taxidermist and his Columbia Falls shop, warrants that were denied the first time around.

Other than that, the only clues they had were boot prints in the woods at the scene of the crime that the tribal police were following up on. There were no breaks in the perimeter fencing and nothing out of the ordinary had shown up on the many cameras installed on the property.

The funeral proceedings began. Loretta turned her attention to the spiritual elder, Naapi Yellow Calf, Keeper of the Buffalo Bundle. Dressed in a ceremonial buffalo robe with his long braid of hair wrapped in red cloth, he had his back to the mourners.

"Ninastoko," he called out, addressing Chief Mountain by its Blackfoot name, "you are the one who watches, the one who waits." The old seer's voice was worn and strained. "Today we deliver to you our sacred son and brother, Siksikáyo Chogan Stimson. Though he had his eyes stolen from him, we have faith that you will show him the path forward, that you will guide him into the next world."

A young teenage boy—Chogan's nephew, Nínnaa—began beating a hand drum and singing the most mournful dirge Loretta had ever heard. "*Oh-oh-oh, ah-um-wahey . . . Oh-oh-oh, ah-um-wahey . . .*" Another voice joined in, then another, until the melody of grief resounded across the ridge. A young woman wailed, crying out in unsettling shrieks. Loretta looked left to see Chogan's fiancée, Mika, sobbing and howling for her lost Siksikáyo.

Naapi Yellow Calf raised a thick braid of sweetgrass in one hand and a sage smudge stick in the other, and lit the ends from the coals of the sacred fire. The fragrant smoke drifted through the guests as the elder spirit guide spoke of Chogan's accomplishments and dedication to the Blackfeet Nation. When the sweetgrass and sage had burned down, Naapi moved among the gathering, touching the charred ends to foreheads and cheeks, encouraging each mourner he touched to share their prayers for the deceased. Loretta felt the charred sweetgrass brush her forehead and said a quick prayer. Bryan followed, but Paul, Ethan, and Lianne waved Naapi away, uncomfortable with the notion. Loretta rubbed Lianne's shoulder and reassured her children that it was okay to remain silent.

Spiritual elder Naapi kneeled next to the bundled shroud and said loud enough for all to hear, "Siksikáyo Chogan Stimson, your name is spoken. Your people are here. They have prayed for you. Go with fire. Find your way to the Sand Hills and be with your ancestors. We will sing you there."

The drumbeat started up again followed by the ethereal chant-like singing.

Chogan's mother, Wawetseka, approached the buffalo robe that shrouded her son. Loretta barely recognized the woman. In her grief, Wawetseka had shaved her head of her beautiful waist-length hair. She held the long strands in her hands, the midmorning sunlight highlighting her dark smooth head covered in raw cuts and razor burns. Dried blood tracked down her cheeks. Wawetseka showed little emotion as she knelt and tossed her hair on her son's shroud along with a pouch of tobacco and Chogan's flint knife. She then leaned in and spoke to Chogan in hushed tones that Loretta couldn't make out. After several minutes, she stood and returned to her family.

Apisi Lyttle approached next. The Gilliam's remaining ranch hand used a hunting knife to dramatically hack off one of his long braids and gently place it on Chogan's body. Then, loud enough for everyone to hear over the rhythmic singing and drumbeat, he said to his departed friend and coworker, "So you won't ride alone, Cho-cho. Ride hard, brother and don't wait for me."

Several others made their way to the buffalo shroud to pay final respects and then Naapi Yellow Calf closed out the proceedings.

"We give you back to the land, Siksikáyo. Even though they took your head, Ninastoko will see you through. Our mountain remembers every *Niitsitapi* soul who ever passed this way. But we will not rest until your death is answered.

"Amen," she heard Bryan mumble, anger in his voice. Loretta looked at him and saw he had his fists clenched.

And then, three young Blackfoot men came forward to lower Siksikáyo Chogan Stimson into the grave.

The Gilliams' longtime ranch hand was off to the Sand Hills.

The Guidepost wouldn't be the same without him.

Loretta tried to hold back her tears but failed.

Lacroix's Return

June 20: Outbound Flight

Gilliam's Guidepost Heliport

PETER LACROIX SAT IN THE PILOT'S SEAT. Jitters zipped through his gut in electric currents. A rivulet of cool sweat trickled down his spine. Today's flight marked his return to the air, his first time piloting a helicopter since the crash ten months ago.

He had been off the dope for two weeks, two days, eleven hours, and thirty-seven minutes. Quitting the oxy cold turkey had been one of the most difficult challenges of his life.

He had Brinshou to thank for his journey back to sobriety. Of course, Peter's fellow addicts at Power of Choice Narcotics Anonymous had helped him, too. But it was Brin who did most of the heavy lifting. His wife had been there for him when he was puking in the toilet. She had been the one to give him comfort and support when he woke in the middle of the night drenched in sweat and suffering from nausea and abdominal cramps. Brin was the one who stuck by him when his moods took him down a dark path, those many times when he became surly and demanding. She had been his redeeming angel. Things were going so well she felt secure in returning home to relieve her mother of childcare duties, leaving Peter to his work at the Guidepost. Kachina had been caring for Kimi and baby Jake for ten days and desperately needed a break.

Peter focused on the preflight checklist. He tried to still his shaky hands as he recorded instrument data on his tablet: Garmin Wide Area Augmentation System GPS, fuel valve, fuel pump, throttle, altimeter, attitude and airspeed indicators, flight controls, oil pressure, starter, transponder, pedals, radios.

All systems were go. The aircraft was ready.

A queasiness soured his stomach knowing they were just minutes from takeoff. The big day had finally arrived.

This will be the real thing, Peter old boy, not a cyber flight on the simulator in the hangar.

Those harbingers of doom—the evil winged pterosaurs that had downed his chopper in Idaho—floated through his mind.

His adrenaline battled his fears.

"You okay, Peter?" he heard his copilot, Walter Mingus, say.

"Yeah, I'm good," he mumbled, thinking: *Are my nerves showing that much? Get a grip, Lacroix! You've got to be on top of this. We've got important passengers aboard.*

"Great day for flying isn't it?" Mingus said.

"*Every* day is a great day for flying, Walt."

Walter Mingus was the most experienced of the three pilots Peter had hired and trained. Like Peter, Mingus was in his late thirties with a wife and two young children. Over his fourteen year career he had piloted a wide variety of rotorcraft, including Bell, Airbus, and Sikorsky helicopters. Mingus had come to Fowler-Lemoyne Aviation from Skybound Ops in Bozeman, where he was Chief Pilot flying aerial firefighting missions, mountain search and rescue, and logging transport operations. Before that he flew for Montana Disaster and Emergency Services out of Helena and was known for his precision longline skills. Peter missed the hell out of his late flying partner, Larry Bing, but he knew he was in good hands with Walt Mingus in the copilot's seat.

Peter heard muffled voices and thumping in back as their two passengers settled in with their gear. Peter checked the passenger manifest on his tablet: Two state game wardens—Montgomery Bridges and Clifford Twitchell—would be scouting reported elk and bighorn sheep poaching activities. And of course, everyone on board would be on the lookout for dinosaurs.

Peter peered through the bubble at the other Fowler-Lemoyne helicopter parked across the tarmac. Newly hired pilot, Kenny Bernacki, turned and gave Peter a thumbs-up. Peter returned the gesture before Bernacki climbed into the cockpit. Bernacki and his copilot, Randall Hoving, were flying out geophysicists from Bitterroot Mining Company for geophysical surveys and mapping of potential mining sites. Fowler-Lemoyne Aviation was back operating at full capacity now with two new Bell 407s. Peter had checked the flight scheduler earlier and was happy to see they were fully booked for the next three weeks.

He donned his headset and radioed Air Control Dispatcher Nancy Diehl. "Hey, Nance, this is Peter in SkyHawk One. We've completed our preflight instrumentation check. All systems are go. Our transponder code is one-niner-five-three."

"Copy that, Peter." A slight pause, then, "You are cleared for takeoff. Happy trails to you and Walt. Be safe. We'll be with you all the way," she said, meaning Dispatch would maintain radar and radio contact.

They lifted off from the Gilliam's Guidepost Heliport at 9:30 AM for the flight that would cover nearly 200 miles.

Once in the air, Peter's nervousness vanished. He felt like his old self again, in complete command of his aircraft. Feet on the pedals in sync with his right hand on the stick, his left on the collective lever. No back or shoulder pain. No oxy brain fog.

He was back in his element.

They flew over the north woodlands that separated the Gilliam ranch from the Blackfeet reservation. Peter thought about the headless body of the ranch hand found in the cottonwoods below. He hadn't known Chogan Stimson very well, had just greeted him a few times in passing. Even so, the violent way the man had met his end had rattled him. A brutal murder so close to him and Brin. It was frightening. A gloomy air had settled over the Guidepost the past three days. Bryan and Loretta certainly weren't themselves, nor was Apisi Lyttle, the head ranch hand and Stimson's good friend. The funeral yesterday on Chief Mountain seemed to have brought some closure, but the ranch still seemed enveloped in sadness.

They flew over the small, tightly clustered town of Heart Butte, mobile homes, trailers, and vehicles scattered across open lots. Yellow school buses—out of commission for the summer months—were parked around the Heart Butte School. They passed over the tribal offices, clinic, post office, and senior center. The sides of a few boarded up buildings were decorated with colorful Blackfoot artwork depicting animals sacred to the tribe: buffalo, eagles, bears, wolves, horses. Interspersed among the striking paintings were symbols portraying tribal legends and Native heritage.

The plains stretched out before them, dotted with sagebrush and crisscrossed by creeks and streams. Blackfoot wheat farms with tumbledown barns and open-sided metal hay sheds sat on either side of Highway 89, sectioned off by miles of barbed wire fencing. Tarp-covered hay bales lined long stretches of the fencing. Tractors, balers, pickup trucks, and horse trailers were in varying stages of disrepair. Small, ranch-style, wood-frame homes spread out across the prairie along with Airstream trailers and dilapidated mobile homes. Horses were everywhere, grazing in spacious corrals. To the west, Peter took in the immense Rocky Mountain Front, jagged and imposing, rising sharply from the grasslands.

They headed north, the landscape transforming from rolling prairie to hills and deep ravines.

Still thinking about Chogan Stimson's murder, he recalled Brin's words:

"I'm betting the entire Gilliam's Guidepost is haunted after what happened there," and "That ranch is jinxed," and "Some kind of negative karmic juju is infiltrating the Gilliam ranch."

Is there any truth to Brin's omens? Is there a curse on the Gilliams and their ranch?

No, of course not. The whole idea is preposterous. Just my wife's Native superstitions.

But then he thought about the Idaho crash and the way she kept harping on her fears of him flying out of Gilliam's Guidepost, the haunted ranch. She had been right about that, hadn't she?

No. That was just a dreadful coincidence. The crash would have happened regardless of where the flight originated.

A voice in his earpiece intruded on his thoughts.

"Captain? Monty Bridges here."

"Yes, Officer?" Peter said into his mic. "Have you spotted something?"

"Affirmative. We picked up what looks like three hunters field dressing a bull elk near the riverbank. Could you loop back around?"

"Sure thing," Peter said, working the cyclic stick to roll the chopper back around, reversing direction. The Marias River now appeared on Walt's side.

Peter looked out over the grassy highlands to where the river wound through thickets of cottonwoods and willows. "You guys have eagle eyes back there," he said, motioning for Walt to get out the binoculars. "I'm not seeing anything."

"Yeah, they're pretty well hidden under tree cover, but a sun glint off their vehicle tipped us off. Can you take us down?"

"Can do." Peter scanned the terrain below, spotting several level landing areas.

Walt glassed the river with the binocs and sat up straighter. "I see them now," he said. "That's one hell of a monster elk."

The elk carcass lay splayed out on the riverbank, splashes of blood painting the rocks, clumpy entrails scattered about.

As they flew closer, Peter could see three orange clad hunters eyeing the approaching chopper warily. Then, suddenly, one of them bolted, sprinting for the Dodge Ram pickup parked a hundred yards downriver. The other two frantically snatched up rifles, knives, bone saws, bloody tarps, coolers. One of them hastily threw a blanket over the slaughtered elk.

"They're scrambling like spooked sheep," Monty Bridges said in Peter's ear. "They're wasting their time. We've got 'em bloody handed with that carved up animal there for all the world to see."

Peter radioed Dispatch and gave Nancy Diehl their landing coordinates. He maneuvered the chopper to a clearing near the river, low-growing bunchgrass blowing in the downdraft. The skids touched down with a gentle thump.

Peter shut down the engine. The rotors slowed, then stopped.

The passenger doors crashed open. Peter heard boots hitting the ground, then watched through the cockpit bubble as Bridges and Twitchell pursued the hunters, guns drawn.

Cliff Twitchell's voice boomed, "Halt! Montana state game wardens! You are under arrest! Do not run or we will use force!"

The two hunters—white males in their late teens or early twenties—stopped in their tracks and turned, looking at the guns drawn on them with the proverbial deer in the headlights look.

Twitchell kept his gun leveled at the two hunters while Bridges pulled his binoculars from his belt and zeroed in on the Ram pickup. The hunter on the run climbed into the truck and peeled out in a cloud of smoky exhaust, accelerating down the dirt lane that ran parallel to the river, kicking up a cloud of dust in its wake.

"You get that plate number, Monty?" Twitchell asked, eyes never leaving the two hunters he targeted.

"Yep. He's as good as booked along with these two."

The two detained hunters looked on in despair at their traitorous friend fleeing in the truck. Their buddy had screwed them over. All chances of escape were gone. Their heads swiveled between their vanishing ride and the game wardens, their expressions shifting from red hot anger to fear.

"It would appear there's no honor among hunters," Bridges said, clipping the binocs back on his belt and drawing his Smith and Wesson duty pistol. "Down on your knees and hands up over your heads, both of you."

The taller of the two hunters dropped a canvas duffel bag along with a couple boxes of ammunition. Emptyhanded, he raised his arms high as he dropped to his knees. The other man cradled a pair of rifles and stood in erect defiance.

"You," Twitchell shouted, waving his pistol at the man with the rifles. "Lay down those weapons. NOW!"

A tense moment ensued as the man stood motionless, his rebellious stance and determined expression hinting that he thought about firing at the officers. He peered down at the kneeling hunter, then back at Twitchell and Bridges.

"Don't even think about it," Bridges said. "You'll only add more years to your jail time. Drop the rifles and get down!"

The young hunter checked out the two Smith and Wesson semi-automatics aimed in his direction and thought better of it. His defiance melted away. His expression said he knew the jig was up. There was no way out of this. They were busted. His shoulders slumped. He tossed the rifles to the ground with a metallic *thunk* and raised his hands in surrender.

"Down on the ground! Do it!" Twitchell boomed.

"Don't shoot me," the man whined, falling to his knees.

Bridges and Twitchell approached the hunters cautiously.

Peter and Walt watched the encounter unfold through the windshield bubble. Peter felt safe in the cockpit. He'd made sure their two new helicopters were equipped with bulletproof glass, known in the aviation world as ballistic glass. Some of the clientele that chartered Fowler-Lemoyne Aviation services were known to operate in risky environments so such protections were necessary. This outing certainly fell into the high-risk category.

Peter watched Officer Twitchell gather up the rifles and ammo, and search through the duffel bag. The officers had the situation under control; it was now safe for him to leave the aircraft and make his way to the crime scene. He needed to know the details for the post-flight log that the FAA required be filed for each flight.

He said to Walt, "I'm gonna go have a look. Radio Nancy and give her an update, will you?"

"Will do, Pete."

Peter stepped down out of the cockpit and walked through a patch of short needlegrass to where officers Bridges and Twitchell were interrogating the hunters. The two rustlers sat on a large river boulder, their hands zip-cuffed in front of them.

"This is complete bullshit!" one of them snarled.

"Quite the contrary, Mr. Luther M. Haddix," Bridges said, reading the man's name from the hunting license attached to his clipboard. "You are under arrest for killing a mature elk out of season. Normally that's a misdemeanor but," he thrust an elbow at the animal's remains, "this guy is a big branch-antlered bull. You need a special permit to kill one of these, and only if it's *in season*. You don't have such a permit, which makes this a felony offense that brings a thousand-dollar fine each and potential jail time. Adding to your troubles, Mr. Haddix, is the fact that your hunting license is expired. That will bring another fine and probable loss of your fishing and hunting privileges for a couple of years." Bridges looked at the other hunter. "At least you don't have *that* to worry about, Mr. Grantham. Your license checks out. As far as your partner who bailed on you guys, he will be cited with resisting arrest and leaving the scene of a crime in addition to taking an animal out of season. His fines will be much steeper than yours."

"Good!" Grantham spit in the dirt. "The asshole deserves it, the way he split on us. Bo's a coward, you ask me."

Officer Twitchell spoke up. "You say his name is Bo?"

"Yeah. Bowman Kelleher. Biggest douchebag that ever lived."

"What else can you tell us about Bowman Kelleher?"

Grantham said, "Will it get me a lesser sentence?"

Twitchell smirked. "That's above my pay grade, sir. Your sentence depends on the judge you get."

The other hunter, Luther Haddix, spoke up. "C'mon, officers. Have a heart. There're huge herds of elk in these parts. Thousands of 'em. What does one measly bull elk mean in the long run? Give us a break. At least we didn't leave the scene like Kelleher."

Monty Bridges moved in front of Haddix, looked down at him. Gave him a mocking smile. "You want leniency for not running from us? That's really rich, Luther. And you say, oh, it's just one measly bull elk so what does it matter? I'll tell you why." He pointed at the ravaged elk corpse. "A bull elk that size will sire offspring for thirty-five to forty cows during the upcoming breeding season. So you didn't just slaughter a single elk, you potentially killed forty elk. Probably many more than that. *Out of season* I might remind you. So excuse us for our lack of compassion."

"And something else, gentlemen," Twitchell said. "It's pretty brainless to be field dressing a large animal like this out here. It attracts the dinosaurs—the carnivores—the Tyrannosaurs and Dromaeosaurs. They've got a keen olfactory sense, able to smell drops of fresh blood from miles away. If the Rexes and Dromes had shown up, you guys would have had a lot more to worry about than fines and jail time."

Luther Haddix spoke up. "I've heard all about the T-Rex attacks on elk herds. Those meat eaters have killed way more elk than we would in a lifetime. We get arrested for taking a single bull but the government protects the dinosaurs when they kill dozens. What gives with that shit, huh? It's horseshit is what it is."

Bridges said, "We don't make the laws. We just enforce them."

Peter liked these two wildlife agents. They were competent and obviously took pride in their work. He was glad to see people like Monty Bridges and Cliff Twitchell out protecting Montana's wildlife. They served an important function in overseeing the balance of nature and preserving the rustic beauty of his home state.

Twitchell turned to Grantham, who squirmed uncomfortably on the rock. "So how about telling me about your friend, Bo Kelleher."

"That asshole ain't my friend," Grantham said, annoyed. "I don't owe that son of a bitch anything now. I'll tell you everything you want to know about that traitor Kelleher."

As Officer Twitchell got the skinny on Bowman Kelleher, Monty Bridges pulled Peter aside.

"Captain Lacroix, we need to take these two to Toole County Detention in Shelby. We've confiscated their weapons and their wrists and ankles will be cuffed so they'll be immobile."

Peter nodded. "Sure, no worries. Criminal transport is part of our contract with Montana FWP," he said, referring to the state's Fish, Wildlife and Parks department.

"We just need to get some photos of the crime scene and load the evidentiary materials into the cargo hold. Shouldn't take but thirty minutes or so."

"You've got it, Officer. Good work with these two wingnuts."

Bridges sighed. "These guys are a product of today's lost generation. Gen Zers truly believe they are entitled to anything and everything. Unfortunately we see this kind of thing all too often."

Peter said, "I thought there might be some gunplay there for a few scary moments."

"We're well trained in apprehending folks who are eager to shoot things."

"You ever have to fire your weapon during an arrest?"

Bridges shook his head. "No. Been lucky in that regard. Twitch has, however. Last year he mortally wounded a man who was hunting bison out of season. Young guy. Mad as a rabid rat. Shot at

Cliff with a crossbow but missed. Year before that Twitch shot a hunter who pulled a knife on him."

Peter let out a low whistle. "Wow! And I thought flying a helicopter was dangerous."

The game warden looked over at the Bell parked nearby, its blue fuselage gleaming under the bright afternoon sun. "Your work *is* risky. I couldn't do what you do, Captain Lacroix. You have my utmost respect."

Peter said, "And I would never want to be in your boots, going after armed poachers. The respect is mutual."

"Just another day in nature for Cliff and me, Captain. Now if you'll excuse me I need to help Twitch process the crime scene."

AN HOUR LATER THEY WERE IN THE AIR making the 30-minute flight to Shelby with the offenders shackled in back. They flew east, crossing over the precipitous granite peaks of the Rockies. The mountains soon gave way to the rolling hills of the Blackfeet reservation. Fifteen minutes in, hill country leveled out into the rectangular grids of wheat fields and cattle ranches. Rows of grain elevators and hay silos appeared on the outskirts of Cut Bank. A network of railroad tracks cut a silver swath across the plains. Windmills and oil derricks dotted the horizon.

Walt Mingus scanned the terrain below through binoculars, searching for other hunters or anything out of the ordinary. Peter knew officers Bridges and Twitchell were also perusing the land-scape through the high visibility windows in back.

Peter heard Walt in his ear. "You think those two elk murderers will do any jail time?"

"Hard to say. They'll definitely get hit with hefty fines and lose their hunting licenses for an extended period. That's as bad as jail time for avid hunters." Peter thought about his father, Pierre, who would be lost if his hunting privileges were revoked. His dad lived for bird hunting each fall in the forests of New Brunswick.

"What is it with people who get turned on killing defenseless animals?" Walt said.

"I've been asking that question my whole life." Peter thought again of his father, whom he loved deeply but never understood his hunting obsession.

"You ever come up with any answers?"

"No. Still searching for one that makes sense."

They flew eastward in silence for several long minutes before Walt let out a yelp.

"Oh, my god, Pete! Surely my eyes are deceiving me. This *can't* be happening!"

Peter looked at his copilot, who was turned away, head bowed, peering through the side window with the binocs.

"What? What is it, Walt?"

"Two T-Rexes. Oh Jesus, god! One of them is feasting on what looks like an adult human near a hiking trail. The other one's chasing some kids through a wheat field."

"What the—?" The unwelcome news sent a jolt through Peter. "Let's get a video read on what's going on down there, Walt."

"Sure thing." Co-captain Mingus set his binoculars aside and touched the control screen to activate the electro-optical videocam. The video feed gave them a view of the ground directly below the aircraft. Using a joystick, he zoomed in on the hiking trail. A grisly scene came up in the center of the display panel—an alarmingly large Tyrannosaur bent over, dipping its snout and twisting its head, ripping chunks of flesh and intestines from a downed hiker. Walt toggled the camera to get a view of the nearby wheat field. The screen showed a number of small bodies zig-zagging through rows of wheat trying desperately to evade a second T-Rex.

Peter felt his nerves short circuiting.

His heart thumped in triple time.

Memories of the Tyrannosaurs he had encountered at the Idaho crash site came rushing back—the big one that took Jackson Lattimer and the Rex that he and Bill Carlton had killed. Peter could taste the oily, rancid taste of roasted Tyrannosaur meat he had eaten to survive. Bile flooded the back of his throat.

He heard Monty Bridges' voice in his headset, shaky, urgent. "Captain, trouble below. We're seeing a pair of Tyrannosaurs."

"Yeah, we've spotted them," Peter replied, trying to control his rising panic.

His mind raced.

Quick decision time. I can't let those children die.

"Buckle in and hold on back there, guys," he yelled into the mic. "We're going down and it's gonna be rough sledding."

Please forgive me, Brinny but I have to do this. Good Lord above, please be with me.

Walt gave him a long stare, his eyes ignited with adrenaline. "Are you sure?"

"Absolutely," Peter said with authority. He reached with his left hand and jammed the collective lever down.

The chopper dipped sharply and they plummeted in a gut-dropping descent.

They were in freefall.

The floor seemed to drop out from beneath them, taking Peter's stomach with it.

Walt pushed back against his seat and grabbed his harness straps, pulling them tight.

Peter worked the cyclic stick and pumped the yaw pedals, the coordination and concentration required to pull out of the quick descent bringing a calm to him.

The chopper leveled out thirty feet above the wheat field.

They flew directly at the T-Rex that was flattening the green shoots in its frenzied pursuit.

Peter heard anguished screams over the *thwop-thwop-thwop* thump of the rotor blades and steady hum of the turbine engine. He looked at the video feed from the undercarriage camera, picking up quick flashes of frightened young faces.

"Definitely children," he told Walt.

"Yeah, unfortunately."

The beast pulled to a stop, fifty yards away.

Forty yards . . . thirty . . .

The Rex turned, casting its crimson-gold eyes on them.

"Careful, Pete," Walt warned.

"I've got this," he uttered, hands steady as he worked the stick and the lever, flying in low and tight, buzzing the Rex, clearing the creature's head by a mere ten feet.

The beast swiped at the chopper's landing skids with one of its short forelimbs.

"Oh, sweet Jesus!" Walt called out, breathless, white-knuckling the sides of his seat.

Peter circled back and flew at the beast a second time, expertly maneuvering the chopper around the big animal but getting in close enough to unsettle it.

The Rex snapped its mighty jaws at the passing aircraft, showing off its deadly rows of teeth.

"That's one big bastard," Walt said.

"Yeah, and he's not happy with us interrupting his hunt."

Peter circled around yet again, lining up the Rex. Spoke into his headset. "Everybody okay back there?"

"A little scrambled but we're all right," Monty Bridges said.

"Hang tight. We're going at him again. Third time's the charm."

Peter shoved the stick forward and the chopper responded with a jolt, gaining speed, the wheat stalks waving in the downdraft.

The Rex eyed the children running through the field, then turned to challenge the oncoming aircraft.

Peter zeroed in on the creature's head. He prayed the beast would dash off.

Forty yards . . .

Thirty yards . . . the Rex remained planted.

Walt's voice in his ear: "Um, whaddaya doing, Pete?"

Twenty yards . . .

Ten yards . . .

At the last possible second Peter pulled back the stick and the craft lifted, narrowly avoiding a disastrous collision.

"Holy motherfucking shit!" Walt yelled. "Damn, that was a little too close for comfort, Pete."

"Looks like it was effective," Peter said, pointing to the rear-facing camera screen on the display panel. They watched the Rex lumber out of the wheat field and disappear into the woods.

"Are you shittin' me?" Walt bellowed, gasping. "Man oh man, you've got balls of chromium steel."

Peter let out a deep breath, his heart still hammering. "If I didn't do something those kids would've been killed, Walt. I couldn't live with that on my conscience."

Walt offered a nervous smile. "I just lost a couple of years off my life but I've gotta say, that was a piece of world class flying there, Pete."

"Thanks, but we're not done yet. We still have another dragon to slay before we push on to Shelby."

"God help us," Walt intoned.

"What's the matter, Walt? I thought you piloted disaster and emergency rescue missions for Skybound Ops."

"I did. But I never experienced anything close to this."

"Your first dinosaur?"

"Isn't it obvious?"

Peter grinned at him. "Welcome to Fowler-Lemoyne Aviation."

He banked and flew away from the wheat field, toward the hiking trail and the second Tyrannosaur. The animal had its head down, still absorbed in its meal of the hiker, oblivious of their approach. Peter brought the copter in about fifteen feet above the creature and hovered in place. The Rex looked up, a bone in its mouth, blood coating its snout, seemingly not bothered by the heavy downwash of air or crisp snapping of the rotor blades.

They spent agonizingly long minutes hovering over the carnivore as it devoured what was left of the hiker. Peter and Walt watched the camera feed in disbelief.

Peter said, "We got here too late to save this poor man. At least I *think* it was a man."

They sat staring at the brownish-green reptilian scales lining the creature's back, the jagged scar running along its flank. Peter was glumly transfixed by the way it threw its head back to gobble down portions of its prey.

A few more minutes passed before Peter said, "Hovering isn't working. We're burning too much fuel sitting here. I'm gonna try a controlled oscillation. Hopefully it will run this bad boy off. Nobody is safe here until we chase this guy."

Walt looked at him doubtfully. Controlled oscillation was, in effect, bouncing the chopper from side to side while hovering in place. A difficult maneuver. Not many helicopter pilots had the skills to pull it off. The slightest miscalculation could take them out of the hover and spin them corkscrewing to the ground.

Peter moved the cyclic stick and pumped the pedals in an exaggerated rhythm. The aircraft responded with a quick left lean, then abruptly tilted back to the right. Two more side-to-side judders caught the attention of the Rex. The beast twisted its thick neck around, looking up at the erratic movement of the chopper, confused, bellowing an annoyed roar. Then, sensing danger, it sprinted into the forest near where the other Rex had disappeared.

Peter heard cheering from the back.

Walt said, "You're gonna give me heart failure before this is all over, Pete. But nice work. I'm impressed."

Peter was all business, saying to Walt, "Radio Nancy and tell her to get 9-1-1 Emergency Rescue out here. With paramedics. We've got at least one dead adult and a number of children, conditions unknown. See if there's a child psychologist available, too. Those kids are gonna need a lot of emotional support."

"Roger that, Captain."

As Walt radioed Dispatch and spoke with Nancy Diehl, Peter set the craft down near the north end of the wheat field, well away from the hiker's corpse. He shut off the engine and unbuckled his harness. Grabbed his holstered Smith and Wesson .44 Magnum from the utility drawer under his seat. Stepped out. Went to the passenger section and recruited Monty Bridges to accompany him in finding the children. Bridges strapped on his rifle. Officer Twitchell remained in the chopper with the two bound poachers.

Peter and Bridges began walking along the perimeter of the wheat field.

"That's a wicked rifle you've got there, Officer," Peter said as they walked along a barbed wire fence.

"It's wicked all right. Like a cannon. A Weatherby Mark Five. Safari guides use them in Africa. I'm told they can put down a charging rhino at eight-hundred yards."

"Good to know. We'll need that kind of firepower if those

Tyrannosaurs return."

"Well, I hope I don't have to use it. The recoil is heavy enough to dislocate your shoulder if you don't set up right."

"We've got a pair of T-Rexes running loose—the most feared predator ever to roam the Earth—and you're worried about rifle recoil?"

Monty Bridges let out a self-deprecating laugh. "Yeah, I guess that was an idiotic statement."

Peter slid his revolver out of the holster. "I'm not a big fan of guns. Only reason I have this is because my boss insists his pilots fly with some protection. I believe it has something to do with our insurance requirements."

"That's smart. You never know what you'll run into out here."

They continued their walk, calling out, trying to locate the missing children.

The first child appeared. A boy, maybe nine. Crying, his arms badly scratched. Then a pair of girls around the same age, timid, spooked, faces red, cheeks wet with tears. Gradually, one by one, terrified children emerged from the wheat. Eight of them in all. Five boys and three girls. Some with backpacks, all wearing identical t-shirts with CUT BANK COMMUNITY BIBLE CHURCH HIKE-A-THON printed across the front.

"Are you the guys in the helicopter?" one of the boys asked.

"Yes we are. I'm Captain Pete and this is Officer Monty."

Peter asked them if all were present and accounted for. One of the older boys, maybe twelve, spoke up. "Yessir, we're all here. All except for Mr. and Mrs. Withers. They're our hiking leaders."

"There were two adults leading you?" Peter inquired.

"Yeah," the boy said. "We got separated when those dinosaurs showed up. The Withers are deacons in our church. They've been our hike-a-thon leaders the past four years. I hope they're okay."

No such luck, young man.

"What's your name, son?"

"Rusty."

"Well, Rusty, we'll do our best to find Mr. and Mrs. Withers," Peter said, feeling bad about not being truthful with the kid but knowing it was the only way to handle it.

Bridges said, "Are any of you hurt?"

They all shyly shook their heads, no.

A major miracle, Peter reasoned, thankful for it.

"We're just scared, mister," one of the older girls said. "Those dinosaurs came out of nowhere and we took off running. I thought we were gonna die."

Peter felt a deep stab of sympathy for these poor children. They would never be the same after experiencing something like this.

"Well, you're safe now, kids. We've got help coming and we'll get you back with your families soon."

"You saved us!" one of the girls shouted. "You saved our lives! Thank you, thank you, thank you!"

And then all three girls and two of the younger boys swooped in, huddling around Peter and Bridges, throwing their arms around them. The kids jumped up and down amid tears of joy and shouts of happiness.

They won't be this jubilant when they learn the fates of the Withers.

As Peter stood there in the middle of highly-charged grateful kids, their arms pulled tight around his legs and waist, he thought:

I just saved eight children from certain death.

I did it with some fancy flying.

I've got my pilot mojo back!

And I'm transporting two lawbreakers to a detention center.

If only we'd arrived sooner to save Mr. and Mrs. Withers.

Hell of a first day back on the job, Peter, old boy.

A Promise of Wings

June 22: Selway-Bitterroot Wilderness

Kooskia, Idaho

"WOULD YOU CLASSIFY THIS AS DINOSAUR PORN?"

Hayden Fowler posed the question to wildlife biologist Bill Carlton while zooming in on a pair of Ankylosaurs in the ravine with his videocam.

They sat in a blind of subalpine fir. Carlton remained silent, peering through the telephoto lens of his high-powered Nikon at the two big herbivores mating down in the wooded glen.

The scene was primal, prehistoric.

Surreal.

Hayden estimated the male Ankylosaur to be fifteen feet and weigh in at close to a ton. The female was slightly smaller.

The male had mounted her from behind and was riding her hard, ramming his big armored body into her with frenzied thrusts, accenting each push with low-pitched, resonant yawps. She remained still, compliant, raising her clubbed tail, accepting him, bracing herself with her strong forelimbs. The male's thick hind legs flexed with each push, his powerful tail raised to counter-balance the forceful coupling. The air was thick with their musky scent, even from this distance.

Carlton lowered his camera. Stared at Hayden with a look of amusement. "*Really*?" he said softly, knowing how sounds carried across the hollow. "*That's* where your head is at?"

"Well, you can see what's going on."

"You're such a perv, Fowler. That's *not* porn. It's a thing of beauty—a biophysical and zoölogical phenomenon. What we're witnessing is truly a miracle."

"Well you seem to be taking an extreme prurient interest in that miracle," Hayden said with a snide grin. "Admit it, Carlton, you have an animal porn fetish."

"I assure you, my interest is purely scientific, my friend."

"Sure it is. Keep telling yourself that, Bill."

The two men lapsed into a comfortable silence as they observed the armor-plated, tanklike Ankylosaurs coupling. The male released low-pitched, guttural exhalations with each thrust, sounding to Hayden like an enormous bellows compressing and expanding. The female emitted rhythmic baritone huffs that reminded him of a bull walrus under stress. Their clubbed tails intertwined and twitched through their spirited coitus.

Hayden broke the silence. "Remarkable specimens. Look at those osteoderms and fused scutes," he said, referring to the bony plates lining their flanks, backs, and tails. "It's like two heavily armored earthmovers copulating."

"Your mind works in strange ways, Hayden."

"I assure you, my mind is purely scientific, good buddy."

Carlton could only shake his head.

"And my scientific mind tells me the fucking is consensual."

"Dare I ask how you know?"

"Can't you see the smile on her face? That beaked mouth of hers is grinning in multi-orgasmic pleasure."

Carlton laughed. "You need help, Fowler."

Time spent with Bill Carlton did Hayden good. They had developed an easy rapport during their joint outings the past year. Their friendship had grown after surviving last summer's helicopter crash in the River of No Return Wilderness area, a hundred miles south of here. Three of their colleagues had perished in that accident. A death defying experience like that tended to forge a close bond between people, and that certainly held true in their case. Carlton respected Hayden as the celebrity paleontologist dinosaur tracker and celebrated bestselling author while Hayden appreciated Bill Carlton's nature experience picked up in his nineteen years as Regional Wildlife Biologist with the Idaho Department of Fish and Game. The two had done field work together several times over the past year, the last being at Tally Lake two weeks ago when they witnessed a Deinosuchus kill a grizzly bear. Hayden hadn't enjoyed a relaxed buddy-buddy friendship like this since his good friend Jackson Lattimer was taken by a T-Rex.

He continued to film, his videocam whirring. Carlton's digital camera clicked and whined. The grunting and huffing of the fornicating dinos carried across the valley.

"Unbelievable," Hayden said. "*Ankylosaurus Magniventris.* The stiffened lizard. Just the second sighting of them since the Cretaceous rebirth, as far as we know. I told you about Nora's and my experience last year didn't I? Seeing those Ankylosaurs run off a pair of Tyrannosaurs?"

"Yeah, you did. I saw the video you shot, too. Pretty wild stuff. Who'd have thought passive herbivores could inflict so much damage on apex predators."

"They're not passive when attacked. They get their backs up. Literally. Those clubbed tails are brutal. They pack a wallop."

Carlton said, "They're equipped with physiology not seen in today's animal kingdom."

"Yeah. They're built like tanks, squat and low to the ground. Difficult for Tyrannosaurs to get at them. I wrote that they were like otherworldly armadillos in our new book. The publishing folks loved that description."

Carlton smiled. "It's fitting, though there's a bit of a size discrepancy."

"Just a bit, yeah. And you, my friend, are just the third set of human eyes to see an Ankylosaurus. And look at us. We're lucky enough to catch them in the act. In flagrante maximus!" Hayden peered through the viewfinder. "Man, those two have some serious stamina. Look at 'em go at it!"

"Now I'm convinced you're a perv, Fowler."

"I don't see you shutting off *your* camera, Mr. self-righteous."

"How about we change the subject before you get overheated, Hayden. When is your book coming out?"

"That's a forbidden topic, Bill."

"Is it? Why?"

"I'm beginning to wonder if it'll ever be published. It was supposed to be released next week, but they've pushed it out into late October. Lots of delays. Some of them due to my procrastination. I pushed a lot of the work off on Nora, which backed things up, not to mention pissing my woman off. My fault entirely."

Carlton nodded. "I thank my lucky stars I wasn't with you and Nora on that dive trip. Those videos you showed me are harrowing. That first Deinosuchus we saw from our treetop stand was frightening enough. But you ran into *three* of them on the dive?"

Hayden nodded.

"I can't imagine. It must have been chilling. "

"It was. I thought for sure we were goners a couple of times. It's a miracle the boat didn't sink. We're lucky to still be alive." Hayden's tone turned glum. "That experience was the proverbial straw that broke the camel's back for Nora. She informed me she's done doing fieldwork with me. She accepted a position heading a Smithsonian paleontology expedition in Canada next month."

"I thought you'd been a bit preoccupied this trip. So you two are—*what*?"

"That's the million-dollar question, isn't it."

Carlton gave him a long questioning look but Hayden kept his eye glued to the camcorder. He'd rather talk about anything other than his relationship with Nora. The purpose of this three-day Idaho trip with Carlton was to get away from his domestic troubles. Communing with nature and tagging dinos for his migration study was supposed to help him forget about Nora and her decision to leave him for two months. And it did to some extent. The tracking had been productive. The past two days they had tagged three Tyrannosaurs, a pair of Dromaeosaurs, and a Triceratops with Argos satellite trackers. They had also collected blood samples and hide swatches from each. But he just couldn't escape thoughts of Nora. She was on his mind constantly, often intruding on his work. He loved that beautiful brilliant, stubborn, headstrong woman more than he could put into words. In two short years, Nora Lemoyne had become the biggest and best part of him.

His satellite phone beeped loudly, startling him. He set the videocam aside and checked the display:

INCOMING CALL: UNKNOWN NUMBER

He was curious as to who would be calling him out here. He stood, telling Carlton he had to take the call. He walked away from the blind and further into the woods. "Hello?"

"Uh, yeah, is this Doctor Hayden Fowler? Dinosaur tracker extraordinaire?"

Jesus! Not another stalker fan.

"Who wants to know?"

"My name is Mick Prescott."

"This is a private number, Mr. Prescott. How'd you get it?"

"I booked a charter on one of your helicopters. Your general manager, Bryan Gilliam, gave me your contact info. He's very personable, friendlier than I would have expected from a celebrity. He ran that dinosaur ranch two years ago, you know, where—"

"Of *course* I know that," Hayden said testily, picturing himself strangling Gilliam. "So Mr. Prescott, you chartered a flight with us and I thank you for your patronage. But I'm quite busy at the moment and don't have time for—"

"Just hear me out. Please. I've got something I'm sure you will have a huge interest in."

"I'm listening. And make it quick."

"Sure thing. I have followed the news reports about the crash of one of your choppers last summer. A flight you were on and survived. I read several of your interviews with the press about the cause of the accident. Winged reptiles. Am I correct?"

"Yeah. More specifically, Quetzalcoatlus. All of that is public knowledge. What's it have to do with you?"

"Well, my wife and I have an interest in Quetzalcoatluses, too."

"Too? Who says I have an interest in them?"

"I read your book, which was an intriguing read, I must say. It really speaks to the fact that you have a keen interest in these dinosaurs that have returned to us and—"

"Get to the point, Mr. Prescott."

"Okay, okay. My wife and I are exotic animal curators. We spend much of our time in remote areas tracking all kinds of species.

Ten days ago we made an extraordinary discovery that I believe will be of great interest to you. At least Mr. Gilliam thought so. That's why he gave me your satphone number."

"Yeah?" Hayden said, his curiosity about the caller growing. "What kind of discovery?"

"I'll answer that with a question of my own."

"You're trying my patience, Mr. Prescott."

"Please, call me Mickey. May I call you Hayden?"

"No! Is that your question, Mickey? I've got my finger on the red button to end this call, so—"

"Wait! Here's my question. Have you seen any Quetzalcoatlus since they brought down your helicopter last year?"

Not something Hayden expected. "That's one crazy-assed inquiry, Mickey."

"Well, have you?"

"Only in my nightmares. Why do you ask? And please get to the point. I'm busy here." Hayden looked out into the glen below, spying the two Ankylosaurs still engaged in heated copulation.

"Okay. Claire and I made a connection on the dark web with a guy calling himself the Quetzal Whisperer. He claimed to be a falconer who has raised a number of Quetzalcoatlus from hatchlings. Said he'd trained them to do extraordinary things. Of course we were skeptical and were surprised when he invited us up to his place, high up in the Bitterroot Mountains near Sula . . ."

Hayden listened to the man talk while glancing at Carlton, circling a forefinger around his ear in the universal *batshit crazy* gesture. But something in Mick Prescott's confident voice and sure delivery told him the man was far from insane. Maybe operating on the wrong side of the law but not crackers crazy.

"Wait a minute, Mickey," he said. "Back up. You say you and your wife are animal curators?"

"That's right."

"For what zoo?"

"We're independent operators, though we both used to work at the Denver Zoo. We still do some animal trapping for them and we've got some open-ended contracts with a few other zoos."

"But you and your wife also trap dinosaurs, I'm assuming?"

"Yes, but—"

"No zoo I know will take them. And the fact that you're operating on the dark web tells me you must be traffickers."

"No—no, *not* traffickers. *Curators*. We sell to traffickers. We respect these animals and don't do them any harm. Our trapping practices are very animal friendly. We find them good homes."

"Their homes are in the wild, Mickey."

A slight pause, then, "Funny you should point your finger of blame at me for that, Doctor Fowler, when two years ago you and a bunch of other scientists studied hatchlings you kept caged at the Gilliam's Guidepost ranch. Like I said, I read your book. A couple of times, in fact."

"Fair enough," Hayden said, appreciating Mick Prescott's grit. "Tell me more about this Quetzal Whisperer dude."

Prescott told him all about the falconer with the milky blind eye and deeply scarred face who lived on a compound nestled high in the mountains. He went on at length about the man who had a bizarre special relationship with the flying reptiles. Eight of them to be exact. Frighteningly wide wingspans of fifteen feet or more. Long pointed beaks and giraffe-like necks. Tall, bladed head crests running across the top of their skulls, similar to a cassowary's casque. Prescott described the way they perched at attention before the Whisperer, patiently waiting for instructions from their master, then carrying out every command issued by the falconer.

"I don't think I should say any more over the phone," Mick Prescott said finally. "No telling who might be listening in. I believe it would be best if we met face-to-face. Somewhere in public."

"We can talk now," Hayden said. "My satphone is encrypted."

"Oh, okay. Great. So is my cell."

"So let's continue. You say these Quetzals actually obeyed this Whisperer's commands and carried them out?"

"Yes. Absolutely."

"Give me an example."

"Well, he ordered three of them to fetch him a small animal—rabbit, squirrel, possum. He was specific about the animals he wanted brought to him. The Quetzals flew off and returned quickly with the exact animal he called for. Dead of course."

Hayden was doubtful but intrigued.

"Claire and I were quite surprised at how the Whisperer opened up to us and showed us around his compound."

"And why exactly would he do that?"

"Because we showed an interest in buying one of his Quetzals."

"He's selling them?"

"Yeah. The Whisperer has five adults up for sale on the dark web. He's keeping the three juveniles for further training."

"And you're buying one for a customer of yours?"

"We were until he quoted us the price."

"How much?"

"Suffice it to say it's way above our budget. But you, on the other hand—"

"Wait a minute. You want me to bankroll this insanity?"

"No. No bankrolling necessary."

Hayden thought, *What is this guy's angle?*

After a moment's pause, he said, "Who the hell would want one of these Quetzalcoatlus, anyway? Without the trainer they'd be impossible to contain. And they're gonna grow to an immense size. Their wingspans will spread to thirty-five feet or more and weigh in at four-hundred-plus pounds. You would need a huge covered habitat to house them. Who wants that kind of headache?"

"You must understand, Doctor Fowler, these ultra wealthy collector types are a strange breed. They all want something completely unique so they can brag about the distinctiveness of their collection. It's a competition du jour amongst the rich elite. They'll pay any price to obtain these dinos. They don't give a damn about the headaches. Or the price. It's a lucrative business, even as a wholesaler, which is what we are."

"So what is it you want from me, Mickey?"

"He wants to meet you, Doctor Fowler." He knows all about you. There's admiration in his voice when he talks about you. The deep knowledge you have of these Cretaceous creatures. The way you survived the crash. He wants to show you his cast. That's what he calls his Quetzals, a *cast*. He wants to talk dinosaurs with you."

Hayden thought for a beat. "And what's in it for you?"

"He said if Claire and I got you up to his compound he would give us a substantial discount on a Quetzal. A price we can afford. We've got a customer lined up and he's chomping at the bit to get one of these birds."

"They're not birds, Mickey."

"I know. But they sure fly like birds. *Big* birds"

Hayden tugged on his beard, thinking. "Why would this guy ask you to get in touch with me? You and I have never met. He could have reached out to me on his own. You didn't lie to him about us having some kind of relationship, did you?"

"No."

"Mickey, come on, man. I didn't just fall off the back of a logging truck. You fabricated some kind of a story for this Whisperer, didn't you?"

A brief pause, then, "Okay, maybe I embellished things a little."

"And how am I supposed to trust a liar?"

"I'm *not* a liar, Doctor. I told him I knew a way to get in touch with you before I knew I actually could. Just a tiny stretching of the truth. Nothing more. I swear to you, these things I've told you about this man are true. Claire and I saw everything with our own eyes."

"Is this trip up to the Whisperer's compound the reason you chartered one of my helicopters? Because there's no way I'm letting either one of our choppers get close to those flying demons again."

"No, oh no! You misread me. I chartered your copter only to get your contact information. You'd ride with my wife and me up the mountain."

"That's pretty devious, Prescott. Disingenuous at best. And might I ask, what's in it for me? A healthy cut of your Quetzal revenue, I hope."

"No. Your payoff would be getting an up-close look at these flyers for your studies and your next book. You could check them out from head crest to tail, from wing to wing. Whisperer promised you would have complete access to his cast to do complete anatomical examinations. It would be a treasure trove of information for you. Where else can you get this kind of data on these rare flying reptiles."

Hayden frowned. "Why would this guy want me anywhere near his reptiles, knowing their siblings caused our crash and my near demise? I would think he'd fear I might be out for revenge."

"He knows you're an internationally famous paleozoologist and a true professional scientist who respects these winged reptiles despite what their kind have put you through. Truth is, I think he wants a piece of your fame."

Since vaulting back into the international limelight of celebrity two years ago for being one of the first humans to encounter dinosaurs, Hayden had been approached numerous times by people wanting to get close to him. The fame magnet had a powerful pull. He understood that attraction, but it didn't make it any easier. Did this Quetzal Whisperer want a piece of his celebrity? Maybe it was actually Mick Prescott who wanted to get close to the fame flame. Or was this whole thing one giant hoax?

"You still there, Doctor?"

"Yeah," Hayden said. "Still here. Just thinking." He looked through the latticework of limbs at Bill Carlton sitting in the blind, his back to him, now videoing the mating Ankylosaurs with Hayden's camcorder. "I'll tell you what, Mickey. Your pitch has me greatly intrigued. What you're telling me is extremely implausible, but then, we're living in surreal times. How about we schedule a meeting and discuss it further?"

"That would be fantastic! Can I call you Hayden now?"

"No. But if you and your wife take me up to that mountain compound and there really is a Quetzal Whisperer and not a great and mighty Oz behind the curtain pulling levers, then you can call me whatever the hell you want."

"That would be awesome, Doctor Fowler."

They made plans to meet tomorrow at a coffee house on South Huggins Avenue in Missoula. Hayden disconnected and returned to the blind.

"What was that all about?" Bill Carlton asked. "The part I heard sounded pretty strange."

"It was," Hayden said, taking a seat next to him. "An animal trapper claims to have a line on the flyers that almost killed us. A place in the Bitterroot Mountains where I can go to see them up close and personal."

"And you believe him?"

"I don't know. But it's too weird to pass up. I'm meeting with him tomorrow. I'll know then if he's completely full of shit or not."

"Just be careful, Hayden. Lots of whack jobs and grifters running around these days."

"Don't I know that." Hayden looked out over the hollow and didn't see the Ankylosaurs. "What happened to our porn stars?"

"They finished up in an explosive climax while you were gabbing. Never fear, I caught it all on video. They're probably having a postcoital smoke in the woods right now."

Hayden chuckled. "And you have the audacity to call *me* a pervert."

A Raid on Antiquity

June 24: Vista Hills Custom Taxidermy

Columbia Falls, Montana

THEY ROLLED INTO THE PARKING LOT like a small invading army. Mike Mathews steered his Grand Cherokee in behind three Flathead County Sheriff Department cruisers.

No bubble lights or sirens.

They opted for a surprise, quick-hit approach.

Better late than never.

Mathews felt the search warrant should have been issued immediately after the murder and beheading of the Blackfoot ranch hand, Chogan Stimson. The facts of the case were clear. Same MO in the Stimson murder as with the decapitated T-Rex head. Both severed heads delivered to the Gilliam family via FedEx from the same fictional sender, Western Adventures. Both heads showing the same clean, precise cutlines of a professional butcher. Mathews reasoned the heads could have been done by a hunter experienced in field dressing wild game, but he really didn't think so. His money was on a taxidermist. And the IP addresses of the computers used to hack into the Gilliams' private network were traced to this location at Vista Hills Custom Taxidermy.

Adding to that, proprietor Kyle Birnham had pulled a short-barreled shotgun on him eight days ago on Mathews' visit to the shop. Birnham had gone off the rails when he suspected Mathews was a cop. An innocent man would not have acted in that manner. And a nonviolent man would never pull a weapon on someone in his own place of business unless it was in self-defense, which it wasn't. The incident was telling.

Kyle Birnham is definitely our guy.

But bureaucracy had prevailed once again, gumming up the works as it always did in legal matters.

It had taken eight long days after Stimson's brutal death to acquire a search warrant and organize a search team. And it had been more than three weeks since the T-Rex head had been delivered to the Gilliams. Far too much time had passed.

After nearly a month, they were finally taking action.

Mathews was pumped up, infused with an adrenaline rush. He felt a swagger coming on that usually hit him when he got to this bringing-it-all-home point in an investigation.

From behind the wheel of his Grand Cherokee, he watched Deputy Sheriff Stuart Fenski park and exit the first black-and-white. Fenski was the lead on this raid and Mathews believed he was the right man for the job. They had a history, having worked together last summer on the missing and murdered Indigenous women cases. Mathews knew Fenski to be competent and tough.

Car doors opened and slammed shut. Five other uniformed police officers got out and followed Fenski up the front steps, several with hands at the ready on their holstered weapons. Mathews got out and followed them into the shop.

They went through the front door, hard and fast. The off-putting stench Mathews recalled from his first visit—an overpowering blend of formaldehyde, adhesives, and musky glandular animal smells—slapped him in the face.

Deputy Fenski called out Birnham's name. An employee, a man in his late twenties with oversized, misshapen ears and prominent ledge of a forehead, looked up from where he sat working on a taxidermied Golden Lab. His eyes widened with surprise as the six police officers and Mathews approached.

"What's this all about?" he asked, intimidated as he scanned the uniformed officers surrounding him.

"Are you Kyle Birnham?" Fenski said.

"No. He's, um . . . he's not here."

Mathews had seen this man. He was the sleepy-eyed taxidermist with a receding hairline whose photo he'd seen posted on the shop's website. He couldn't recall his name.

Mathews spoke up. "I know Mr. Birnham lives here and I saw his truck parked out front. Go get him for us, please."

The man stared blankly, struck dumb by the situation in which he suddenly found himself. Mathews had seen that stare many times over the years when questioning suspects. The *buying-time-while-trying-to-figure-out-the-next-move* stare.

"What's your name, son?" Fenski asked.

"Andre. Andre Johnson," he said meekly.

"Well, Andre," Fenski said, "you don't bring us your boss right away we'll go find him ourselves. We've got a warrant that gives us the right." He pulled the five-page search warrant from his back pocket and waved it around like a flag. "You don't cooperate you might find yourself charged with interference of a lawful search and seizure. In simple terms, obstruction of justice."

Andre Johnson put down the brush he was using on the Golden and got up off his stool. "Can I ask what this is about?"

Deputy Fenski raised his bushy gray eyebrows. "We will fill Mr. Birnham in on all the details. Go get him please."

Johnson headed toward a beaded curtain that led to the back area of the shop.

"Hold on, son," Fenski said, looking around at his fellow officers. "Lindstrom and Capehart, accompany Mr. Johnson and make sure he doesn't get up to any shenanigans."

"Yessir," they replied in unison, then disappeared into the back with the taxidermist.

They returned three minutes later, Officers Lindstrom and Capehart on either side of Kyle Birnham, Andre Johnson trailing with a hangdog expression.

Birnham was bigger than Mathews remembered. Well over six feet tall with a solid girth. The scars on his arms and the left index finger that was missing down to his knuckle gave him an even more imposing look.

He's definitely big enough to lop off heads unassisted!

"What the hell is this bullshit?" Birnham roared, then noticed Mathews amongst the police officers. "You!" he bellowed, pointing a stumpy forefinger at him. "I knew you were bad news. I figured you were a fucking cop! I told you to never darken the doorway of my shop again."

"I'm a private investigator and *not* a police officer," Mathews said. "But these gentlemen are and they have something to say to you." He nodded at Deputy Fenski.

"Are you Kyle Rupert Birnham, owner-operator of Vista Hills Custom Taxidermy?"

"As I live and breathe. Suppose you tell me what the fuck's goin' on here."

"Certainly," Fenski said with an amiable smile. "First, you'd best keep quiet so you don't implicate yourself further."

"*Implicate* myself? For what?"

"That's what we're here to find out. I hold in my hand an official search warrant issued by the Honorable Senior District Court Judge, Franklin S. Adamson, of Flathead County, Kalispell, Montana." Deputy Fenski held the paperwork out in front of him. "Would you like to read through it, Mr. Birnham?"

"Am I under arrest for something? Do I need a lawyer?"

"You're not under arrest and a lawyer cannot stop us from going through with our search. Here, read through the warrant. It'll answer all your questions."

"No thanks. Why don't you just tell me on what grounds this warrant was issued."

"I'm not required by law to give you the specifics of our investigation, but I do have to inform you what this warrant allows us to do. It spells out that we have the right to search your entire premises, including your living quarters, the shed out back, and surrounding woodlands. We have the right to view all of your store security camera footage. We can search your vehicles and seize all computers and phones, both personal and business. We can also confiscate any firearms and tools of your trade we feel might have some bearing on this case. This document also states that you are to cooperate fully by giving us logon IDs and passwords to your computers and phones. You must also share with us your financial records, including but not limited to, bank statements, outstanding loan information, credit card activity, investments, the mortgage on this property, and tax returns."

Birnham glanced behind him at his employee, Andre, who shrugged his shoulders in an *I can't help you with this* attitude.

Then, face flushed in deep anger, Birnham turned back to Deputy Fenski. "This is a goddamn outrage! You come barging in here like a fucking SWAT team and put me on trial for who knows what. This is America! It's unconstitutional. I know my rights."

"What we are doing is *absolutely* constitutional," Fenski said evenly. "We're following search and seizure by probable cause decrees detailed in the fourth amendment of the United States Constitution. And you're not on trial for anything. At least not yet. This is merely a fact-finding mission."

Birnham, puffed up with hostility, face beet red, said, "I'm not gonna cooperate. No fuckin' way! Not when you won't even give me a clue about probable cause."

Deputy Fenski gave him a lazy smile. "Your choice, Kyle. But if you don't cooperate with the terms of the warrant, I'll be forced to arrest you. Why make a bad situation worse?"

"Christ!" Birnham shook his head at the unfairness of it all, his long greasy ponytail swishing across the back of his broad shoulders.

Mathews observed the taxidermist, his facial expressions and his mannerisms. Underneath the bluster and pushback, he saw a frightened man. A man who was in coverup mode. Years of interrogating suspects had honed Mathews' skill of interpreting body language of the guilty.

Fenski turned to him. "Anything else you'd like to add, Detective, before we start hunting and gathering?"

Mathews had a raw burn in his gut looking at the guy who had pulled a loaded shotgun on him. "Yeah," he said, trying to keep his anger in check. To Birnham he said, "You didn't do yourself any favors pulling a scattergun on me when I was in here a week ago."

"*What?* I don't have a clue what you're talkin' about, asshole."

"Oh, I believe you do, Kyle," Deputy Fenski said. "In fact I *know* you do. And so do all of us standing here. Your entire interaction a week ago with Detective Mathews was recorded in glorious video technicolor. The sound is crystal clear, too. It's one of several key pieces that got us the search warrant."

"No way," Birnham uttered, hunching his shoulders and squirming, looking more like a cornered animal now. "No way that's possible. It was just me and him," he said, pointing at Mathews, "alone here the day he came in."

"I recorded you with a minicam tucked in my hatband," Mathews said. "One of the new SpyFocus recorders. It's an amazing little gadget. Got the entire ugly scene recorded for posterity and shared it with my law enforcement friends here."

Birnham fumed. "What? Filming me without informing me? That's gotta be illegal!" He made a move for Mathews. "Why you son of a fucking—"

Officers Lindstrom and Capehart grabbed the taxidermist and held him back, struggling with the effort of keeping the big man contained.

"Snap the cuffs on him," Deputy Fenski ordered. "Cuff his ankles, too, and then let's get on with the search. The first thing we'll look for is that sawed-off shotgun. My guess is it's down behind one of these counters. And I'm figuring you don't have a current federal ATF tax stamp for it, do you, Kyle?"

Birnham didn't answer, only glared at Officer Lindstrom who was applying the cuffs.

"I didn't think so," Fenski said. "That illegal weapon will be your first charge and will get you probable jail time. On with the search, gentlemen."

"Wait," Birnham said, twisting his hands and shaking his shackled legs, trying to get comfortable with the restraints. "You're gonna find my shotgun so I know I'm up shit creek without a paddle. But I think it's only right that you let me know what you could possibly have on me that would get a judge to put out a search warrant on me. Due process and all."

Fenski looked at Mathews. "Care to share any of your findings with our animal stuffer, Detective?"

"Can't hurt now," Mathews said. He faced Birnham. "Let me ask first, what do you have against the Gilliams?"

"Who?"

"Bryan and Loretta Gilliam and their children."

Birnham gave him the side-eye. "No idea who they are. I don't know anyone named Gilliam."

"Oh you *definitely* do, Kyle! You hacked their private network server to steal family photos you included with the severed T-Rex head you FedExed to them."

"Computer hacking? T-Rex head? You have a hyperactive imagination, Detective—what was it?—Mathews?"

"That's right. Detective *Mike* Mathews. And you can stop your lying now, Kyle. I picked up four IP addresses off the Gilliams' server logs that mapped back to you at this address, which we got through a subpoena issued to your internet service provider, MontanaLink Networks. I'll give you credit for a few things you did right. You set up your computers to generate masked proxy IP addresses. That was a good move on your part, I'll give you that. It would throw off most people. It was also to your benefit that you used dynamic IP addresses rather than static addresses that most businesses use. But your mistake was leaving those IP addresses exposed. If you had set up a VPN and hidden the internet protocol addresses behind that wall, we wouldn't be having this conversation. Not even MontanaLink would know of them and hence your identity. Actually your biggest mistake was packaging those same photos with the dino head. Um, permit me to rephrase that. *Everything* you have done has been a mistake, Birnham. So I ask again, what is your beef with the Gilliam family?"

Birnham locked eyes with Mathews and held his stare for several long beats, then said, "Do I need a lawyer?"

"Probably wouldn't hurt," Deputy Fenski said.

Mathews said, "There aren't many lawyers who can get you out of this mess."

Birnham looked spooked as the reality of things sunk in.

"Okay, time's wasting," Fenski said. "Let's get this party started, fellas."

The deputy instructed Officer Capehart to lock the front door and hang the closed sign in the window.

THEY SPENT THE NEXT FIVE HOURS sweeping every nook and cranny of Vista Hills Custom Taxidermy, including Birnham's upstairs living area and the half basement below. A younger officer, Rennie Hilton, watched over Birnham and his employee, Andre Johnson, as Mathews accompanied Deputy Fenski and the other four officers in the search.

They worked the main floor, finding the sawed-off shotgun and box of shells first, under the counter at the customer checkout area. Fenski and three of the officers worked cohesively, pulling items from shelves, opening drawers and cabinets, collecting soiled rags, stained aprons, and work gloves while Officer Lindstrom walked behind them documenting the search with a video recorder. The deputy put Mathews to work packaging, sealing, and labeling each piece of evidence. He had done a lot of this kind of search and seizure documentation during his time with the Billings Police and was honored Fenski had faith in his competence. Mathews knew the importance of putting together thorough documentation for a warranted search and seizure operation. He'd seen too many searches deemed inadmissible in court due to poorly documented chain of custody evidence collection.

The back room—the main work area—was much more spacious than Mathews would have thought judging by the smaller sales area out front. The officers combed through four work areas dominated by long stainless steel dissection tables with water hoses and drains. Each area had hanging racks draped with animal hides, bundles of twisted forming wire, jars filled with glass eyes, epoxy, paints, and prep and mounting chemicals such as borax, hydrogen peroxide, tannic acid, phenol, and formaldehyde. The search team scraped the drains and sponged the dissection table gutters for blood and hair samples. They tagged and bagged numerous items of interest— pneumatic skinning tools, knives, scalpels, bone saws, fleshing machines, bone drilling kits, heavy duty sewing needles, rolls of sinew, molding materials including silicone, latex and resin. They found spreads of bones soaking in acid baths. Mathews was certain that evidence pulled from these work stations would tell them whether Chogan Stimson's body or dinosaurs had ever been processed here.

The team moved on to the three large walk-in freezers where they discovered body parts of questionable origin. Human or animal? The pieces were too mutilated to make an immediate identification. Of particular interest was the cremation incinerator with vents leading out through the back wall of the shop. Officer Lindstrom shoveled out a small mound of ashes, which were bagged for examination. They found two laptops and a landline phone in Birnham's office along with many files containing personal notes and financial ledgers.

The basement didn't reveal much as it served as a storage area for supplies and wasn't well traveled. The upstairs living area, however, gave them two cheap burner cell phones to add to the one Birnham already turned over. They pulled two pairs of boots from Birnham's closet to compare with the boot prints the Blackfoot tribal police discovered leading away from Chogan Stimson's headless body strung up in a treetop at Gilliam's Guidepost. They also found a pair of expensive cameras—a Nikon Z8 and a Canon camcorder—and more weapons: two 9mm Glock pistols and a deer rifle, a Winchester Model 70. They did a check, running the serial numbers through NCIC, discovering none of them were registered.

The day pushed on to five o'clock and the search team moved outside, where they went through Birnham's two vehicles: a Chevrolet Silverado pickup parked out front, and a Mercedes-Benz G-Class SUV out back, covered by a tarp. Mathews admired the luxury features of the Benz, thinking, *Where does a backwoods taxidermist get the cash for that kind of expensive ride?*

As the day approached six o'clock, the team escorted Birnham and Andre Johnson out to the large metal shed to finish up the search. The group stood in front of the high-walled shed, staring at the pair of heavy padlocks on the double doors.

"Two monster padlocks, Birnham?" Fenski asked. "Must be some precious cargo inside."

"Nah, just a bunch of old taxidermy mannequins," Birnham said, the cuffs clinking as he continuously twisted his hands and pulled at his fingers.

A nervous tell, Mathews thought. *His edginess is giving him away. Same with the way he's avoiding direct eye contact.*

"Open it up," Deputy Fenski demanded.

"I already told you. I don't have the keys."

"So how do you get to your mannequins?"

Birnham gave the deputy a withering look. "We don't. They're old and retired. Not needed anymore."

Mathews noticed an air conditioner compressor humming on the far side of the shed. "Pretty high-end outbuilding you've got here," he said. "Why would you need air conditioning for storage of crap you don't need anymore?"

"He's obviously lying," Fenski said, impatient. "Open it up, Birnham."

"I told you I can't. I guess we'll just have to call in a locksmith, won't we?" Birnham smiled at the deputy, a mocking gesture.

"No, we won't," Fenski said. He looked around at his officers. "Hilton, go get the bolt cutters and sledgehammer."

Birnham took offense. "Hey, that's destruction of private property. That's fuckin' low."

"What's low is you impeding our investigation, Birnham. Now I'm giving you one more chance. Get the keys for these locks or we cut them open and I cite you on an obstruction charge."

Kyle Birnham let out an exasperated breath and looked skyward, perhaps praying to a higher power to come to his rescue. It was obvious to Mathews and everyone there that Birnham was hiding something inside the shed. After an awkward long minute, his eyes met Fenski's. "I lost the keys. Do what ya gotta do."

"Get the cutter and hammer, Rennie," Fenski said to Hilton.

Birnham noticeably deflated. His previous bluster had vanished, knowing he was doomed.

Rennie Hilton returned with the tools and cut off the first lock with the bolt cutters. The second lock proved to be more stubborn and Officer Lindstrom stepped in to finish the job with the sledgehammer. Deputy Fenski swung the doors open.

Rows of overhead lights snapped on.

Mathews heard several audible gasps—a "Whoa, holy shit!"

He had a difficult time processing what he saw.

Taxidermied dinosaurs. A menagerie of seven full-bodied, mature animals—three Tyrannosaurs and four Dromaeosaurs—their glassy eyes lifelike, their gazes intense, as though sizing the police officers up for their next meal. Sitting on a shelf running the length of the back wall were a Triceratops head and a T-Rex head, along with several suspicious looking skulls.

Mathews' attention was drawn to the left wall, where the strangest looking bird he'd ever seen was posed with its enormous wings spread wide. The sheer magnitude of its size shocked him. He was mesmerized by its slender spear-shaped head with the bright blue crest fanning across the top, the long, sharp beak, the elongated telescoped neck. This assemblage of ancient creatures unsettled him with their alien reptilian visage. He looked around at the search team. Every one of the six police officers stood gawking in open-mouthed silence.

Deputy Fenski turned to Birnham. "Kyle Rupert Birnham, you are under arrest for violation of the Endangered Species Act as it pertains to the state of Montana's amendment protecting Cretaceous Period reptiles. You are also hereby under arrest on one count of possession of an illegal firearm for the short-barreled shotgun, and three counts of unregistered weapons for the pair of Glocks and your rifle. So tell me. What is this stuffed zoo all about?"

"Customer orders waiting to be delivered," Birnham said. "Dino taxidermy has become big business in these parts. Ask your PI there," he said, giving Mathews a baleful stare. "He knows all about it."

Deputy Fenski nodded at Lindstrom. "Phil, you and Capehart take him in for booking and lock him up."

As the officers escorted Birnham to one of the cruisers, Andre Johnson spoke up. "What about me? Am I under arrest?"

Fenski said, "Not yet. You're free to go for now, son. But don't travel anywhere. If we find you were involved you'll be on the hook for conspiracy at the very least. And you'd best be looking for new employment because this place of business is closed."

When everyone had cleared out and Officer Lindstrom began

videoing the taxidermied dinosaurs, Deputy Fenski said to Mathews, "Good work, Detective. Thanks for bringing us this case. Sheriff Dunstable will be pleased. The PR on this will be immense."

Mathews was also pleased, but he knew it was far from over. "That's all well and good, Stuart, but we still don't have a motive. We nailed Birnham on a couple of transgressions, but we don't know for sure who killed Chogan Stimson. And we don't know why the Gilliams were targeted."

"We collected a mountain of valuable evidence today," Fenski replied. "I'm sure it'll bring us some answers."

"Maybe so, but my gut feeling is that Kyle Birnham is a pawn in all of this. A middleman."

"Time will tell, Mike, time will tell." Fenski pointed at the shed, where Lindstrom was filming. "Have you ever seen a weirder collection of animals?"

Mathews glimpsed the enormous bird. "Never in my life. These are strange times we're living through."

Officer Lindstrom hollered from inside the shed as he videoed the stuffed T-Rex, "I second that emotion, Detective."

It Takes Two to Tango

June 27: Eden Prairie, Minnesota

NORA'S RELATIONSHIP WITH HAYDEN had taken a big hit. He didn't care much for her decision to go to Canada and work another paleontology dig. It was maddening to her how his disposition kept fluctuating. One day he'd be a tearful, needy victim accusing her of abandoning him, and the next he'd return to the self-assured Hayden of old who loved her unconditionally.

Why can't he be a grownup about this?

After a week of his mercurial ups and downs, Hayden left for Idaho to do field work with Bill Carlton. Nora felt immense relief when he departed, finally free of his messy mood swings. But after a couple of days the house felt cavernous and empty, absent his booming voice and bearlike presence. Nora filled the lonely hours FaceTiming with her Cretaceous sisters, Brin Lacroix and Loretta Gilliam. She felt much closer to Brin and Lor than she ever had with her estranged, flesh-and-blood sisters, Cate and Debra, who spent their childhoods ridiculing Nora and trying to crush her self-esteem.

But things were looking up. Hayden returned from his Idaho trip relaxed and loose, more animated and responsive to her than he'd been when he left. He had even regained his twisted sense of humor as he recounted his and Carlton's luck in stumbling upon two Ankylosaurs copulating. While showing her video clips of the mating Ankylosaurs, he got Nora laughing until her chest hurt with his hilarious play-by-play narration of the dinos' lascivious coupling. It felt good to laugh together again; the grins and guffaws had been in short supply the past few months.

Viewing the video clips of the horny Ankylosaurs led to a scientific discussion of the sexual maturity of this second coming of the Cretaceous species. The animals' surprising ability to reproduce at a young age was now a major buzz in paleozoology circles. Hayden and Carlton had found a nest of Dromaeosaur newborns in the Nez Perce-Clearwater National Forest near Kooskia that couldn't have been more than a month old. They had also tracked a pair of juvenile Triceratops in the Columbia Plateau region that were less than a year of age. These young animals were obviously the offspring of the two-year-olds that returned to Earth two summers ago, now referred to in the scientific community as *The Late Cretaceous Meteorite Resurrection Genus.*

"It all comes down to the extremely rapid growth of their medullary bones," Hayden said. "That's the key to hyper-young reproduction that we could never find in skeletons and fossils."

Nora sighed. "You're not downplaying the importance of paleontology again, are you? Because it sounds like you are."

"No, not at all. I'm only saying that live specimens hold the key to growth rates and sexual maturity. Paleontology is of great import for many other things. Until the meteorites landed, the discipline was all we had to go by for understanding these beasts of antiquity."

They sat on the living room sofa drinking coffee, watching the national news with the sound turned low. Nora had always enjoyed talking science with Hayden and today he was definitely in his element. He draped his arm over her shoulders and she wiggled in closer, snuggling up against his broad chest. His closeness felt good. Reassuring.

But there was one new dark cloud on the horizon. Hayden had been going on and on about an oddball falconer who raised and trained Quetzalcoatlus. Listening to him, Nora thought the whole tale had to be a mythological fantasy.

"So you're definitely making the trip with the trappers, Prescott and his wife?" she said. "You're really going to see that alleged Quetzal Whisperer?"

"Yeah, I am. Mick Prescott is making the final arrangements."

"Hayden, surely you're not buying into that ridiculousness. I know you're smarter than that. You have advanced degrees in paleontology and paleobiology. You've got decades of field experience. How can you be so naïve to fall for something like that?"

"I *have* to check into it, *mon amour*. My restless intellectual curiosity beckons."

"Oh, honey. That whole thing sounds so preposterous it almost has to be some kind of a scam or setup. At the very least it's people trying to take advantage of your fame. I worry about you going up into the high Bitterroots with people you don't know."

"You worry about me? Really?"

She pulled away from him. "Are you friggin' kidding me? Yes, of *course* I worry about you. How could you ever doubt me? In case you forgot, I spent four days by your bedside worrying, wondering if you would ever come out of your coma . . . if you would ever come back to me."

"I know. But you couldn't be *that* worried about me when you're planning to leave."

Oh Jesus, here we go again!

The look on his bearded face was so clingy and needful she didn't know whether to cry or tell him to grow a pair. Nora let out a frustrated breath. "I'm only going to be gone for two months. You keep acting like I'm leaving you permanently."

"Well, aren't you? Isn't that's what will ultimately happen? A two-month paleontology dig will lead to another and another?"

"*What?* What the hell are you saying, Hayden?"

"You'll get out there in the Canadian wilderness on your expedition and get the lonely blues, and then fall for somebody on your team. Same way you did with me."

Nora couldn't believe this. She stared at him for an extended beat, then said, "Jesus Christ, Hayden. You're the absolute last person I would ever expect to be insecure or jealous."

His tawny-brown eyes glistened with a hint of tears. "I've never met anyone like you, Nora. The effect you have on me is, dare I say it, *profound*. If that makes me insecure or jealous then so be it."

She sipped her coffee, collecting her thoughts, then set her cup on the saucer. She scooted closer to him and rubbed his shoulder. "Listen to me, you big dumb adorable oaf. I love you and care about you more than any man I've ever known. You remember what I told you about me being an obsessed fangirl of yours back in college, right? When I was an undergrad and you were the boy wonder of paleontology?"

He nodded. "Yeah, I remember you telling me that. But that's all you told me. You didn't expand on it."

"Well then, I guess maybe it's something you need to hear now. I fell hard for you back then. I used to gaze at your author photos on your book dustjackets like a pathetically obsessed fangirl. I read those books cover to cover and referenced quite a few of your theories in my master's thesis and dissertation in grad school. I thought you were brilliant and hot looking and rebellious and mysterious. I checked you out on the internet like a deranged stalker—your interviews, your photos, your early videos. I fantasized about you, never dreaming I would meet you and work with you one day, let alone sleep with you. I wasn't looking to get involved when you charmed me into bed and ultimately into living with you. Hell, I sold my Wisconsin home to come to Minnesota to shack up with you." She slid her hand down his arm and rubbed his thigh. "You have to believe that no other man could ever measure up to you in my eyes, Hayden. You have to trust me on that. It's just that we've been doing your thing for the past two years and now I want to get back to doing *my* thing for a bit. I'm going to Canada to work. Nothing else. Just two short months that will fly by. And then I'm coming back here to be with you in September. In plenty of time before the book tour."

"You're still planning on going on the book tour with me?"

"You bet your ass I am. I put in too much work to pass up fancy hotels, fine dining, and fan worship."

"That's great news! You're wonderful, Nora," he said, pulling her close.

"So you see, I'm not leaving you, big guy. I just need some time to do my thing."

He peered at her, his eyes shining with unveiled admiration now. "Damn but you're an amazing woman, Nora Lemoyne."

She smiled. "I'll remind you that my offer for you to join the dig team still stands. You would be a tremendous asset. Greg Dulowski is returning. You liked working with Greg on the Choteau dig, didn't you?"

"Yeah. Dulowski is a preeminent geologist. I respect him."

"So how about joining us? We'd have the nucleus of the old Choteau team back together again."

"I appreciate that, sweets, but I would be miserable digging up fossils knowing that live Cretaceous animals are roaming the Great Divide."

"So that's it?" Nora said. "Your mind is made up?"

"I'm afraid so. You know I'd love nothing more than to be with you, but I just can't leave my paleobiology work and migratory study behind. I'm too invested in it."

"I understand, Hayden. I truly do." She shook her head in a gesture of sudden awareness. "I guess we're just a pair of stubborn old fools."

Hayden nodded. "Stubbornness is one trait we share, for sure, my love. I'll just have to put on my big boy pants and set aside my insecurities for a couple of months. Besides, someone has to run Fowler-Lemoyne Aviation. And I need to get started on my—*our*—next book," he said with a sly wink. "I'm accumulating lots of great data and story ideas with each field trip."

"Next book? We don't have a contract yet."

"True. But I spoke with Henry this morning and he says Random House is ready to make a deal for our third book. It's about ninety percent certain, he says. Is there any possibility you would write with me again?"

"I don't know at this point, Hayden. I'm really burned out on the writing and editing and dealing with New York book publishing. Our second book hasn't even been published yet so let's wait and see, shall we?"

"Sure. Absolutely. And I really appreciate you opening up to me the way you just did. You're amazing," he said, bending over and kissing her.

She grabbed on to him and leaned into his kiss, reveling in the feel of his whiskers tickling her cheeks, the thrill of his tongue play.

When they came up for air, Hayden said, "I apologize for my behavior of late. I've been carrying on like a spoiled child. Very self-centered of me to not grant you the space you want and need."

Nora tried to collect her breath after the intense clutch and kiss. "Apology accepted. Especially after a kiss like that. Whew!" She ran her fingers through his beard and scooted closer. "Not that I want to turn down the heat, but I *am* concerned about you going on this quest, Hayden. These trappers? The Prescotts? You don't know much about them."

"I got a positive vibe from them. They know what they're talking about when it comes to wildlife, especially the Cretaceous kind. And they were honest about the illegal trapping they do, which tells me they're straight shooters. It's this Quetzal Whisperer I'm not so sure about. But when Mick and Claire talk about this odd duck mountain man falconer, I sense they're sincere. I don't see either of them being creative enough to make this shit up out of thin air. We'll see. If by some chance this guy is for real and he can do what the Prescotts claim, the implications would be enormous. I can't pass up an opportunity like this. It's so outlandish I *have* to check it out."

"And you should. To scratch that restless curiosity itch of yours. Just be super careful is all I ask."

He reached for her hand, caressed her knuckles. "Come with me, love," he pleaded. "Let's go up the mountain together to see this falconer. One last dino tracking outing together. You've got time before you leave for Canada. We'll write about it in our next bestseller."

"No, absolutely not." She saw his eyes pooling with tears and her heart broke. *Stay strong, Nora.* "You talked me into going to Tally Lake with you and we saw how that turned out."

"That was different."

"Was it? Are you forgetting that these Quetzalcoatlus—if they actually exist—are the same winged monsters that brought down our helicopter? The beasts that put you in a coma?"

"Of *course* I know that. It's even more incentive for me to go see them, Nora. This Whisperer dude is giving me the opportunity to study these animals up close."

"According to the Prescotts. You haven't talked to this falconry wizard directly."

"Well, no, but—"

"Wait!" Nora said, holding up a hand, her attention diverted to the big flat-screen TV. "It's another news segment about Peter."

A headshot of Peter Lacroix filled the screen. She grabbed the remote off the coffee table and boosted the volume.

> ". . . In these dark and dangerous times, a bright light shines on America's newest hero. One week ago today, 39-year-old Peter Lacroix—lead pilot for Fowler-Lemoyne Aviation in Heart Butte, Montana—saved eight children from certain death with his daring helicopter maneuvers. The children, ages eight through thirteen, were on an annual hike sponsored by their church. They were south of Cut Bank when they ran into a pair of hungry Tyrannosaurs, better known to most as the apex Cretaceous predator, T-Rex. The beasts chased the kids deep into a wheat field where they ran for their lives and screamed for help. Ever vigilant pilot Lacroix, flying en route to Shelby, spotted the trouble and flew directly at the creatures, distracting them from their hunt, eventually sending them scurrying off . . ."

The male newscaster continued reporting on the terrifying chase. Video clips shot from the chopper showed the creatures trampling the five-foot-high wheat in pursuit of the shrieking children. The rolling, herky-jerky video made Nora dizzy. The swooping dives at the Rexes had Hayden cheering Peter on: "You go, Lacroix! You da man, Pete!"

The footage ended with the beasts scrambling out of the wheat and hopping away into the forest in that quirky way they ran, springing off their muscular hind legs in a birdlike bounce.

The view switched back to the reporter, Justin Rafferty, in the studio:

"I'm here with one of the children who were rescued that day, Darcy Millgate, who's eleven, and her mother, Pamela. Thank you both for being here today. I realize how difficult this must be for you after what you've been through this past week and I appreciate you agreeing to share your experience with our viewers. Darcy, I'll start with you. Can you tell us what happened in that wheat field?"

"Yeah. We were all scared, running and running and running until I thought my legs would fall off. I remember hearing those big animals behind us, snorting and thumping the ground. The wheat kept slapping me in the face and I couldn't see where I was goin'. I thought I was gonna die. But then Mr. Lacroix's helicopter flew over us. It was like an angel with propellers and all the noise scared the dinosaurs away. Mr. Lacroix is my helicopter pilot angel. He saved our lives. And then he stayed with us until another helicopter came and picked us up. I have cried a bunch the last few days thinking about it."

The girl's mother, Pamela Millgate, started sniffling. She dabbed at her eyes with a tissue and leaned in closer to the microphone.

"It's been hard on our family, realizing what almost happened. My Darcy was so brave through it all. Peter Lacroix and his crew were godsends for those children and my husband and I thank our Lord and Savior Jesus Christ for sparing our Darcy and her fellow hikers. We only wish they could have saved Stanley and Annie Withers, their hike leaders. The Withers have done so much for our church and community over the years. It's such a tragic loss. They were both the kindest, most giving people I have ever known and they had so little for themselves. Our church—Cut Bank Community Bible Church—is taking donations for their family. And I just want to add that I think it's past time our Montana state politicians put an end to the protection of these deadly dinosaurs that have caused so much death and destruction. I mean, why are these beasts on the endangered species list? There have already been twenty-two human deaths by dinosaur this year, which is ahead of last summer's pace, and we're still a week away from the July fourth holiday. I believe it's the people of Montana and Idaho who are endangered, not these Cretaceous abominations."

Nora and Hayden continued watching as Justin Rafferty put up information on the screen as to where viewers could send donations for the Withers family. He then played a taped interview with Peter Lacroix. Peter was his usual humble self, giving much of the credit to his copilot Walt Mingus and Montana game warden, Monty Bridges. Peter came across with an *Aw, shucks, just doing my job* kind of no-big-deal attitude that made Nora smile. He mentioned Fowler-Lemoyne Aviation several times, which pleased Hayden. But when the interviewer tried to get Peter to talk about last year's famous Idaho helicopter crash he politely begged off.

Nora was so proud of their lead pilot. Peter had successfully kicked the drugs and was back on track. And they really needed him as their bookings were solid over the next month thanks to the hard work of Bryan and Loretta Gilliam.

Hayden said, "Lacroix is looking good. He's come a long way."

"Yes, he certainly has."

"This is great publicity for us, Nora."

"Hayden!" she said, jabbing him in the side with her elbow. "You are so uncouth sometimes. Two people died and eight children might never be the same again, and all you can say is *this is great publicity for us*?"

"Well, it *is*, Nora. Sorry that I'm so corporate aware, but somebody needs to be." Nora's glare told him he was being insensitive. "Okay then. You're right. How about I make a hefty donation to the Withers family?"

Nora smiled. "I'm sure they would appreciate that."

Peter's interview concluded and Nora shut off the TV. "You know what *I* would appreciate, Hayden?"

"No. Tell me."

"That you take me upstairs and fuck me like you mean it. My Mister Happy isn't doing the trick anymore. I need a real man to douse the fire. You think you can handle it, sailor?"

He gave her a raised-eyebrow smile. "I love it when you talk longshoreman speak to me. This sailor is ready, willing, and able, babe."

She stood and grabbed his hand, pulled him up from the sofa with a husky laugh. They stumbled up the stairs, kissing and groping and peeling off clothes as they went. By the time they reached the bedroom they were both naked.

She peered at his bearish physique through her steamed up glasses. It had been a long time since Nora had seen Hayden this aroused.

She ached for him.

Nora pushed him down on the bed and mounted him.

She wasn't going to let him fail to launch this time.

Kill Shot

June 30: Salmon-Challis National Forest
Eastern Idaho

BIG GAME FATHER-SON HUNTING WAS A TRADITION in the Mortensen family.

Seventeen-year-old Robby Mortensen was on his third summer hunting trip with his dad, Rick, traipsing the Idaho wilderness, stalking elk and moose. Last summer they bagged three trophies, decorating their finished basement in Pocatello with two moose heads and a full-bodied bull elk. The taxidermist in Boise had done an amazing job with the three mounts.

In years past, going back a dozen years, Robby's older brothers, Rendell and Riley, had joined the old man on these summer jaunts. Robby's siblings had families of their own now and had moved away, leaving Robby to carry on the legacy.

Robby knew that hunting out of season was a risky game. He was aware they could face severe penalties if caught. Elk and moose season didn't open until September but that never deterred Rick Mortensen. Mountain lion and gray wolf seasons opened today but Robby's dad wasn't interested in smaller prey. Same with fox, badger, wild hog, coyote, and squirrel, which were open season year round. Too much trouble for very little return, Rick Mortensen had always told his sons. He wanted the big animals with impressive racks and intimidating physical size. He wanted hunting *challenges.* Robby's dad considered anything less than seven-hundred pounds to be a waste of time and energy. When Robby would ask him about the legality of what they were doing, Rick assured his son that this remote wilderness was rarely patrolled. Too much inaccessible real estate for the Fish and Game authorities to cover. Recent government cutbacks in funding meant fewer conservation officers.

But Rick Mortensen's dream trophy had been elusive through the first three days of this hunt. Robby knew his dad wanted a dinosaur in the worst way. A Cretaceous creature was Rick's great white whale. Father and son had scoped a few last summer—several Dromaeosaurs and a T-Rex—but they hadn't been able to get close enough to get off a kill shot. The two species were wily and evasive, smarter than elk and moose. Their survival instincts were sharp.

Robby wasn't as thrilled as his father about bagging a dino. Moose and elk could be dangerous if riled, but they didn't devour human beings the way Cretaceous carnivores did. He wasn't quite sure he wanted to tangle with a Tyrannosaur or Dromaeosaur.

They had struck out through the first three days of this hunt. No trophies. Quite a few errant shots.

But now they were hot on the trail of a huge Triceratops and Robby felt their luck was about to change.

They had tracked a solo Triceratops for more than a mile over rock-strewn backcountry trying to get in position for the kill. The animal was well aware it was being hunted. The low-slung, waddling creature continually frustrated them, weaving through stands of thick pine and hiding behind large boulders. At one point it splashed through the shallows of the Salmon River, intuitively knowing his pursuers wouldn't shoot it in the water. And they wouldn't. Robby had lost a deer last year—a large 10-point buck—when he shot it in knee-deep water and the whitewater rapids carried the carcass downriver, never to be seen again.

Father and son remained two-hundred yards behind, trying to keep a low profile, waiting for the right moment to open fire.

"He's onto us, son," Rick said in a breathless whisper. "He's hyper-alert but he'll eventually make a mistake and give us our shot."

The Tri-horn wedged into a stand of aspen, aggressively grinding his beaked snout and three horns against the trunks, shaving off large strips of bark. The animal's sturdy mass and vigorous rubbing shook the trees. A covey of gray partridge took flight.

Robby and his father took a knee behind a granite outcropping, watching the back end of the creature shake and shimmy. The treetops swayed with each powerful thrust.

Robby raised his Browning .30-06 rifle and peered through the Swarovski scope. The high-powered view took him close enough to count the number of scales on the creature's hide and clearly pick out the bristly quills dotting its thick tail.

Rick raised his hand. "Hold off, Robby," he whispered. "Don't get impatient. He's got an armored ass. You hit him in the ass and he'll take off. We'll never find him. Wait 'til he comes out of the trees and shows us his frill. Then you can pop him."

Robby kept his eye on the scope. "What's he doing in there?"

"Marking his territory. It's mating season. He's a big-un. Gotta weigh in at half a ton. That head is gonna look great on our wall."

"Sure will."

The animal—finished with leaving his calling card for potential female mates—backed out of the aspen grove and turned toward them. The late afternoon sun caught the Triceratops' iridescent frill that crowned the back of its massive head, shining in a kaleidoscopic array of colors—red, green, yellow, purple—the hue changing as it rotated its head.

"Wow! Awesome!" Rick exclaimed. "Looks like he's toting a stained glass window on his head." He placed his hand on Robby's shoulder. "Wait for him to turn so you can take him down with a side shot. We don't wanna mess up that beautiful head. We want a perfect mount on our wall."

Suddenly, Robby heard gunshots—*BOOM-BOOM-BOOM*—in quick succession, thundering across the grassland like cannon shots.

Confusion.

He hadn't pulled the trigger.

Is somebody else hunting our Tri-horn?

His father gasped next to him, a sharp intake of breath, then cried out, "Oh no! Oh shit, I've been hit!"

A spray of blood wet the side of Robby's face and he instinctively wiped it off with the palm of his hand.

He watched in horror as his dad keeled over and plopped to the ground with a loud grunt. Robby was alarmed at the damage. Rick had taken a shot in the side and one in the head. Blood gushed from both wounds, puddling in the grass.

A stunned unreality rolled over Robby.

This can't possibly be happening.

Shock paralyzed him; his arms and legs were frozen. In his peripheral vision he saw a quick greenish-gray flash as the Triceratops took off in a sprint. He didn't think it possible that a lumbering creature that big could move so fast.

He wanted to help his father, but couldn't, then realized with an encroaching sense of dread that his dad was beyond saving.

Robby remained kneeling, crushed, frightened, immobile. Some unseen assassin had murdered his father. He was all alone out here in a vast wilderness with some crazed gunman on the loose. Maybe more than one.

Four more shots ripped up the turf around him and his flight response kicked in. Cautiously he popped up behind the stone barrier, head swiveling frantically, attempting to see where the shots were coming from.

Where are you, asshole?

He glanced at his fallen father who lay in an expanding pool of blood. One side of his face was blown away. Nothing but a charred, bloody cavity and an empty eye socket.

Robby's eyes blurred with tears.

This is a waking nightmare.

Two more shots, one kicking up dirt in his face.

His adrenaline kicked in.

Time to move!

He took off running for cover, a stranglehold on his rifle. Shots trailed him as he ran.

Robby headed for the dense section of forest. The pines enveloped him and he collapsed on the mossy floor, heart jack-hammering in his chest, his lungs burning.

Who in the hell would want to kill us? he thought, fumbling for his cell phone to call 9-1-1.

He pulled his phone from his belt pouch, hands shaking

uncontrollably. Looked at the display.

No service.

He cursed his phone.

It felt like something had come loose inside him, something broken and rattling around deep in his soul. A lonely, frightened emptiness. He felt disconnected from reality.

His father was lying dead out in the field and unknown lunatics were on the prowl.

He fretted over how he would tell his mother about this. That is, if he made it out of these woods alive.

Robby wondered if he would ever see Mara again, his steady girlfriend through the past schoolyear. His first real love.

This would be the last Mortensen father-son hunt.

Dead father and a dead phone.

So suddenly shocking, like a thunderbolt from hell.

So devastatingly unfair.

Dad is gone! How could this happen?

Robby curled into a fetal position and cried. Deep wracking sobs that he did his best to muffle to avoid revealing his location.

After a time, he realized he had to focus.

He sat up, leaned back against a tree. Wiped the tears from his eyes.

Listened.

Cradled his rifle, safety off, finger on the trigger.

How did we go from being the hunters to the prey?

It was a question for which there were no immediate answers.

Robby Mortensen waited for his assailants.

Hunting the Hunters

July 3: Gilliam's Guidepost

Heart Butte, Montana

BRYAN SAT IN HIS LA-Z-BOY RECLINER. Loretta and Mike Mathews sat across from him at opposite ends of the sofa. The three of them were in the living room waiting on Joint Terrorism Task Force FBI agents coming from the Salt Lake City field office. The special agents were forty minutes late and Bryan was getting antsy.

He said to Mathews, "Whaddaya think this is all about, Mike?"

"Don't know the specifics but I called them and spoke with an information officer. She told me they want to know about recent events at your ranch."

Loretta said, "That's a seven-hundred-mile trip. It's gotta be pretty important to them."

"It is," the detective said, rubbing his hawkish nose. "I think they're trying to get closure on a few of their terrorist watchlist suspects."

"Terrorist watchlist?"

"Yeah, heavy stuff, right? But let's not forget what happened here two years ago, Loretta."

"How could we?"

"Yeah, I know. I feel for you guys. Animal activists storming your ranch, setting free carnivorous dinosaurs and torching buildings. Gunshots. Fires everywhere. I can't imagine it. And it had to be particularly difficult not knowing if this guy would make it," Mathews said, lifting his chin at Bryan.

Bryan wrinkled his forehead in a grimace. "It was definitely touch and go for a while. Just an unimaginably horrible day. We've tried to put it behind us but I don't know if we've succeeded."

"Yeah," Loretta said. "That was without question the worst day of my life. So many of our Blackfoot friends lost. My hubby almost—" she glanced at Bryan, eyebrows raised, "*—leaving us.* My poor brother Jimmy taken by a T-Rex. No, we'll *never* forget that day, Mike. Not a chance."

Mathews nodded. "Quite frankly, I'm surprised it's taken the FBI counterterrorism folks this long to pay you a visit."

"Well the FBI did show up when it counted," Bryan said. "I wouldn't be here right now if it wasn't for their SWAT teams. I owe my life to them."

Loretta said, "Everything's been insane here at the Guidepost since that damned meteorite hit our property and those godforsaken creatures hatched out. And the trouble never ends. Our two longtime ranch hands have been targeted. They're our Blackfoot friends and their families are practically Gilliams in spirit. My god, they certainly didn't deserve what they got—Apisi's wife, Kanti, abducted last summer and now Chogan Stimson murdered in a most horrific way. I mean what have we ever done to deserve all this? I just don't know how much more we can take."

Loretta shook her head and spoke to Mathews. "You know, I'm not embarrassed to tell you I have had this recurring dream since that disastrous cookout, where I gather up all those Dromaeosaur hatchlings and shove them back into the meteorite, then kick the meteorite into the stratosphere. I watch the space rock soar, its bright golden-yellow tail of light trailing, getting smaller and smaller until the sky swallows it up. Dreams usually don't make much logical sense and this one's no different, but it sure makes me feel better. Makes it easier to cope."

Bryan considered his wife's rather specific dream. This was the first he'd heard of it and he wondered why she was sharing it with the detective.

"I'm truly sorry for all you've been through, Loretta," Mathews said. "You, too, Bryan. I'm doing my best to get to the bottom of these current crimes against your family."

"I know you are, Mike," she said. "Bryan and I appreciate all you've done for us. Your hunches about that taxidermist were spot on. Thanks for taking him down."

Mathews smiled. "Thanks, but I worked on solid evidence, not hunches. And it was a team effort nailing Kyle Birnham and his two accomplices. I can't say enough good things about the sheriff's deputies I worked with. We still have a ways to go to get solid convictions but we're well on the way."

"However you did it, we're grateful. I feel a little safer now."

Bryan, too, was indebted to Mike Mathews for his role in the arrest of the Columbia Falls taxidermist, Kyle Birnham, and two of his employees.

The search team deputies had made multiple key discoveries during the raid on Vista Hills Custom Taxidermy. What they found would almost certainly be tied to the decapitated T-Rex head and Chogan Stimson's murder. At least Bryan hoped so. They had confiscated a number of taxidermy tools from the shop, all crusted with dried blood: an electric bone saw, a reciprocating saw, three scalpels, two fleshing blades, and a pair of skinning knives. In the bed of Birnham's truck they found burlap bags, a thick roll of broadloom carpet, and a small pile of cedar chips, all stained with blotches of blood. The blood samples were sent to the Montana Department of Forensic Sciences Lab in Missoula, but Mathews told Bryan and Loretta the lab was so backed up it could take months to get results, even with pressure being levied by Flathead County Sheriff Dunstable and the Blackfeet tribal police.

The search team also took two laptops and a desktop computer that matched three of the IP addresses Mathews found in the Gilliams' VPN server logs. The Flathead County Sheriff's Department cyber criminology techs uncovered several suspicious large payments from payors absent any transaction details when most transactions (legal?) were well documented. They also cracked the encryption on a pair of burner cell phones that showed incriminating text messages between taxidermy shop personnel and dubious recipients. Flathead County Sheriff Detective Talton Boone was in the process of tracking down those recipients. Also turning up in the search: a large cache of unregistered weapons and ammunition.

And then there was the biggest discovery of all, hiding in plain sight. The large storage shed packed floor-to-ceiling with dinosaur mounts. If authorities couldn't get the taxidermists on Chogan's murder, the multiple violations of the Endangered Species Act and possession of illegal firearms was enough to keep them behind bars for quite some time.

"The search was an all-day effort," Mathews said. "That shop is one of the strangest places I've ever been to. And that's saying a lot when you consider some of the stuff I encountered in my ten years patrolling the streets of Billings. Vista Hills Taxidermy is all dark shadows and spooky vibes, stuffed animals staring at you with those freaky glass eyes. And Birnham and his employees are both odd individuals. Kind of like evil undertakers. I was worried we might run across a taxidermied human or two in the basement or the shed. Fortunately we didn't."

Bryan's cell phone exploded with a song by son Paul's band, Moonrise. The loud, bass-heavy distortion startled Mathews.

The front gate guard: "Your guests have arrived, Mr. Gilliam."

"Great. Send them on up."

Special Agents Veronica Chavez and Trent Borden were not what Bryan expected. They looked more like casually dressed salespeople than wary counterterrorism federal agents.

Chavez, the lead investigator, was in her early forties, five-foot-eight and lean with olive skin, a narrow nose, penetrating dark brown eyes, and long black hair twisted into a no-nonsense bun. She wore a fitted blazer over a light blue button-down blouse, charcoal jeans, and low-heeled boots. Borden was a few years younger and five inches taller than his partner. He sported a wiry build, sun-weathered face, and a well-groomed two-day stubble across a lantern jaw. Alert blue-gray eyes and sandy brown hair cropped close to his scalp. Navy blue polo shirt, khaki pants, scuffed hiking boots. Neither were carrying weapons that Bryan could see. If it wasn't for the lanyards hanging from their necks identifying them as FBI, he never would have pegged them as federal agents.

Agent Chavez started the conversation while Agent Borden entered notes on an iPad.

"First of all, thank you for inviting us into your home, Mr. and

Mrs. Gilliam. I'll get right to it."

No small talk. Bryan liked that.

"I'll start things off by asking, have you watched the news recently?"

"No," Bryan said. "We don't follow the news much anymore. It's all pretty much doom-scroller pornography and celebrity du jour puff pieces. Editorials masquerading as fact, or I should say, *alternative* facts. It's just sensationalistic twaddle in search of ratings boosts or online clicks. We've got better things to do with our time."

Agent Chavez let out a boisterous laugh. "I see I hit one of your hot buttons, Mr. Gilliam." She exchanged glances with Agent Borden, who smiled back at her. "Why don't you tell us how you *really* feel."

Bryan had to laugh at himself. "Yeah, I guess I tend to get on my high horse about the media."

"I don't necessarily disagree with you but that's quite an interesting take."

"Yeah, we've had our time in the glare of the national spotlight. It was exhausting. Nowadays we go out of our way to avoid reporters and TV news personalities even though they keep pestering us. Always hammering on us, wanting to discuss our dinosaur zoo and the AEF attack. The only time I'm interested in talking with those nosy bastards is when it comes to our son Paul's band. I'll talk to them all day long about Moonrise, the hottest power trio in all of Montana if I do say so myself. They're playing the Zootown Music Festival in Missoula tomorrow if you're interested."

Veronica Chavez offered a faint smile. "I'm sure they're quite good, Mr. Gilliam, and I applaud you for supporting your son, but rock 'n roll really isn't my thing. And I understand where you're coming from concerning the news media, but I have to say I believe there is still a lot of truth and validity in TV broadcast journalism. You just have to winnow out the alternative facts these days."

"Maybe so," Bryan said, "but I'm too old and too busy to bother with the winnowing part of it."

"I get it, Mr. Gilliam, but we're not here to discuss the news media, are we? Since you haven't been *winnowing* lately, I'll bring you up to date. There has been a string of murders the past six weeks in northwest Montana and eastern Idaho. A half dozen so far, all following the same MO. All six murders have targeted hunters. Six long-range assassinations of men illegally hunting dinosaurs. The most recent happened just three days ago, a father and son on a hunting trip in Idaho. The father was killed with a head shot from a Barrett MRAD rifle using .300 Norma Mag cartridges, a precision long gun and rounds that give the shooter extreme accuracy up to fifteen-hundred yards—"

"What does MRAD mean?" Loretta asked.

"Multi-Role Adaptive Design. The Barrett rifle was originally designed for military use, but is now favored by police snipers and hunters targeting large game. More importantly, it's the same caliber gun used in the other five hunter murders. The son got away, evading a barrage of shots. He hid in the woods waiting for his father's killers to come after him, but they never did. When darkness fell, he hiked two miles back to their vehicle, scared witless. The boy, Robby Mortensen, is only seventeen. We interviewed him yesterday and he was understandably shaken, as was his mother. He's experiencing a lot of survivor guilt, you know, questioning why his father was taken and not him. The boy said he never picked up anything that would be useful to us. All he saw were tracers of shots fired from the forest atop a bluff. Too busy running for his life, he said."

"That's awful," Bryan said. "I feel for the kid and his mother. But what does it have to do with us?"

Special Agent Borden looked up from his iPad. "Our records indicate the same type of rifle was used by at least one of the interlopers during the invasion of your ranch two summers ago. That attack by the AEF put several of their members on our TSDB—"

"TSDB?" Bryan asked.

"Sorry. TSDB is shorthand for Terrorist Screening Database, better known to the public as the FBI Terrorist Watchlist. As you know, a few of those AEF attackers were killed in the assault. A couple were captured and are now doing hard time at Montana State. A few that we suspect were there escaped and we think our dinosaur hunter killer might be among them. After all, that was the impetus behind their attack on Gilliam's Guidepost, the protection of those prehistoric animals."

Bryan ran a hand through his long salt-and-pepper hair. "Pardon me for saying this but I once thought the FBI was a collection of bumbling bureaucrats. Please don't take offense. I thought the same of all federal agencies. After two tours of Afghanistan, I saw how inept and deceitful our government was, especially the military and law enforcement branches. But then, two summers ago, your SWAT teams came to my rescue. I thought I had seen the last of my days but your guys saved my ass, and I'm forever grateful to the FBI for that. You're one of the few federal agencies that does good work."

The two agents looked at each other, then at Bryan.

"I must say, Mr. Gilliam," Agent Chavez uttered, "you certainly have no shortage of opinions."

Loretta smiled wanly, looked at Bryan. "Yes indeed, my husband was born with opinions. He has opinions about opinions."

Bryan gave her a mock smirk, thinking, *God how I love this woman.*

Agent Borden said, "Well, thank you for that, Mr. Gilliam. We at the Bureau haven't been held in the highest regard in recent years. The current administration has been down on us, accusing us of being incompetent and untrustworthy and politically biased. That low opinion has caught on with a large portion of the public. Your comments mean a lot to me."

Agent Chavez said, "And a big thank-you from me as well. But let's move forward. I apologize if I sound insensitive here, but your ranch hand who was murdered, Chogan Stimson? He was beheaded in the same manner as the Tyrannosaur head that was delivered to you. There could very well be a connection between those two events and we'll soon find out thanks to your perceptive work, Detective Mathews. Good work in putting that together and tracking down the taxidermist."

Mathews waved his hand at Chavez. "Actually it was Hayden

Fowler who gave me the idea of a taxidermist being involved."

"*Doctor* Hayden Fowler? The paleontologist bestselling author and dinosaur chaser?"

"Yep. One and the same. Hayden told me the precision cuts and separation of the T-Rex head had to have been done by a pro."

Mathews went on to tell the agents about the Gilliam family photos hacked from the VPN server and finding the IP addresses left behind by the hackers—IP addresses that led to Vista Hills Custom Taxidermy.

"That was a brilliant piece of detective work."

"There was quite a bit of luck involved, too, as well as the stupidity of the criminal mind."

Agent Chavez chuckled. "I agree with you about the low level intelligence of most criminals. It makes our work easier. But you did some fancy sleuthing and unveiled the culprits quickly. You're to be commended for that."

"*Alleged* culprits. They've been arrested but aren't convicted yet." Mathews scratched his cheek, thinking. "I'm confused about something, Agent Chavez. What does the arrest of a few taxidermists and closing down their shop have to do with your cases?"

"Good question, and I'll answer it like this. Taxidermists' main clientele are big game hunters and hunters tend to be cliquish. They're a tightly knit group, a fraternity if you will. Your taxidermist, Kyle Birnham, with his experience mounting dinosaurs, could be a critical key to our serial killer cases. He obviously has worked with many dinosaur hunters and more than likely has heard a few things about the hunter murders. He could possibly know when and where dinosaurs are being hunted. He might even know the killer and could be setting up the kills in exchange for lucrative payments." Chavez addressed Mathews. "We understand the sheriff's department found some large, undocumented payments on the computers confiscated during the search."

"Yes," Mathews said. "That's correct."

"Our experience tells us taxidermists are not the most honorable citizens. Hell, the guy pulled a scattergun on you,

Detective. What does that tell you about him?"

"That he's a loose cannon with an itchy trigger finger."

"Right, not exactly a Boy Scout. But maybe this loose cannon would be willing to talk with us with the hope of catching a break on his sentence. His employees, too. Maybe work a plea deal with one or all of them in exchange for information about our killer."

"I wish you luck with that, Agent," Mathews scoffed. "Kyle Birnham is one of the most standoffish people I've ever had to deal with. He's reckless and has a taste for violence."

"We're meeting with Sheriff Dunstable and Deputy Fenski in Kalispell tomorrow for a briefing on what you and the deputies found at Birnham's shop. We'll see what that reveals before we do a jail visit with him. After that, we'll continue chasing down AEF members." Chavez looked at her partner. "Tell them where we're at with that, Trent."

Agent Borden read from his iPad. "You all are very familiar with the leader of the mob that attacked your ranch—Leonard Sheridan of Bend, Oregon—who's incarcerated at Montana State Prison in Deer Lodge. He's doing twenty to thirty on a group of charges related to the attack. Also there are Richard Bevere and Travis Wooledge, both of whom also participated in the raid on your property. Bevere and Wooledge are charged with arson and felony criminal mischief and are serving ten years each."

Borden looked up from his iPad, glancing first at Bryan then Loretta. "We already talked about the large settlement paid out to you by the AEF last year in the civil suit. We understand you elected not to bring individual lawsuits against Sheridan and his cohorts to avoid having to go through long and tedious courtroom trials. Is that true, Mr. Gilliam?"

"Yes, it is. Loretta and I didn't want to put our kids through that stress, and we didn't want the media spotlight shining on us again. Besides, we already have more money than we could ever spend in ten lifetimes."

"That's true," Loretta said. "But that money, even though substantial, doesn't begin to compensate for what we lost. What many of our Blackfoot friends lost that day."

"I understand completely," Agent Chavez said. "We believe many AEF members might still be harboring ill will over the lawsuit you brought against their organization. There is also a large contingent of animal rights activists who are AEF sympathizers. The list of persons of interest we need to track down is long. Vengeance is a strong motive so we can't rule out any of them at this point."

"The main suspects being the three AEF members that went to prison?" Bryan asked.

"Them and a few others with prior convictions," Chavez said. She pulled a notecard from her blazer pocket and handed it to him. "Do any of these names mean anything to you, Mr. Gilliam?"

Bryan checked them out: Scott Hammond, Timothy Rugger, Burgess Flood, Leslie Graham. He glanced up. "No, I don't recognize any of them," he said, handing the card to Mathews. "How about you, Mike?"

The detective looked over the names and shook his head, passed the card back to Chavez. "Not familiar to me either. Who are they?"

"Longtime AEF members with deep criminal histories. We found Timothy Rugger. He's lawyered up and giving us the fifth amendment runaround. The other three are ghosts in the wind. We think any of these AEF people could be our dinosaur hunter assassin. Or maybe assassins, plural. There's a good probability they're also involved in the threats against your family and the murder of Chogan Stimson. We know from testimony that Stimson had your back the day of the invasion of your ranch, Mr. Gilliam. It's on record that he shot and killed a couple of those bulldozer thugs."

Mathews spoke up. "Excuse me but let me interject here. Something's not adding up. These AEF terrorists are all about protecting the dinosaurs, right?"

Chavez nodded.

"I get why they might be after the Gilliams and Chogan Stimson. But then, why would they kill a Tyrannosaur, decapitate it and send the head to my clients? That doesn't fit the Animal Emancipation Faction declaration of animal rights."

Chavez said, "If it *is* the AEF, we believe their thinking is that killing and beheading a T-Rex will take the suspicion off of them. It's a classic distraction maneuver. A *look over there it's not us* switch-the-suspect ploy used by lawbreakers since the beginning of time."

"That might be so," Mathews concurred, "but there is another set of possible suspects we haven't discussed yet. A couple of people who were involved with the kidnapping of Indigenous women last year in a botched ransom attempt. They would have a more recent bone to pick with the Gilliams."

"Are you talking about Thomas "Hoops" Terrell?" Agent Borden inquired.

"Yes. Hoops and his fellow conspirators, Jason Blackmire and Gregory Crandelini."

Chavez said, "We have knowledge of those cases. Special Agents Clevenger and Morrissey worked them and they briefed us yesterday. All three are being housed at the Flathead County Detention Center in Kalispell awaiting trial. They expect to finish up Terrell's jury selection next week. Blackmire and Crandelini's trials have yet to be scheduled. We don't see any of the three being good for the hunter sniper, however. They don't have the reach or wealth of the AEF."

"What about the threat against my clients and Chogan Stimson's murder?" Mathews asked.

"Terrell and his partners are locked up and hamstrung. They could orchestrate something from the inside, but it's difficult to commit serious crimes from behind bars. Especially without a good bit of money. The AEF is a better bet for the T-Rex head threat and Stimson's murder. Either them or people in taxidermist Birnham's network. We'll know more after our meeting with Sheriff Dunstable."

The conversation went on for another thirty minutes with the two FBI agents questioning Mathews about his two trips to Vista Hills Custom Taxidermy and his encounters with proprietor Kyle Birnham.

When they were gone Bryan said, "Well, wasn't that special?"

Mathews shook his head in consternation. “Yeah. The Fibbies keep it close to the vest. I get the impression they’re keeping a few key pieces of information from us. That’s how they operate. But what they did reveal tells me I need to contact Deputy Fenski.”

“What for?” Loretta sked.

“To see if any of the calls on Birnham’s burner phones were from Montana State Prison. And to see if their cyber techs uncovered the sources of those large payments to Vista Hills Taxidermy.”

Welcome to the Zoo

July 4: Zootown Music Festival
Missoula Fairgrounds
Missoula, Montana

A GLORIOUS DAY FOR AN OUTDOOR CONCERT.

Paul Gilliam stood in the wings on the shadowy side of the stage and peered out over the sun-drenched crowd. He couldn't have asked for a nicer Independence Day.

It was ideal playing conditions for what would be the biggest gig his band, Moonrise, had ever played. Sunny, 78 degrees. Cloudless pale azure skies. Soft breeze whispering across the fairgrounds. Mouthwatering smells of chili dogs, barbecue, and kettle corn perfuming the air. Seeing how this was a rain or shine event and could have gone either way, Paul took it all in and thanked Mother Nature for delivering such a fine day.

He'd never seen so many people in one place. An endless sea of music fans stretched across the grounds, seemingly all the way to Mount Sentinel. And they were still streaming in. One of the promoters told him they had sold 18,000 tickets for this first day of the Zootown Music Festival. Some well-known acts would be performing during the two-day event—Kacey Musgraves, Hozier, Jason Isbell and the 400 Unit, Lake Street Dive, Mt. Joy, Modest Mouse, and many more.

He was excited. Amped up.

Maybe a little too amped up.

A lump formed in his throat every time he looked out over the immense crowd. He tried not to let it overwhelm him, but a wave of dizziness overcame him. Butterflies fluttered in his stomach.

Moonrise had never performed for an audience this big. Not

even close. A big show for them was a hundred. Most of their gigs to this point had been college frat parties with thirty or forty drunken bros screaming for covers of Fall Out Boy, Paramore, and Shaboozey tunes.

They were scheduled to go on at four o'clock, in the third slot. The opening act—The Dead and Down, an Americana roots rock quintet from Bozeman—had launched into their second song. Paul focused on the music to pull his mind away from the monster crowd, tapping his foot and bobbing his head in time to their soul-tinged grooves and prog rock syncopation.

Talented players. The lead guitarist has some interesting licks. But what were they thinking with that band name? With a name like The Dead and Down they could be the house band at a funeral home!

He couldn't help but smile at that.

Paul knew this kind of exposure was a golden opportunity for the band. Moonrise had worked hard on their new album the past seven months, doing off-hours recording sessions at The Vault and The Recording Center in Missoula when they weren't playing University of Montana party gigs. The college scene and recording chores kept their weekends packed. Then on Sunday nights they would trek back to Heart Butte for another week of high school classes and nighttime rehearsals in the barn. Through the school year the 460-mile round trip between Heart Butte and Missoula put thousands of miles on the band bus and an equal amount of wear and tear on each of them. But they got better. Tighter. More professional. The songs became more polished, their performances more relaxed and natural. Then, finally, a month ago, after an eternal schoolyear, Paul graduated, barely passing with a 2.0 GPA. His bandmates had another year to go but Paul was free. He had kept his end of the deal he'd made with his parents despite the grueling challenges of his senior year.

And his parents had more than lived up to their promises.

Paul had come to appreciate what Mom and Pops were doing for them. His parents bankrolled the band completely: the luxurious tour bus, upgraded instruments, unlimited studio time, vehicle gas and maintenance, hotel stays and meals on the road, improvements to their barn rehearsal space. Mom took care of legal contracts and accounting. Pops booked their gigs and handled publicity. Paul had to admit the old man had a knack for selling something he believed in. And, without question, good old Dad was all-in on Moonrise. Pops loved telling booking agents that they would be "Over the moon for Moonrise." Another of his favorite pitch lines was "Your audiences will rise and shine with Moonrise." In the beginning, Paul laughed at Pops' cheesy sales pitches thinking they were embarrassingly ridiculous. But then the gigs started rolling in, and he began to see the genius behind the old man's approach. Paul knew that without his parents they would still be playing their music in the rehearsal barn for a handful of their friends. Mom and Pops were the sole reason Moonrise was playing the Zootown Music Festival today. Without question they were the driving force behind the band's early regional success.

During reflective times, Paul dogged himself over the way he had treated Pops early on. He had doubted his father's abilities, telling him to his face he was a delusional, broken down old rancher mechanic who didn't know a damned thing about rock and roll. How could the old man possibly make Moonrise famous? How could Pops ever get their music radio play when he wasn't hip to that world? Now when he thought about the abuse he'd heaped on his father, he became choked up.

Jesus, what an arrogant, clueless, childish prick you were, Pauley! Pops is proving you wrong every day.

Their new record, titled *Moonscape Moodies*, was released three weeks ago. The lead track, "Rockin' Me With Your Vibe"—a Doobie Brothers inspired rocker—was already in heavy rotation on college radio. Paul thought the album was the perfect complement to their 4-song EP that they had released in January. Nine songs at a running time of 43 minutes. Every track a mini masterpiece.

At least Paul thought so.

Kit and Ox weren't completely happy with it, however. They argued there wasn't enough of their influence on the record.

When they started playing music together a year and a half ago, Kit Reeder and Hass Oxendine had been his two best friends. Kit and Ox were dirt poor Blackfoot boys from Browning with a fierce dedication to achieving the rock 'n roll dream. The first six months were laughs and partying. Best buds playing cover tunes badly. They were having fun and enjoying each other's' company, playing every chance they got, hosting small parties for their friends in the rehearsal barn. The constant practice made them better musicians. They improved, becoming more proficient on their instruments. They supported one another as a team and worked for a common goal.

But then, while recording the EP, jealousies and egos started surfacing. Kit accused Paul of being a control freak, accusations that erupted into heated arguments and several near band breakups.

Paul knew that most popular bands had an alpha dog leading the way. He had done his homework. The highly successful bands weren't democratic. They were guided and motivated by a strong leader—Dave Grohl with Foo Fighters, Josh Homme with Queens of the New Stone Age, Nine Inch Nails' Trent Reznor and Radiohead's Thom Yorke, Jack White, and going further back into the archives of rock history, Tyler, Petty, McCartney, Townshend, Ian Anderson with Jethro Tull, John Fogerty with Creedence Clearwater Revival, Cobain with Nirvana, Jeff Tweedy with Wilco. Those bands would never have achieved what they did without their alpha dogs. He thought it only made sense that he should be Moonrise's alpha dog. He was the one carrying the load—main songwriter, lead vocalist, arranger, lead and rhythm guitars. Plus he designed and maintained the band website and spent the most time behind the wheel of the band bus, driving them all over Montana, Idaho, and Wyoming. Paul knew he was quite literally the driving force. Without him, Moonrise would be going nowhere. Most of their original material consisted of his compositions. They played his songs and he made out the setlists, choosing the cover tunes they would do. He ruled with a steel fist and it had begun to get under the skin of the other two.

Kit and Ox made it clear they weren't thrilled with being Paul's backup band. They pushed back on him, wanting more of a voice in band decisions. Demanding that more of their original compositions be played and recorded. Paul pretty much tuned them out. Kit and Ox both felt they had surefire hit songs he was ignoring and they made it known they didn't like being shut out. Paul thought things might be different if they had any songwriting skills. He found their originals to be simplistic rehashes of old hits and shallow lyrics he would be embarrassed singing in public. Just because all four songs on the EP and seven on the new album were his compositions didn't give them the right to bitch at him. Songwriting wasn't easy and he felt he deserved more credit. Bass player Kit even had the audacity to suggest they bring in a second guitarist or keyboardist, saying Paul's playing was threadbare and left too much empty space. That had chapped Paul's ass for weeks and caused a good bit of friction within the group. And drummer Oxendine had never been cool with Paul's girlfriend Sinopa singing backup vocals. Ox had taken it too far in saying Sin's voice sounded like an alley cat that had inhaled too much helium. That had set off another storm of internal squabbling.

The hell with them, Paul thought. *It's me people are talking about, not my two-bit rhythm section. And screw Ox. Sin has every right to sing with us. She has a beautiful voice and fills out our sound nicely. Hass Oxendine is tone deaf. That's why he's a fucking drummer!*

He suddenly remembered where he was and realized now was not the time for negative thoughts. Today was the day Moonrise would advance to the next level. Today's performance would be the litmus test for the new songs. Paul planned to wow the audience, maybe even pull out a few new stage moves. Thousands of people would be seeing them for the first time. After today's set, Kit and Ox would realize he was the star who was taking them places and they were just along for the ride.

Perusing the huge crowd, he felt his nerves return. His family was out there somewhere—Mom and Pops, his sister Lianne who had been excited for weeks about seeing her big brother playing on the same stage as all these well-known musicians. Little bro Ethan was even missing one of his precious baseball games to check out the scene, even though he continued to rag on Paul about how much Moonrise sucked. Paul wrote it off to younger sibling jealousy, but the barbs definitely hurt. *We couldn't suck that much if we're playing the prestigious Zootown festival.* And Pops told him last night that Hayden Fowler and Nora Lemoyne had flown in and were excited about seeing the band live. Dr. Fowler had been one of their earliest fans and had used his celebrity status to get two of their EP songs airplay on a Minneapolis radio station, which had brought some new Minnesota subscribers to their website.

"There's my guitar hero! I wondered where you'd wandered off to." The voice came from behind him, the line delivered with thinly veiled condescension.

He turned to face his personal bodyguard, Lou Goolsby, dressed in all black like a Johnny Cash wannabe. The skinny jeans, hipster boots, backward baseball cap, aviator shades, and earring in his left ear were the pathetic efforts of a man in his sixties attempting to recapture his youth. At least the gun tucked in his waistband under his chambray shirt saved him from looking like a complete geezer loser.

Paul yelled to be heard over the music. "Well if it isn't my ball and chain. I thought I'd finally ditched you. You're like my suffocating six-foot shadow for Christ sakes."

"Your father is paying me the big bucks to make sure no harm comes to you, junior. Just doin' my job."

"I'm not a junior!" he shouted. "Back off, would ya? I can take care of myself. You are so goddammed paranoid."

"My paranoia is what keeps you alive, Bucko."

The Dead and Down continued their set, the stage vibrating under Paul's feet. He did his best to ignore Goolsby, his eyes drifting over the gathering of music fans. So many hot babes strutting around in their slinky sundresses and Daisy Dukes shorts. Cowboy hats and alligator boots everywhere he looked. Crop tops and tank tops and fringed vests. Colorful band t-shirts. Vendor tents billowing in the breeze.

"Are ya feelin' the jitters yet, superstar?"

Lou Goolsby loved to bust his balls. Paul gave him the stink eye, but the bodyguard ignored it, just kept staring out over the horde of concertgoers. Goolsby thought Paul was a spoiled, entitled rich kid who was full of himself. It had been obvious since the day they were introduced three weeks ago. Most every comment out of his mouth was a patronizing jab, a disrespectful punch. Paul complained to Pops about him and his father had responded that bodyguards were paid for protection, not friendship. There were serious threats against the Gilliam family and Pops was convinced Lou Goolsby was doing a good job of protecting his oldest son.

Paul was sick of the guy. Three long weeks of this wiseass cloying shadow. The band had been on the road and away from the Guidepost much of the time since school let out, and Goolsby rarely let him out of his sight. The bodyguard rode with the band in the bus. Ate with them in restaurants. Always got a connecting room in hotels. He even followed Paul into bathrooms, did everything but hold his dick for him when he peed. He and Sin had to get creative to get any alone time together. They certainly couldn't find any intimacy on the bus. The best they'd been able to do was rushed and cautiously quiet sex when they'd stayed in hotels and Goolsby retired to his room next door for the night.

But Paul did have to admit he was intrigued by Goolsby's stories of his days with the U.S. Secret Service. It all sounded so exciting in an international espionage kind of way. His work involved protecting foreign dignitaries on their Stateside visits. Goolsby told the tales with such flair and authenticity Paul figured some of them might even be true. He loved to throw out big names, sharing stories about his work on security teams for Nelson Mandela, the Dalai Lama, Pope Francis, Queen Elizabeth, King Abdullah of Jordan, and French President Emmanuel Macron, among others. Paul figured it was probably those stories that sold Pops on him. Paul smiled every time he thought about what a huge comedown it must be for a man with Goolsby's pedigree, to be chaperoning a teenage band on the road. The guy must be living his own brand of hell with this assignment.

The Dead and Down finished their set amidst modest applause.

Wow! How disappointing. I hope we get a better response than that.

Roadies swarmed the stage. Longhaired inked-up dudes reeking of body odor rushed around frantically, dismantling the drum kit, winding up cables, grunting and groaning as they pushed amplifiers down ramps at the back of the stage. A guy wearing a Dead and Down t-shirt put guitars on a rolling cart and unhooked a pair of pedalboards. Another broke down the keyboards and stands and packed them away in heavy duty Anvil cases. They cleared the opening act's gear quickly and a second wave of road crew hit the stage, rolling out new equipment for the next act—Cole & the Thornes—an R&B-infused reggae group that Paul had heard good things about, especially their female lead singer. As he watched the roadies work, he wished Moonrise had an efficient road crew like this. As it was, they had one roadie, Todd Bellows, a Blackfoot friend who had been a dedicated Moonrise disciple from the beginning. Todd did a great job, but it was a lot for one man to handle, so the bandmembers had to pitch in and help. They all appreciated Bellows, especially Ox, whose enormous 10-piece drum kit was a pain in the ass to break down and set up.

Paul checked his watch. A little over an hour until showtime. He wanted to stick around and check out the Thornes, but it was time to head to the bus to get his head into performance mode.

He turned and headed backstage, descending the steps leading down to the backlot where rows of festival performers' vehicles were parked. He sauntered past trucks, buses, vans, and trailers with license plates from all over and plastered with colorful band logos.

Sure enough, Lou Goolsby was right on his heels.

A carnival midway ambiance permeated the parking area. Music of all styles and genres poured out of the trailers. Raucous laughter came from a van as he passed. A chick sang over piano accompaniment from inside a converted school bus.

The earthy, skunky smell of weed hung in the air. "Hold your breath, old man," he said to Goolsby over his shoulder. "Wouldn't wanna have to report to my folks that you're gettin' high on the job. You might lose your high security clearance."

"Ha-ha, junior. You need to work on your comedy quips."

They passed a group of musicians playing acoustic guitars, jamming on a song that sounded familiar to Paul but one he couldn't quite place. Further on, three older guys were slapping out syncopated beats on brightly painted hand drums. One of them greeted him, "Hey, it's Dinosaur Boy!" he said, without missing a beat. "Fed any Tyrannosaurs today, DB?" He'd been branded as *The Dinosaur Boy.* It was a familiar callout Paul had heard several times since their soundcheck yesterday. Paul didn't like it but it was something he couldn't escape. And the Gilliam dinosaur association had opened many doors for Moonrise, so he couldn't really hate it. But it seemed that here on the fairgrounds he was better known as one of the famous Gilliam clan—the wealthy family of the ill-fated dinosaur zoo and AEF attack—than he was as the talented singer-songwriter-guitarist and leader of Moonrise.

And then there were the journalists who wanted to interview him about his dinosaur days and his relationships with the famous people who had first come in contact with the meteorite dinos. The media types had stalked him yesterday before and after soundcheck. They were like hordes of locusts buzzing around him, every one of them wanting an exclusive interview, making a difficult day even more stressful. So today he hid out in the bus until he ventured out an hour ago to check out the crowd and opening act.

He turned the corner and arrived at his home away from home, the big silver and black Prevost tour bus with the flashy Moonrise logo splashed along its side, a brilliant orange crescent moon suspended over the Rocky Mountains, the band name in fancy script underneath. Mom and Pops had spared no expense in setting them up with this luxuriously appointed tour bus. WI-FI enabled with a router linked to 5G cellular data plans. Multizone Bluetooth audio connectivity and HVAC system. A sleeper suite with four privacy-curtained bunks, all equipped with entertainment screens. A lounge area with facing leather sofas, two recliners, and a dinette booth. A kitchenette with a Sub-Zero fridge, microwave, and cooktop. A half-bath with a tiled shower stall. An attached trailer that held their gear.

Paul only had a vague idea how much the band's tour bus had cost his parents. The vehicle was ten years old and a long way from having that new bus smell, but he suspected the price tag ran in the high six figures. He sometimes felt guilty that Moonrise traveled in such luxury when more experienced bands traveled in cramped, beat-up rides.

He grabbed the door handle, then paused, turned around to face Goolsby. "You wanna case the bus first? There could be assassins lurking."

Lou Goolsby just shook his head, as if dealing with a toddler.

Paul stepped up into the bus and entered the lounge. Kit and Todd played cards in the dinette booth and Sin sat in a recliner scrolling on her phone. He went to Sin and kissed her softly on the mouth. Pulling back he saw trepidation in her dark eyes and the firm set of her jaw, the nervous way she fidgeted with her phone.

"You okay, baby?"

"There're a lot of people out there. This won't be like playin' private parties."

"No it won't. It'll be a hell of a lot better. C'mon, you can do this, Sinny. You're a real trouper. You're a great vocalist and we're gonna kick ass," he said, trying to come across as confident when his own nerves were casting doubt as well. "Let me feast my eyes on my girl," he said, pulling her up out of the chair.

She looked smoking hot in her stage outfit—brown corset halter top, metallic-gold high-waisted shorts, fishnet tights, heeled ankle boots, choker with a dangling crescent moon charm, fingerless gloves. Sinny looked much more like a rock star than Ox, who always wore that stupid Western shirt and turquoise bolo tie ensemble.

He pulled her up from the chair and hugged her. "You're gonna be great, girl, I just know it. You'll feel better after our pre-show warmup. Where's Ox?"

"He's back in the bunks," Kit said. "Probably jerkin' off."

"Eww, you're dis*gust*ing, Reeder," Sin said.

"I think he's in your bunk."

"If he is I'm gonna castrate him!"

That got laughs from Kit and Todd. Even Goolsby showed a reluctant smile.

Paul went to the back of the bus to get Ox and found him lounging in a bottom bunk, watching a Rush concert video. Hass idolized the late great Neil Peart, Rush's legendary drummer.

"Let's go, Hass. Time for pre-show warmup."

"Christ, Gilliam," Ox said, annoyed. He sat up and shut off the video with an angry flair. "You and your fucking New Age kumbaya bullshit! Why do I have to be involved? I don't even sing."

"You're a bandmember, aren't you? This isn't just about getting our voices tuned up. It's about group unity. You know that."

Ox rolled his eyes as he climbed out of the bunk. "Unfortunately I do. Such horseshit, Gilliam! I'll come, but I ain't holdin' hands with anybody. No how, no way."

"You don't have to," Paul said, thinking what a handful Hass Oxendine was. "You don't even have to sing. You just need to be there."

Paul knew Ox would be good to go once they hit the stage. He'd learned by now his drummer was dedicated to his craft but just liked to bitch and make life more difficult for him.

They stood in a circle in the lounge area, Paul, Kit, Sin, and Todd holding hands, with Ox and Goolsby standing off to the side. Paul, Kit, and Sin launched into the Eagles' "Seven Bridges Road," singing a capella just as the Eagles did in concert.

"There are stars in the southern sky
Southward as you go
There is moonlight and moss in the trees
Down the Seven Bridges Road . . ."

Paul loved the way their voices blended—Kit filling out the bottom end with his brassy baritone, Paul with his crystal clear tenor, and Sin with her mezzo-soprano. Together they produced a rich, layered sound that elevated their recordings and live performances to another level. The three of them singing together had seemed magical from the beginning.

Ox can kiss my ass, Paul thought as he sang. *Sin has a beautiful voice. She gives our sound a polished sheen and you want to silence her? What a dumb fuck you are! Drummers have no sense of melody or harmony. You're only good for pummeling away on those skins like a mindless caveman, Hass.*

They followed it up with "It's All Right" by Huey Lewis and the News, a song that Kit's baritone carried.

"Sounding great, guys," Paul said, breaking the a capella circle. "We're gonna kill 'em today."

There was a knock at the door and he walked to the front of the bus to answer it.

"You folks are on in forty-five minutes," an event coordinator told him. "Time to get your equipment backstage."

The group filed out of the bus and went to the trailer. Todd Bellows directed the unloading of gear, drums out first, followed by amps with the guitars and effects pedalboards last.

"You know, old man, it might be helpful if you pitched in and helped out once in a while," Paul told Lou Goolsby. It pissed him off that his bodyguard stood around gawking at them as they lugged equipment. "Afterall, you're bein' paid a lot more than us."

"That might be true but physical labor is *not* in my contract, junior," Goolsby said with a demeaning smile.

Paul wanted to punch that belittling smirk off his face.

With Todd's organized approach, they had all their equipment unpacked and backstage in twenty minutes. They waited in the wings as Cole and the Thornes played the last song of their set. Paul felt the sweat trickling down his back and beading on his forehead. The load in and out of band gear always exhausted him and he made a mental note to see if Mom and Pops would spring for a professional road crew. He felt sapped of energy but fueled by surging adrenaline and the sight of that huge crowd out front.

He knew he had to deliver today.

Sin's comment came back to him: *"This won't be like playin' private parties."*

Cole and her Thornes took their final bows to a warmer response than what the opening act got. As the band moved offstage, Paul and Sin congratulated them on a good set.

At 4:15 Moonrise was announced and a low buzz crawled

through the crowd as they walked out on the stage. Ox climbed up on the drum riser and took his seat behind the kit. He pounded the kick drum and hit the snare, announcing their arrival. Kit strapped on his bass and plucked the low E string a couple of times, setting his levels. Sin moved to her spot and adjusted her microphone, grabbed her maracas and gave them a shake. Paul picked up his Les Paul and moved to the front of the stage. Scanned the crowd looking for family and friends but couldn't locate anyone he knew. A vast ocean of strangers stared at him in anticipation, their looks seeming to say, *So you think you can entertain us? Prove it.*

Thousands of music lovers waited on them to show their stuff and the number of eyes on him paralyzed him for a moment.

He had trouble getting air into his lungs. The lump had returned to his throat. His mouth was dry and he felt like he had to pee.

Can I do this? Can we pull this off?

He looked at Sin, then Kit. Turned and looked back at Ox sitting on his throne.

You're the alpha dog here, man. Pretend like you own the place and do your thing.

An old trick. Imagining he owned the venue had always worked for him. His doubts evaporated. He stepped up to the mic. "Hello, Zootown!" he yelled, his voice echoing back at him through the floor monitors. "We are Moonrise from Heart Butte and we're here to rock your asses off!"

And with that they kicked into "Reptile Rock" the lead song from their EP. Paul could hear a noticeable roar from the audience. As he sang he wondered if the response was to the song or to the knowledge of who he was—the oldest son of the famous Gilliam family and one of the few humans who had fed dinosaurs. "Reptile Rock" had received substantial airplay on college radio stations and had garnered a good number of downloads from Spotify and Apple Music. Even so, he wondered about the loud reception. After all, Moonrise was still largely an unknown band.

His fingers were stiff on the fretboard and his voice sounded thin due to his nervousness. But as soon as they hit the chorus and Sin and Kit came in behind him with their harmonies, he relaxed and just let it flow.

They closed out "Reptile Rock" with the searing lead break, Paul trying out his Michael Jackson moonwalk and not missing a note. The place erupted in cheers and whistles and enthusiastic applause. The slap-back from the crowd response reverberated through his chest with the power of an earthquake. A much more enthusiastic response than either of the first two bands had received. He smiled at Sin and gave a thumbs-up to Kit and Ox. He turned back to the mic and thanked the audience.

Without delay they launched into "Rockin' Me with Your Vibe," the lead song on the new album. The crowd went crazy as Paul delivered the first blistering lead break, going down on his knees at the edge of the stage and cradling his guitar like he was coaxing every last possible note out of that Les Paul.

He had them under his spell now.

But in the back of his mind a small voice asked, *Is it our music or is it because I'm one of the celebrity Gilliams?*

They closed out the song with a blazing crescendo, Paul leaping in the air and pulling a Pete Townshend windmill strum as he struck the final chord. His feet hit the floor and the crowd thundered their approval.

He grinned, his entire being swelling with pride. He felt great. The band sounded fantastic. He was on his game.

Paul switched out guitars, replacing the Les Paul with his Taylor acoustic. He stepped up to the mic, completely in control now. "We'd like to slow things down for a moment and pay tribute to our hometown. This is a sweet, soulful ballad off of our EP called 'You Can't Take the Heart Out of Heart Butte.' Hope you enjoy it."

He started with the soft fingerpicking intro and the audience quieted, hanging on every plinking note. Fans in front began waving their arms above their heads, slowly, back and forth, in time to the music. Kit came in with a sweeping flanged bassline on the second stanza. Ox laid out a soft, swishing beat with brushes. Paul began singing, low and intimate, amazed that the crowd seemed to be mesmerized by his melody and the band's laid back playing. And then, when they hit the chorus, their three voices merging and the music intensifying, the crowd stirred again with whistles and shouts. He was amazed to see some people near the stage singing along with them, knowing all the lyrics.

They closed out the ballad to cheers and applause.

"Thank you," he said. "Now you know we can play the soft stuff, too. But right now we're gonna get back to rockin' your faces off!"

More whistles and hoots and hollers.

Paul traded out his acoustic for his Fender Strat while Kit and Ox crashed into the intro of "Running with the Spirits." This fourth song in the set was a bit of a gamble. The first three tunes had enjoyed some regional exposure but this one was a deep cut from the new album that had received no airplay and only a handful of downloads or streams.

Paul let the rhythm section go on with an extended intro, Kit laying down the catchy running bassline and Ox entrenched in the pocket with accentuating snare rimshots and kick drum/hi-hat combinations. Paul went to the edge of the stage and clapped his hands high over his head, encouraging the audience to join in. Within thirty seconds he had them. The fairgrounds literally shook with thunderous bass, drums, and hand-claps.

Paul broke into the frenzied intro lead, using his fuzz box and chorus pedal to get a dirty, dreamy sound he had worked on to fit the mood of his song about ghostly spirits. He whipped his long hair around as he played, grinning, bending the strings dramatically, his guitar wailing like a screeching phantom.

And then trouble started.

Paul was immersed in his guitar playing and didn't spot the commotion at the rear of the fairgrounds at first. But after singing the first verse he picked up on what looked like a fight breaking out amongst a large group in back.

A group of fans appeared to be scuffling.

Lots of pushing and shoving. Almost like a heated mosh pit.

Then he saw it wasn't a fight or a mosh pit. People were running away from something, knocking down others in their frantic attempt to escape.

Paul kept singing but it was difficult to focus with the distraction.

He could hear shrieks and piercing screams over the music.

More people running through the main gathering, bowling over others in their haste to escape. But escape what?

Thousands of heads turned in unison to see what the ruckus was about, their attention drawn away from the stage.

The dread in the air was palpable.

A stampede was taking place! People were being trampled and crushed.

What the hell is going on? Paul wondered, losing track of his lyrics.

He stopped singing when he finally picked up the source of the disturbance. He suddenly felt deathly ill. An icy chill ran down his spine and froze his testicles.

Three large Tyrannosaurs crested the knoll at the rear of the crowd. Could have been more than three, he couldn't tell in all the chaos.

The beasts lumbered down the slope, collapsing two of the big vendor tents as they chased down concertgoers. People scurried, confused about which way to run. The side bleachers emptied, a tide of humanity coursing down the rows of aluminum bench seats, trampling people on the way down.

The fairgrounds had erupted into panicked hysteria.

Kit and Ox quit playing, both staring out in disbelief at the ugly scene unfolding down on the field. Sin screamed and ran to the back of the stage.

The eerie tuba-like calls of the attacking T-Rexes mixed with the shrieks and cries for help, made for a disturbing soundtrack.

Paul stood in front of his mic, transfixed, immobile. Terrified. He looked out over the tragic carnage taking place in the midway, watching in a stunned stupor as a Tyrannosaur delivered killing blows with its deadly jaws, then drug two corpses off where it could devour them. More T-Rexes entered the fairgrounds. Paul spotted three Rexes stumbling around with bloodied, broken bodies in their drooling maws, shaking them viciously before throwing back their heads and swallowing them down their long throats.

Gunshots echoed across the grounds. *Festival security guards? Concertgoers with carry permits?*

Paul saw one of the Tyrannosaurs take three bullets, the beast falling on a woman, crushing her.

God help us all! This is way worse than our picnic two years ago. The monsters are so much bigger now.

He fretted over whether his family and friends were safe. If they were able to escape. Mom and Pops. His little sister. Ethan. All their Blackfoot friends. *Jesus!*

He started trembling, shaking so bad he thought he might be having a seizure. He couldn't move but thought he would be safe up here on the stage; Tyrannosaurs couldn't climb. Apparently the people fleeing the bleachers didn't know that.

Paul picked up a black blur coming at him in his peripheral vision. He turned in time to see Lou Goolsby come at him and roughly throw his arms around him, causing his guitar to come loose and hit the stage with an electrified boom.

"C'mon, kid," Goolsby huffed, grabbing Paul by his shirt collar and yanking him, "We gotta get you outta here."

Paul dug in his heels and resisted. "But it's safe up here. Rexes can't—"

"No it's *not*!"

And then, in the blink of an eye, a pair of Dromaeosaurs leaped up on the stage and came at them. Goolsby let go of Paul and pulled his weapon, firing several shots at the lead Drome, bringing it down mid-leap as it swiped with its deadly sickle claw. The creature slammed against the stage floor in a spray of bloody entrails.

Then, quicker than Paul could ever imagine a sixty-year-old man moving, Goolsby turned and shot the second Dromaeosaur coming at them from the other side of the stage. Two bullets caught the Drome in the throat and the dying animal gurgled on the blood filling its lungs, fighting for air as it hit the deck, then died.

Paul glanced at the two dead creatures, their blood staining the boards where just minutes ago he had performed for thousands of appreciative fans. He couldn't make sense of it.

It was like some kind of surreal filter had been lowered over the fairgrounds.

He didn't remember Goolsby getting him back to the bus.

Paul sat in one of the recliners, staring dumbly at his bandmates and Todd Bellows. No words were exchanged. Everybody sat looking at each other in a stunned stupor.

After many long minutes, Ox said, "Jesus Christ, what the fuck *was* that out there?"

Nobody answered. They were all in stunned zombie land shock.

Kit tried for a little humor. "So I guess this means there won't be any fireworks show tonight."

Nobody laughed.

Paul could hear Lou Goolsby talking on the phone back in the bunk area, but he couldn't make out the words.

The guy I can't stand just saved my life!

It was quite the sobering thought.

Sin came to him. Kissed his cheek and plopped down in his lap. No words were exchanged. What could possibly be said that would make sense of it all?

Soon they were both sobbing.

Today was supposed to be a celebration of music. It was supposed to be Moonrise's big break, an introduction to the rock-n-roll bigtime.

Instead, it turned out to be an epic tragedy.

A Life-Saving Migraine

July 7: The Lacroix Home

Florence, Montana

THEY LAY IN BED, NAKED, SNUGGLING. Peter and Brin liked to watch movies *au naturel* once the kids were asleep.

They had just finished watching *Eternal Sunshine of the Spotless Mind*, and the late news played softly on the flat-screen.

Peter ran his hands up and down her back. "Kimi and Jake are asleep. What say we turn off that crap and fool around."

Brin luxuriated in Peter's deft, feathery touches. She wanted to have sex as much as he did but that would have to wait. The news correspondent was reporting on the Zootown Music Festival tragedy that had become the talk of the entire country. The entire *world.* She was curious to know if there was any new information. Brin sometimes cursed her restless curiosity.

"It's not crap, Peter," she said, pulling out of their snuggle. "It's horrible what happened, and right here in Missoula, too."

Peter propped up on an elbow. "Look, I know this has really affected you, Brin, but our friends escaped. The Gilliam boy and his band got out all right. Everyone we know is okay. So why dwell on this? It only gets you all worked up."

She looked at him, his chiseled face taking on the flickering blue glow of the TV's light. "Many people didn't get out. Don't you have any empathy for those who died?"

"Of *course* I do, but—"

"Just let me watch this and then we can make love," she said, reaching out and gently stroking his neck.

"You won't be in the mood then," Peter grumbled.

Brin let out a deep breath. "I believe you can wait five minutes, dearest hubby."

She picked up the remote and increased the volume. Watched NBC News reporter Stella Grunfeld standing in the middle of the now deserted Missoula Fairgrounds with a handheld microphone.

> "This is the scene of the worst dinosaur attack since these prehistoric creatures invaded Montana two years ago. Three days ago this area was packed with music fans who traveled here from all over the country to see and hear pop and rock acts perform live as part of the Zootown Music Festival. 19,000 strong according to ticket sales. But a horde of attacking Tyrannosaurs and Dromaeosaurs prematurely ended the event in a terrible tragedy.
>
> "What is it about Independence Day celebrations that attract these malevolent creatures? Just two short years ago at the Park County Fairgrounds in Livingston, sixteen people lost their lives and twenty-one others were seriously wounded as a pack of Tyrannosaurs descended upon the annual Fourth of July Roundup Rodeo during the fireworks display. Four of those wounded eventually died. The massacre here in Missoula was much worse. Two years on, the animals are much bigger and more deadly. Fifty-four music fans died. Another twenty-nine were rushed to area hospitals with critical injuries. Four of the dead were killed by errant gunshots as patrons fired at the attacking beasts. Authorities are still trying to get an exact count of how many victims were crushed to death during the stampede of fleeing concertgoers. Four Tyrannosaurs and three Dromaeosaurs were killed in the onslaught, and were hauled away to an undisclosed location for research . . ."

The report continued as Stella Grunfeld interviewed witnesses who were at the event. They described the pandemonium as "being in the middle of a war zone," gunfire going off all around them and otherworldly beasts bounding through the crowd, bellowing and randomly picking off music fans. Others spoke of trying to elude the tsunami-like waves of humanity attempting to escape. One interviewee described the gunshots, desperate screams for help, and tuba-like roars of the beasts as "the soundtrack for a tour through hell."

As the Zootown coverage continued, Brin thought about her FaceTime calls yesterday with her Cretaceous sisters, Nora and Loretta. They had both been at the concert and Brin was concerned about their wellbeing. Nora was especially distraught, telling Brin it brought back the horrors of the Livingston Roundup Rodeo slaughter that she thought she had put behind her.

"One of the Rexes passed within ten feet of us," Nora told her. "So close we could smell its foul breath and rank wild animal stench. I didn't know if we were going to be eaten or shot or trampled. It was horrific, Brin. I'm leaving for Canada next week to head up my Smithsonian dig, and I can't get away fast enough."

This was Nora's second brush with death by dinosaur in the past month after she and Hayden had faced off against the lake-dwelling Deinosuchus in early June.

And then Brin had been surprised to hear Nora say, "I don't know, Brin, but lately I think Hayden might be a bit too reckless for me. I'm beginning to think too much of Jackson Lattimer has rubbed off on him."

The confession surprised her. It was the first time Nora had shared anything that intimate with her about her relationship with Hayden. Loretta Gilliam was a little more composed but was concerned about her son Paul, who was mired in a deep depression after witnessing the dire events from his bird's eye view onstage, saying he might not ever play music again.

"Could we please shut this off and enjoy each other?" Peter said, sliding in close to her, wrapping his arms around her and swinging a leg up over her thigh.

"Just a few more minutes, honey, I promise. Nora told me there would be an interview with Hayden tonight, and I'd like to see it."

Peter groaned, frustrated. Sulkily he sat up with his back against the headboard. Crossed his arms and listened to survivors relating their harrowing tales.

Brin and Peter had been lucky. They had planned to attend the concert, wanting to see Paul Gilliam's band play. Peter bought two general admission tickets and her mother was going to watch the kids. But fate had intervened. Unfortunately (however, she now thought of it as fortunate) Brin awoke the morning of the Fourth with a hard-edged migraine and she begged off, knowing that loud rock music would likely crack her skull wide open. Brin knew how much Peter had been looking forward to it, and she urged him to go alone. The fairgrounds were only a twenty-minute drive. But he said he'd rather stay home with her. He had been away working in Heart Butte the past week and wanted to spend time with her, which she thought was really sweet of him.

Brin had never in her life been so thankful for a splitting headache.

Stella Grunfeld came back onscreen:

> "We have accumulated lots of video that people shot on their cell phones at the event, but we have decided not to show any of it out of respect for the friends and families of the victims. Trust me, they are much too graphic to share. We do not want to add to the hysteria already affecting the public. Most of it is on the internet for those who wish to view it. Instead we'll go to preeminent paleontologist, Smithsonian dinosaur tracker and esteemed bestselling author, Dr. Hayden Fowler, live from the undisclosed site where the T-Rex and Dromaeosaur carcasses were taken. Dr. Fowler and his co-author, Dr. Nora Lemoyne, were at the event and witnessed the carnage first-hand. Interestingly both dinosaur experts were also at the Livingston rodeo two

summers ago. Dr. Fowler, thank you for joining us today."

Hayden Fowler's wide face and unruly beard filled the screen. He was in a cavernous building, a warehouse with a high ceiling and dim lighting.

Hayden Fowler: "Thanks for having me on, Stella. First, Nora and I want to give our condolences and prayers to the victims and their loved ones following this horrific tragedy. We are grieving with you and I'm sure it will take years to dislodge from our minds the sights and sounds of what occurred. One of your eyewitnesses summed it up best—a bizarre hellscape. So true. As you mentioned, this unfortunately was Nora's and my second experience attending a mass calamity caused by prehistoric carnivores. As you also brought up, this one was much worse than the one at the Livingston rodeo. Twice as many casualties. And we still don't know the status of most of the wounded. These creatures are much bigger, more agile, and more fleet of foot now. They make grizzly bears seem like puppies."

Stella Grunfeld: "I can't imagine being there and going through that. So, Dr. Fowler, the events at the Zootown Music Festival have pushed the Montana state government to consider reopening the bounty rewards system on Tyrannosaurs and Dromaeosaurs, and removing them from the Endangered Species lists. The governor has even said he would like to bring in the military to rid Montana of these invasive and deadly beasts. What are your thoughts on that?"

Hayden Fowler: (Stroking his beard). "Well, that's a slippery slope and I must choose my words carefully here lest I come off sounding like I'm defending the killers. These animals are eating machines with high metabolic rates and fast cellular respiration. They burn enormous amounts of ATP—adenosine triphosphate—which is their cells' main energy currency, and as such, they need to keep ingesting large quantities of protein, fats, and sugars to maintain a biological balance. I'm by no means taking their side here, and I'm wearing my genetic science hat when I say that when Tyrannosaurs and Dromaeosaurs show up at large public events and attack humans, they are doing what comes naturally to them. They're doing what they need to do to survive. Their DNA has been refined over millions of years to make them efficient predators, an efficiency that allowed them to survive for millions of years. And now, by some mysterious quirk of nature, they have returned to Earth and coexist with us humans. It's been an uneasy relationship, to say the least. So when you ask what I think about the state considering returning to open season on these creatures, removing their protected status and paying game hunters to slaughter them, I must say I'm on the fence. My human side says they are a scourge and imminent threat to the public and should be, um . . . *controlled*. My scientific side, however, shouts to me that we would be doing a grave injustice wiping out these species that were here long before we came along.

"One aside about the music festival attack, and my apologies in advance to those who lost loved ones at the concert, but I am speaking as a paleontological scientist here. It's very unusual to see Tyrannosaurs and Dromaeosaurs going after prey in the same space. They are different genera entirely. Both are theropods but they are distinct at the family and genus levels. T-Rex belongs to the Tyrannosauridae family while Dromes are raptors in the Dromaeosauridae family. They share a lot of the same characteristics. Both are super carnivores with insatiable appetites and both are highly territorial. I've seen Dromes and Rexes stake their claims to feeding grounds and defend them to the death. What is puzzling about the Zootown attack is that there were no territorial skirmishes. The Dromes and Rexes worked together in a coordinated effort, as if the attack was preplanned. That kind of collaboration between apex predators is unheard of, suggesting that these animals possess a high level of intelligence and critical thinking.

"Anyway, I'm working alongside two of the most respected zoologists in the country—Addison Marketti from Alaska and Susan Phelps from Maine. They agree with my assessment about the intelligence levels of these carnivores. We are also unanimous in our thinking that there needs to be a middle ground between bountied killing and protected status. The government always seems to work in extremes, and they have been wildly inconsistent on this issue, waffling between killing or protecting these animals. The state of Montana has bounced back and forth a couple of times. Idaho has had their own problems dealing with it. There are strong animal rights lobbies on one side who agree with the scientific community, and angry scared citizens, farmers, and ranchers on the other who want to eliminate all dinosaurs."

Stella Grunfeld: "Correct me if I'm wrong, but Isn't there a movement afoot to create a national park for these animals? Somewhere far away from civilization?"

Hayden Fowler: "Yes, you're right. I'm glad you brought that up, Stella. That has been an ongoing effort for more than a year now, spearheaded by my partner, Dr. Nora

Lemoyne. Trouble is, there has been a lot of pushback from conservation groups and difficulty finding enough acreage for the animals, not to mention the cost of such an ambitious endeavor. There have been battles over who would pay for it and how. My colleagues and I would certainly love to see something like this come to fruition, but it's difficult. Right now that idea is hung up in a bureaucratic civil and legal quagmire."

Stella Grunfeld: You mentioned you have been working with wildlife zoologists examining the dead creatures. Do you have any new discoveries to share with our viewers?"

Hayden Fowler: "Yes. But first let me say how honored I am to have been invited to work with my esteemed colleagues on this autopsy project. We are gaining extremely valuable knowledge about these animals. Our first big discovery has to do with their sense of smell. All seven of these creatures have unusually large olfactory bulbs. We estimate the Tyrannosaurs could pick up the scent of their prey from many miles away, perhaps as far as ten miles, the smaller Dromes maybe a couple of miles. A large outdoor gathering like the Zootown Music Fest would register with both Dromes and Rexes from quite a distance. It could explain why they showed up in such big numbers—possibly as many as fourteen Tyrannosaurs and eight Dromaeosaurs by our estimation. Also, they have extraordinary hearing capabilities. Both species have complex elongated cochlear ducts and exceptionally thick auditory nerve bundles running from inner ear to brainstem. We estimate they could pick up sounds within certain ranges from several miles away.

"Lastly, we made a disturbing discovery: all four of the Rexes had bloated ticks the size of golf balls embedded in

> soft tissue areas and enlarged yellowed livers with mottled bone marrow, indicating some type of systemic infection. We're still working on that. The three Dromes seemed to be clear of infection but we are worried that a tick-borne virus like Rocky Mountain Spotted Fever or Anaplasmosis or Lyme disease could spread not only throughout the dinosaur kingdom, but possibly transmit to domesticated species as well . . ."

As Hayden's husky voice filled the bedroom, Brin felt Peter slide closer and take her into his arms, his hardness rubbing against her back. His close intimacy warmed her, chasing the cold reality of the news segment. She moaned softly, feeling his hands massaging her breasts. Peter's fingers expertly tweaked her nipples and kneaded her skin in ways that thrilled her.

She shifted in the bed, turning to face him. A surging heat gripped her. She kissed him, a long, slow, tantalizing kiss, mouths and hands exploring, bodies writhing. She brushed his chest with her hand, then trailed down between his legs. He responded, which turned her on; she loved the hard feel of him in her hand.

"Oh, god how I love you, Brinny," he whispered, his breaths coming quicker.

"I love you, too, Petey," she said.

And then they showed each other just how deep their love went.

Get Your Wings

July 9: Bitterroot Mountains

Darby, Montana

THEY WERE IN THE PRESCOTTS' FORD TRANSIT VAN, on their way to see Quetzal Whisperer. Mick Prescott drove with his wife Claire in the passenger seat. Hayden sat behind them in the cargo section, next to a large wire cage for use in transporting the Quetzalcoatlus the Prescotts planned to buy from Whisperer. Tree limbs scraped the sides of the vehicle as they made their way through the dense forest up the unpaved Forest Service road.

Mick and Claire talked excitedly about the deal they'd made with Whisperer, in which Whisperer would extend them a substantial discount on their purchase of a Quetzal in exchange for bringing Hayden to his mountain hideaway. Hayden would also benefit from the deal, getting complete access to Whisperer's flying reptiles. The Whisperer would get a large under-the-table cash sale, avoiding IRS scrutiny. He would also be authenticated on the international stage with Hayden promoting him for his work raising and training pterosaurs. He saw it as a win-win-win deal, with all three parties getting something out of the arrangement.

That is, if this whole thing isn't a royal charade, Hayden thought.

He had to admit to being jittery about this trip. He was still reeling from his and Nora's close call at the Missoula Fairgrounds—the big 12-foot-tall T-Rex bounding past them within an arm's length and scooping up a young couple in its fearsome shovel mouth, flinging them around like they were stuffed dolls. But they weren't dolls. They were flesh-and-blood, biological human beings.

Until they weren't.

Claire twisted around in her seat to speak to him. "We saw your interview on the news a few nights ago. Your zoological conclusions are fascinating."

"Thanks. I enjoyed working with Marketti and Phelps. They're blue chip zoologists and we learned a great deal. I just wish it had been under different circumstances."

"We also saw some of the videos taken by concertgoers on social media," Mick said, cigarette dangling from his lip bobbing up and down as he spoke. "Really harrowing stuff. It must have been hell on Earth,"

"It was," Hayden said, "and if you don't mind, I'd really rather not discuss it right now."

"Oh sure, Hayden, I didn't mean to—"

"Just focus on your driving, Mick."

Up the mountain they went, Hayden thinking about Nora. She was leaving for Canada in four days, which made him initially question making this trip with the Prescotts. She would be gone for two months. Jesus! At one point he'd even given serious thought to joining her on the expedition. Those thoughts vanished quickly, however, when he realized what he would have to give up in terms of his research. The dinosaur population would be in the beginning of winter hibernation when Nora's expedition finished up. He just couldn't pass on the chance of getting an up close look at these Quetzalcoatlus. So here he was, in a van with a pair of wrong-side-of-the-law animal traffickers riding up a bumpy mountain road to visit a mythical man and his pack of flying reptiles, the same reptiles that had nearly killed him last summer.

You're finally losing your marbles, Fowler!

A pothole caused the cage to bump his shoulder. The crate seemed on the small side. He rapped the wire siding with his fist. "Is this enclosure big enough to contain a mature Quetzalcoatlus?"

Mick tipped his head back. "We'll sedate it and strap its wings. Most of a Quetzal's size and heft is in their wings. They're more compact when their wings are banded. It'll be a good fit."

They rounded a bend and the tree cover fell away. The interior of the van brightened. Hayden peered through the windshield at a heavy wooden gate swung open between a pair of large stone pillars. Strange winged figures—half animal, half human—and weird pictograms etched into the rock columns made him skeptical.

"I feel like we're paying a visit to the Addams Family," he said.

That brought a chuckle from Mick and Claire.

"You never know," Mick said, smiling, lighting up another cigarette. "We just might run into Lurch and Uncle Fester up here."

"Yeah," Claire agreed, "maybe Wednesday and Pugsley, too."

Hayden laughed, enjoying the couple's freeform sense of humor. "Ah, I see I'm privileged to be traveling with connoisseurs of classic American television."

Mick blew out a lungful of smoke. "Yes indeed. The streaming era is a great thing, is it not?"

"Can't argue with you there, Mick. Where would the world be without ridiculous old TV sitcoms?"

"Yeah, *Gilligan's Island, The Beverly Hillbillies,* and *The Three Stooges* have certainly boosted the collective IQ."

They were all laughing now.

Hayden kept it going. "This guy certainly couldn't get much farther away from civilization. We might run into Bigfoot out here."

Claire giggled. "Maybe Chupacabra and Mothman, too."

It felt liberating to laugh again after the heaviness of the past week. Hayden wished Nora was here. She would definitely appreciate the Prescotts' twisted sense of humor.

The levity was cut short by a dark shadow falling across the van, extinguishing all sunlight. Hayden looked up, seeing a large Quetzal lazily flapping its enormous wings, escorting them down the earthen lane at a leisurely pace.

So much bigger than the creatures that took down our helicopter.

"Is that—?" he said, surprise lifting his voice.

"Yes, it is," Mick said, slowing the van to a crawl. He looked up at the underside of the creature coasting overhead. "Don't be alarmed. It's just Thrall doing his thing."

"Thrall?"

“Yeah, Thrall. Whisperer’s sentinel. His guardian of the gate.”

Hayden followed Thrall’s flight above the opening in the treetops. “Christ, its wingspan has got to be twelve feet.”

“*Seventeen* feet, according to Whisperer,” Claire said.

Hayden shook his head in wonder, keeping his eyes on the pterosaur. “Mighty impressive. And he’s trained to lead visitors to Whisperer?”

Claire nodded. “That and much more.”

“As in dealing with unwanted visitors?”

“You got it.”

What the hell have I jumped into here?

They reentered dense forest, the heavy treetop canopy blotting out the sky. Another two minutes of rough road and they pulled into Whisperer’s open courtyard. Hayden spotted Thrall roosting on a heavy duty, deeply grooved falconer’s perch made of railroad ties. The Quetzal sat motionless, observing them through its predatory eyes. Hayden marveled at the creature’s long giraffelike neck that had to be five feet in length, and its equally long, pointed beak.

What an odd yet magnificent creature.

The front of the lodge came into view, a mix of weathered, jagged-cut timber and smooth river boulders. The back of the manse disappeared beneath a colossal shelf of granite. A jacked-up black Ford Ranger sat nearby, with padded perches in the rear bed, all-terrain tires, and large animal bones serving as bumpers. Attached was a horse trailer displaying the name *THE WINGMASTER* in fancy blue script.

They parked in the shade of a tumbledown shack. Mick and Claire got out and Hayden followed them across the weedy yard to the lodge. The air was thinner here, high up in the Bitterroots, and the temperature had dropped considerably. Hayden kept a wary eye on Thrall as he walked.

“You guys have any weapons in case this thing goes sideways?”

“There’s no need for firearms, Hayden,” Mick said, tossing his butt on the ground and stomping it out, lighting up another.

“No? That Quetzal is eyeing us like we’re soon to be his lunch.”

Claire gave him a knowing smile. “Oh, Thrall is harmless. He would only hurt you if Whisperer commanded him to do so."

"If you say so, milady."

Mick and Claire walked across the courtyard. "Whisperer doesn't allow firearms," Mick said. "Says they upset his Quetzals."

Hayden walked behind them, the chilly mountain breeze tickling his cheeks and ruffling his beard. An unnerving squawking cacophony broke out in the distance. Deep bass cries, a blend of honking and mooing with a trailing whooshing sound like air forced through large bellows. The noise sounded like Canada geese in migratory flight mixed with moose rutting calls.

"I'd say his Quetzals are already upset," Hayden said, eyes never leaving Thrall, who joined the bellowing chorus. "This is the freakiest thing I've ever heard, even more strange than the T-Rex tuba calls."

Mick said over his shoulder, "They're not upset. They're just excited about our arrival."

The front door opened and Quetzal Whisperer stepped out on the front stoop, carefully descending the steps between stone statuettes of winged animals in flight. He was almost as tall as Hayden but blade thin. Late fifties with a milky, blind left eye. Deeply bronzed complexion. A wicked white scar running across his cheek. Long salt-and-pepper hair touching his shoulders. Dressed in some kind of cosplay medieval outfit—white long sleeve linen shirt, black knee-length tunic embroidered with cryptic feudal symbols, mustard-colored leggings, pointy-toed, elfin-like shoes Hayden knew as poulaines.

"So I finally meet the great Dr. Hayden Fowler," the man said with great panache.

This guy is either an eccentric genius or a whack job grifter, he thought as the falconer approached.

"It's a great honor to have you here at Quetzal Villa," Whisperer said, extending his hand in greeting. "I've read all of your books and seen you on television with your fascinating videos. You have done some groundbreaking work, Dr. Fowler. And you're about to see some of *my* amazing work. I hope you brought your camcorder."

Hayden clasped his hand, trying not to look at the man's dead eye. "Of course. I never leave home without it. But I must say, I thought you were all about keeping your Quetzal training under the radar. My friends here told me you confiscated their cell phones on their first visit, that you didn't want any recordings leaking out."

Whisperer rubbed his sightless eye. "Yes, I did. I wanted to wait for the right moment to announce my genius to the world. Your arrival marks the right moment. *You* will be my megaphone."

"Why me?"

"You need to ask? You are the world's most distinguished Cretaceous era dinosaur scholar. You have millions of readers who have been following you since you first started working with Dromaeosaur hatchlings. You are my mouthpiece to the world, Dr. Fowler. You are going to make me very wealthy and internationally famous. You agreed to this, remember?"

"Yeah, I do. So when do I get to see your genius at work?"

"Soon. I've got business to transact with your friends first."

Mick stepped up. "You got our Quetzal ready for us?"

"Only if you brought the cash."

"Of course we did," Mick said, touching Claire's elbow. "We don't make empty promises."

"Where is it?"

"In the van."

"Go get it, please. Once I count the money and am sure it's not counterfeit, I'll take you out to the Aerie. Talgarin's ready to go to his new home."

"*Counterfeit?*" Mick said, offended.

"Yes. No disrespect intended, Mr. Prescott, but I've had amateurs try to rip me off with really poor reproductions of U.S. currency. No rag content paper. No watermark. No security thread running through the bills. *Counterfeiters.* The lowest of the lowlifes. I'm sure you can understand my need for caution."

"Talgarin's the Quetzal we agreed on?" Claire asked.

"Of *course* Talgarin is the one we agreed on, little lady," Whisperer said with a sneer. "I don't make empty promises either."

Mick went to the van and returned with the duffel bag containing the payoff. Strapped bundles of twenties and fifties.

They traipsed into the house behind the falconer. Hayden was itching to see the Quetzals and whether this crazy man dressed for a day at a Renaissance fair could live up to his advance billing.

They settled around a marble slab table in the great room. An expansive cathedral beam ceiling arched overhead. Whisperer served the Prescotts his homemade wild plum brandy in carved horns while Hayden opted for black coffee in a pewter cup etched with enigmatic pictographs.

Hayden checked out the great room's interior. The place smelled of pine resin, leather, smoke, and a peculiar musky scent. A Quetzalcoatlus skeleton hung from the ceiling beams, posed as if in flight, the bones lacquered and wired together. Wolf pelts and bearskin rugs covered the floor. The shelves contained bison, elk, and eagle skulls adorned with bird claws and feather charms. A massive river rock hearth took up one wall, bearing the remains of an animal that had been roasted there: Deer? Elk? Wild boar? Something else?

Everything about this place is as strange as its owner.

"I would like to propose a toast," Whisperer said, lifting his horn of brandy. "To the Prescotts, who are finding a good home for my beloved Talgarin, and to the honorable Dr. Hayden Fowler, who will spread the word about the special relationship I have with my Quetzal Aeroguild. Welcome, one and all, to my home here, high in the Bitterroot Mountains."

The Prescotts clinked their drinks against Whisperer's brandy horn in tribute. Not one for ceremony, Hayden sat back and sipped his coffee, thinking, *Are those Triceratops horns they're drinking from? They're certainly not from cattle or bighorn sheep.*

As they enjoyed their libations, Whisperer gave Hayden the same background he'd given the Prescotts on their earlier visit. He told him about finding the Quetzalcoatlus hatchlings (on the banks of Trapper Creek); what he fed them (lots of fish, primarily cut-throat trout and graylings); how he had raised them and taught them to return to the Aerie (using a feeding reward system, falconry creance training, and geolocation monitoring from an ultralight gyrocopter). He also told him about the Quetzal named Rhazek he'd sold back in May.

"Rhazek was the most aggressive of my Aeroguild. He riled up the rest of 'em somethin' fierce. Caused a few injuries with his temper. My brood has been much calmer since Rhazek left the sanctuary, but I do miss him. He had a colorful personality and kept things interesting."

Hayden said, "Your buyer was okay with getting an overly antagonistic Quetzal?"

"It's what he wanted."

"Oh yeah? For what purpose?"

"I didn't ask. I just smiled and took his cash."

Hayden observed the old man sitting at the table, slurping down his wild plum brandy, entertaining them with tales about his brood of Quetzalcoatlus flyers. Mick and Claire had told Hayden about the young Quetzals that had hatched out here in captivity. Whisperer called them his *second generation*.

"I hear you've got a few juveniles here that are less than a year old," Hayden said.

Whisperer's craggy face glowed with pride. "Indeed we do. A trio to be exact. They're a little over nine months old."

"Any trouble getting the adults to breed in captivity?"

"No, not really. It just kind of happened, though I will say it surprised me. I thought my Quetzals were too young to reproduce. But then, Ashara laid three eggs late last October, the week before Halloween. Ashara was only a year and a half at that time. And then, a miracle! All three young'uns hatched out, healthy and ready to snarf down some fish. Minnows at first, but soon they were eating frogs and lizards and good size trout. They're whip smart, too. Catch on quickly. They can't fly yet, but it won't be long. Their wings are nearly ready for liftoff. They're eager to take to the skies."

"Will I get to see them?" Hayden asked.

"Of *course*," Whisperer said, as if there should be no question about it. He tilted his head back and drained his brandy horn. "The youngsters are part of our deal. And I'll have you know that Novera is now gravid and about to deliver more second generation eggs. Refills anyone?" he said, pushing away from the table and holding up his empty horn.

Mick and Claire declined. Whisperer went to a hearthstone bench and lifted the lid, pulled out a stoneware jug. Refilled his horn and returned to the table.

Hayden said, "I have to ask because I'm curious. You've been going on and on about your Quetzal . . . what'd you call it? Your *Aeroguild*?"

"That's right. My Aeroguild."

"Well, it's obvious you have a fondness for your flyers. One might even say you possess a *love* for them. They seem like family."

"That they are, Dr. Fowler. They *are* my family, superior in many ways to my useless flesh and blood relations."

"And you also talk about how you have put in a lot of hard work raising and training them. So why, then, are you selling them off?"

"I'm sure everyone seated at this table knows part of the answer. These animals grow at an alarming rate and my feed bill is already astronomical. You can imagine how many hundreds of pounds of fish and amphibians we go through feeding five mature Quetzals and three juveniles. When fully grown they'll be fifteen feet tall with thirty-five-foot wingspans and weigh in at around four-hundred pounds. I also have a number of falcons and hawks here at the Villa that gobble down twice their weight in raw meat. It's quite an expensive food budget and I need the revenue to keep going.

"Secondly, I will be sixty-one years young next month and I'm not as spry as I once was. Rooster and Joanie are a big help, but they're merely ranch hands and work more with my falcons and hawks. *I'm* the brains behind this Quetzal operation, the genius with the magic training touch. When I'm gone, pterosaur training will be a thing of the past. I want to be recognized for my brilliance before I shuffle off this mortal sphere and . . ."

Hayden listened to the man as he rambled on, stopping only long enough to gulp down more grog. *The man is certainly quite taken with himself—a self-absorbed legend in his own mind.*

Hayden was getting impatient. He peered at the duffel sitting on the floor next to Whisperer's elfin shoe and wondered when the old man was going to shut his yap and count his money so they could get on with it.

He cut in on Whisperer's long rambling monologue. "Look, I traveled all the way from Minnesota to be here. I'm a very busy man and we're on a tight schedule. It's time for you to show me your genius you brag about."

"No brag, just fact," the falconer said, giving Hayden an annoyed look with his good eye. Huffily, he reached down and picked up the duffel bag, set it on the table and unzipped the top with an irritated flourish. Pulled out a handful of banded bills. "I'll take you out to the Aerie after I add up my loot. Why don't you go fetch your camcorder while I count. You're gonna be astonished by what I have to show you and it's time for the world to see it, too."

As Hayden got up to go out to the van, Mick said to him, "Believe him. He's not wrong."

TWENTY MINUTES LATER, WHISPERER, having determined the Prescotts' payment was legal United States tender, took them through a low-ceilinged, dark hallway of black stone, leading out into the Aerie. Hayden filmed as they walked.

They entered the open-air sanctuary, a vast bowl of dusty stone enclosed by towering walls of granite and striped gneissic rock. Hayden estimated the Aerie to be somewhere between ten and fifteen acres. He breathed in the gamy, feral animal smell scented with the hint of animal dung. The Quetzals restarted their uncanny moose-geese calls, the squawking sounds raining down on them from atop the cliffs. He looked up, spotting three of the winged reptiles lining the crest of the ridge, their bodies appearing as dark cutouts against the sunny backdrop. They stood rigid and regal, their long stork-like beaks pointed downward as they carried on with their bellowing and honking. Hayden zoomed in with the videocam, getting clear shots of each. At the bottom of the cliff, a hundred feet below the Quetzals, were the remains of what looked like two deer, their ripped and bloodied carcasses hanging from a wrought iron feeding rack.

Hayden lowered his camera, focusing on the deer carrion. "I thought you said your Quetzals ate fish," he said, his eye not leaving the viewfinder.

"Their diet *is* primarily fish. But being scavengers as they are, they never pass up an easy meal. Deer and elk meat are special treats for them. But they have to earn it. I've got them trained. They know the feed rack is off limits until I give them permission to indulge."

Hayden spotted the gyrocopter parked beneath a rocky ledge, a small, open cockpit, single-seater aircraft that looked more like a wheelchair with rotor blades than anything that could fly.

He heard Whisperer's voice over the calls of the Quetzals. "I see you admiring my *Whispering Windjack*, Dr. Fowler."

"*Admiring* isn't the word I would choose. I would never go up in that contraption."

"Oh, it's quite safe. Much more stable than larger copters in the high winds we get up here in the mountains. The *Windjack* is perfect for working with my Quetzals."

Hayden gave him a sardonic smile. "I just hope your insurance premiums are paid up."

Mick and Claire snickered behind him.

"No need to worry about me, Dr. Fowler."

"Oh, believe me, I don't," he said, his impatience growing. "When are you gonna show me your training magic tricks?"

"Ask and you shall receive, Dr. Fowler. The show is about to begin." Whisperer raised his right arm high and brought it down in a slashing motion. The Quetzals went silent. The only sound was the wind whistling across the clifftops. "You see, they know who's boss," he said with a cockeyed grin. "C'mon, folks, follow me."

Whisperer led them to a group of training platforms constructed of thick wooden beams and rebar piping. The units were anchored in a deep sand pit and contained heavy duty perches, wide swings, and giant iron hooks.

The falconer reached into a cedar chest and pulled out a large bone whistle. He took a deep breath, then turned toward the cliffs and blew the horn, emitting a high-pitched foghorn sound that echoed through the Aerie.

Five mature Quetzals flew in from all directions, circling the training arena. Round and round they flew, gliding down in a circular descent. Hayden followed their flight with his camera, impressed by the grace of the big reptiles, how they skillfully rode the thermals and crosswinds. The air stirred as they came in one by one, each hooking onto a perch with extended talons.

Remarkable animals, Hayden thought. *So agile and fluid for creatures their size.*

They roosted on their perches and focused on their master through shimmering tawny eyes. They were hyperalert, vigilant. Waiting for instructions.

Hayden was blown away. The scene was beyond belief. Very ethereal and alien.

And if he was being honest with himself, a little scary.

A vision of the pack of Quetzalcoatlus that attacked their helicopter flashed through his mind. *These guys are related to the winged demons that nearly killed me!*

Whisperer introduced them to Hayden: Thrall, Talgarin, Crayth, Ashara, and lastly Novera, with her wide hips and a distended abdomen heavy with eggs.

As each was introduced, they dipped their long, thin beaks in a courteous manner, and gave their visitors a wing-wave. Hayden recorded every sensational moment.

How is this even possible?

Whisperer turned and faced the camera, introducing himself and giving a brief history of his Aeroguild Quetzals and his methods of training.

"And now my pterosaurs will demonstrate just how well I have coached them. Each one of these fine specimens is an apex hunter, capable of understanding over two-hundred English commands. For this exercise I will command three of them to fly out and kill an animal of my choosing, then bring it back to me. I'll start with the biggest and most accomplished hunter, Thrall. Please say hello to the world, Thrall."

Thrall obediently lifted a foot from his perch and pointed his claws at the camera, then let out an extended baritone honk that sounded like an arctic seal, his long neck vibrating with the effort.

Whisperer spoke to the camera. "If you think that's impressive, we're just warming up." He turned back to Thrall. "Okay now, Thrall, I want you to fetch me a raccoon."

Thrall nodded, showing his blade-thin crest. He spread his wings wide, beat them a couple of times preparing for liftoff, then launched from his perch, honking and squawking as he soared up and away, his powerful wings taking him up over the Aerie rim.

Whisperer then sent two other of his Quetzals out on the hunt. "Crayth, fetch me a chipmunk. Ashara, fetch me a gopher."

Crayth and Ashara flew out of the canyon, screeching excitedly.

Hayden filmed their flight, not believing his own eyes.

I wish Nora was here to see this. If even one of these three Quetzals returns with the right animal—or any animal for that matter—I'm going to make an appointment with a shrink to have my sanity tested.

Whisperer addressed the camera. "As you can see, these are very intelligent animals. Thrall, Crayth, and Ashara will be back within twenty minutes with their prizes. I have trained them by calling on their natural predator instincts. They think they're honoring me by bringing me a gift of a dead animal. They're like cats in that regard."

Hayden said, "How can we be sure you haven't planted a dead raccoon, chipmunk, and gopher somewhere near here and the Quetzals are just going to pick them up?"

"Excellent question, Dr. Fowler! And even if that was true, it would still be impressive if they returned with the *proper* dead animal, would it not?"

"I reckon," Hayden said, still not quite convinced that this was anything but a carnival sideshow act.

"So, to disavow you of your skepticism, I ask that *you* pick an animal and I will have Novera fetch it. Please make it a small mammal. Their slender beaks can only carry so much weight."

"Okay. How about a hoary marmot?" Hayden said, coming up with the most unusual small mammal that he knew populated northwestern Montana.

Whisperer laughed. "Oh how I love your inventiveness, Dr. Fowler." He gave Novera the *fetch* command and she took off to hunt for a hoary marmot.

Hayden followed Novera with the videocam. *If these Quetzals pull this off, I will gladly acknowledge Whisperer's genius.*

Seventeen minutes later by his watch, Crayth returned with a chubby chipmunk clasped in his swordlike beak. He dropped the bleeding animal in front of Whisperer, who rewarded his Quetzal hunter with a plump brook trout. Crayth took the fish to his perch and gobbled it down his long gullet in one hurried swallow.

Next came Thrall, dropping his prize raccoon on the stone floor and accepting his fish reward. Five minutes later, Ashara flew in, delivering her assigned prey, a dead pocket gopher with bulging cheek pouches.

Are you shitting me? Hayden thought from behind the lens. *It can't be possible to train prehistoric animals to do these things.*

"That's *really* impressive," Mick Prescott said. "Bringing in a burrowing animal like that gopher in less than a half hour."

"I agree," Hayden said. "And all three brought in the right animals. Most extraordinary!"

The four Quetzals made soft clucking noises from their perches as if acknowledging the compliments.

They waited on Novera's return in the biggest test yet—the hoary marmot.

Five minutes slipped to fifteen, and Whisperer's demeanor went from supremely confident to a restless anxiety. He paced back and forth in front of his Quetzals, their dark golden eyes following his movement. "Novera is a superlative huntress," he said. "She'll return with a marmot, you'll see. I'm sure of it."

Is Whisperer trying to convince us or himself?

And then, as if Novera could hear Whisperer's compliments, she flew in over the canyon rim, struggling with keeping the marmot secured in her thin beak. She came in for an awkward landing, tumbling a bit trying to stick the landing with her belly full of eggs, and dumped the hefty two-foot-long marmot at Whisperer's feet.

Hayden was thunderstruck. A real hoary marmot hunted down and brought back to the Aerie in less than forty-five minutes. He trained the camcorder on the marmot, its thick black and gray fur splotched with blood.

"Very good, Novera," Whisperer exclaimed, reaching into his fish bin. "You deserve a couple of treats for that effort." He tossed a pair of trout to Novera, which she snapped out of the air with two lightning-fast jabs with her sword beak.

"Simply amazing, Whisperer," Hayden said, incredulous by what he just witnessed and recorded.

"Thank you, kind sir," Whisperer said, taking a dramatic stage bow for the benefit of the camera.

Hayden shut off the camcorder. "Okay, now for your part of the bargain. Where can I examine these fine performers of yours?" he said, tilting his head at the five Quetzals, casually grooming themselves on their roosts.

"I'll get them to the Aerofirmary and you can take as long as you need with them, Dr. Fowler."

"Excellent," Hayden said, thrilling to the thought of looking under the hood of these miraculous creatures. "I need to go out to the van to get my instruments. Will they tolerate a xylazine-ketamine tranquilizer mix?"

"Oh, my Quetzals don't need to be sedated. I can hypnotize them into a deep twilight sleep so you can examine them freely."

Hayden looked up at the Quetzals sitting high atop their roosts, preening. A stab from one of those long beaks could puncture an internal organ or put out an eye. "Are you sure? I'm going to have to draw a lot of blood and get into their private parts."

"You doubt me? I've got you covered, Dr. Fowler. You've seen how much control I have over my Aeroguild."

Claire Prescott said, "That might be true, but we'll have to sedate Talgarin for the trip out."

"You are correct, little lady. Damn but you're smart!" he said, his tone blatantly patronizing and sexist. "I must remain in the vicinity when I induce twilight sleep. But as far as Talgarin goes, I'll have to oversee the dosage. These animals have very hollow bones and thin arteries. Getting the dosage just right is a delicate balance. It doesn't take much tranq to kill them."

Whisperer gave a *drop-and-walk* command to his Aeroguild and one by one they hopped down off their perches, following their master to the Aerofirmary.

Hayden filmed the otherworldly parade. As graceful and agile as Quetzals were in the air, they were awkward on the ground, their gait stilted and clumsy. Their powerful hind legs propelled them forward and they used their folded wings as stabilizing arms, walking on all fours. It was almost comical watching them lift their folded left wing and advance their left leg, then bring their wing down to steady themselves before bringing their right limbs forward for the same action on the other side. This deliberate machination created a slow, side-to-side robotic motion. Adding to the clumsiness, they walked with their hind feet planted flat on the ground, making a dull slapping sound against the stone floor. Hayden knew it as plantigrade feet, which differed from many other dinosaurs and birds that walked on their toes in a locomotion known as digitigrade gait.

THEY SPENT THE AFTERNOON and early evening in the Aerofirmary, a sprawling room constructed inside a cave on the far side of the Aerie. Thick cedar planks covered the rock walls and floor. The expansive treatment room smelled of resins and herbs that helped mask the strong musk of the Quetzals. Racks of diffused lighting extended from the ceiling. A pair of flexible gooseneck LED light fixtures mounted on mobile stands flanked a long exam table, a low platform of timbers covered in layers of animal hides. The table was wide enough for a Quetzal to half-recline with its broad wings spread along grooves in the floor so bones and hide could be inspected without strain. A carved stone water trough sat next to the table. Large falconry jesses and padded harnesses hung from pegs along one wall. Oversized versions of avian care instruments were scattered everywhere: hooks, clamps, beak and claw files, suture needles as long as a man's forearm. Whisperer told them the bundles of sage, yarrow, and wild willow bark hanging from the overhead rafters were used as antiseptics, anticoagulants, and pain relievers. The clay jars sitting on a wide shelf held poultices and salves used to treat infections. Fermented honey and plum contained in hanging wineskins were used as antiseptics and pain-killers.

Hayden worked steadily, thoroughly examining all five adult Quetzals and the three juveniles. He drew vials of blood, charted heart rate, body temperature, weight, bone and muscle health, respiration, and arterial blood flow. He also checked every inch of their leathery hides, combing through their pycnofibers (hair-like filaments) looking for parasites, wounds, and infections. The Prescotts took turns videoing the proceedings while Whisperer kept the animals calm and composed using his enigmatic hypnosis spells. As he worked, Hayden kept a close eye on the pterosaurs' beaks, not fully trusting Whisperer's twilight sleep hypnosis. Should one of the creatures awake from the "sleep" startled, one quick thrust from the sharply-pointed beak could eviscerate him.

Hayden spoke to the camera, sharing his discoveries during his full body examination of Thrall:

"Their long, narrow swordlike beaks are lacking teeth and their jaws are surprisingly weak. Therefore, they can't chew. They gulp down their prey whole, much like herons, storks, and pelicans. Like those aquatic animals, Quetzals have two-part stomachs to aid in digestion. They do, however, use their toothless beaks for hunting and defense. As you can see here, the tip is razor sharp, perfect for stabbing small prey. It's why they are such skilled fishermen. They use that beak as a harpoon when fishing and as a formidable weapon to defend against larger attackers. One quick jab from that long beak can blind or kill a Tyrannosaur."

Hayden moved to the other side of the exam table and Claire followed with the videocam.

"Quetzals have advanced respiratory systems like modern-day birds, with large air sacs that exchange oxygen efficiently. Their eyesight is much more keen than eagles and hawks. Their big telescopic eyes and wide-set eye sockets give them the ability to see straight ahead and peripherally simultaneously. And let's take a look at their wings. Unlike birds, which have feathers, Quetzal wings are made of a tough fibrous membrane. They have four fingers at the midsection of the wings that aid in their walking, three of them small with claws. The fourth phalange is much more prominent, giving the wing strength and durability. You have seen the mechanical way they walk by folding their wings in and using those wing fingers as walking canes, for lack of a better analogy. Their hind legs are stout and all muscle. They use them as a propulsion mechanism to get those huge wings up off the ground and into flight. Moving down to the feet, these Quetzals and other advanced pterodactyloids have four clawed toes on each foot as opposed to the five-toed hind feet of earlier pterosaurs. These are claws, not talons, which is a significant distinction to be made here. As a ground-walking pterosaur, Quetzals' feet and claws are adapted for terrestrial movement rather than for grasping and killing prey like the longer, sharper talons of raptors. And if you bring the camera in a little closer, you'll see some webbing between the toes. This is to keep them from sinking in muddy marshlands, which is their favored hunting terrain."

THEY FINISHED JUST BEFORE eight o'clock with Hayden and Whisperer making closing remarks on video. Long shadows stretched across the Aerie floor like a tangle of dark arms as they loaded a very sedated Talgarin into the travel cage in the back of the Prescotts' van. The Quetzal fought them as they attempted to band his wings. They'd had to give the creature an additional tranquilizer dose before they could get him strapped and into the crate.

Hayden was exhausted from the day's activities. His neck was sore and his lower back hurt from hours of leaning over the exam table. His eyes kept blurring and his legs were shaky.

You can't keep burning the proverbial candle at both ends like this, old man.

Whisperer pulled him aside as the Prescotts climbed into the front seats and buckled up.

"Now you be sure to let me know when you're gonna release the video to the world, Dr. Fowler."

Hayden looked at the falconer, whose milky eye gleamed in the setting sun like a white marble "Oh, I will for sure," he said, wondering whether Whisperer knew that the video would most likely bring the authorities and an arrest warrant up to his mountaintop sanctuary. Nothing was recorded about the sale of Talgarin to the Prescotts, but it was illegal to keep dinosaurs on your property without a permit. His Quetzal Villa was a direct violation of the Montana Endangered Species Act.

And if that wasn't enough to get the law up here, what Hayden had uncovered during his examinations certainly would.

Three of the Quetzals—Thrall, Crayth, and Novera—were sick with nontuberculous mycobacteria, *Aeromonas hydrophilia* bacterial infections, and an unidentifiable animal-borne virus. Fortunately Talgarin, the Prescotts' purchase, tested healthy.

He could not, in good conscience, let it slide. These pterosaurs were capable of flying long distances and could spread disease not only through the dinosaur population, but also to domesticated animals and most likely to humans. It could quickly become a public health crisis, spreading respiratory disease and salmonella all along the Great Divide and well beyond.

Is Whisperer aware of this? Does he know several of his Aeroguild have contracted zoonotic infections? Does he care?

Hayden thought about bringing it up in the exam room, and would have if Talgarin been infected. But he held back. He didn't know what kind of reaction he'd get from Whisperer, a brilliant but sketchy and roughhewn mountain man with questionable ethics. They might not have gotten off this mountain alive if Hayden had thrown that kind of wrench into Whisperer's ego party. Much safer to contact Montana Fish, Wildlife, and Parks when he got back to civilization. FWP agents would swarm Whisperer's sanctuary like stormtroopers once they got this information.

Let the FWP do their jobs. No need for me to stick my neck out.

As they made their way back down the mountain in darkness, Hayden told the Prescotts of his discovery.

"Are you sure, Hayden?" Claire said from the passenger seat. "Three of them are infected?"

"Yeah, I'm pretty sure. All three were showing excessive foamy salivation and respiratory distress, a waxy discharge from the eyes. Thrall, Crayth, and Novera also displayed signs of encephalitis. At first I thought it might just be head trauma from knocks they had taken. But I couldn't find abrasions or bruising on their heads. I'll know for sure after running the bloodwork through PCR and ELISA testing. The blood doesn't lie."

"Polymerase chain reaction and enzyme-linked immunosorbent assay blood panels?" Mick asked.

"You know about that kind of testing?"

Hayden saw Mick nod in the faint dashboard light. "Sure do. Claire does, too. We both did a lot of zoonotic disease testing during our time at the Denver Zoo."

"And I'm sure with your wildlife backgrounds you know what kind of a problem we've uncovered here."

"It's a major league problem, for sure," Claire said. "But you say our Talgarin isn't infected?"

Hayden looked at Talgarin, sedated and drawing ragged breaths in the cage. "As best as I can tell. Like I said, the bloodwork will tell the story."

Mick said, "How long do you think it'll take to get results?"

"I'll be able to get it pushed through in a day or two. I have a connection at the Montana Veterinary Diagnostic Laboratory in Bozeman. Martina Jessops. She helped Nora and me when we were working with Dromaeosaur juveniles."

Claire said, "Do you think Whisperer knows there is disease running through his Aeroguild?"

"Yes, I absolutely do. I think he's rushing to unload his treasures before they die. He sold one of his mature Quetzals in May and now he's sold Talgarin. Three of the other four Quetzals are sick and it won't be long before the disease spreads to the three juveniles. Time is of the essence for our Quetzal Whisperer. He might be a genius level animal trainer but he's also a devious, shifty character."

Mick crushed out his cigarette in the dash ashtray. "I think he knows of the disease in his brood, too. But one thing I don't get is if Whisperer is aware that his Quetzals are sick, why would he give you an open invitation to examine them?"

"Because he knows his time is running short for showing the world how brilliant he is. He wants international acknowledgment for being the only human to successfully train dinosaurs. Whisperer wants to ride the fame train before it's too late. I'm his only hope for that outcome, regardless what I uncover through my biological testing. You heard the man. His ego and personal quest for glory far outweigh his sense of responsibility."

They rode in silence for ten minutes, before Claire said, "You know, I agree with you, Hayden. The Whisperer is kind of shady and fly-by-night. He's also rude and sexist, and um, more than a little dangerous." Hayden saw her look across the front seats at her husband. "I think this might be a good time to tell Hayden, don't you think, Mickey?"

"Claire, we talked about this," Mick responded sharply, obviously perturbed. "I don't think we should—"

"Tell me what? What's going on?"

"Well," Mick said, lighting up another smoke and shooting Claire an annoyed look, "when we came up here the first time and Whisperer did his show and tell for us, two of the Quetzals returned from their hunt with some, uh . . . shall we say, unorthodox prey."

"What *kind* of unorthodox prey?"

"Body parts."

"Body parts? You mean like *human anatomy* body parts?"

"Yes, I'm afraid so," Claire said. "The Quetzal named Ashara returned with a human hand and Novera came back with a human forearm. Whisperer gave them the fetch command, telling them to surprise him, to bring back something of their choosing. He was quite pleased with his two female flyers and what they retrieved."

Hayden could almost feel steam coming out of his ears. "What the fuck! You witnessed this and just ignored it? You knew this and you're just telling me now? Why would you keep something like that from me?"

"Well," Claire said, looking anxiously at Mick. "We didn't think you'd work with us if you knew."

"Jesus fucking Christ!" Hayden said, bubbling in a stew of emotions. "Never mind me. At the very least you should have immediately reported it to the authorities. What the hell is wrong with you two?"

The dim dashboard light cut a stark silhouette of Mick Prescott, both hands on the steering wheel, ever-present cigarette dangling from his lip. Hayden wanted to punch him in the mouth. He looked at Claire, slumped down in the passenger seat and he wanted to slap some sense into her.

Mick pulled the cigarette and blew out a cloud of smoke. "You have to understand, Hayden, that with the work we're doing in the dinosaur trade, it could be disastrous for us to get too close to law enforcement."

"I *know* that," Hayden said angrily. "I never mistook you two for law abiding citizens. But those Quetzals could start an epizootic or worse, a human epidemic. You saw Whisperer being pleased with his Aeroguild for bringing him human body parts and you just turned your backs on it? Unbelievable! You just pretend like it didn't happen and continue on with your illegal trafficking? That's completely fucked up!"

Mick looked at Claire, anger torching his words. "I told you he would react this way, but you just *had* to bring it up. Christ!"

"You both should be ashamed," Hayden said, a molten fire burning in his chest.

Claire said, "We didn't know his Quetzals were diseased."

"What the hell does that have to do with it? We're talkin' human body parts here. That's a police matter. And you knew *he* was off-kilter. Rewarding his *Aeroguild* for fetching human hands and arms? Jesus!"

"Hey, we didn't have to tell you about it," Mick said, his tone threatening. "We could have kept it to ourselves and you would have been none the wiser."

"But I *do* know about it and now I'm gonna have to report it."

"You don't have any proof that it happened," Claire said.

Mick nodded. "Yeah, it would just end up being our word against yours. We would deny it ever happened. So don't go stirring up a hornets nest."

Christ, Fowler, who are these people you've thrown in with?

Nora was right. I never should have gotten involved with them.

He looked at the Quetzal, Talgarin, jammed into a much-too-small crate, wings banded tightly to its body with rawhide straps, drugged within an inch of its life and breathing laboriously. He felt a deep empathy for the animal. It was traffickers like Mick and Claire Prescott and the many more like them operating in this new dinosaur milieu who robbed these creatures of their freedom to live in the wild as the laws of nature decreed. The Prescotts and others saw big paydays while losing sight of the big picture.

His anger was reaching the tipping point and he wanted to lash out at them. But he decided the smart move would be to clam up. Saying more might find him kicked out of the van and stranded in a dense forest on a dark mountain road late at night. Or worse. That's the kind of people he was dealing with here.

You really misread this couple, Hayden old boy.

He let out a deep breath and sat back, deciding that when he got back to civilization, he would report both the Quetzal Whisperer and the Prescotts.

Hayden settled in for the jarring ride down the mountain and listened to Mick and Claire bitch at each other up front.

Talgarin let out a long, somnolent sigh from inside the cage.

Hayden leaned in and whispered, "I'm with you, buddy. Hang in there."

Calls from the Cloud

July 11: Montana State Prison
Deer Lodge, Montana

MIKE MATHEWS LEFT INTERSTATE 90 and pulled onto Conley Lake Road, a narrow two-lane of buckled asphalt framed by gravel ditches, cottonwoods, and scrub brush. He passed a time-worn sign—**Montana State Prison – Authorized Entry Only**—that was pockmarked with bullet holes.

The prison came into view with its mix of old and new architecture. The old sections, which the detective knew were built in the late 1800s, were medieval in appearance, with castle-like crenelated towers, gray sandstone walls, battlement style roofs, and arched windows. Ancient cellblock 1 and surrounding areas were now designated as historical sites and housed several museums. The newer cellblocks contained the 1,600+ male inmates, and stood like a fortress, surrounded by coiled razor wire and with guard towers overlooking rooftops.

He pulled up to the first checkpoint. A correctional officer wearing mirrored sunglasses and a bored expression asked for his ID and reason for his visit.

"Private Investigator Michael Mathews here to see inmate Leonard Sheridan," he said, handing over his credentials. "It's been approved by Warden Dickinson."

The officer checked a clipboard, made a quick radio call, then waved him through the gate.

Mathews parked as close as he could to the processing center. He locked his gun in the glovebox and walked to the entrance, hearing earthmoving equipment groaning in the distance, hammers pounding and clanging.

More expansion? In a state with just a million people it's incredible to think they need more jail cells.

Inside, he went to the check-in window where a reception officer stated in a bored rote, "Sign in. Empty your pockets. Off with your belt and watch. Anything metal goes in the tray. No cell phones allowed past this point."

Mathews placed his belt, watch, wallet, keys, and phone into a bin. A second officer did a quick pat-down, running his hands down his sides and legs, then checked the contents of his manila folder. Satisfied it contained no contraband, the guard handed him the folder and a plastic visitor badge, told him to walk through a body scanner arch.

A third officer escorted him to the visitation area. "You've got twenty minutes with prisoner Sheridan. No physical contact. No passing items across the table. If he gets out of line, we cut it short. Clear?"

"This isn't my first prison visit, Officer."

The young guard was apologetic, "I figured, but I'm required to inform you."

They walked down a long corridor that smelled of disinfectant and old paint, doors sliding open with a buzz then clanking shut behind them.

After walking for what seemed like miles, they finally arrived at the visitation room. Steel chairs and tables were bolted to the floor. The large space was half full, voices carrying across the room in a low hum, punctuated by the occasional sharp bark of a guard.

The escort officer pointed at an empty table. "Wait here. We'll bring him in."

Mathews sat, opened his file folder and reviewed his notes. The Flathead County Sheriff's Department had given him a list of calls they found on taxidermist Kyle Birnham's burner phones that were traced to the prison. In particular to this cellblock. Even more specifically to Leonard Sheridan himself.

With Sheriff Dunstable's backing, Mathews worked with Warden Dickinson to connect the dots. All inmate calls were routed through a third-party vendor, ICSolutions, on their ENFORCER platform. The warden had complete access to those inmate calls, and Dickinson had given Mathews an early Christmas gift—audio recordings of Leonard Sheridan instructing Kyle Birnham to "deliver a prehistoric heads up" to his rancher friend (Bryan Gilliam), and to include something personal, such as recent family photos to "really stir up interest." They also uncovered recordings of Sheridan speaking to an as yet unknown male subject about taking the Gilliams' longtime ranch hand, Chogan Stimson, on a "permanent vacation." Attempts to track down the murderer had so far been unsuccessful. A more recent call, made just two days ago, had Sheridan in discussion with a different male voice, talking about ways in which to kill Bryan Gilliam "without leaving a trace." That's the call that got prison officials' attention and the call that brought Mathews here. All of Sheridan's conversations were heavily steeped in encrypted language and oblique semantics, but it didn't take a professional codebreaker to know his intentions.

The door buzzed, then swung open with a robotic hiss. Leonard Sheridan entered accompanied by a pair of guards, shackles clinking on his wrists and ankles. Though he wore the general population uniform of blue short sleeved shirt and gray pants, he carried himself with pride, like a man who refused to be diminished. He was well over six feet with a lean, hardened frame. Close-cropped hair. Colorful tats of animal iconography swirling up his forearms and biceps. Flinty pale gray eyes, sharp and restless, intense.

He sat across from Mathews, the chains clanking against the steel chair. A wolfish grin crossed his face. Mathews knew it as an expression of someone who was convinced he was still in control even when shackled.

"Thank you for seeing me today, Mr. Sheridan."

The inmate shrugged his shoulders. "It beats hell outta laying in my cell bunk."

"I imagine so, yes."

"So you're the private dick?"

"Yes. Private *Investigator* Mike Mathews from Billings."

"Hmmm. I expected more."

Mathews let the vague insult go. He'd seen this ploy hundreds of times before, where suspects tried to get the upper hand early in the interrogation.

"Look, I know Deputy Stuart Fenski and the FBI have already been out to talk with you and—"

"I *didn't* talk with them. I never talk to pigs. Especially Fibbies. That sheriff's deputy wasn't any prize either."

"Did any of them tell you about their findings?"

"Those assholes didn't tell me shit. I clammed up, too. Tit for tat, you know. Shit for shat. We sat at the table and stared at each other for twenty minutes."

"Well, you're talking to me, Mr. Sheridan. Why is that?"

"Because you're working for Bryan and Loretta Gilliam, a couple of animal abusing scumbags who should be locked up instead of me. I'm hoping a few of the things I say will get back to them."

"I know you've got a checkered past with them, Leonard. May I call you Leonard?"

"I've been called worse."

"Okay, *Leonard*, For the record, I understand that you are a lieutenant in the Animal Emancipation Faction, best known as the AEF, an organization the FBI has denoted as a domestic terrorist group. You're in here doing a stretch of twenty to thirty for your part in the AEF attack on Gilliam's Guidepost ranch two years ago. Am I correct in my statement?"

"No, you're way off. First, I'm not a lieutenant. We don't use hierarchical military rankings in the AEF. Yes, I led the attack on the Gilliam ranch, but I have no title. I'm just a proud member of an elite organization. Second, we're no more a terrorist group than are the Boy Scouts of America. The Fibbies are masters at spreading propaganda that aligns with their agenda."

Mathews gave him a grim smile. "I would say invading an innocent family's ranch with bulldozers and gun-toting assassins lends a whole lot of truth to the FBI's claim. Let's see," he said, consulting his notes, "you were convicted of criminal trespass to property, felonious criminal mischief, first degree arson, and conspiracy to commit murder. That's quite a crime spree. All in a single day, too."

"Fuck you!"

"And court transcripts indicate that you showed no remorse during the proceedings."

"Listen, Mathews. I *didn't* feel bad about anything we did that day and I still don't. The Gilliams kept those dinosaurs in deplorable conditions in that godforsaken zoo of theirs. They ran inhumane tests on them. They profited immensely from their abuse of those animals. I shouldn't be locked up for that. Nor should my AEF brothers, Bevere and Wooledge. No fuckin' way! We liberated those poor creatures. They belong in the wild, not cooped up in some greedy rancher's shit-stained habitat. And to top it off, the greedy Gilliams and their shyster lawyer took my organization for ten million bucks! Tell the Gilliams to watch their backs."

"You'd better watch what you say, Sheridan."

"Or what? They might throw me in jail? You're a scream, private dick Mathews! I'm proud of what we did. We all were. The Gilliams asked for it and we gave it to them."

Mathews had long been incredulous at how hardcase sociopaths justified their criminal actions by gaslighting their victims. He'd interviewed hundreds of malignant narcissist suspects over his long crimefighting career. He recalled a case he was called out on as a Billings patrolman years ago. He and his partner had answered a 10-80 call (domestic disturbance) arriving to find the father had shot and killed his wife and two kids. When Mathews asked the man why he'd murdered his family, his answer was "It's their fault. They annoyed me. They just wouldn't shut up, always blaming dear old dad for everything under the sun. They just wouldn't shut their whiny, complaining mouths and I couldn't take it anymore, so I shut them up for good." Mathews would never forget how the man spoke so calmly, how he'd stood there tall and proud, wearing a crooked grin, like he believed he'd done the world a big favor.

When he looked across the table, he knew he was dealing with a similar personality. Leonard Sheridan was indeed a malignant sociopath.

"Leonard, I'm not here to discuss your previous convictions.

I'm here to inform you of new charges being brought against you."

"What the hell are you yammering about?"

"I'm not yammering. I'm telling it like it is. Surely you must know all calls here at the prison are monitored and recorded."

"Yeah, that's common knowledge through gen pop here. So what's your point?"

"The prison has recordings of you setting up the dinosaur head delivery to my clients. Let's see," Mathews said, consulting his notes again, and reeling off two phone numbers that were Kyle Birnham's burner phones. "There were four calls to those numbers the week before the T-Rex head was delivered to my clients. It was your voice on all of them. You told the taxidermist to include something personal with the head. Something like family photos to quote, "stir up their interest," end quote. Too bad the guy you trusted to do that work isn't real savvy with computers. If he hadn't botched the hacking of the Gilliams' VPN server, I wouldn't be here right now. How do you know Kyle Birnham, Leonard? It doesn't seem like you two have much in common, with him killing and stuffing animals while you're all about protecting them."

A long pause, then, "You're talking gibberish, Mathews. I don't know any taxidermists. And I certainly don't know anything about a T-Rex head."

Mathews gave him a *do you really want to go there?* glance. "C'mon, Sheridan. You're toast and you know it. We also have you on record instructing someone to take the Gilliams' employee, Chogan Stimson, on a permanent vacation. Was it your idea to decapitate Stimson or was it a creative impulse by the killer?"

Sheridan's face flushed a deep crimson, his cool demeanor giving way to anger. "That Blackfoot savage killed two of my AEF brothers that day. He deserved what he got."

"Thanks, Leonard. You just gave me your confession."

"I did no such—"

"You and your Animal Emancipation friends were trespassing. Bulldozing fences and torching buildings. Watching innocent people be devoured by those carnivores you let loose. I'd say your two buddies got what *they* deserved."

“Fuck you, Mathews!”

A guard shouted out to them. “Hey! Keep it down over there or we’ll end your visit.”

Mathews said in a quiet voice, “So how do you know Kyle Birnham, Leonard? You two seem like an odd couple.”

Sheridan shook his head, disgusted. “I don’t wanna talk about that dunderhead. I’m sorry I ever got involved with him. He’s pissed on everything we had planned.”

“*We?* Who is we?”

“I’ve said enough. I’m not saying another word without my lawyer present.”

“Oh, one more thing, Leonard. We have you on a couple of calls two days ago setting up a hit on Bryan Gilliam. Those two calls are what flipped the switch and caught the prison brass’s interest. You really need to work on your phone conversation coding. Even the most clueless jury member would know exactly what you’re talking about. The best defense attorney in the world isn’t going to protect you on these recent maneuverings of yours. The sheriff’s department has all the proof they need.”

That one stung Sheridan, lighting a fire behind his eyes. Mathews saw him getting him worked up and knew it was time to go for the close.

He said, “Flathead County deputies will be here soon to serve you with these new charges. You’re now facing life without parole. You can, however, lighten your sentence by working with the police. Who are your outside accomplices, Leonard? Who murdered Chogan Stimson? Who is the hitman you contacted to go after Bryan Gilliam? Give me some names and addresses and Sheriff Dunstable says he’ll be willing to cut a deal.”

Sheridan glared at him for a long, intense beat, then slammed his shackled wrists against the tabletop, shouted, “GUARDS! GET. THIS. ASSHOLE. OUT. OF. MY SIGHT!” the restraints clanking like blacksmith hammers, emphasizing each pointed word.

Two guards rushed in, grabbing Sheridan. Another pair of guards pulled Mathews up out of his seat. The inmates and their visitors quieted, all eyes on the sudden commotion.

Mathews heard Sheridan yelling, "Fuckin' Birnham, that douchebag stooge! I'll kill the bastard!" as his two escort officers struggled to control him. "And I'll get you, too, Mathews, Mr. private dick!"

"You better call off your executioner dog, Sheridan," Mathews shouted back. "I don't think you want to spend a lifetime in here."

And then Leonard Sheridan was gone. All conversations had stopped. You could hear a pin drop in the spacious room.

The guards gave Mathews time to gather his papers together and stuff them in his folder. Then they escorted him back down the long winding corridor to Processing. He retrieved his belongings and made a call to Sheriff Dunstable on his way out to his car, quickly giving Dunstable the high points of his interview with Sheridan.

The last thing he told the sheriff before ending the call was that his deputies and the FBI needed to accelerate their search for the assassin Leonard Sheridan had hired to kill Bryan Gilliam.

While My Guitar Gently Weeps

July 16: Gilliam's Guidepost

Heart Butte, Montana

LORETTA COULDN'T CONCENTRATE on the Colleen Oakley novel. Her thoughts kept drifting to last night's phone call from Mike Mathews, when the detective recapped his prison visit with Leonard Sheridan. The news was shocking. The jailed AEF terrorist had actually issued a direct death threat to her husband. Neither she nor Bryan had gotten much sleep after that call.

Mathews apologized for having to be the messenger of such disturbing news, but he said they needed to hear it to be on their guard. She could still hear the detective's raspy voice laying out the grim warning, hitting her like a sledgehammer between the eyes.

Truth was, the possibility of a death threat had been the elephant in the room ever since FedEx had delivered the T-Rex head. Then Chogan was beheaded and strung up in the trees on their back forty.

And now they faced another direct threat.

Mathews went on to say that Sheridan had brought up the Gilliams' ten-million-dollar civil suit settlement, calling Bryan and Loretta greedy and Atlee Pinnaker a shyster lawyer. But the real kicker was that Sheridan had all but confessed to orchestrating Chogan's murder. The knowledge of that made the threat to Bryan all the more terrifying and real.

"So we don't know who Sheridan's accomplices are?" Bryan inquired.

"We don't, no," Mathews said. "Our discussion went south before I could interrogate him completely. He went ballistic and the guards swooped in to break it up. I believe that was by design."

Bryan said, "You seem to have a knack for pissing off these criminals, Mike. First the taxidermist and now Sheridan."

"It comes with the territory."

The call with Detective Mathews added yet another layer to their troubles. Loretta was still struggling to get past the nightmare at the Missoula Fairgrounds a week ago. She shuddered when she thought how close they'd come to losing their first-born son. The terror Pauley must have felt with those hungry Dromaeosaurs leaping onto the stage and charging him. If Lou Goolsby hadn't been there . . . well, she refused to let her mind go there.

And now Leonard Sheridan had admitted to ordering a hit on Bryan.

Loretta had asked Mathews, "Isn't that enough to charge him with attempted murder?"

"With my testimony, maybe. But he's already doing time. He doesn't have much to lose. The key now is finding his co-conspirators. The FBI has phone numbers and recorded voices. They'll get those involved, sooner than later."

Detective Mathews had also queried them about their protection. Was their current security enough? Before the music festival tragedy, Loretta thought their security detail might have been overkill, with four personal bodyguards wandering the house and grounds, shadowing their every move, riding along with them when any of them left the ranch. But things had changed.

A week ago, Lou Goolsby had saved her son.

And now they faced this serious threat on Bryan's life.

I don't think we could have enough bodyguards at this point.

Loretta looked up, surprised to see Paul enter the den and plop down in the recliner across from her. "Do you have a few minutes, Mom?"

He had spent most of the past week depressed and fearful, closed off in his room, listening to sad music.

She set her book aside. "Sure. I have all the minutes you need. What's on your mind?"

"I think Moonrise is history," he said, a weepy flutter in his voice.

Earlier in the week Paul told her he didn't think he would ever pick up a guitar again. The rehearsal barn had been quiet since the festival.

"So, you've definitely decided to quit playing your music?"

"Yes and no," he said, looking away, shoulders hunched, eyes brimming with tears. "Jesus, I don't know. Everything's so messed up right now."

"Talk to me, Pauley. Maybe I can help."

"Well," he said, turning to her and rubbing his eyes with the heel of his hand. "It's not me so much. It's Oxendine. Hass quit the band. He says his folks don't want him out playing music where there're big crowds. I think that's a huge pile of horseshit. I'm pretty sure it's more that *he* wants to check out on us. There's a couple of other bands on the rez looking for a drummer and I think he got an offer."

"Have you tried talking with him?"

"Yeah, I have, but he always shuts me down with some wiseass comment. He's gotten really nasty lately. Ox bitches about everything. He says he deserves more of the songwriting credit because he creates all the drum parts. Says his percussion work made a couple of our tunes radio hits and that he should be recognized for that. And get this. He wants his kit moved to the front of the stage and not in back where he says his fans can't see him. *His* fans, not *our* fans. He wants a mic so he can talk to the audience. No telling what would come out of his mouth if I gave him a microphone. I said no to all of it. Ox's ego has gotten out of control."

"He's jealous of you, Paul. You're the front man of the band and you get most of the attention. Rightfully so. Hass is too young to understand some things. He doesn't realize that with the attention comes responsibility and additional burdens."

"That's what I tried to tell him, but he doesn't wanna hear it. Just keeps calling me a control freak. We'd never get anything done if I didn't push Hass and Kit. It's exhausting. All the complaining and nit-picking. The finger-pointing and fighting. We started off as friends and the music was fun. It was like a party when we got together to jam. Now it's a business and becoming a drag. The Zootown festival was supposed to be our big break. Instead it was one of the biggest tragedies in years. We'll forever be known as the band that was playing when the attack happened. We're like that band that went down playing on the Titanic."

She looked at him, slumped in the chair, hangdog expression. Downcast, defeated, *dejected.* She wanted to go to him and throw her arms around him, tell him things would work out.

She said, "Moonrise is *nothing* like the Titanic band, Pauley. You're not on a sinking ship, as bad as things might seem."

"They *died*, Mom. Those musicians died a horrible death. Just like I almost did," he said, visibly shaking. His eyes were swollen and bloodshot. His cheeks glistened with tears. "One minute I was singing and the crowd was really into it. I felt on top of the world. Next thing I know, everything went to hell and I saw a couple of Dromes comin' at me." He twisted in his chair. "I almost died!"

"But you didn't, son. That's the thing. You're still alive and well. All of us are—you, your father, your brother and sister . . . your bandmembers. We should all be grateful that we made it out unscathed. There are dozens of other families who didn't."

"I know, you're right," he said, sniffling. "It's just that I don't think I'll ever be able to play guitar and sing again. It'll take me right back to that horror."

"You've been through a lot, Pauley."

He gave her a faint smile, swept his hair away from his face.

My boy is eighteen but he still needs me, Loretta thought, her gray mood lifting.

She said, "You've certainly been through some horrible stuff, darling, but you're strong and you'll be back playing and singing again soon. I just know it. You love it too much to give it up. In fact, I'm pretty sure you'd be miserable without your music. And you're too good to just up and quit. Think about those thousands of people singing along with you at the festival, singing songs that you wrote. Think about the studio work you've done and getting college radio airplay. God gave you a special gift and you don't want to let it fade away. And speaking of God, did you ever stop to think that maybe the good Lord intervened when those Dromes came at you?"

"Oh, don't hand me that religious crap, Mother. Lou Goolsby

came to my rescue. Not God."

"Maybe it was God who put Lou there on that stage with you. Did you ever think of that?"

Paul waved her off. "Okay, yeah, *whatever*."

"And it's *not* religion, Pauley. Religion is a human construct, a tool used by mortals to gain power over the masses. It's politics in sheep's clothing. Religion divides people just as much as it brings them together. Probably more so. We've never talked about this but your father and I are not fans of organized religion."

"Yeah, I sorta figured you and Pops were atheists."

"We're *not* atheists, Paul. No, what gets us through is *faith*. The spiritual side of things. Faith in a higher power. Faith in family and friends. Faith in *ourselves*."

Paul stared at her for several beats, thinking. Loretta could see the wheels turning in his head and thought maybe she had gotten through to him.

Then he said, "I appreciate what you're tryin' to do, Mom. I really do. But I've got a band with no drummer and I don't know that I'll ever get over what I went through at the festival. Everything is just so messed up."

She could see Paul trying hard to hold back his emotions. He hung his head and emitted several soft whimpers, trying to hang on, but failing, broke down in tearful sobs.

Loretta rose from the sofa and went to him, kneeled by his chair and rubbed his hand. "It's going to be okay, Pauley. Things will work out, you'll see. Just have some faith."

He pulled his hand away and wiped his face, attempting to regain his composure. "Look at me," he muttered, "crying like a little baby. How friggin' embarrassing!"

"You're never too old to cry, Pauley," she said, caressing his arm. "It's good to let out your emotions. Much better than holding it all in. How is Sinopa taking all this? I haven't seen her all week."

"Sin is going through her own issues," he said through sniffles. "But we're tight. She's a great girl and really good for me."

"That's wonderful. How does she feel about the band?"

"Sin's a trouper, Mom. She wants to carry on. She says it won't be that hard to replace Ox, that there are plenty of drummers on the rez who would want to play with us. She wants to start holding auditions right away. Truth be told, I think she's glad that Hass is gone. She never got along with him from day one."

Loretta smiled. "That's great. Sinopa has a good head on her shoulders for someone so young."

"Yeah, she's awesome. We're great together. We've even talked about getting married."

What? Loretta tried to mask her shock. *Sinopa Harwood just turned seventeen! They're much too young for marriage.* She wanted to interject her thoughts on the subject but understood that now was not the time or place to fight that battle.

Further discussion was cut short by Lianne's appearance. Loretta's youngest entered the living room wearing a Moonrise tee and a wide smile. She padded into the room holding Paul's acoustic guitar by the neck.

Paul stiffened in the recliner and glared at his sister. "Hey, what the hell are you doin' with my guitar, Lee-lee?"

"I brought it for you to play me a song."

"No! Absolutely not! Put that down before you drop it, little miss klutzy. That ain't a toy, it's an expensive instrument."

Lianne stopped. Her smile faded. She thrust her lower lip out in a disappointed pout.

Loretta told her, "It's okay, Lee. Bring me the guitar. I'm sure your brother would be happy to play you a song."

"No, I wouldn't!"

Lianne dutifully brought the guitar to Loretta, then looked at her big brother. "I just wanted to hear you play that new song you wrote for Sinopa."

"No, Lee! It's a stupid song."

"It is *not*!" Lianne said, stomping her foot. "It's pretty. Just like Sin."

Loretta held the guitar out to Paul. "C'mon," she pleaded. "Just one song for your sister. She's your biggest fan."

Paul looked at the guitar like it was radioactive, then looked away. "No! I can't do it. I have to be in the mood and I'm just not.

She's got our CDs to listen to."

"I wanna see you play, Pauley, I—"

"Stop bugging me, Lee-lee. And do *not* call me Pauley!"

"Let your sister talk, Paul," Loretta said. "You didn't stop me when I called you Pauley."

"That's different."

"No, it's really not," she said. "Go ahead, Lee-lee. Tell Paul what you wanted to say."

She started shyly, unsure of her temperamental brother's mood. "Well, um . . . I just wanted to tell you how much I loved seeing you up on that big stage last weekend. I was so proud of you. You sounded so good. I bragged about you to my friends. I told them you are my rockstar brother. And Marnie is really jealous. She wanted to come see your band but Aunt Livvy said it was too far to drive. I wish I could play guitar and sing like you, Pauley."

Paul's eyes brightened. "You really mean that?"

Lianne nodded enthusiastically, her smile returning. "Will you teach me how to play?"

"Well, I don't know about—"

"I think that's a splendid idea," Loretta exclaimed.

Paul let out a deep sigh. "I don't know. I don't have the time."

Loretta leaned the guitar against the side of the recliner and stood. "Oh, I think you have plenty of time for your number one fan now that Moonrise is on hiatus."

"Mom, you're not helping."

"Sure I am. I think it would do you a world of good to give Lee some lessons. And I think it would do Lee-lee good if you'd play a song or two for her."

Lianne's face lit up, shining with hope and expectation. "Yes! Please, Pauley. Please, please, *please*!"

Paul sat there, head swiveling back and forth between his sister and his mother. Finally, with a deep exhale, he got out of the recliner and grabbed the guitar.

"All right, I'll play for you, Lee-lee, you being my number one fan and all. Just not the song I wrote for Sin. 'Sinful Love' is too personal, and it has lyrics no little sister of mine should hear." He moved to the sofa where he had more elbow room.

"I've heard the song before," Lianne said with an air of annoyance. "Lotsa times."

He started tentatively, halfheartedly fingerpicking the intro to "Dreamtime," a deep cut off of Moonrise's new album.

Lianne clapped excitedly as she recognized the melody. She watched Paul's hand moving up and down the fretboard, love and admiration evident in her gaze.

Paul launched into the first verse, a light seeming to illuminate within him, as if the music was a personal vibroacoustic therapy session. He was all smiles, in performance mode, caught up in the tune, bobbing his shaggy head as he strummed and sang.

Lianne mouthed the words to "Dreamtime." The girl had been listening to the Moonrise CDs nonstop the past week, and knew every lyric. She was obviously delighted by this command living room performance, and it warmed Loretta's heart to see her kids interacting like this.

Paul strummed the final chord of "Dreamtime" and went into "You Can't Take the Heart Out of Heart Butte." Loretta knew the words to this one and sang along with Paul and Lianne.

Paul was midway through a Beatles cover tune, "Here Comes the Sun," when Bryan slipped into the room, recording the merriment on his cell phone, with bodyguards Lou Goolsby and Phil Marsden entering behind him. Loretta thought Paul might object to being filmed by his dad and would halt his performance, but surprisingly, he grinned at the camera and kept playing.

Loretta glanced at Bryan, who gave her a knowing smile.

An hour later, Paul was still at it, picking and strumming and singing, grinning his way through a mix of Moonrise originals and cover songs, entertaining his family like he had never done before. The music washed over Loretta like an auditory massage.

My son is back in his groove, his happy place.

She only wished that his brother Ethan could be here, but the baseball diamond was Ethan's happy place.

It was a joyful celebration of music and family.

If only for the moment.

The Bone Fields

July 17: Smithsonian Expedition

Northern Alberta, Canada

DAY FOUR OF THE EXPEDITION AND NORA was thrilled about their first find—a well preserved Pachyrhinosaurus skull.

The enormity of it took her breath away! Five feet across the top, the skull had to weigh 500 pounds if an ounce. It had taken the team two and a half days to dig the matrix trench around it to where they could hoist their prize out of the earth's tight grip.

Nora projected they could do the extraction this afternoon.

The dig was off to a smashing start.

The Smithsonian curators will be pleased.

They were in the Grande Prairie wilderness, 280 miles northwest of Edmonton, known to be one of the densest dinosaur bone beds in North America. This outcrop valley of shale, sandstone, and weathered gravel covered fossils and skeletal remains of hadrosaurs, tyrannosaurs, nodosaurs, and pterosaurs as well as ancient lizards, turtles, and crocodiles. Nora knew the skull wasn't a unique find in this valley. Two years ago, paleontologists from the nearby Philip Currie Dinosaur Museum extracted a 600-pound Pachyrhinosaurus skull and named it "Big Sam." Their extraction proved difficult, due not to size and weight, but because Big Sam's skull was intertwined in a cluster of hundreds of other bones. Nora was relieved her team hadn't run into that hassle here.

She observed her field crew applying plaster-soaked burlap around the skull and framing it with wooden planks. A specimen this large had to be encased carefully to give it stability during the lift out. The preparation was every bit as important as the hoist. One small oversight could damage the specimen, not to mention cause a fatal accident.

Nora was familiar with the horned Pachyrhinosaurus, the older cousin of Triceratops. They thrived in what is now northern Canada and Alaska during the Campanian-Maastrichtian stage of the Late Cretaceous. They shared many characteristics with contemporary mammals like the Indian elephant and rhinoceros. But instead of having a horn on their snout like a Triceratops or rhino, they sported a big bony bump called a *boss,* and bone growths over their eyes.

She breathed in the heady mix of scents associated with paleontological dig sites—musky sphagnum moss sweetened by fireweed and yarrow in bloom; shale dust and freshly turned earth wafting from spoil piles; wet plastered burlap; burnt diesel fuel from earthmoving equipment. She loved that unique blend of aromas, a fragrant reminder that she was where she belonged.

She scanned the site, taking in the dozen trailers that served as sleeping quarters, the trackhoe excavator, hydraulic crane, pickup trucks and other passenger vehicles. The nylon tents that held supplies and drinking water, the popup shelter where the crew ate and cataloged finds. Two propane powered generators droned behind a tarp wall. Large spoil piles of earth and rock surrounded the matrix trough. This was a much bigger operation than the one Nora headed up two summers ago. She looked on with pride at her team preparing for the extraction. They all knew their roles and worked well together. She hadn't been able to cherry-pick this team as she did two years ago, and that had worried her at first. But here on the fourth day out it was obvious the Smithsonian folks had done a good job with recruitment.

There was one holdover from that expedition two summers ago—internationally renowned geologist Greg Dulowski, who had assumed leadership after Nora left to track dinosaurs with Hayden. Dulowski had also been selected to lead this outing before Nora's arrival. She had a good working relationship with him. Everyone called him *The Professor*. He possessed none of the sexist male ego that was so prevalent in the industry. He was completely at ease with a woman heading up the dig. It made Nora's job so much easier.

Being out here in the Canadian wilderness unearthing prehistoric relics charged her up like nothing else. It's what she dreamed of doing ever since she started digging up bones in the woods as a little girl growing up in rural Wisconsin. Nora much preferred this over going out on what Hayden called *tracking safaris* chasing after dangerous T-Rexes, Deinosuchus, and Dromaeosaurs.

He had been weepy and down in the dumps the day she left. She had to admit to being a bit crestfallen herself on the flight out of Minneapolis, wondering if she had done the right thing. *Have I been too selfish? Too self-absorbed with my career?* But then she had chuckled as she recalled Hayden kissing her goodbye, checking to make sure she had packed Mr. Happy, her trustworthy dildo. He was obviously still worried about her taking up with another man on this trip. Nora thought it was cute, Hayden showing his jealousy that way. She even felt a bit sad for him, the way he'd gazed forlornly at her with those puppy dog brown eyes as she got in her car to leave for the airport.

Nora had worried about Hayden's frame of mind before his trip up Bitterroot Mountain to meet with the weird falconer. She thought he might be losing it, the way Hayden completely bought into the Prescotts' tales of the trainer who could bend wild Quetzalcoatluses to his will. But those worries disappeared when Hayden returned from his visit with his astonishing video clips. She watched them, not believing what she was seeing. She had been struck by the unreality of the footage, the oddness and incongruity of the recordings, similar to when they'd watched the first Dromaeosaurs hatching out of the meteorite at Gilliam's Guidepost.

"It all looks and sounds like a Hollywood production. A CGI special effects extravaganza," she had told him on her initial viewings.

"True enough. But hasn't all of this return of the dinosaurs had a doctored digital feel about it?"

"Well, yes. But this is something drastically different, Hayden."

"I certainly won't disagree with you there."

The day she left for Canada, he was still going on about the extraordinary things he and the Prescotts had witnessed at

Whisperer's mountaintop ranch. Hayden even called the pterosaurs sentient beings.

"They possess a large vocabulary and are able to follow specific commands," he'd said. "I'm telling you Nora, they are intelligent, sentient animals. They're extraordinary. And so is Whisperer, even if he is a dickhead."

"Did getting up close and personal with them bring back your visions of the crash?"

"At first, yeah. They're intimidating, odd-looking creatures, but beautiful in their own way, too. I actually felt a bit of compassion for them when I discovered the diseases they were carrying. And I felt nothing but disgust for Stanley Murchison," he said, referring to Whisperer by his real name. "Murchison's ego is so humongous he's chasing fame in spite of knowing his Quetzals are carrying serious diseases. He *had* to know I would be turning him in."

"Fame is a powerful aphrodisiac," Nora said. "Some people will do literally anything to achieve it."

Hayden had phoned Montana Fish, Wildlife, and Parks, giving them precise coordinates for locating the difficult-to-access ranch. FWP officers had swept in and shut down the operation, charging Murchison and his workers with numerous wildlife violations. Unfortunately they'd found just three of the eight Quetzals. Two adults and one juvenile. Where the other five had gone was anybody's guess, and Hayden worried about the very real danger they posed to the public.

Nora had FaceTimed with Hayden several times since she had been in Canada. Between his pleas for her to come back to Minnesota, Hayden railed about Mick and Claire Prescott. The trapper couple had kept critical information from him, namely that the pterosaurs had returned to the sanctuary with human body parts.

"They told me that *after* we were done with the Whisperer and on our way down the mountain with their Quetzal in a cage in the back of the van. They didn't think I'd work with them had I known."

"I'm surprised they told you at all."

"Yeah, me, too. I think Miss Claire had a case of the guilts."

And so Hayden had also reported the Prescotts, giving

authorities a description of their van and license plate number. Despite intense questioning he couldn't give them any more than that since they dropped him at his hotel before taking their Quetzal purchase—Talgarin—either to the buyer or a holding area. The last Hayden knew, Mick and Claire Prescott had disappeared into the ether and could not be located.

"The Fish and Wildlife people asked me if I knew anything about the Prescotts' clients," Hayden said. "I told them no, that I had just met them and they were secretive about their business. I wouldn't have worked with them had I known about the body parts. I wouldn't have risked my career on something like that. That crosses a line for me."

"Come on, Hayden. This is me you're talking to," Nora said to the image of his face in her small cell phone screen. "You knew they were lowlife traffickers the first time you met with them. Admit it. The Prescotts did you a favor connecting you with Whisperer. Look at all the Quetzalcoatlus research you've been able to do."

Hayden had given her a wry smile. "Always so direct."

"When I need to be, yes."

"You've always been the glass half full type, Nora."

"You should try it sometime. It works wonders."

That awkward conversation had taken place two days ago.

Just now her phone buzzed and she checked the display. Hayden FaceTiming her again. She connected and held the phone up where he could see her.

"Hey, Nora. Are you digging your scene up there in the north country?"

She grinned. "I never thought I would miss your terrible puns, but I do."

He told her he had been working steadily on editing the videos he'd taken, readying them for public release. The Smithsonian had first right of refusal and *National Geographic* had shown interest along with a host of other publications and docuseries platforms.

"These clips are going to go viral in a big way. Bigger than anything Jack ever did," he said, referring to his late friend, Jackson Lattimer. "And they'll make Whisperer a celebrity. Just not in the way Murchison wanted. He'll be public enemy number one once word gets out his escaped pterosaurs are diseased."

He went on and on about his video editing project, how it helped take the edge off his loneliness, repeating how lonely he was without her several times.

"I'm lonely, too," she told him, looking around to make sure nobody was within hearing distance. "I miss you, my big cuddly teddy bear."

"Do you?"

She didn't want to get into his loneliness pity party with him again and so told him she had to go, hearing his frantic "Wait, Nora, WAIT!" as she disconnected.

She was making her way to the popup shelter when Greg Dulowski and Addie McDougall, a grad student intern, approached.

"Look what we found, Nora," Dulowski said, holding out his hands, showing her long fossilized teeth that looked like serrated steak knives. "Any idea what they are?"

She took them from him and recognized them immediately. "Yes. They're Boreonykus teeth," she said, excitement lifting her tone. "Very rare. Where'd you find them?"

"Pipestone Creek. Not far from here." Dulowski turned to the grad student. "Show her what you found, Addie."

She held out a fossilized claw, her young face shining with the thrill of discovery.

Nora took it from her and held it up, examining it. "It's a Boreonykus sickle claw. Findings of these are rare."

"I'm not familiar with Boreonykus, Dr. Lemoyne," Addie said, embarrassedly. "What were they?"

Nora smiled at the girl. "They were a small but vicious feathered carnivore that roamed these parts during the Campanian stage of the Late Cretaceous, around seventy-three million years ago. They're a member of the dromaeosaurid family, cousins of *Velociraptor mongoliensis*." She looked at Dulowski. "These are remarkable finds, Greg. Take me out there. Show me where you found these."

Nora went to find the team's senior vertebrate paleontologist, Garrett Finch, and the four of them climbed into Greg Dulowski's jeep.

On the drive out to Pipestone Creek and the Boreonykus bone bed, Nora fondled the sickle claw and thought this expedition might be blessed by the paleontology gods.

Graveyard Guardians

July 20: Selway-Bitterroot Wilderness
Northern Idaho

HAYDEN AND BILL CARLTON RODE in Carlton's Jeep Wrangler, traveling east on the Magruder Corridor, a 100-mile single lane unpaved road that ran between the River of No Return Wilderness to the south and the Selway-Bitterroot Wilderness to the north. The dirt thoroughfare was more of a glorified trail, the high mountain road steep and winding with several hairpin turns that kept Carlton alert at the wheel. Naturalists considered this part of Idaho one of the loneliest and most remote areas of the continental United States. Twenty-five miles north of this area is where they lucked into spotting a pair of fornicating Ankylosaurs while doing dinosaur migration studies a month ago.

Two of Carlton's wildlife biologist colleagues from the Idaho Department of Fish and Game—Gunther Reese and Dell Waymond—followed in a Chevy Silverado 6500. The IDFG had appointed Carlton the lead in a dinosaur census to comply with their federally mandated wild game survey.

The state had been doing aerial flyovers the past couple of weeks, spotting unusually heavy dinosaur activity in the area. Especially predominant were T-Rexes. The problem was, IDFG fleet helicopters unsettled the creatures, sending them scurrying for cover, making it impossible to get accurate counts of each species. Bill Carlton's team was tasked with tabulating accurate counts of the various species and studying their behavior to determine what was drawing them to this desolate part of Idaho. Part of their assignment required them to set up motion activated trail cameras for long term observation. Carlton, knowing Hayden was working on his dinosaur migration study, had invited him to join the team after getting approval from the Fish and Game brass.

Carlton said, "You realize we could be walking straight into the fires of hell."

Hayden grinned. "Good times, right? I say, bring on the beasts, ol' chap, and let the fun begin. Couldn't be any worse than tangling with those crocodilian monsters at Tally Lake."

Bill Carlton gave him a dubious glance. "Sometimes I think you're angling for a Darwin Award, Fowler. You're one reckless son of a bitch."

"Only the dead win that award. I'm very much alive and well, thank you very much."

"Yeah, well you better not do anything wild and crazy on my watch, Hayden. There'll be hell to pay if you do."

"Relax, Bill. I'm just thinking about my time out on Tally Lake in that dive boat, going after those Deinosuchus," Hayden said, a lilt of fondness in his voice. "That was the ballsiest of ballsy adventures. Better than an amusement park thrill ride."

Carlton looked at him askance. "Sometimes I think you're crazier than a shithouse rat."

Nora had also called him crazy and reckless along with a few other derogatory names after their close call with the Deinosuchus on the lake. He didn't think he was crazy or reckless. Intellectually curious? Yes. Scientifically obsessed? Sure. Reckless? No way. Crazy? Maybe, but he was always careful and well prepared when approaching dangerous species.

How am I supposed to learn about these animals if I don't get close to them?

That difference of opinion was the biggest reason why Nora was in Canada digging bones and he was in Idaho chasing prehistoric beasts.

Hayden had immediately accepted Carlton's invitation to join the IDFG survey team. Nora had been gone for five long days and he couldn't take another minute in the claustrophobic confines of his Eden Prairie home where so many memories of her remained. Her sweet floral jasmine perfume floated on the air like a ghostly aromatic scent. The kitchen table where they'd shared many meals, laughs, and deep conversations, was empty without her. The living room couch where they'd cuddled and fooled around like hormonally crazed teens mocked him with her absence. The den where they had watched movies and listened to music while munching takeout pizza echoed with loneliness. Their bed where they'd scratched each other's carnal itches was a constant reminder of lost intimacy. He missed her bright giggly laugh that filled the house with joy. He missed gazing into her mesmerizing jade green eyes, so large and seductive behind those sexy designer frames. He missed Nora's cerebral, scholarly mind that always challenged him. He'd needed a getaway and a deep dive into his work to heal the ache of her absence. Escaping to the wilds of Idaho to track T-Rexes seemed like the perfect antidote for his overwhelming loneliness.

But it wasn't just Nora's being in Canada that had Hayden out of sorts. Three days ago he'd received the lab results from his annual physical. Doc Martin had called him with the bad news—his eGFR and blood creatinine levels showed a startling decline in the health of his lone kidney. His urinalysis also showed a high level of proteinuria. He knew what it all meant. Dialysis was probably in his future. He'd lost a kidney in the helicopter crash and sustained significant damage to the remaining one. His nephrologist had put him on a donor wait list even though Hayden was deemed "healthy" with the one functioning, albeit faltering, kidney.

Doc Martin said he would try to pull some strings to get him a kidney, but told him not to expect a miracle—the national wait time for a healthy kidney was three to five years. As if that wasn't enough, Hayden's liver wasn't in great shape either. All those younger years of heavy drinking were coming back to haunt him.

So goddamned depressing, all this declining health bullshit!

I will NOT allow it to slow me down!

Truth be told, he hadn't really noticed much in the way of symptoms. Just a bit of fatigue and weakness once in a while that he attributed to having just turned 49. Considering his near death experience last summer and four days in a coma, Hayden thought he was faring quite well.

He had not shared his lab results with Nora. He didn't think he could handle her sympathy right now. More importantly, he didn't want her to think he was using his poor health diagnosis as a means to lure her back home.

"You still with me, Fowler?"

Bill Carlton's voice yanked him out of his reflections. "Yeah, yeah, I am," he said, his mind lost in a fog of regrets. "Just thinking about those Ankylosaurs we saw fucking out here last month."

Carlton looked across the center console, eyes narrowed, studying him. "Really? *That's* what's on your mind?"

"Yeah. It was wild, wasn't it? And our video is getting lots of attention, as I knew it would. It's clocked in at over two-hundred-thousand views on YouTube." Hayden gave him a snide smile. "It must give you some comfort to know you're not the only pervert who's into animal porn."

"*Me?* For Christ's sake, *you're* the one who did all the filming and editing. Face it, Hayden, you're the Steven Spielberg of zoological porn. I was just an innocent bystander."

"I'd prefer to be Martin Scorsese. And you were no innocent bystander, my friend. You're a dino Peeping Tom. You were absolutely *riveted.* Admit it."

Carlton let out a husky chuckle. "Okay, you got me. All ball-busting aside, yes, I *was* riveted. Who wouldn't be? I mean, we witnessed something no human eyes had ever seen before."

"Agreed."

"Speaking of weird video footage, what's the latest on your clips of the Quetzalcoatlus and their genius trainer?"

"I finished editing them yesterday. My people at the Smithsonian are reviewing them now. They've got first rights. Another couple of days probably before I can post them on the internet."

"You say you turned that Quetzal Whisperer in to Montana Fish and Wildlife?"

Hayden nodded. "I had to. He's keeping dinosaurs without any kind of permit. His sanctuary is a giant petri dish of communicable diseases with those Quetzals flying in and out. Not to mention his ego is off the charts. So arrogant. I despised the man at first sight."

"And what about those trappers who took you there?"

"The Prescotts? They're not my favorite people either. They call themselves exotic animal *curators* so they can feel better about themselves. But really, they're just scumbag dinosaur traffickers. They don't give a damn about these creatures, Bill. Dinosaurs are just a hefty paycheck for them."

"So you reported them, too?"

"Yeah, I did. Felt good about it, too."

"Are they in custody now?"

"No. They're dust in the wind. I should have seen the situation for what it was, but I didn't. They're smarter than I gave them credit for. But they'll be found soon, I'm sure of it."

They bumped along the uneven road as they approached Observation Point, Hayden surveying the wide swaths of burned out ponderosa pine and Douglas fir.

Carlton filled Hayden in. "This is the section that burned three years ago. The Magruder Ridge fire, caused by devastating lightning strikes. Burned nearly four-thousand acres before torrential downpours extinguished it. It'll take another twenty years to restore this area to its previous beauty."

They passed fire-blasted jet-black tree trunks rising from mossy green carpets dotted with fuchsia, fireweed, and blue lupine. The sight was desolately beautiful and raw with the greenery regeneration process well underway. Hayden had long marveled at the revitalizing powers of nature.

They drove in silence for another ten minutes, the Silverado half a dozen car lengths back. The landscape changed from gray ash, blackened skeletal trees, and fire-charred stumps to dense forestland of healthy pine and western larch. They came to a winding S-curve and Carlton slowed to negotiate the twisty turns, his colleagues remaining a safe distance behind. A breathtaking view opened up on their left—a sheer drop-off plummeting more than a thousand feet down into a panoramic canyon where the wilderness rolled out in folds of forest and stone to the base of the Bitterroot Range and Trapper Peak.

They came out of the final turn to see a pair of huge Tyrannosaurs ahead, feasting on a bighorn sheep carcass in the middle of the road.

Carlton hit the brakes, bringing the Jeep to a stuttering halt. “Holy shit! That’s a male ram they’re devouring. Gotta be over three-hundred pounds. Don’t see many that size out here.”

“Never mind the ram, Bill. Check out those Rexes. I’ve never seen any that size.”

The beasts straightened, checking out the two vehicles, bloody sheep parts dangling from their massive jaws. The bigger of the pair threw its immense head back and swallowed his take. Hayden watched in fascination as the carrion bulge moved down the creature’s long gullet.

“They’ve gotta be fifteen feet tall,” he said. “Probably close to eight-hundred pounds.”

“Yeah, mighty big boys for sure,” Carlton said, peering through the windshield in awe.

Spooked, one of the Rexes turned and lumbered into the woods. The second Rex hesitated, continuing to stare them down, then bent to clamp on to the sheep’s spiral rack, and dragged the ram by the horns into the woods through the wide opening where the other Tyrannosaur had vanished.

Hayden looked on in disbelief. The big Tyrannosaurs had seemed to fear their vehicles and the loud engine noise. Highly unusual behavior for these apex carnivores to be fleeing. His experience with T-Rexes had shown them to be highly aggressive and usually in attack mode.

Something isn’t right here.

Carlton got on the two-way radio and spoke to Gunther Reese, the biologist driving the Silverado. “Okay, Gunther. Time to park it and hike in. You and Dell grab the gear. Make sure we’ve got enough tranquilizer to sedate several big animals. And bring plenty of ammo.”

Hayden heard car doors opening and slamming shut. Suddenly his attention was drawn to large shadows fluttering across the dirt road. Curious, he leaned forward, peering up through the windshield.

Quetzalcoatlus!

Five winged pterosaurs slowly circled the summit, above the escape trail the Rexes had taken.

"Mother of God, take a look, Bill," Hayden said, pointing.

Carlton gripped the wheel and pulled himself forward, dipped his head and squinted. "Eagles?"

"Guess again. They're way too big to be eagles. They're Quetzalcoatlus. Very large specimens. It's odd the way they're circling up there."

The two men sat in reverential silence, watching the Quetzals glide overhead in a wide loop.

"It *is* odd. Whaddaya make of it, Hayden?"

"Don't know, but they seem pretty focused on something. A food source maybe?"

Carlton looked at him doubtfully. "If it was a food source they'd be diving to get at it. Why are they staying airborne?"

"I don't know. It's puzzling."

Carlton moved the Jeep off the road and shut down the engine. He opened his door with a creak. "Let's go check it out."

Hayden felt giddy with anticipation as he strapped on his camera case and gathered with the biologists in front of the Jeep. Carlton was cool and composed, but his two young colleagues looked petrified.

"We'll be following the path those Rexes took," Carlton said. "Hayden and I will lead with tranq guns. Gunther, you and Dell follow with your long guns. Use them only if absolutely necessary. Same goes for us, Hayden. Our etorphine-xylazine sedative mix is a thousand times more potent than morphine. A dose of just ten milligrams will immobilize an African elephant."

Hayden held out his rifle. "What kind of dosage are we carrying?"

"Five mils. So don't use it on juveniles unless you intend to kill."

Carlton perused the entrance of the dinosaur path, then tilted his head to scan the hillside up to the pinnacle. "No idea how far it is to the top. Let's place a couple of trail cams on the way up. And let's get a few scat samples while we're at it. There's bound to be some." He looked at Reese and Waymond. "You guys have your gloves and tubes?" he asked, referring to latex gloves and plastic collection tubes.

Gunther Reese and Dell Waymond gave him fidgety nods.

"Any questions about our mission here?"

Silence.

Hayden worried about Reese and Waymond's readiness for this job. It was obvious they had no experience with dinosaurs the way he and Carlton did. He had little confidence in them watching their backs. They looked like green army recruits going into their first battle. Scared. Darting eyes. Slick sweaty faces. Rigid postures. Hands white-knuckling their rifles. This was no job for novices, but Carlton didn't seem too concerned.

"Okay, let's hit it," Carlton said. "Stay alert and keep cool heads. We don't want any accidents up there."

They entered the break in the trees where the Rexes had disappeared. Dense stands of lodgepole pine and Engelmann spruce engulfed them. Sunshine filtered in through small gaps in the canopy, illuminating the dim passage with streaks of light. The ceiling was high, giving them good clearance; Hayden was thankful they didn't have to hack away at heavy vegetation. The path was springy underfoot and their footfalls fell into a syncopated rhythm. An industrious woodpecker hammered in the distance.

Hayden quickly recognized that this wasn't an old deer trail. The wide route up the gradient was forged by dinosaurs. The underbrush was trampled and flattened. Large piles of fresh dung had them watching where they stepped. Broken limbs and fractured branches all around where the tall beasts had taken down foliage on their way through. Large tridactyl (three-toed) footprints were embedded in the loamy soil, the clawed inner toes clearly visible. The distinctive odor Hayden had come to associate with T-Rex trails was prevalent—a gamey decomposed meat stench with the reek of freshly deposited manure. He'd trekked these dinosaur trails many times the past three summers, and he knew to be wary at what they might find at the other end. These beasts defended their food and water sources to the death.

They reached a place where Carlton wanted to set up the first trail camera. Hayden was winded and feeling faint. He took a seat on a boulder. His legs were rubbery and his lungs burned. Granted, they were hiking at high altitude, but he shouldn't be feeling this kind of strain after such a short slog.

"You okay, Fowler?" Carlton inquired as he assisted Reese with the camera setup. Waymond stood guard while the two men worked.

"Yeah, I'll live." Hayden was embarrassed that his partner had picked up on his poor conditioning. "Anything I can do to help?" he asked, attempting to salvage a little dignity.

"Thanks, but no. We've got this down to a science."

Carlton inserted an SD memory card in the camera and secured it to a tree with a steel bracketed tree mount, ten feet up, then activated it. Gunther Reese walked past it, back and forth, testing the motion sensor from several different angles. Assured everything was in working order, they resumed their hike up the slope.

Five minutes later they stopped to place another trail cam near a couple of large piles of newly deposited excrement. Hayden and Waymond put on gloves and used forceps to collect scat samples, slipping the muck into sterile vials while Carlton and Reese set up the camera. It was a smelly, thankless job, but important. Fresh scat like this could tell them much about the health of these animals. Critical things like levels of cortisol and other stress hormones, the presence of parasites and pathogens, the existence of toxins or poisons, nutritional status, and much more. A silica desiccant in the collection vials would prevent DNA degradation while they were in the field.

They moved on, hiking another ten minutes up the slope. As they neared the summit, Hayden heard what sounded like the bleating of raspy throated goats.

Dozens of bleaters, a baritone drone coming at them.

A disturbing, melancholy sound.

A sorrowful chorus of low-pitched moaning.

The four men stopped, peering at each other in the dim light, questioning with their eyes while they listened.

"What the hell is that?" Reese asked, his voice a fearful whisper.

Dell Waymond said, "I've never heard animals make noises like that. It's eerie as hell."

"It sure is," Hayden said, getting a bad feeling in his gut.

"C'mon," Carlton said. "Let's head on up and see what the ruckus is about."

The ground leveled out as they reached the highpoint. Hayden huffed and puffed noticeably. He was exhausted. His muscles felt like they were melting. Carlton looked at him, a knowing glance of concern and pity. Hayden turned away, humiliated by the way his body seemed to be failing him.

They walked out of the woods, the trees falling away like curtains drawn back. They were in an open hollow, a meadow with knee-high beargrass and mountain aster, the air smelling of sun-warmed pine. They came to a stop, their rifles raised, squinting against the harsh sunlight, ready for anything.

Bleating groans and whimpers seemed to come at them from all sides, louder, more raucous and discordant out here in the open.

They were the sounds of extreme suffering.

Hayden looked across the way, spotting the origin: a ragged grouping of sick and dying animals, laid out under the plentiful shade of subalpine fir trees at the far end of the glen. More than a dozen T-Rexes and Dromaeosaurs. He also spotted a Triceratops, an Ankylosaurus, and at least two Quetzalcoatlus, along with a couple of carcasses he couldn't identify from this distance.

It's a mountaintop graveyard where they come to die, Hayden thought forlornly. *What compels them to come here? More importantly, what is killing them?*

Carlton lowered his tranq rifle. "Please tell me this isn't what I think it is."

"I'm afraid it is," Hayden said, looking up, seeing the Quetzals circling overhead. He set his tranq rifle aside and pulled his videocam out of the case. Began recording. "It's a dinosaur cemetery. And I think our Quetzal friends winging it overhead are graveyard sentries."

"Sentries?" Reese asked. "For what purpose?"

"I don't know," Hayden said. "Maybe they're guardians of the graveyard? Looking out for their fellow Cretaceous brothers and sisters? Letting them die dignified deaths."

"That's absurd."

"Is it?" Hayden said, scanning the sky above, taking in the wide wings gliding on the thermals.

Carlton pointed his rifle across the glen, at the rows of downed animals. "What do you think is making them sick?"

Hayden thought back to the autopsy he'd performed on two T-Rexes after the Zootown Music Festival disaster in Missoula two-and-a-half weeks ago. He told the biologists about the bloated golf-ball-sized ticks he'd found embedded in their hides and the systemic infections he'd discovered in them.

Carlton said, "So you think maybe these animals have picked up those infections?"

"I do," Hayden said, looking above. "And I believe our Quetzalcoatlus sentries might be the carriers."

Gunther Reese said, "You think they're dying from tick-borne viruses, Hayden?"

"Not sure about the origin of the viruses or even what the viruses are. Could even be bacterial in nature instead. But there is certainly deadly diseases being passed among the dinosaur population. The big question is whether it's transmissible to domesticated animals and humans. We could have a real public health crisis on our hands, gentlemen."

"I agree," Carlton said. "Let's set up a couple more trail cams and get some blood samples to take back to Boise."

"You think it's safe?" Dell Waymond said, nervously scrutinizing the hollow.

Hayden said, "These animals are either dead or in the final throes of dying. I doubt they are in any condition to attack."

Reese pointed to the sky above. "Maybe. But I still wonder what those pterosaurs are doing up there."

"We can't let them deter us from what has to be done," Carlton said. "We've got work to do, so let's get to it."

They slowly, cautiously, began making their way across the meadow, searching for a spot to install a trail camera. Hayden had his videocam out, recording every step of the way. The mournful bleating increased in volume as they neared the sick creatures.

Hayden kept an eye on the two Rexes who had preceded them up the trail, watching them gnawing on what remained of the bighorn sheep. They looked sluggish and listless, like they might be in the early stages of whatever disease had felled their brethren. But if there was to be an attack, he thought it would come from them. He cradled the tranq rifle under his right arm, his finger on the trigger, filming with his left as he walked.

He tried to reason why these animals had chosen this site high in the Bitterroot Mountains as their dying place. *Five completely different species of Late Cretaceous dinosaurs gathering here in their final days? Why? What is drawing them here? It's not exactly accessible.* But then he thought, *Maybe that's the attraction.*

He knew of other locales in the natural world where animals died in groups. Scientists had found sites in Yellowstone National Park where clusters of bears and bison had died due to carbon dioxide and hydrogen sulfide gas leaks. And hundreds of birds—a large percentage of them upland sandpipers—fell dead each September and October in the high altitude Ozogoche Lakes in Ecuador. Their deaths were thought to be caused by volcanic steam.

But this situation was something completely different. These deaths weren't caused by poisonous gases. There weren't any volcanic steam vents up here.

Suddenly, one of the Quetzalcoatlus circling overhead dropped out of the rotation and swooped down, landing between two sick Quetzals. It quickly went to work grooming them, using its long, swordlike beak to pluck parasites from their hides.

Hayden zoomed in with the camcorder. "Unbelievable!" he said, squinting through the viewfinder.

Carlton edged up next to him. "What are you seeing, Hayden?"

"Those dying pterosaurs are carpeted with large ticks, and the sentry Quetzal is acting as a caregiver, stripping them off. That kind of intimate care is unheard of in paleontology circles."

Carlton looked despondent. "We need to rethink this. We shouldn't move any closer. There's no telling what we're getting into here. We don't know what kind of diseases are infecting these animals, whether they are potentially zoonotic. We're woefully unprepared to deal with it. We'll need protective gear—N95 respirators, chemical-resistant jumpsuits, heavy duty boots and gloves. We'll need to come back with efficient PPE. That said, we could already be in trouble from airborne pathogens."

"I highly doubt this thing that's infecting them is an airborne contagion," Hayden said. "But at the very least, these animals have advanced cases of Rocky Mountain Spotted Fever. Possibly even anaplasmosis or some other serious bacterial infection." He pointed to a small pond behind the listless creatures, a layer of algae scum covering the surface. "Maybe something they picked up from that body of water back there. We'll need to bring in antibiotics . . . some doxycycline. Maybe we can save a few of these creatures."

"You're dreaming, Hayden," Gunther Reese said, perusing the suffering beasts. "Antibiotics won't be effective, especially if we're talking about viral infections. There's no saving them at this point. The best we can do is to stop the spread."

Reese's negative comment angered Hayden. "That is *not* the best we can do, Gunther. You're right about stopping the spread. We have the health of Montanans and Idahoans to consider, not to mention livestock and farm animals. But we have to do everything in our power to prevent the Cretaceous dinosaur population from going extinct again. It's our duty as overseers of the natural world. It's our pledge we made as scientists."

Dell Waymond said, "I don't remember making any pledge to save those monsters. Those things are evil. They kill people and eat them for lunch."

Hayden scowled at Waymond. "You made a pledge to protect *all* creatures in the animal kingdom when you became a biologist, Dell. You can't pick and choose which ones you want to save."

Without warning, quick as a lightning bolt, a Quetzal dropped from the sky and took a furious run at them. A wide shadow fell across them as the large beast descended, coming in low and hard, making a close pass that had them all ducking. The pterosaur then looped back around for a second charge, clacking its beak and emitting low-pitched growls that reminded Hayden of agitated ostriches or alligators.

Hayden shoved the camcorder back in the case and took off running with the others, heading for the safety of the woods. A second Quetzal divebombed them and caught Gunther Reese in the shoulder with its sharp beak. Reese screamed out in pain and went down hard in a bed of prairie grass, his wound bleeding profusely.

Dell Waymond halted, turned and fired an errant shot that missed badly. He backpedaled, falling on his ass, getting off a second shot from a sitting position that clipped the Quetzal's wing. The blast knocked the pterosaur off its flight, and it struggled to stay aloft with one wing before tumbling awkwardly to earth.

Hayden backtracked to help Reese to his feet when a third Quetzal entered the fray, coming hard and fast at them. Hayden fired his tranq rifle, hitting the pterosaur with a precision shot in the soft-tissue pouch under its jaw. The Quetzal kept coming, swooping in and raking the side of Reese's face with its extended claws, then wheeling away with a loud shriek, the sedation dart dangling from its jawbone.

Hayden helped Reese into the forest, joining the other two. The four men gasped and wheezed, trying to tamp down the adrenaline surge and get their wind back. Hayden looked at Carlton, who was bent over, hands on his knees, trembling noticeably, his face a sickly pasty white.

"Are you okay, Bill?" Hayden asked.

"No, I'm uh . . ." and he let loose with a gush of vomit near Dell Waymond's boots.

"What the hell, man!" Waymond cried out, stepping back, out of harm's way. "What's wrong?"

Carlton, still bent over, wiped his mouth and turned his head to his colleague. "What's *wrong*?" he said, his voice a croak. "You have to ask, Dell?" He spat a couple of times, then looked at Hayden. "Those Quetzals took me back to the crash. Christamighty, they're terrifying."

"I can relate," Hayden said as he checked out Reese's shoulder wound. "I've spent some time with Quetzalcoatlus nightmares myself."

"How're you holding up, Gunther?" Carlton asked Reese.

Reese touched his shoulder and grimaced. "Not so good. Their beaks are razor sharp. He stabbed me good and deep."

Hayden applied direct pressure to the wound with a towel. "He's bleeding quite a bit. I believe that Quetzal nicked a major vessel. We need to get him down the trail and to a hospital."

Dell Waymond said, "Closest hospital is in Grangeville, a ninety-minute drive. Including the hike, we're looking at two hours, minimum."

Carlton scratched his scalp, thinking. "It would take a fleet medevac chopper at least that long to get here from Boise. Believe it or not, it would be quicker to drive to Grangeville."

"That's cool," Reese said, wincing. "I can make it."

Hayden wondered about that. The towel he held on the wound was soaked through. The gouges along the side of his face were ragged and bleeding.

"You're a real gamer," Carlton said to Gunther Reese. "Let's clean the wounds and get some antiseptic on them. Then we'll strap a tourniquet on that shoulder to hopefully hold it through the trip. You want a bullet to bite on, Reese?"

"I'd rather have a cigar."

Hayden dressed out Reese's wound and the four of them hiked back down the trail, the sorrowful bleating of the dying Cretaceous creatures fading behind them.

An hour and fifty minutes later they arrived at the Syringa Hospital ER. Reese had lost a lot of blood and was barely conscious.

The admissions clerk, a gray-haired older woman in white nursing scrubs, peered over her half-glasses at them with a puzzled expression, and asked, "How did your friend get that shoulder wound?"

Hayden said, "We ran into a few graveyard guardians who didn't take kindly to our trespassing."

"Graveyard guardians?"

Carlton frowned. “We don’t have time to go into the details, nurse. This man desperately needs a doctor.”

Hayden spoke up from the chairs where he was tending to Reese. “And I think we all need to be checked out. It’s possible we’ve been infected.”

“Infected by what?”

“Pathogens of an unknown origin. That’s what we’re here to find out.”

They were quickly escorted back to a quarantined exam room. Hayden wanted to get Gunther Reese the help he needed and then get the hell out of here.

There was much work to be done.

His Cretaceous creatures were in trouble.

And maybe humanity, too.

Homesick Blues

July 23: En Route to Ruby River Valley
Southwest Montana

PETER KNEW HE SHOULDN'T BE FLYING when he was this tapped out, but he didn't have much choice. The client company that had chartered the week with Fowler-Lemoyne Aviation—Beaumont Mining—had requested him personally to transport a group of engineers on geological surveys out to the Alder Gulch, north of Nevada City. Peter wondered why they had requested him considering he'd been the pilot of the highly publicized crash in Idaho last summer. When questioned, Beaumont officials pointed to Peter's exemplary history flying Bell choppers for the Montana Forest Service, and his recent heroic piloting skills that saved the lives of eight children who were on a church group outing. The work took the Beaumont geologists into treacherous mountain terrain, and they believed Peter was the most qualified pilot to get them there. In his more cynical moments, he thought they might have chosen him and Fowler-Lemoyne Aviation due to the celebrity surrounding him and the other three executives of the company.

Peter was discovering that fame had a way of attracting clients with deep pockets.

Business was booming this summer. His schedule had been insane, working thirteen-hour days piloting scheduled flights and handling paperwork left behind by Hayden and Nora, both of whom had been away and incommunicado the past ten days. Hayden was in Idaho working with the state on tracking down diseases among the dinosaur population. Nora was in Canada heading up a Smithsonian paleontology expedition. That left it up to Peter and Bryan

Gilliam to run Fowler-Lemoyne Aviation's day-to-day operations at a time when client charters jammed the calendar. Both company choppers had been in constant flight. A couple of long flights into Wyoming and North Dakota further piled on the workload for the company's five pilots.

Peter was bleary-eyed and exhausted Luckily, he had Walter Mingus in the copilot seat to take over when needed. Walt was the most experienced of the four helicopter pilots he had recruited, and Peter trusted him implicitly.

This was their third consecutive day out with the Beaumont Mining geologists. Today's flight took them over the Tobacco Root Mountains. Hollowtop Peak loomed straight ahead, its uppermost reaches snow-streaked even now in late July. The craggy summit cast its long, triangular shadow across the sweeping valleys below. Echo Lake shimmered below, a turquoise pool cupped in a wide stone bowl. A small band of mountain goats tightroped the jagged cliffs. Two meandering rivers—the Madison to the east and the Jefferson to the west—curved around the range.

Peter spoke into his headset mic. "It sure is rugged country out here."

"Gorgeous, isn't it?" Mingus responded. "Quite a view from up here. I pinch myself every day that I get to do this for a living. Fourteen-plus years flyin' choppers and it never gets old."

Peter couldn't argue with Walt's sentiments. But as much as he loved flying, he disliked being away from his family for long stretches. He hadn't been back home in nearly two weeks, and his homesickness was beginning to drag him down. He longed for Brin and the kids. He missed playing peekaboo with six-month-old Jake and reading him stories like *Goodnight Moon* and *The Very Hungry Caterpillar* before tucking him into his crib for the night. And he loved watching their three-year-old, Kimi, emulate her idol, Ms. Rachel, the YouTube sensation and Taylor Swift of the toddler world. Peter's heart soared every time Kimi came to him with that look of hopeful anticipation dancing in her dark-brown eyes, saying, "*Mizz Way-chill music, Dada! Mizz Way-chill songs, please, please, PLEASE, Dada! I wanna sing with Mizz Way-chill!*" He never had it in him to turn down her passionate requests (demands?). He would open YouTube on his iPad and queue up their Ms. Rachel playlist. Most of the time it was "I'm So Happy" and "I Love a Rainbow" and "Walking at the Zoo," Kimi's three favorite Ms. Rachel tunes that she wanted played over and over, repetition being a preschooler's modus operandi. He and Brin would smile at each other, watching their little diva Kimi attempt to copy Ms. Rachel's dance moves while singing painfully out of key.

The time he was able to spend with his family was precious to him, and being away so much carved a deep hole in his psyche. The extended absences made him yearn for his old flying gig with the Forest Service that allowed him to be home every night. He'd even considered contacting his former boss, Gary Ralston, to see about returning to the Forest Service. But then he thought about the cut in pay he would have to take, and that was only if Ralston agreed to take him back, which would be a long shot considering the way Peter had left and then hired (stolen?) two of his Forest Service employees—dispatcher Nancy Diehl and fleet mechanic Carl Lacey.

Peter knew Walt had a wife and children and wondered how he handled being away from them. He glanced at Mingus, who was busy monitoring aircraft instrumentation and charting navigational data. "Question for you, Walt."

"Ask away," Peter heard in his headphones.

"You have kids, right? Two if I remember correctly."

"Yeah. A boy and a girl, just like you and Brinshou." Peter was impressed that Walt remembered Brin's Kootenai name. "Our two are a good bit older than yours. Kevin's twelve and Dee is nine. Why do you ask?"

"Well, I was just wondering. How do they deal with you being away from home so much? How do *you* handle it?"

"I've been doing this going on fifteen years so they're used to me being gone by now. They accept it as our way of life. Marlene is my queen, the greatest wife a guy could ever hope for. She keeps the household running smoothly and is independent by nature. Mar has a lot of serious hobbies to keep her entertained when I'm gone. The kids also keep her plenty busy."

"She doesn't work?"

"Oh, she works her pretty ass off. Being a housewife and mom is more than a fulltime job."

"True enough. Don't you miss her and your kids?"

"Ah, I see where this is coming from," Mingus said, eyeing Peter with the hint of a grin. "I believe Captain Lacroix has the homesick blues."

"No, I, uh . . ."

"It's okay, Pete. I get them, too, now and then. Especially when I'm missing one of Kev's soccer games. And last week I missed Dee's very first dance recital. She's my pretty little ballerina and I missed out on her big moment. That got me feeling the blues, let me tell ya."

"Yeah, I can relate," Peter said. "I FaceTime with Brin and the kids, but it's just not the same. I just want to lean into the screen and kiss my wife and reach out and hug the kids, but I can't. It's frustrating."

Mingus smiled knowingly. "True that. But what pulls me through is knowing the time away makes the time I'm home that much sweeter. It's strange, but being apart for long periods actually strengthens my marriage."

Peter thought about that. *It must be comforting to have that kind of relationship. Brin and I certainly don't roll that way. Hayden and Nora don't either.*

"Anyway," Mingus said, "we have discussed moving the family to Missoula when the new heliport opens there. Speaking of which, how is that project coming along?"

This was a sore subject with Peter. He had been making good progress on establishing a second heliport in Missoula up until three weeks ago when he had to start putting in a lot of overtime hours in Heart Butte. The new heliport close to his home in Florence would solve a lot of his own problems, but he couldn't get much done with Hayden and Nora being out of the loop.

"Unfortunately it's stalled right now," he said. "We've purchased a plot of land just outside of Lolo and gotten FAA approval. All the state and local permits have been filed. I finished drafting the blueprints and sent them to Hayden, but he's got other things on his mind these days. Until he and Nora get back in the fold, we can't move forward on site preparation and construction."

"Sorry to hear that."

"Yeah," Peter said. "At this rate we'll be lucky to be operational by Christmas, maybe not even until late spring. It's killing me commuting between Gilliam's Guidepost and home every weekend. That is, when I can get a weekend off. Those have been rare lately."

"How far is your commute?"

Peter frowned. "Two-hundred and fifty miles, as the crow flies."

Walt Mingus nodded his understanding. "It's about the same for me getting home to Bozeman. Flying cuts the trip down a good bit, but with this crazy schedule, neither chopper has been available on a weekend since mid-June."

They continued on, heading west, toward the Ruby River Valley. Mingus radioed dispatcher Nancy Diehl, updating her on their location. Peter listened to the static-drenched exchange as he took in the beauty spreading out below them.

They crossed over a high, open plateau before the land dropped dramatically into a valley of steep ridges, narrow draws, and dark patches of timber. Soon they were flying over a long green corridor that snaked toward Twin Bridges, widening into high country meadowlands. The Ruby River wound through cottonwood groves and sagebrush flats, a silvery thread against a patchwork of hay fields and rangeland. Pronghorn antelope scampered along a rocky bench trail a few hundred feet above the valley floor. A large herd of elk grazed in the foothills. They passed over the Ruby Reservoir, the surface a sparkling deep aquamarine, the dam's spillway flashing white in the morning light.

A strong crosswind pushed through the canyon and buffeted the aircraft. Peter checked the torque, Ng, TOT, and manifold pressure gauges. Out here, in a mountainous canyon, shifting winds could be deadly if the aircraft's power margins dropped below the safety line. Fortunately, all looked good.

The four geologists sitting in back were flying out here to do the on-the-ground work at a potential copper and silver mining site.

Beaumont Mining had done the preliminary survey work—the topographic, boundary, and mineral surveys—using satellite high-resolution imagery, drone aerial mapping, and radiometry. Having discovered a rich vein of copper, the company filed a claim with the Bureau of Land Management for drilling rights. Now, this week, Peter's four passengers were doing the required fieldwork, collecting rock and soil samples, and mapping out the dimensions of the site. The past two days Peter and Walt had watched the geologists head out wearing hardhats, goggles, and gloves, using rock hammers, chisels, shovels, pickaxes, and a small-core drilling machine to fill their collection bags with earth and stone chips. They jotted down findings in their field notebooks, speaking to each other in heavy mining jargon that, to Peter, might as well have been a foreign tongue. The engineers walked around endlessly, scanning the ground with various handheld instruments. Peter had asked what the portable devices were and he was told they were using X-ray florescence analyzers to evaluate the elemental composition of rocks, and laser scanners to generate 3D mapping models. They also used magnetometers to detect the presence of magnetite, a magnetic mineral that is often found clustered around large copper deposits.

As they neared the Beaumont Mining claim, Peter felt the dread coming on. Another long boring day sitting around engaging in small talk with Mingus while the geologists did their thing. Another day of listening to them jabber to each other in their acronym-laden, nearly incomprehensible language. Yes, he was being paid well, but the hours sitting idle at the site stretched out like days. Peter was a man of action. He didn't like sitting on his ass watching other people work. He'd much rather be out flying over Montana's panoramic landscapes.

Ruby River glistened off to their left. The claim site came into view, a pale scar tucked into the west side of the valley, just below the first step of the Gravelly Range. Peter checked conditions on the approach—density altitude 8,000 feet; variable crosswinds of 15 knots; power margin less than 10%. They were approaching the claim site in less than favorable conditions due to these high altitude airstreams.

He approached into the wind, keeping the aircraft low and shallow, regulating the descent rate. Powerful squalls bumped and tossed the chopper. Peter fought to keep on course, strong-arming the controls through three minutes of gusty winds. Then, as they dropped into the ravine, the ridgeline cut off the howling wind, and Peter could breathe easier. He brought the chopper down gently, the skids settling in loose dirt. The rotor blades whipped up spiraling clouds of dust.

He heard Walt's voice in his earphones. "Good work, Captain."

Peter pulled the throttle back to the closed position, shutting down the engine, then flipped the fuel valve switch to cut off the fuel supply and shut down the generator. The rotors slowed to a rhythmic *thump-thump-thump*, then stopped.

"I tip my hat to you, Pete," Mingus said. "You showed some crackerjack skills there, partner. You really greased the landing."

"Thanks. It's a lot more windy than yesterday. I hope none of our passengers crapped their pants back there."

Mingus snorted out a laugh, then radioed Nancy Diehl to confirm their safe landing.

Peter got on the intercom to inform the geologists they could unbuckle and move out. Not for the first time since he'd been flying for Fowler-Lemoyne Aviation, he was thankful for the privacy partition between the cockpit and passenger area. The barrier didn't come standard on Bell 407s, but Hayden and Nora thought it would be an attractive selling feature, ensuring clients maximum privacy during flights. Peter also liked the privacy wall as he wasn't fond of conversing with passengers while in the air.

Hayden and Nora had always placed a high priority on class and distinction. Their business model called for offering clients luxurious and elegant air transport. They had given Peter carte blanche when he was shopping for their two choppers (three when including the aircraft lost in the crash). In all three purchases he had gone with the deluxe 407GXi model that came with a VIP luxury interior suite. Fowler-Lemoyne copters were equipped with Italian leather seats and interior panels, plush carpeting, advanced noise reduction, and flat-screen TVs for inflight entertainment, as well as many other lavish amenities. Nora said from the beginning that Fowler-Lemoyne Aviation helicopters should offer customers the extravagance, comfort, and smooth ride of a Rolls Royce limousine. Bryan Gilliam, being the creative one of the partners, ran with it, coming up with a catchy slogan that had become the message behind their brand: *Fly Fowler-Lemoyne, the Rolls-Royce of helicopter transport. You'll think you're floating on a magic carpet.*

Peter heard garbled voices in back, bumping and clanking as the mining engineers gathered up their equipment and disembarked.

Mingus completed the post-flight log entries and looked at Peter. "Well, partner, another exciting day watching the eggheads do their thing."

Peter unbuckled and removed his headset. Peered through the windshield at the geologists walking through the settling dust, setting up their equipment. "Yeah, I can barely contain my enthusiasm," he said, shaking his head dejectedly.

Mingus removed his comm headgear. "I feel your pain, Pete. Good thing we're getting paid well for this charter. Look at the bright side. Only two more days of this tedium."

"*Three*, counting today."

"Cheer up, partner," Mingus said, tapping him on the shoulder. He opened his door to get out. "I've gotta stretch these old legs of mine. You coming?"

"I'll be along soon. I wanna give Brin a call."

He checked his watch and saw it was close to when Brin usually took her lunch break at the store. He pulled the satellite phone from the dash-mounted cradle and punched in her number.

She answered after two rings. "Petey!" she called out enthusiastically. "To what do I owe this unexpected call?" His wife's ebullience lifted him from his doldrums.

"Hi, hon. We just touched down out here in God's country and I wanted to hear your voice. How're things at Brinshou's Baubles and Jewelry today?"

"Really good. *Great*, actually. We sold that mahogany obsidian bison piece with the hematite inclusions you said you liked. The one with the hand carved jasper horns."

"Wow, that's fantastic, hon. How much did you get for it?"

"Five grand, before tax. And if that wasn't enough good fortune, we also sold a diamond western stirrup pendant for four thousand, and a gold apple ring with Montana sapphires and diamond accents for six thousand."

"Fifteen grand? A banner morning for the shop."

"Yes! This is the best day we've had since we had that stock of Cretaceous meteorite jewelry. Nuna, Luanna, and me are ecstatic. We're planning to celebrate after we close tonight. Drinks and dinner at the Top Hat."

"That's wonderful, babe," he said, her excitement boosting him up. "Just be careful with the drinking."

"We've got it covered. Luanna doesn't partake in the evil alcohol. She's our designated driver."

"What about the kids?"

"Oh, they're not old enough to drink," she said with a breathy giggle.

Peter chuckled. "You're a scream, Brin."

"Mother is taking care of Jacob and Kimi tonight. I swear, she has been going above and beyond the call of duty. I don't know where I'd be without her."

"Yeah, Kachina is the gift that keeps on giving," he said. "She seems reborn since she got clear of your asshole father."

"Please, let's not bring that man into the conversation. I'm in too good of a mood for Nash Taleka. What I *do* want to talk about is when you'll be getting back home again."

"Soon. *Very* soon." He wanted to switch topics. "How are the kids? Is Jake sleeping better?"

"Not really. Jacob's first teeth are coming in and he's been waking up at all hours crying in pain. Mother and I take turns rubbing his gums, which seems to comfort him for a few hours."

"His first teeth, eh? Sorry I'm missing that."

"No you're not, Peter Lacroix," Brin said, teasingly. "Don't hand me that nonsense."

"How about Kimi? Is she eating better?"

"Hardly. I can't pay her to eat her scrambled eggs or oatmeal.

She turns her nose up at those every breakfast. Says they're yucky. The only things she'll eat in the morning are Pop Tarts and Fruity Pebbles."

"We've got to get her off all that sugar."

"*We*, Peter?"

That one stung. "Okay, fair enough."

"Kimi will eat bananas and blueberries and cheese and crackers for snacks. But the only meat she'll eat is chicken nuggets. I made her a vegetable puree blended into a smoothie last night and she made a big scene like she was about ready to puke."

"Well, that's our darling little diva. I'd say it's all pretty typical for a three-year-old, Brin."

"I worry she's gonna starve to death."

Peter smiled. *My wife, the worrywart.* "Kimi is *not* going to starve, love."

"Well, she certainly isn't getting balanced nutrition. I think she has an eating disorder, Peter."

"She does *not* have an eating disorder," Peter said, his exasperation coming through. "She's a three-year-old child. Her tastes will expand as she matures."

"You think so?"

"I *know* so."

"I think part of her eating problem is that her father isn't around much. Every day Kimi asks, Mummy, where's Dada? When will Dada be home?' I wanna sing with Dada and Mizz Way-chill."

Hearing that brought on the guilt trip.

Okay, it's time to let Brin in on what I've been thinking.

"Well, I might have a solution."

"Really?" she said, a hopeful lilt in her voice.

"Yeah. I've been giving it a lot of thought lately. Simply put, I miss you and the kids more than I can put into words. I'm beginning to think maybe this job isn't for me anymore. Sure, the money and benefits are great. But I'm so unhappy being away from you."

"You sound really down."

"I am, yes, but—"

"You're not back on the oxy are you?"

"Oh, hell no! How could you even say that to me, Brin? That shit is ancient history to me. Just hear me out, okay?"

"Okay. Sorry. My bad. Go ahead, love."

"What would you think about me going back to my old job?"

"At the Forest Service? Working for Gary Ralston?"

"Yeah. I'd be home every night."

"I would absolutely *love* that. But wait. Aren't they mostly using drones now?"

"I don't know. I haven't spoken with Gary since he called to cuss me out for stealing his employees last year."

"I forgot about that. How do you think Ralston will respond?"

"Don't know, Brin. Maybe you shouldn't get your hopes up."

"Would you be happy operating drones? I know how much you hated that before."

"I've gotten to the point where I would be happy doing *anything* that would keep me close to you and the kids. Keep in mind it would mean a cut in pay. A mighty *big* cut."

"We'll manage," she said. "We always have. But what about Hayden and Nora. How do you think they'll feel? They've been awfully good to us."

"Screw Hayden and Nora! They ran off to do their own things and dumped all company business on Bryan and me. I recruited and trained four very competent pilots for them. This is an opportune time to leave. Fowler-Lemoyne Aviation will be fine without me."

"I love you so much, baby. Thanks for doing this."

"I love you, too, but I haven't done anything yet. I'll call Gary Saturday, after this dreadful mining charter finishes up, and see what's up with the Forest Service these days. I'll let you know how it goes. I'd better let you get back to your work. Give Jake a kiss for me and tell Kimi I'm thinking about her. Tell her I'll be back soon for singalongs with Ms. Rachel. Take care, honey."

"You, too, love. Be safe."

"Always."

He disconnected and jumped down out of the chopper, feeling a thousand pounds lighter.

Twitchy Eye and Mr. Chill

July 25: Absaroka-Beartooth Wilderness

Northern Wyoming

MICK PRESCOTT WAS HAPPY TO BE BACK out in the wide open spaces. He and Claire had finally escaped the mildewed confines of the tumbledown hunting shack where they had been holed up the past ten days.

A week and a half hiding from state and federal wildlife agents thanks to that two-faced asshole, Hayden Fowler.

Fowler had the gall to report them to the authorities.

After all we did for him.

Mick discovered through sources on the dark web that Fowler had contacted Montana Fish and Wildlife, informing them of the illegal dinosaur trafficking operation the Prescotts had going. FWP had issued a BOLO on their Ford Transit van, their Colorado plates tracked back to their Denver home address. Two-plus years of successfully evading state wildlife authorities, and now he and Claire were directly in the crosshairs of the law. And now the feds were in on the hunt as well. He and Claire were wanted for questioning about the human body parts they had seen the pterosaurs bringing back to the Whisperer's highland ranch. Mick wasn't surprised to learn Whisperer's villa had been raided. The falconer and his employees had been taken into custody, and the Quetzals were rounded up. What did surprise him, however, were their dinosaur-trapping competitors who were angry at them for their part in bringing the law out in big numbers. One anonymous tracker had even posted *You'd best be watching your backs!*

All because Fowler had blown the whistle on them.

Asshole!

So they had shut down their operations and gone into hiding. They took Forest Service roads to the Wyoming border where they stashed the van in a thick grove of lodgepole pine, then hiked until they found the dilapidated hunting cabin. Sagging leaky roof, bullet-tattooed walls, family of chittering raccoons nesting under the floor-boards. No electricity or running water. They lived by lantern light and water from a nearby creek. The deplorable conditions were enough to crush anyone's spirit.

Throughout the first week, they frequently heard helicopters and planes flying overhead, but the abundant forest kept them shielded. They avoided detection in what Mick called their *little outhouse in the woods.* After an interminable week, aircraft traffic finally dwindled. They waited it out another three days before Mick reasoned it was safe to venture out and get back to work.

They'd thought about returning home to Denver. But that trip would expose them over a 550-mile route through the entirety of Wyoming. And it would be risky to return to their Denver residence; their license plate that Fowler reported had sent authorities there. Their work was here, along the Continental Divide in Montana and Idaho. This is where the money was to be made. They had client business to honor, and the only place to do that was here.

After leaving the shack, they risked driving twenty-five miles to a no-tell motel near Bozeman. It had been an unnerving twenty minutes out in the open, with Mick white-knuckling the wheel and Claire watching the skies for Fish and Game aircraft. They paid cash for a cramped room that smelled strongly of disinfectant and insecticide. Far from world class accommodations, but still a huge step up from the hunting shack. They also rented a car to take them to and from their hidden van. They had work to do and couldn't remain on the lam anymore, regardless of the risk. They were a week behind in satisfying a contract for a pair of Dromaeosaurs and had to make a move. Mick called their contract employees—Ray Yount and Max Baker. Gave them instructions on where to meet and what to bring.

The Prescott trapping team was back in action for the first time in two weeks, chasing Dromaeosaurs in the Custer-Gallatin National Forest. The van sat in the shade of a thick stand of cottonwood, well concealed from any searching aircraft (fortunately the skies had been quiet all day). Mick perched on the front bumper cradling a tranquilizer rifle while Claire trained her binoculars on a trio of Dromes they had tracked to a small pond. Cicadas and grasshoppers buzzed. A soft breeze blew through the trees making a rustling, clattering sound. Yount and Baker were two-hundred yards down shore, in their line of sight, both shouldering tranq guns, still as statues and well cloaked in a thicket of brush.

Mick watched the Dromes drinking from the pond, the three of them lowering their narrow snouts to the water. They flicked the surface with their glistening pink tongues, lapping up the water in darting, birdlike motions. One of them glanced up, golden eyes alert, nostrils flaring, testing the air for trouble. Mick thought the creature might have picked up their scent, but then it bent and resumed drinking.

He knew from experience that Dromes could go days without water, then gorge themselves to rehydrate. The best time to take them down was when they finished replenishing their fluids. They tended to be lethargic after hydrating, taking away their lightning-fast quickness and making them easier targets. Sticking them with a tranq dart when they were bloated got the tranquilizer into their systems more quickly and made the capture easier, which could sometimes be dicey. But they had to be careful not to hit them while the creatures were wading in the shallows. The xylazine-ketamine mix they used was quick acting, and Dromes were susceptible to drowning if they went down in the water. It had happened once last summer on Avalanche Lake in the Northern Rockies.

As Mick watched them drink, his thoughts returned to their experience with Hayden Fowler. Two weeks ago, following their trip to the Quetzal Whisperer's mountain sanctuary, they had dropped Fowler off where he was staying at the Darmont Hotel. Fowler had wanted to travel with them to Laramie to deliver the Quetzalcoatlus to the Prescotts' client. But Mick didn't want the world renowned paleontologist and bestselling author anywhere near their client. His presence at the delivery site would only hurt future business, especially with the bad blood currently being directed at the Prescotts over the dark web.

He and Claire got along well with Fowler in the beginning, quickly striking up an easy alliance. Like lifelong friends it had seemed. But all that changed when Claire let it be known that they had witnessed Quetzals bringing bloody human body parts back to Whisperer's sanctuary. Fowler became argumentative, the three of them getting into a shouting match on the ride down the mountain.

In hindsight, Mick thought it would probably have served them better to keep that information close to the vest. He still hadn't gotten over his irritation with Claire for bringing it up. He loved her, but she often ran her mouth before thinking things through.

Mick had entertained thoughts of killing Fowler. But those thoughts quickly evaporated into nothing more than fleeting morbid fantasies. Mick knew he was no murderer. He was a pacifist. He couldn't kill another human being no matter how much he wanted to. And even if he could, killing a high profile celebrity would only bring them more trouble. Much *bigger* trouble.

Claire's whisper brought him out of his reverie. "I think Ray and Max are happy to be back at work."

"Aren't we all," Mick said with a tired smile. "Another day in that outhouse in the woods and I would have been ready for the loony bin."

"You and me both." She lowered the binocs, letting them dangle on the strap. Glanced at him. "Do you really think this is a good life for us, Mickey? Running from the law? Living in the forest like unwashed survivalists?"

"We made a bundle on that Quetzalcoatlus sale." He pointed his rifle at the pond. "And those Dromaeosaurs are going to net us another few hundred grand. So I'd say yes, this is a *great* life."

"Well, I'm tired of living like a pioneer woman. Tired of being considered outlaws and having to always watch our backs. It's exhausting. What good is money if we have to live like this?"

Mick was dying for a smoke. Cigarettes were his stress reducer.

But no way could he light up this close to their prey. Dromes had a keen sense of smell. One whiff of cigarette smoke and they would be gone in a flash.

"You signed up for this, Claire," he said. "You've been saying for three summers now that you're with me on this."

"I know, but I miss our house and our comfortable bed. I miss our Denver friends. I miss living like normal human beings, Mick."

He took his cigarette pack out of his pocket and shook one out, lipped it. The unlit smoke dangled from his mouth. The feel of it there soothed him.

"Tell me Claire, what other profession pays this well for eight months work a year? We've got the winter months together in Denver, that is when we're not spending our hard earned cash on luxury cruises. I'd say we've got it pretty good."

"You don't hear what I'm saying, Mickey," she said with a pout.

Mick turned back to the slurping Dromaeosaurs, a sadness blooming in his chest. His wife was slowly checking out on him and their lucrative business. She had become increasingly bitchy about their dinosaur trapping as the summer wore on. But he knew anything he said right now would only throw another log on the fire of her burning discontent.

Damn, I wish I could fire up this smoke!

Then, suddenly, three quick gunshots exploded behind them.

BOOM-BOOM-BOOM—a crashing sound like a roll of thunder.

Mick ducked and slid off the front bumper, kneeled behind the van, his head on a swivel, his senses in overdrive, watching disconsolately as the Dromaeosaurs bounded into the forest.

What the hell?

His mind raced.

His heart punched like an erratic piston.

He peered around the side of the van, pointing his rifle into the trees, searching for the shooter. Couldn't pick up any movement. It suddenly dawned on him that he was defenseless; a rifle loaded with a tranquilizer dart might as well be a BB gun.

Keeping his eyes on the forest behind the van, he called out, "Claire? You all right, baby?"

No response.

He looked around frantically. Under the van. Around the sides of the van.

And then he saw her, lying face down in the dirt, two bullet wounds seeping blood from her back.

Lots of *flowing* blood.

Fear gripped him in a stranglehold.

"Claire?" he whisper-shouted. "You okay, baby? Talk to me!"

No response. No movement. She didn't appear to be breathing.

Oh, please, God, NO! Fuck, no! SHIT NO! Don't check out on me, baby! Please, Lord, don't let this be happening! Please don't take her from me!

His breaths came in wild, ragged gasps.

His pulse thrummed in his ears.

His sight dimmed and a wave of dizziness knocked him down on his knees. He wanted to go to her but he couldn't move.

He heard boots crunching through the duff.

Multiple boots. Approaching.

Mick glanced at his motionless wife, the entire backside of her blouse now blood-soaked. He was close to losing his shit.

A hoarse voice called out to him. "Come out from behind the vehicle. NOW!"

He was trapped. There was no way out. His only hope was Yount and Baker coming to his rescue. He prayed for them to find the courage to rush in and save him.

Two more shots slammed into the van's rear doors with loud *THUNK-THUNK* thuds. A third shot tore out a chunk of earth near Claire.

"You've got five seconds. Toss your weapon and come out."

Mick was shivering, though the day was quite warm. He heard footsteps crunching through the underbrush, getting closer.

He couldn't breathe. *Where are Yount and Baker?*

He tossed his rifle onto a strip of pinegrass. He stood, unsteady on his feet. Took a deep breath and walked out into view, hands held high, arms shaky, a fierce quiver running through his legs.

He faced two disheveled men in their mid-twenties. Both with military style buzzcuts. Dressed head-to-boots in full camo fatigues. Both aiming long guns at him.

Mick's voice cracked as he asked, "*Please*, will you allow me to help my wife?"

"There's no need, dude. She's dead. Your wife is on her way to hell where she belongs."

The talker had a noticeable twitch in his left eye. He was jumpy, skittish, a look of deadly intent etched on his narrow face as he stamped his feet nervously. His partner stood next to him, calm and collected, staring at Mick with an unsettling glacial stillness.

These killers aiming their rifles at him were a double vision nightmare. Mick felt helpless, lost. Scared and vulnerable. His eyes blurred with tears. His dear sweet e-Claire lay dead behind him, gunned down by these two unhinged lunatics.

A furious anger took hold, pushing him to voice his resentment and outrage. "You fucktards murdered my wife! Jesus Christ, you're a couple of whack job psychos."

Twitchy Eye spoke. "I'd watch how you talk to us if'n I was you, dude."

Mick tried to tamp down his rage, realizing he needed to keep Twitchy Eye talking and give Yount and Baker time to get here. He pointed behind him at Claire's body. "Why'd you kill her? You didn't know her."

Mr. Chill entered the conversation, his voice quiet and calm. "Oh, we know her quite well, Prescott."

His name coming from the mouth of this deranged stranger was surreal.

"We've known about your wife and you for a while. You are animal abusers. You torture these prehistoric treasures for ludicrous profits. Shoot 'em up with your paralyzing drugs and cart them off to the highest bidder where they live trapped in inhumane conditions so wealthy pricks can show them off and brag to their equally disgustingly rich friends how special they are. You and wifey are capitalist pigs, Prescott. We sent your wife to hell and you will be joining her shortly."

Mick felt a lump form in his throat. A bead of sweat trickled down his back. He could no longer control his outrage. "You're *insane*. Just a couple of worthless, maniacal assholes." He trembled uncontrollably, feeling like he was in the throes of an emotional and physical breakdown.

Twitchy Eye spoke again. "You're pushing your luck, Prescott."

"Who the fuck are you?" Mick sobbed, spilling tears.

"We were sent by Leonard Sheridan of the AEF," Mr. Chill said calmly.

"Who the hell is Leonard Sheridan?"

"Mr. Sheridan is one of the supreme leaders of the Animal Emancipation Faction," Twitchy Eye answered. "He was wrongly convicted and serving time in Montana State for doing the right thing two years ago, freeing imprisoned dinosaurs."

"You mean the guy who led the invasion on that rancher who had the dinosaur zoo up north of here?"

"One and the same, yeah," Mr. Chill said. "A rancher named Gilliam who was working with the feds, torturing those poor creatures. And it wasn't an invasion. It was a *liberation*. Mr. Sheridan is a great man. He has put the AEF on the map. He's one of the top architects of change, leading the charge in stamping out animal abuse and eliminating those who choose to partake in the practice."

Mr. Chill's meaning wasn't lost on Mick, who was close to pissing his pants. "Uh—*eliminating*?"

"Yeah, eliminating," Twitchy Eye said, shaking his rifle at Mick. "Mr. Sheridan sent us to rid the world of you and your wife. Time to join your beloved Ms. Claire in the deep dark abyss. Goodbye, Mr. Prescott."

"Please, please, *please* . . . have mercy on me," Mick pleaded.

The first shot clipped Mick in the shoulder, the second in the chest. A burning pain ripped through him as he went down. A third shot slammed into his back.

His vision faded. His consciousness dimmed.

The last thing Mick Prescott saw before he died was Ray Yount shooting Twitchy Eye in the ass with a tranq dart, and Yount and Baker chasing the two AEF vigilantes into the woods.

The Hunter Killer

July 28: Mathews Investigations

100 North 27th Street

Billings, Montana

MIKE MATHEWS SAT AT HIS BATTERED OAK DESK watching the passing traffic from his third floor office window. A hook-and-ladder fire truck passed, its horn blasting a clear-the-way warning. The MTN Afternoon News played on a small flat-screen at low volume on the far wall. Longtime anchorwoman Amelia Hatcher's mellifluous voice floated through the room like a spoken word song. Clips of an ongoing phone conversation drifted in from the reception area, his personal assistant Naomi Newell taking care of business.

He checked the time on his laptop: 4:33.

That late? Where did this day disappear to?

He had enjoyed an extended lunch, wining and dining a potential client at Jake's Downtown Bar and Grill. He was paying for it now, finding it difficult to concentrate on his case notes. Jake's sourdough baguettes with hot crab dip and bison medallions served over garlic mashed potatoes always did this to him. Made him feel logy and unmotivated. The day drinking only added to it; a couple of three-finger bourbon blackberry smashes always put him off his game.

Though he was fuzzyheaded and unfocused, Mathews thought his "lost" afternoon had been worth it. He had signed the client, Sam Nettlebaum, whose wife of fourteen years had disappeared after cleaning out their joint bank accounts. She had taken all of her jewelry and two suitcases, but had left her phone, credit cards, and passport behind. Strange. Intriguing. Just the kind of case Mathews could get into. He would be assisting the Billings Police Department in the search for Jessica Nettlebaum.

He wanted (needed?) an investigative challenge now that the Gilliam case was stalled. Mathews was waiting on results of blood samples scraped from the taxidermy shop knives and saws confiscated during the execution of the search warrant. It was a source of extreme frustration with Mathews as the lab worked at a glacial pace. But until those blood results were in, he had done all he could for Bryan and Loretta Gilliam.

More than two weeks had passed since Mathews' prison visit with Leonard Sheridan. The AEF leader had admitted to his association with the taxidermist, Kyle Birnham. Did that relationship involve setting up Stimson's murder? Did it involve planning a hit on Bryan Gilliam? Sheridan wasn't saying. Nor was Birnham, who was still being held at the Flathead County Detention Center, and hadn't uttered more than two words since being incarcerated there. Prison officials had Sheridan on recordings using amateurish code language to set up the snuff of Bryan Gilliam, but those calls didn't go to Birnham. Both had gone to burner phones and were untraceable, which was most unfortunate. And Sheridan wasn't about to blow the whistle on any of his associates. The man was already serving thirty years with little chance of parole, so why would he cooperate? Mathews had not been able to obtain a formal confession from Sheridan. Certainly nothing that would stand up in court. But the AEF leader's volatile reaction was affirmation in his mind that Sheridan had the necessary motive and reach to kill Chogan Stimson and threaten the Gilliam family.

If only I could have recorded our conversation.

Despite the known contract put out on Bryan Gilliam, there had been no more threats to the Gilliam family since the mid-June Stimson murder. Was it possible that taxidermist Birnham had been Bryan Gilliam's selected executioner and it all had been called off after Birnham's arrest. Mathews didn't really think so. He thought Birnham was probably the one behind the beheadings, but didn't think the man was a murderer, even if he was a hemorrhoidal asshole.

Bryan Gilliam had asked him numerous times: "Why'd they go after Chogan and not me and Loretta?" The answer was simple, really. Chogan Stimson was more accessible than the Gilliams. He and the other ranch hand, Apisi Lyttle, spent a lot of time out in the pastures with the Gilliams' half-dozen horses. They were easier targets than Bryan and Loretta, who were protected by a security detail that would do Fort Knox proud. The family had round-the-clock perimeter patrols, motion detection cameras at key points around the property, and personal bodyguards for each member of the family. The best 24/7 security money could buy. And the Gilliams had piles of money for private security.

Things were under lock and key at Gilliam's Guidepost right now. Mathews felt confident they were safe to the point where he could work his other cases.

But the long stretch between threats at the Heart Butte ranch still left him uneasy. *Are we in the calm before the storm? Will whoever Sheridan tapped to kill Bryan Gilliam make their move soon?*

He yawned and leaned back in his chair. Stretched his arms and flexed his fingers, glancing around the office, his workplace for the past ten years. The walls were lined with framed photos of Montana landscapes: the Yellowstone River swollen during a spring flood; the Beartooth Mountains under a carpet of snow; Flathead Lake with Wild Horse Island centered in front of a dazzling sunset. He looked at the faded clipping from the *Billings Gazette* announcing his first case, a black-and-white photo of himself ten years younger, smiling under the bold headline. It had been a cheating spouse case that embarrassed him now. But he owed a lot to that newspaper interview. It had launched his PI business, the local exposure bringing him a stream of lucrative cases. A tall metal filing cabinet sat below the rows of picture frames, the four drawers labeled in yellowed masking tape: *Active, Closed, Unsolved, Personal.* He and Naomi always seemed to have more important business than digitizing the copious stacks of paper documentation. A Keurig coffee machine sat on an end table next to a mini-fridge. A conversation pit with three chairs and a couch took up the far wall. Nothing fancy or ostentatious, but the two-room office was comfortable and tidy enough to meet with clients. These walls and the squeaky flooring held many memories.

Naomi entered from the front room, purse strapped across her shoulder. "I'm calling it a day, Mike. Heading home to fix dinner for my lazy ass hubby."

He flinched, the suddenness of her entrance yanking him out of his contemplations. "You should really teach Herb how to cook."

"No way," she said, waving him off. "He's a lost cause. Anything my Herbie made would taste like charred roadkill."

Mathews laughed. "My stomach just did a back flip. Thanks for planting that image in my head, Nay."

"Anytime," she said with a crafty smile.

"I guess it's time for me to call it a day, too. Thanks for your work putting that dossier together for me."

"I enjoyed it. Makes me feel like a spy in one of those *Mission Impossible* movies. That Carruthers fella is a pretty strange character."

"That he is. We get all kinds here. Keeps things interesting."

"Sure does. Have a good evening. See ya tomorrow, boss."

No sooner had the door closed behind his Girl Friday than his attention was drawn to the TV and Amelia Hatcher's news report.

> ". . . Breaking News! The Dinosaur Hunter Killer has struck again, but his murder spree might finally be at an end. And is it possible these hunter murders might have been the work of a team and not a solo operator as first suspected? On Saturday, the infamous hunter of hunters claimed two more victims in the Absaroka-Beartooth Wilderness area, thirty miles north of the Wyoming border. The victims have been identified as Michael and Claire Prescott of Denver, ages thirty-nine and thirty-seven. The deceased were known dinosaur traffickers, and were wanted for questioning by authorities about the illegal transport and sale of a large winged pterosaur—a Quetzalcoatlus—and their relationship with a reclusive falconer named Stanley

Murchison, aka, the Quetzal Whisperer.

"Two of the Prescotts' associates—Raymond Yount and Maximilian Baker—were working on the other side of a small pond trying to trap Dromaeosaurs when the murders occurred. According to Yount, they hustled to the murder scene to find not one, but *two* killers, sitting on the bumper of the Prescotts' van, laughing, their guard down as they gloated over bundles of large denomination bills in a duffel bag. Armed with only tranquilizer guns, Yount and Baker managed to bring down one of the killers, Scott Hammond, twenty-eight, of Boise, by shooting him in his backside with a powerful sedation dart as they chased him through the forest. The second killer got away unscathed.

"As if this story isn't bizarre enough, it takes an even more strange turn. When Hammond woke from his sedation sleep, he bragged about his killings that he claimed were ordered by none other than Leonard Sheridan, a convict who is currently serving a thirty-year sentence at Montana State for his involvement in the invasion and destruction of Gilliam's Guidepost Ranch in Heart Butte two years ago. Sheridan was a top lieutenant with the Animal Emancipation Faction, an animal rights activist group the FBI has identified as a domestic terrorist organization. Our viewers might recall our coverage of those crimes that took place at the famous ranch where the first dinosaur hatchlings were housed. Sixteen people lost their lives that day as the AEF stormed the ranch with bulldozers rolling and guns blazing, setting free the captive dinosaurs.

"The Prescotts were murdered with thirty caliber magnum bullets fired from a Barrett MRAD rifle, matching the weapon and ammo used in the other six hunter murders. Scott Hammond is being held at the Park County Detention Center in Livingston. Any doubts that he was at least one of the shooters in the previous murders were cleared up when he claimed credit for them and boasted that he was proud to be a member of a worthwhile organization like the AEF. Despite pressure from Park County sheriff's deputies and the FBI, Hammond has not revealed the identity of his homicidal partner in crime, though it is thought his accomplice was also a member of the AEF. And though many would see Raymond Yount and Maximilian Baker as being heroes for their roles in bringing down one of the dino hunter killers, they both are also being held at the Park County facility for violation of the Montana Endangered Species Act amendment, which outlaws the trapping, sale, or killing of Cretaceous reptiles. We have learned the two men are refusing to cooperate with Montana Fish and Wildlife agents in turning over information about other exotic animal traffickers in the state. We here at MTN News will keep you informed of new developments as we get them.

"In a somewhat related news story, Montana and Idaho wildlife agents are reporting an alarming number of dinosaur carcasses throughout the two states, killed not by hunters or predators, but dying from some unspecified disease. Experts are unsure at this point if the disease is viral or bacterial in nature. If you see a dead dinosaur, stay clear of it. It is not known at this time if the disease they carry is transmissible to humans. For more on this developing story we go to Christy Clark, Director of Montana Fish, Wildlife and Parks ..."

Mathews shut off the TV, an adrenaline spike zapping him. Scott Hammond was one of the names brought up by Special Agents Vasquez and Borden of the FBI Joint Terrorism Task Force at Gilliam's Guidepost a month ago. Could Hammond and his AWOL accomplice have been involved in Chogan Stimson's murder? Did Leonard Sheridan tap either one or both to snuff Bryan Gilliam?

And just who is Hammond's partner who got away?

Mathews knew he had to get to the Park County Detention Center to interview Hammond. He was sure there were lots of answers there.

He picked up his cell phone and punched in Bryan Gilliam's number. Waited for him to pick up.

"Hey, Mike. Long time no hear. What's up?"

Mathews said, "Have you heard the news?"

"Naw, I don't follow the news anymore. Too much of a downer."

"Well it looks like we might have found Chogan's killer. And maybe the hitman who has you in his crosshairs."

"Really?"

"Yeah," he said, his excitement building. "Too much to go into now. I've got a little more digging to do. We'll talk soon."

Homeward Bound

July 29: Gilliam's Guidepost Heliport Offices
Heart Butte, Montana

THE HANGAR WAS DESERTED THIS NOON HOUR. No high-pitched whines of pneumatic drills or clanking hammers in the maintenance bay. No staticky radio communications coming from the dispatch room. No whirring swish of chopper rotor blades or the roar of revving engines. Carl and Nancy were out at lunch with Bryan (accompanied by a pair of bodyguards), and the four other pilots were out on chartered flights, leaving Peter alone in his office.

A perfect opportunity to make his pitch to his former boss Gary Ralston. Time to see if he could get his old job back with the Forest Service.

He had FaceTimed with Brin this morning and she had boosted his confidence, telling him Gary just *had* to take him back because Peter was the best pilot the Montana Forest Service had ever employed. But now that he was about to make the call, much of that morning self-assurance had abandoned him.

His hands shook as he punched in Ralston's number on his cell phone, putting it on speaker so he didn't have to hold it to his ear.

Why is this so difficult?

One ring . . . two rings . . .

His palms were sweaty.

He found it hard to swallow. *Come on, man, get your act together!*

Third ring . . .

"Peter, you old rotorhead you," Ralston answered, a friendly articulation in his voice. "How have you been? Making millions with that startup outfit?"

Doesn't sound like he's holding a grudge. That's a good sign.

"Hey, Gary. No, not millions, but I'm doing well. How about you?"

"I'm good. Thanks for asking. Hey, I read about you saving those church hikers. That was some good flying, bud."

"I didn't *save* anybody. That was a lot of journalistic hype."

"Ah, Peter Lacroix. Mister Modesty, as always."

"Yeah, maybe so."

"So, what's it been? A year or more since I last heard from you?" Ralston said. "I seem to recall the last time we spoke it was me cussing you out for stealing two of my best employees,"

"Well, I still don't see what I did was *stealing* per se. I—"

"Let's not beat around the bush here, Peter. I'm a busy man. What do you want?"

The harshness in Ralston's voice hit him like a slap in the face. "Um, well . . . I called wanting to crawl back into your good graces, Gary," he said, embarrassed by his obsequiousness. "I think I made a big mistake last year leaving the Service, and—"

"You're right. It was a *huge* mistake on your part."

"I know. But I want to come back and fly for you again."

"Really? Why?"

"Because my current job keeps me two-hundred and fifty miles from my wife and kids most of the time. Because two of my business partners in this venture have flown the coop and dumped the business end of things on me and the other partner. It means sixty-hour work weeks and total exhaustion. That's a recipe for an air disaster."

"Yeah, about that. I heard about your crash, Pete. Did overwork and exhaustion cause that?"

"No—*no*! That was back before things got really insane around here. We ran into a pack of aggressive pterosaurs. I did the best I could to save us."

"Have you recovered from it?"

"You know as well as I do a pilot never fully recovers from a devastating crash. I went through some rough times. A long stretch of hell, to be honest. But I'm back on track now. I really miss flying for you, Gary. And I'm really unhappy where I'm at now. I've been flying some of the most boring charters you could ever imagine. I just got done piloting a weeklong charter for mining company engineers. Let me tell you, that kind of—"

"Look, Pete, I feel for you. I really do. I would like nothing more than to have you back with us, but the reality is that the feds have sliced and diced our funding. This administration has cut us to the bone, the pompous bastards! Apparently they don't think our forests and national parks are all that important. I've had to lay off two pilots and cut our UAS drone operations in half. Sorry, bud, but no can do."

Peter's entire soul plummeted. He tried to talk but his vocal cords wouldn't cooperate. All he could produce was a hiss of air.

"I wish I could help you out, Pete. I'd love to have somebody with your skills and experience, but I just can't swing it right now. But please keep in touch."

He found his voice, but it was a weak mumble. "Sure, Gary. Thanks for hearing me out."

He disconnected and sat, stunned, unable to move. Why had he thought for even a millisecond that he had a sliver of a chance?

This will absolutely slay Brin. I never should have told her about calling Ralston.

"What's the matter, Lacroix? We're not good enough for you here at Fowler-Lemoyne Aviation?"

Peter looked up, startled to see Hayden Fowler lurking in the doorway, all six-feet-four-inches of him. Standing there with his arms crossed and an accusatory look on his face.

"Hayden?" he said, blushing. "How much of that did you hear?"

"All of it," Hayden said matter-of-factly. He scratched at his beard, judgment in his countenance.

"So you were, um . . . you were *eavesdropping*?"

"Not eavesdropping. Just being polite and not interrupting your phone call."

"Wh-what are you doing here? I thought you were in Idaho tracking down diseased dinosaurs."

"I was. But I figured it was time to get back to the company that bears my name. As you so eloquently stated, I 'flew the coop' and 'dumped the business' on you and Gilliam," he said, pantomiming air quotes with his big hands to emphasize Peter's words.

Hayden entered and took a seat in front of Peter's desk. Peter scooted his chair back as Hayden appeared larger and more intimidating than usual in the confines of his small office.

Hayden peered at him, his forehead wrenched into a frown. "You know, it's disrespectful to talk trash about your business partners to people outside the organization. You shouldn't go behind peoples' backs, Lacroix. It'll come back to bite you in the ass."

"Uh, look, Hayden, I uh, I didn't mean to—"

"And it's wrong to discuss our charters with anybody."

Peter squirmed in his seat as Hayden glared at him. The big man could be most menacing up close like this. He looked away from Hayden's angry visage, and said, "B-but I didn't mention the name of the mining company. Or any location."

"Doesn't matter. It was sloppy and unprofessional."

Peter met Hayden's stern gaze, feeling a stabbing sensation in his gut—part fear, part anger. He had tangled with some ruffian thugs on skates during his short-lived professional hockey career, but none of those brawlers came close to knocking Peter off his axis the way Hayden Fowler could do when he was in one of his *put-down-Peter-Lacroix* moods.

Seeing that I probably just orchestrated my termination, it's time to go for broke. "Can I ask you something, Hayden?"

"Sure. Shoot."

"We've never discussed this before but here goes." Peter took a deep breath. "Do you blame me for the crash? Is that why you're always on my case?"

"Say *what?* Are you shittin' me, Lacroix? You're the main reason I'm still alive. Any lesser pilot than you at the controls when we hit that flock of Quetzalcoatlus, and neither you nor I would be here having this conversation. I'm obviously not a chopper pilot, but I know enough to know it was your skills in the cockpit that saved us. I'm extremely grateful."

"Then why do you always ride me? I don't ever see you getting on Bryan like that."

"Christ, Pete. You gotta toughen up some. You're too goddamned sensitive for your own good. I give Gilliam plenty of grief. He just takes it better than you."

"Why do you have to give either of us any grief?"

"Because that's just the way I'm wired. I expect a lot out of the people I work with. Sometimes I go overboard. You should know by now not to take it personally."

"Well, I do," he said, his ire rising. "It's disrespectful."

"Wow, Lacroix, just *wow*," Hayden said, brushing his hair back off his shoulders in a dramatic gesture of disappointment.

"Are you, uh . . . are you going to fire me, Hayden?"

Hayden burst into a peal of laughter. "*Fire* you? Jesus, relax, Pete. I'm just busting your balls. Having some fun with you. You make it easy with the way you're so serious all the time. Lighten up. Enjoy life. And please know I couldn't fire you even if I wanted to. You're an equal partner. You own a quarter of this company."

"Really? It doesn't feel like it most of the time," Peter said, his anger building again. From their very first meeting two years ago, Hayden had always treated him like an underling, lording his fame and fortune over him, taking every opportunity to jab at him. To belittle him. And this kind of bullshit really hit him where it hurt, especially after just having been slammed by his old Forest Service boss.

"Look, I'm sorry about picking on you," Hayden said. "You are extremely valuable to this company, Lacroix. I really appreciate the way you and Gilliam have taken over in my and Nora's absence. I've noticed all the hours you've been putting in, the way you're managing the other pilots. I came back to give you a raise and tell you to take a couple of weeks off to recharge. Go home and be with Brin. Really be present for her. She's a good woman. Play with Kimi and little Jake. Be a husband and daddy."

"Really?" Peter was accustomed to Hayden's sudden mood shifts, but this quick turn left him dizzy. "Two weeks off?"

"Take three if you need it."

Peter gave him a skeptical look. "You're sure? This isn't some gentlemanly way of laying me off, is it?"

"Jesus, Lacroix," Hayden said with a laugh. "I've never been called *gentlemanly* in my life. And I wouldn't be giving you a raise if I had a mind to fire you. For an ace helicopter pilot you sure are insecure. Paranoid, too."

Hayden stood, stuck out his hand for a shake. "I want you to go home and take care of yourself and your marriage for a while. Consider it an investment in one of Fowler-Lemoyne Aviation's most prized assets. And I've also decided that we need a fulltime administrator to take care of all that time-sucking paperwork that's been dragging you and Gilliam down."

Peter stood and took his hand, thinking, *There's a heart and a core of empathy underneath that gruff, irascible exterior after all.*

"Thank you, Hayden," he said, then shook his head in wonder as he watched the big man leave his office.

Northern Exposure

August 1: Smithsonian Expedition
Northern Alberta, Canada

NORA STOOD PEERING INTO THE TRENCH that encircled their most recent prize: an intact skeleton of a Nanotyrannus, a midsized bipedal predator that lived in the Maastrichtian Age of the Late Cretaceous. Long regarded to be a juvenile T-Rex, recent studies of bones unearthed from the Hell Creek Formation revealed that Nanny (as the team had taken to calling it) was a distinct tyrannosauroid genus, sharing the same anatomy (albeit much smaller) and ecosystem as Tyrannosaurus Rex. The growth rings in the thigh bones taken from that dig site indicated it had been a fully mature animal at death, allowing the paleo scientific community to accept the new genus classification as separate from T-Rex.

The afternoon was a gorgeous 73 degrees, the sun beaming down from a cloudless sky, typical early-August weather in northwestern Canada. Nora was flanked on the rim of the trench by her lead paleontologist, Clive Driscoll, and geologist, Greg Dulowski.

"This is quite a feather in our caps, gentlemen," Nora told them. "Our sponsors were thrilled with the photos and video I sent."

"They should be," Driscoll said. "To the best of my knowledge, only four Nanotyrannus skeletons exist in U.S. museums, and none of them are complete. The Smithsonian will have an exclusive with this beauty."

The three scientists observed the field technicians working in the moat, doing the delicate work of chipping away rock and sediment from Nanny's bones.

"I have you guys to thank for your hunch. The move here

certainly paid off," Nora said, referring to Clive and Greg's suggestion that they move the operation ten miles south of the original dig site, where the geologic strata consisted of more permeable sedimentary rock. The sandstone, siltstone, and mudstone here made for easier excavation than the dense metamorphic and igneous rock layers of the bone field where they had spent the first two weeks of the expedition.

"Lucky guess on our part," Dulowski said.

Nora said, "I don't see it as luck at all, Greg. I attribute it to you both knowing the types of geologic formations that are likely to cover rarities. Your insightful scouting led us to this paleo gold. A complete Nanotyrannus skeleton! It's an astonishing find."

Driscoll nodded in agreement. "You know, I have thought from the beginning of this dig that we have been blessed. First, that rare Pachyrhinosaurus skull, then the Boreonykus sickle claw and teeth that led us to two intact skeletons. And now this Nanotyrannus specimen."

"I agree, Clive," Dulowski muttered. "I've felt it, too. This is already one of the most successful expeditions I've ever been a part of, and it's only day seventeen. It bodes well for the next month and a half."

"Yeah, things are going so well I wouldn't be surprised if we stumbled on Iani Smithi ornithopods or a Mirarci Eatoni fossil bird or two," Driscoll said, referring to what were known to be the rarest paleontological finds on the North American continent.

Nora said, "That would be a miracle seeing that both of those discoveries were far south of here, in Utah."

"Well you never know with the kind of winning streak we're on," Driscoll said.

Nora noticed a vehicle approaching from the south, kicking up a plume of dust behind it. She squinted, trying to make out who it might be. All expedition members were here in camp today. It was highly unusual to see any traffic on the dirt road leading to their encampment.

"Looks like we have some company," she said.

Driscoll and Dulowski lifted their heads and looked across the basin at the approaching vehicle, a nondescript Ford F-150 pickup.

"Are our sponsors scheduled for a visit today?" Dulowski asked.

Nora shook her head. "No. It's not Smithsonian reps. It would damage their elite east coast reputation to be seen in a pickup truck."

Clive Driscoll chuckled at that.

"Let's go see who's gracing us with their presence," Nora said, leaving the trench and walking to the camp entrance.

As the truck came closer she could make out the driver, and her heart nearly stopped. She didn't know whether to be ecstatic or deeply sad. She stopped in her tracks, shocked, watching the pickup roll into the camp.

Hayden was behind the wheel, wearing aviator sunglasses and his ridiculous red beret.

What the hell? Nora thought, dumbfounded.

"Is that Hayden?" Greg Dulowski inquired.

"None other," she said, not believing this.

Hayden pulled into the dig site and gave Nora an animated thumbs-up. A wide devil-may-care grin peeked out from under his beard.

Clive Driscoll came up beside her. "You look like you had no idea about this."

"I had absolutely *no* idea whatsoever," she said, stunned as she watched Hayden park the truck and get out.

He strutted toward her. "Greetings, *ma charmante reine*," he called, coming to her and throwing his arms around her, giving her a passionate bear hug and a kiss on the cheek. "God how I've missed you, *mon amour*."

Just great, he's back in his French mode again.

"What, um . . . what are you doing here, Hayden?" she said, stepping back from him, her face a mask of confusion.

"I'm fleeing the deluge of journalists who have been trying to get at me after the Smithsonian released my Quetzalcoatlus videos. I was right. Those clips went insanely viral. Tens of thousands of daily views on social media, the lead story on just about every TV newscast. Didn't matter if I was in Minnesota, Montana, or Idaho, those annoying cockroaches found me and hounded me for interviews. I've had enough of 'em." Hayden scanned the ghostly hills and deep forests surrounding the dig site. "No way they'll ever find me out here." He peered down at her. "What's the matter? You don't look very happy to see me."

"Well . . . I . . . I don't know," she stammered, still trying to make sense of this huge surprise. "Yes, of *course* I'm glad to see you, honey. It's just a little odd that you would travel fifteen-hundred miles to see me without giving me a clue you were coming."

"I would travel around the planet ten times to see you, Nora."

She tried to keep from blushing. "That's sweet, Hayden," she said, studying him. "I hope you're going to tell me you finally came to your senses and are here to join the expedition."

"Oh, no. I'm done with paleontology, no disrespect to you folks." He looked at Dulowski. "Hey, Greg. Good to see you again, my friend."

"Hello, Hayden. It's been a minute or two."

"Sure has. Two years to be exact. The Choteau expedition and the Gilliam dinosaur habitats."

"Yeah," Dulowski said. "Those were strange and exciting times."

"Indeed they were." Hayden turned to Driscoll. "I don't believe we've met."

"Oh, I'm sorry, dear," Nora said. "This is Clive Driscoll, my lead paleontologist. Clive heads the Department of Organismal Biology and Anatomy at the University of Chicago. They have a world class fossil lab there. Clive, meet Hayden Fowler."

"No introductions are necessary with this man," Driscoll told her. He shook Hayden's hand. "It's a great honor to finally meet you, sir," he said gushingly. "Those Quetzalcoatlus vids of yours are incredible. That mountain man falconer who trained them? Wow! You captured the oddness of it all. Well done, sir! And I'll have you know that I have used two of your books as texts in my Dinosaur Science undergrad classes and my Stones and Bones summer program."

"Thank you, Clive. Good to meet you. But let's get one thing straight before we go any further."

Nora saw Driscoll stiffen. "What's that?"

"As far as I know, I haven't been knighted by British royalty, so let's shitcan it with the *sir* formality, shall we? Just plain old Hayden will do."

"Okay, sure," Clive said, obviously taken aback by Hayden's directness.

Nora said to Hayden, "So if you didn't come to join the team, why did you make the trip?"

"What? I need to explain why I want to be with the woman I love? I'm beginning to get the feeling you don't want me here."

"No . . . no, it's not that at all. I *am* really happy to see you. It's just a huge surprise is all. Out of the blue and all."

He grabbed her arm and leaned in, kissed her hungrily, his beard tickling her chin and cheeks, his tongue exploring her mouth. She had missed his kisses, for sure. But they weren't alone and she wasn't one for public displays of affection.

She pushed him away. "Hayden, stop!" she admonished.

"What's wrong?" he said, giving her a wounded look, a look she knew all too well.

"You're embarrassing me, that's what's wrong."

"*Embarrassing* you! That's a fine way to treat someone who's come more than a thousand miles to see you."

She glanced at his pickup truck. "You drove all that way?"

"Hell no. I might be crazy but I'm not insane. I flew into Edmonton and rented the truck. Even then, it's a 360-mile drive." He gazed out over the wilderness, his long hair blowing in the breeze. "I thought Idaho was off the grid, but this place is like another friggin' planet." He looked back at Nora. "I came here to tell you something, *ma cherie*."

"You couldn't tell me during our FaceTime calls?"

"Not this, no."

He dug into his pants pocket and pulled out a black velvet engagement ring box, dropped to a knee and pulled off his beret, held it against his chest.

Oh no! Please don't do this here, you big, sweet romantic fool.

"I've missed you more than I can put into words, *ma douceur.* I can't live without you anymore, Nora. Not one more second—"

"Hayden, you're embarrassing me."

He looked up at her from his kneeling position and removed his shades. "Nora Jane Lemoyne, I've had a lot of time to think about things recently and I have come to the conclusion that life without you is no life at all."

Nora looked at Greg and Clive as Hayden rambled on. They both looked like they'd rather be anywhere but here. Several nearby team members stopped what they were doing to watch and listen.

She turned back to Hayden, looking down at him, seeing the vulnerability in his eyes and her heart broke for him. She couldn't decide whether his pose was pathetically needy or beautifully romantic.

". . . so I kneel before you to ask the proverbial question. Will you marry me, Nora Jane Lemoyne?" He opened the velvet box and pulled out the ring. The diamond cluster glittered in the sunlight.

A burst of applause erupted from around the camp, and Nora wanted to hide. The ring was gorgeous and Hayden's performance was heartfelt. Oscar worthy, even. She was flattered by his show of love, but also angry at him for showing up unannounced and making it into a public spectacle. Especially in front of her employees. Nora knew she couldn't possibly give him the answer he wanted to hear, and that would most likely shatter him.

But seeing him again after nearly three weeks apart stoked the fire in her belly.

Nora wanted him in the worst way.

She extended a hand to him. "Come on, Hayden, get up. Let's go discuss this in my trailer."

The Heat of the Moment

August 1: Smithsonian Expedition
Northern Alberta, Canada

HAYDEN FOLLOWED NORA TO HER TRAILER, holding her hand as she tugged him along, feeling like a disciplined child trailing an unforgiving mother. Expedition members watched the procession with pitying stares. The ring box felt like a hundred pounds in his pants pocket. He had failed with his marriage proposal bid. What had just happened? He felt certain Nora would go for it, that she was finally ready to bless their relationship with a matrimonial bond.

Whatever gave you that idea, you old fool?

I'm on the walk of shame, he thought, doing his best to avoid the gawking witnesses. *Not many guys fail at this. You're such a loser, Fowler.*

A feeling of incompetency washed over him.

He followed Nora up the stoop and into her trailer. She closed the door behind them. His sadness and self-pity heated into a blistering anger.

"What the hell was the meaning of *that*, Nora?"

"The meaning of *what*?" she said, looking up at him, smiling, her innocent demeanor really pissing him off.

"You know damn well what I'm talking about, woman! The way you humiliated me out there."

"Oh, I didn't humiliate you, darling," she said with a snorty laugh. "You humiliated yourself."

"Really? Don't give me that shit! I don't—"

"If anything, you humiliated *me* in front of my team. You knew my feelings about marriage, and yet you traveled more than a thousand miles to make a public spectacle of your proposal. Did you stop to think for even a second how that might make me feel?"

"Jesus Christ, Nora," he said, moving away from her, turning his back and running a hand through his hair. "You're impossible! You don't deserve my love."

She went to him, stood in front of him and rubbed his chest. "Listen, Hayden. What you did was really sweet and thoughtful, though it *was* misguided. The ring is absolutely lovely. I don't know how many times I have to tell you this to get it through that thick, bushy head of yours. I love you more than I have ever loved another man. But the fact remains, you have struck out at marriage three times and I've whiffed twice. Why ruin a good thing between us by legalizing our relationship?"

He pulled her hand away. "You think what we have is a *good thing*? We're living fifteen-hundred miles apart and you call it a good thing? You're delusional, Nora, you know that?"

"Shut up, Hayden," she said, starting to unbutton his shirt. "The more you talk the less I want to fuck you."

"Wh-what are you doing?"

"What does it look like I'm doing?"

She kissed him while her fingers undid buttons. He tried to pull away but she grabbed his shirttail and held him close. "What's the matter, my big cuddly teddy bear? You were fine making out with me outside."

She pulled him down to her and kissed him deeply. Nibbled his lips. He could never resist Nora's kisses. Soon he was into it as much as she was.

Between kisses she whimpered, "I *am* glad you came. It's been too long, honey."

She helped him get his shirt off and she dropped to her knees. Loosened his belt and unzipped his fly. Pulled his pants and boxers to the floor and took him in her mouth.

Hayden moaned.

It wasn't long before he forgot all about his humiliation and the walk of shame.

Prison Rats

August 3: Park County Detention Center

Livingston, Montana

MATHEWS SNAPPED TWO MORE PIECES of the investigative jigsaw puzzle into place, the puzzle being the Gilliam family case.

Flathead County Sheriff Will Dunstable called to inform him that the blood results from the Vista Hills Custom Taxidermy search had come back from the lab. Dried blood on several of the taxidermist implements were shown to be of human origin and matched Chogan Stimson's B-negative blood type. They were still waiting on DNA data, which would ultimately tell the tale, but the initial findings pointed a fat accusatory finger at Kyle Birnham's taxidermy shop as being the site where Stimson was beheaded.

"Two of my deputies took the proof to Birnham in his cell where we're holding him," Dunstable said on the call. "And guess what? Our star taxidermist began squealing like the cornered rat he is. He threw Leonard Sheridan under the bus, confirming that Sheridan orchestrated the Stimson hit from behind prison walls. He gave our guys another name—Scott Hammond. Hammond and an accomplice showed up at Birnham's shop well after closing on the night of June 15 with Stimson's body and instructions from Sheridan to decapitate the corpse. Birnham went into excruciating detail about the beheading. After he completed the gruesome task, Birnham received a fifteen grand cash payoff from Hammond, then Hammond and his unnamed conspirator loaded Stimson's headless body into their van and took off into the night. When my deputy, Stuart Fenski, inquired as to the second man's name, Birnham said he'd never seen him before. Said he didn't know him."

"What about the head? Did Birnham FedEx it to the Gilliams?"

"Yeah. Birnham said he took care of that per instructions from Sheridan. The fifteen G's was for decapitation and delivery of the head."

"Wow! Good stuff, Will. Where did the payment come from?"

"Looks like it came through an AEF shadow organization. To hear Birnham tell it, the Animal Emancipation Faction has their fingerprints all over the Stimson murder."

"Well, we both know this isn't the AEF's first murder rodeo," Mathews said.

"Yeah. That organization is chock full of dark souls. Birnham was very helpful, in a real talkative mood. That's what happens when desperate suspects start bargaining for leniency. He confessed all to my deputies. Went on to say he had earlier beheaded a T-Rex and FedExed it to the Gilliam ranch packed in dry ice along with family photos he had hacked from the Gilliams' private server. Told our guys Leonard Sheridan ordered it."

"Well, we pretty much already knew that from other evidence."

"True," Dunstable said, "but he gave us further information that implicates two others in this mess."

"Like what?"

"He had two of his employees weight the Rex body down with cinder blocks and dump it in the depths of Flathead Lake. That's a direct violation of Montana Endangered Species Act—the um, dinosaur amendment. We've brought those employees in for questioning. We want to see if they were involved in the Stimson murder. We also have a forensic dive team out dragging the lake."

Sheriff Dunstable had more big news for Mathews. Yesterday at Montana State Prison, mid-morning, Leonard Sheridan was jumped in the exercise yard by two gang inmates and stabbed repeatedly in the neck and chest with crude shivs. Sheridan bled out and died two hours later in the prison infirmary.

"Wow! Sheridan got bumped?" Mathews said.

"Yeah. Officials are still trying to sort it all out. We've learned that there has long been bad blood between imprisoned AEF members and a gang known as the Little Valley Locos. After extensive questioning of witnesses, the two Locos were turned over to the Attorney General's office. For safety reasons, four AEF members have been moved into protective custody. We've been told by Corrections that your interviewee, Scott Hammond, will be joining them."

"Maybe it doesn't have anything to do with AEF."

"Whaddaya mean, Mike?"

"It might have everything to do with the fact that Sheridan was a blue chip homicidal asshole."

Dunstable chuckled. "You're right. There *is* that."

Mathews phoned Bryan and Loretta Gilliam immediately after the call with Sheriff Dunstable, giving them the news that Chogan Stimson's killer had been identified and Leonard Sheridan was dead. Needless to say, they were both overjoyed that Sheridan was gone and glad to finally get some closure on their Blackfoot friend's murder. Mathews told them that he was still trying to track down another suspect who might also have been involved.

After a couple of delays, Mathews was finally getting his chance to interview Scott Hammond, the self-confessed murderer of Mick and Claire Prescott. And now he appeared to be Chogan Stimson's murderer as well. *Real standup guy, this Hammond fella.* Mathews had gotten in just under the wire—Hammond was scheduled to be transferred to Montana State Prison tomorrow and put into protective custody due to what was now known to be inside threats to inmates with AEF affiliations. Once Hammond was ensconced in protective isolation it would have been impossible to get a face-to-face interview with him.

Mathews had been frustrated by the delay, but now realized it had worked in his favor. According to Park County officials, Hammond did not yet know of Birnham's ratting him out by name, nor did he have any knowledge about Leonard Sheridan's stabbing death. Mathews planned to throw down that information to get the name of Hammond's mystery accomplice.

Scott Hammond sat across from him in the interrogation room in the basement of the City/County building on Callender Street. Hammond was twenty-five with pale white skin and a buzz cut so close that the pink of his scalp shone brightly under the fluorescent fixtures. The man's face was disconcerting, with a noticeable twitch in his left eye and spasms worming through his forehead and cheeks. *This guy has more facial tics than an advanced Parkinson's patient,* Mathews thought, not able to discern whether the tics were due to a liar's tells or a serious neurological issue.

There were two other people in the room with Mathews and Hammond: Park County Sheriff Grady Barstow and Hammond's public defender, Louis Greenwell, a short, pudgy man with a bulbous red nose who wore suspenders, a bow tie, and a bored expression that said he would rather be anywhere than here defending this client who had openly confessed to several murders. A guard stood outside the door.

Mathews knew going in that Hammond was being represented by a public defender. He thought he could use that knowledge to force Hammond to identify his accomplice in the Prescott murders (and probably the hunter killings as well). He'd used the public defender ploy in two previous cases where he'd been successful in getting obstinate suspects to talk. After meeting Louis Greenwell, he knew it would work here.

The interview had been going for thirty minutes with starts and stops, Hammond bragging about his kills and Greenwell cutting him off with warnings about saying too much. Mathews quickly tired of Greenwell jumping into the conversation, silencing Hammond just when Mathews thought the killer was close to revealing the identity of his partner. Hammond went into great detail about his kills of hunters, repeatedly stating that all of God's creatures deserved to live wild and free. When Mathews asked him if he didn't regard human beings as God's creatures, Hammond just sat there staring at him with a smug, self-satisfied expression.

Mathews was familiar with the type. He had dealt with arrogant young men like Hammond during his many years in law enforcement. Hammond fit the profile perfectly—sociopathic narcissist braggart with a god complex, ramped up on machismo testosterone. He was a cultist personality with a myopic worldview and an obsessive devotion to Leonard Sheridan.

"So tell me again about the Prescotts," Mathews said across the table. "I understand Leonard Sheridan ordered the hit."

"Yeah, he did. Leonard is a great man. We know when he gives an order that it's for a good reason, and we jump to carry it out. Those Prescott scumbags deserved to die. Leonard taught us that all animal traffickers and hunters should be eliminated."

"And you might have gotten away with it if it hadn't been for Ray Yount shooting you in the ass with a tranquilizer dart. Your buddy got away though. How does that make you feel, Scott, you getting the murder rap and him going free? Doesn't it make you angry? Life sure isn't fair, is it?"

Hammond took a long look at his lawyer, then turned back to Mathews, his eye twitching madly. He started to say something, but then held back.

"Come on. Who is he, Scott?"

Greenwell spoke up. "You already asked this, Detective. As I said previously, my client will not be answering that question."

"You're only making things harder on him, Counselor. The law might take it a bit easier on him if he answers that question. If he cooperates."

Hammond said, "Are you offering me a reduced sentence if I tell you who he is?"

"I don't have the authority to do that," Mathews responded. "Sheriff Barstow here is in a position to pull those strings. But that's a long road seeing as how you're on the line for multiple murders. You and your mystery accomplice."

"It's true, Scott," Sheriff Barstow said. "We can help you if you help us."

Mathews said, "Let's move away from the Prescotts for a moment. Did you murder Chogan Stimson?"

"Who?"

"The ranch hand at the Gilliam's Guidepost ranch. Don't give me that blank look, Scott. You'll never win any Oscars."

"I don't have a clue what you're talking about."

His facial tics said otherwise.

"You know damn well what I'm talking about. A month ago you

and your co-conspirator killed the Gilliams' ranch hand, Chogan Stimson. You took his body to Vista Hills Taxidermy to have his head lopped off and delivered to the Gilliams in Heart Butte. You and your buddy then took Stimson's headless body into the north woods of Gilliam's Guidepost ranch and strung it up in the trees."

Hammond laughed, a haughty bark. "That's rich! I couldn't find Heart Butte on a map if my life depended on it."

"Your life *does* depend on it, Scott. You know exactly what I'm referring to. Your taxidermy friend, Kyle Birnham, came clean a few days ago after blood on bone saws and knives taken from his shop came back matching Stimson's blood. He identified you as the one who brought the body to him to do the wet work and gave a description of your helper that night of June fifteenth that is very close to the description given by Ray Yount and Max Baker, the two who witnessed the Prescott murders. They describe your partner as, and I quote, 'deadly chill with ice water running through his veins.' So who is he, Scott? Who is this Mr. Chill?"

Hammond sat still as a mannequin, stunned by the Kyle Birnham revelation. His eye convulsed. He looked like he'd seen a ghost.

"Do *not* answer that, Scotty," Greenlaw said, firm and demanding.

"Your murderous activity is finally catching up with you," Mathews said calmly. "But let's back up a minute. Tell me more about your relationship with Leonard Sheridan. Were you with him two summers ago when the AEF invaded Gilliam's Guidepost and set the dinosaurs free? Were you a part of that?"

Hammond came out of his trance. "No. I went to a few meetings before that great day and was impressed by Leonard's speeches. When I heard what went down at the Gilliam ranch, I was disappointed that I missed out. I joined the Faction after that, to help with the AEF fight. I thought Leonard got a bad rap for doing an awesome thing. Still do." He looked at Sheriff Barstow. "They put a great man behind bars even though he did the right thing."

"You think freeing deadly predators during a picnic and killing large numbers of people is *awesome*? You think burning a man's home to the ground is *doing the right thing*?"

"Yeah. The Gilliams got what was coming to them. Well, sort of. Bryan Gilliam is still walking around, as is that other redskin ranch hand douchebag who gunned down my AEF brothers that day. I think his name is Apisi Lyttle. They're scum—the Gilliams and their hired hands. What they did to those poor dinosaurs was disgusting. Unforgivable."

Mathews said, "So did Sheridan give you orders to kill Bryan Gilliam? You and Mr. Chill?"

"Yeah," Hammond said proudly. He told us to take down that Indian fucker, too."

"Scotty, for Christ's sakes shut your damned mouth!" Greenwell said, exasperated. He stood and turned to Mathews. "We're done here, Detective."

But Mathews was far from wrapping up the interview. "Sit back down, Counselor. There's quite a bit more ground to cover here."

Greenwell gave him a long, annoyed look, then reluctantly returned to his seat.

Mathews turned back to Hammond. "Birnham went on to say this whole thing against the Gilliams was Sheridan's master plan. Do you concur with that?"

"Uh, yeah. He coordinated everything from his cell. The man is brilliant."

"If Sheridan is so brilliant what's he doing in Montana State looking at thirty years hard time?"

Hammond shrugged his thin shoulders. "Men like Leonard get things done no matter where they are. He's been a guiding light for the AEF."

"So besides Birnham, you, and Mr. Chill, who else took orders from Sheridan?"

Lawyer Greenwell slapped the table. "Don't speak, Scotty. He's trying to trick you. There's no need to pull anybody else into this."

Mathews faced Greenwell and said, "I'm not using trickery, Counselor. I'm trying to get to the bottom of a very serious matter. Your client could help himself quite a bit by cooperating." He looked back at Hammond. "I have more news about your so-called *guiding light* Leonard Sheridan, Scott."

"Oh yeah? What's that?"

"His light was extinguished yesterday." He stared down Hammond, letting it sink in.

"What, um . . . what are you saying?"

"I'm saying sociopaths like Sheridan usually run out of time, sooner than later. They usually die horrible deaths. Your iconic animal rights activist went down for the last time yesterday, Scott, killed by two gang members with prison crafted shivs."

Hammond swallowed hard. Both of his eyes were twitching now. "Wait, that can't be true."

Mathews gave him a dour smile. "Oh, it's *very* true, Scott. Leonard Sheridan is dead, stabbed to death by AEF haters in the exercise yard. AEF members are not real popular there. I understand there are orders to transfer you to Montana State tomorrow. You're gonna have a grand old time there without Sheridan to protect you."

"You're lying! Leonard's a survivor. He'd never let gang members take him down. He's too sharp for that. This is just a trick to get me to talk."

"It's no trick," Mathews said. "Sheriff Barstow here will vouch for me."

"It's true, Mr. Hammond," Barstow said from behind Mathews. "Leonard Sheridan died at ten-seventeen yesterday morning in the Montana State Prison Medical Infirmary from multiple stab wounds."

"No! NO! It can't be." Scott Hammond's jumpy eyes filled with tears. "He's a legend among the animal rights activists."

"And now he's a *dead* legend," Mathews said. "So tell me, who all were taking orders from Sheridan?"

"Don't answer that, Scotty," Greenwell nearly shouted.

Mathews glanced at the lawyer, then back at Hammond. "How does it make you feel, Scott, that the organization you kill for doesn't even shell out for a real lawyer? Instead the AEF goes cheap, leaving you to go it alone, running the legal gauntlet with this public pretender, this wannabe attorney," he said, pointing at Greenwell. "Such a shitty way of showing gratitude to a loyal soldier."

"Hey, who the hell do you think you are, Mathews?" Greenwell protested. "Watch your step. One more crack like that and I'll report you for unethical conduct to the Montana Board of Private Security. See how big a man you are when they yank your license."

"Go ahead, be my guest. They'd laugh you out of Helena so fast it'd make your cute little bow tie twirl around like a propeller," Mathews said, keeping his eyes on Hammond. He could see Hammond thinking over the bombshell he'd just laid on him, the unfairness of his situation sinking in. He said, "You know good and well the AEF has done you wrong, Scott. After all you've done for them, that's how they treat you? I know if I was in your shoes, I'd be royally pissed off and want revenge. You know they've got plenty of money to get you a *real* lawyer."

Greenwell looked like he was about to pop a vein in his neck. He jumped up and grabbed Hammond's upper arm, giving it a tug. "Come on," he barked. "This interview is over. This joke of a detective isn't worth our time. Guard!" he yelled at the closed door.

Scott Hammond pushed his lawyer away with his shackled hands. "Don't touch me!" he roared. "You haven't done shit for me since they brought me here. You just keep telling me to keep my mouth shut. Where's the lawyering in that?"

The door opened and the guard entered, but Sheriff Barstow intercepted him. Spoke to him in whispered tones. The guard returned to the hallway and closed the door behind him.

The sheriff turned to Greenwell. "This is my jurisdiction and *I* say when this interview is over, sir. We scheduled for an hour and we've got fifteen minutes remaining. Sit down, Mr. Greenwell." He nodded at Mathews. "The floor is yours, Mike."

"Christ almighty," Greenwell said, plopping down in his chair with a huff. "I've heard of kangaroo courts before but this is absurd."

Mathews ignored him and continued his questioning of Hammond. "So now that your king is dead and your taxidermist friend has sold you out, we're back to Mr. Chill. Are you going to be okay with taking all the heat for the Prescott murders, Scott?"

Mathews watched Hammond, saw the wheels turning behind those twitchy killer eyes, contemplating the unfairness of the situation. After a long stretch of silence, he said, "No . . . no, I'm not okay with it."

"So who is he? Tell us where we can find him."

Hammond looked at his lawyer, who was shaking his head in defeat. "I'll tell you what I know. But only after I get some proof that Leonard was really shanked in the prison yard."

Grady Barstow showed him a few of the news reports on his cell phone. Hammond sat there taking it all in as the sheriff scrolled through the accounts, news reporters' voices filling the interrogation room.

"You believe us now?" Mathews said.

Hammond nodded slowly, clearly stunned and overwhelmed by what he was seeing. A lone tear trickled down his trembling cheek.

How can anyone shed a tear for that monster Sheridan? Mathews thought.

Sheriff Barstow shut his phone down and put it in his pocket.

Mathews slid a legal pad and a pen across the table. "Write down Mr. Chill's name and where we can find him."

Hammond grabbed the pen and stared at the pad, thinking, then raised his head and glared at Mathews. "How the hell am I supposed to know where the dude is? I ain't his keeper. Last time I saw him was when we did the Prescotts."

"So write his name and any place we *might* find him. Certainly you know him much better than we do."

Hammond fidgeted with the pen in his shackled hands for a beat, then said, "Before I write anything, I want something in writing from you, Sheriff, stating that you will give me a little immunity for my cooperation."

Mathews came close to laughing out loud. *This serial killer clown thinks he deserves immunity?* Sheriff Barstow couldn't do much in the way of offering leniency even if he wanted to. That was up to the sentencing judge. *Funny how many hardened criminals didn't understand that.*

"Start writing, Scott," he said. "Any immunity will be determined by what you give us. And keep in mind, any false information you turn over will only add to your sentence."

After a long pause, Hammond dropped his head and started scribbling, his restraints clinking against the tabletop as he wrote. When he was done, he slapped the pen down on the pad and pushed it toward Mathews. "There, that's all I know about him. We weren't actually good buds, just business associates."

Mathews looked at what Hammond had written. The name jumped out at him.

Burgess Flood.

One of the AEF suspects being pursued by the FBI's Joint Terrorism Task Force. Hammond had also scratched out a city, Bigfork, Montana, and a phone number.

"That's his burner phone he used for illegal AEF business," Hammond said, "so I doubt he still has it now that he's on the run. Don't know a street address but Flood talked a lot about his hometown."

Burgess Flood of Bigfork was Mr. Chill, if Scott Hammond was to be believed. The prison rats (Birnham and Hammond) had squealed and justice was soon to be levied.

Mathews stood and tucked the pad under his arm.

"Are we done here?" Hammond asked.

Mathews offered him a sardonic smile. "Yes, *you* are *very* done, Scott."

Mathews hurried out of the interrogation room. Phone calls awaited.

Drums and Dromes

August 6: Band Rehearsal Barn

Gilliam's Guidepost

Heart Butte, Montana

THE AUDITIONS FOR A NEW DRUMMER were not going well. Moonrise was a depleted band.

The guy behind the kit tonight, a 24-year-old Blackfoot named Huritt Night Eagle, was the fourth drummer they'd auditioned this week. Four songs into the tryout and Paul Gilliam realized Huritt would not be the next Moonrise drummer. This process of trying to find a replacement for Hass Oxendine had brought Paul little but mounting stress.

Huritt was a friendly dude, laid back and hip enough. Thankfully lacking Ox's narcissism. Unfortunately he was a long way from Ox's talent. Huritt struggled to stay in the pocket and his kick drum foot was weak. Bassist Kit patterned his runs around the kick drum, and he showed his frustration at not being able to sync with Huritt's faint bass drum and inconsistent rhythms. And the guy relied too much on heavy cymbal crashes, which smothered the vocals. Sinopa made disappointed faces at Paul as she tried to sing a Wolf Alice song over the swish and clatter of Huritt's overly enthusiastic cymbal work.

This just wasn't working out.

Finding compatible musicians in a band was more of a challenge than Paul could ever have imagined. You had to blend musical tastes with skill levels and playing styles. And then there was perhaps the most important element: the meshing of personalities. Paul was beginning to see that the formation of Moonrise had been a lucky miracle. The four of them—Paul, Sinopa Harwood, Kit Reeder, and Hass Oxendine—had come together as friends, and matured musically into a well-rehearsed unit that had quickly found regional fame. Sure, they had worked hard, but they had also been blessed with quite a bit of luck and good timing. That is, until the Zootown Music Festival disaster derailed Moonrise and Hass walked, leaving them scrambling to fill his slot. Not for the first time, Paul cursed Hass Oxendine for the disarray in which he had left the band.

Unfortunately the talent pool for drummers was shallow. Geography was their first problem. Paul had placed ads in music stores in Billings and Bozeman looking for an experienced drummer, but with Heart Butte being so remote, a good four-hour drive away, there were no takers. That left the Blackfeet Indian reservation. All four of the auditioners were Blackfoot, three males and one female, all novices. The whole audition thing exhausted Paul and brought back his spiraling depression.

Cruising on autopilot, he strummed the chords to "Moaning Lisa Smile" and watched Sin belting out the vocal. His thoughts drifted to the first three auditions they'd held. The first guy was a party animal, showing up high and immediately pulling out a vial of Tri-horn blow, snorting the Triceratops horn powder off the snare drum head. He only lasted three songs before he wanted to take a break to enhance his high. Paul told him in no uncertain terms that they only wanted serious musicians in the band. Drugs were forbidden, so this wasn't going to work out. The guy took Paul's dismissal personally, gathering up his stuff and cussing them on his way out, calling them "elitist children" and "amateurs" among other derogatory insults. The second drummer had the rock star look down: chiseled GQ looks, straight coal-black hair that draped his shoulders, white t-shirt with a black leather vest, snakeskin headband and studded wrist-bands, red leather pants, colorful tattoo sleeve running up one arm. He had the energy and the appearance, but zero talent. Couldn't even pull off a simple drum fill without getting hung up. The third drummer was a petite young girl, sixteen if she was to be believed (probably more like fourteen), so tiny she nearly disappeared when she took her place behind the kit. She had some decent chops on the ballads and was undeniably cute. But ultimately she was too young and not strong enough to supply the power needed for the Moonrise rockers.

From the elevated stage, Paul looked out across the barn, to the entrance where his bodyguard, Lou Goolsby, stood, smoking a cigarette, once again keeping watch, protecting Paul from all the evils of the world. The man had saved his life at the music festival a month ago. The ex-Secret Service agent he despised in the beginning had kept him from being torn apart onstage by that pair of charging Dromaeosaurs. Paul shuddered every time he thought about how close to death he had come. How close to dying a ghastly death by dinosaur like his uncle, Jimmy Enright, who was taken by a T-Rex two years ago. Paul had also been mulling over what his mother had suggested, that possibly God put Goolsby on that stage in what might have been some kind of divine intervention. The more Paul thought about it, the more he believed his mother's words might hold some truth. And in the month since that disaster, Paul had gotten to know Lou Goolsby better, and actually enjoyed his company now. Goolsby was always eager to tell Paul and the band tales of his Secret Service days, and his telling of them was always entertaining.

Mercifully, the Wolf Alice song ended. Paul wanted to call it quits and tell Huritt to go home. But for some reason, Kit wanted to keep going.

Does Kit see something in Huritt Night Eagle that I don't?

Sin laid her tambourine down and walked over to Paul. Whispered in his ear, saying she needed to talk with him in private. She had been preoccupied with something the last few days, acting remote and distant, but he'd learned it best to hold off questioning her about what was going on in that gorgeous head of hers. Sin had her moods, but she always opened up to him in her own time. Her serious expression and tone of voice said this was the time.

"All right, Sin and I need to take a short break," he said to Kit and Huritt, unstrapping his guitar and setting it in the stand. "You guys can keep jamming if you want."

Paul took Sin by the hand and led her off the stage, pulling her toward the front entrance.

“No, not out the front,” she said, stopping, pulling him back. “I don’t want Mr. Goolsby hearing our conversation.”

“Okay, sure,” Paul said, his concerns growing about what Sinopa had on her mind. He tilted his head at the door behind the stage. “Let’s head out back.”

They walked out into a glorious sunset, the sky a brilliant fiery red, casting a crimson gleam through the cottonwood trees. Paul led Sinopa out away from the barn, closer to the woods.

He turned to face her, feeling the need to start the conversation. “What the hell are we gonna do, Sin? Moonrise isn’t a band without a drummer. This dude Huritt isn’t gonna cut it.”

“Yeah, I agree.”

“We can’t play gigs without percussion. “It looks like I’m gonna have to program one of those damn drum machines. That would be a huge pain in the ass. It would set us back a few weeks, maybe a month or more.”

She looked away, into the cottonwoods. “It’s not the band I’m worried about, Pauley.”

“Whaddaya mean?” he said, now really concerned at where her head was at. He clutched both of her hands, gave them a gentle squeeze. “What’re you saying, Sin?”

“It’s us. It’s . . .” She paused, reluctant to continue.

Oh hell no, this can’t be happening. She’s breaking up with me! I can’t take this on top of the band situation.

“Talk to me, baby,” he implored. “Tell me what’s wrong.”

“I don’t know any other way to say this so I’ll just come out with it,” she said sadly, a look of guilt and regret playing across her dark features. “I’m pregnant.”

“You’re, uh—you are *what*?”

“Pregnant. You know, with child. A bun in the oven,” she said, touching her belly.

For some reason, it was the last thing he expected, but he really shouldn’t have been surprised. They’d been having regular sex all summer, several times without protection.

Kit and Huritt began laying down a booming rhythm in the barn.

"Are you sure?" he said over the crash and boom, feeling like an idiot as soon as the words left his mouth.

She nodded meekly. "I'm scared, Pauley. *Really* scared. I'm too young to be a mom. Me, a mother? You've got to be freakin' kidding me! I love you, Paul, I really do. But a *child?* I still feel like a child myself sometimes. We're too young to be parents. Let's face it, we're *both* kids really." She took a step back and shook her head in disbelief. Tears glistened on her cheeks, looking like drops of blood in the crimson light cast by the low-lying sun.

Paul huffed out a deep breath as he saw his life going off the rails in dramatic fashion. Suddenly the band's problems seemed inconsequential. Thinking about what was to come for Moonrise was silly considering the heaviness of this news.

Pops is going to kill me, he thought, and then quickly felt guilty for considering himself over Sin. He gazed deep into her chocolate brown eyes, seeing her fear and helplessness there, swirling like two dark storms.

"It'll all be okay, Sinny. Everything will work out, you'll see," he said, taking her in his arms, wishing he could believe it himself. She looked so young and vulnerable. So in need of comforting.

Of course she's young and vulnerable, you idiot. Sin just turned seventeen. You knocked up a seventeen-year-old girl! How to go, moron!

She leaned her head into his chest, her tears wetting his shirt. He held her tight, breathed in her musky floral scent. Felt her lithe body tremble against him, his thoughts traveling in a thousand different directions.

"I'm so, so sorry, Pauley," she sputtered between sobs.

"Hey, c'mon, don't say that," he said, placing his hand under her chin and lifting her head. "It's not your fault. In case you forgot, it takes two to make a baby. If anything, this is all on me. I'm the one who was in too much of a hurry to strap on a skin."

She smiled through her tears. "So, I guess it's my fault that I turn you on that much, huh?"

"Ooh, you definitely do that to me, my sinfully beautiful Sin. I wouldn't call it a fault, though. I'd call it a superpower."

She let out a three-beat giggle and wiped her eyes. "You always know just what to say to me, Paul. I love you so much right now. But seriously, what're we gonna do? We can't raise a child. We're both living at home with our parents. I still have another year of high school."

"I . . . um, I guess . . ." He searched his confused mind, struggling to find the right words to ease the tension of the moment. He wished he could conjure up some magical spell that would make this warped reality disappear. But what could he say that would lighten Sin's mood? 'Let's make it official and get married, have a go at raising the kid?' or, 'Let's put our baby up for adoption?' or, 'I'd be glad to pay for an abortion?' Each of those options seemed ludicrous.

She broke the awkward silence. "I know this is hard for you, love. For *us*. I just need to hear you say you love me. Please tell me you love me, Paul."

He hesitated, surprised by the needful demand in her voice. "I, uh . . ."

Suddenly a loud crashing erupted in the woods. Something stomping through the brush, snorting and gasping. Getting closer.

"What's that?" Sin whispered.

"I don't—"

A four foot tall Dromaeosaur bounded into the clearing, pulling to a halt a mere twenty yards away. Close enough for Paul to catch a whiff of rotten meat and the metallic scent of blood. The creature remained stationary at the edge of the woods, tilting its oblong head, training its rapacious crimson eyes on them. Bloody drool dripped from its quivering maw.

Visions of the Dromes that attacked him at the music festival paraded through his head, bringing an overpowering flush of panic. He pulled Sin close and whispered in her ear as calmly as he could, "Don't move and stay quiet."

Paul knew they were dead if they tried to make a run for it. You couldn't outrun these creatures. He knew that from experience. Dromes were the fastest breed of this second coming of the Cretaceous species. Smallish and lightweight. Streamlined physiques. Legs of muscle and sinew built for covering ground quickly. Their overdeveloped jaws and teeth and killing claws struck fear into their prey.

Paul was feeling that fear aplenty as he stared at this monster.

I can't believe Pops fought off one of these beasts.

The standoff continued. The alien animal sized them up, snorting and snuffling at the edge of the woods while they gripped each other in fear. Paul could feel Sin's jagged breaths against his side while he tried to slow his own breathing.

The minutes ticked by, slow, eternal. Intense. The Drome stood, still as a gravestone, focusing on them with those eerie red eyes. Every muscle in Paul's body was rigid and he thought he might crap his shorts at any minute. He felt Sin shivering in his grasp and he hugged her tighter. Tried to get more of his body between her and the animal without making any quick movements. When—not if—the Drome charged them, he would do his best to protect her.

And their baby.

The beastly eyes continued staring, unblinking, unyielding, as if the Drome had x-ray vision and was peering under Paul's skin and bones, searching through his internal organs, trying to decide what to select for dinner.

The Drome studied them for another few interminable minutes before dropping its head and taking a hop and a skip toward them.

Paul flinched, retreating a step. Sin let out a shriek and he pulled her closer.

He felt certain they were about to die.

But then, strangely, the beast stopped and looked side to side as if confused. It let out a long, low, whining moan, and Paul thought it might be suffering some kind of injury, though he could see no wounds on the animal. It stood, unmoving, head lowered, its powerful legs visibly shaking, then did an about face and charged back into the cottonwoods.

Paul felt Sin relax in his arms. He couldn't believe their good luck. He'd never known a Dromaeosaur to back away from an attack. They were predators with a ravenous appetite for flesh.

"Weird," Paul said, on the edge of hyperventilating, eyes still on the fringe of the woods. "I've never seen them act that way."

"Oh my god, I thought we were gonna die, Pauley."

"Me, too, baby. The only thing I can think of is that was one of the sick ones Hayden Fowler and wildlife agents have been rounding up. Otherwise there's no way that thing would have passed up a sure meal."

"Eww! Do you have to use that word? A *meal*?"

"Yeah, we absolutely could have been a meal. *Should* have been a meal. We raised a few of these Dromaeosaurs back when the meteorites landed, and from the moment they hatch out they are eating machines."

She wrapped her arms around his midsection and leaned into him. "I'm still shaking. So are you."

"Yeah, with good reason," he said, kissing the top of her head.

"I feel so safe when I'm with you."

Paul issued a thin chuckle. "You might want to rethink that, Sin. This is the second time in a month I've come close to becoming a Dromaeosaur meal. My guardian angel Goolsby wasn't here to bail me out this time. Jesus, we got damned lucky."

"If Mr. Goolsby is your guardian angel like you say, then I think you might be mine," she said, smiling up at him.

He kissed her, long and hard, then pulled back. "I was about to tell you something before we were rudely interrupted."

"Yes, you were," she said, her face shining with anticipation.

"So, better late than never. I love you so much, my gorgeous Sinny girl."

She let out a delighted squeak and hugged him. "Hold me, Paul. *Please* hold me."

He gave her a quick hug, looking over her shoulder to where the cottonwoods started, then said, "I think we should get back inside before another one of those things comes out of the woods. It sounds like our rhythm section needs us."

They walked back into the rehearsal barn, hand in hand, Paul thinking, *It's gonna take a whole lot more than love to make it through this pregnancy thing.*

Wakeup Call

August 9: Fowler-Lemoyne Aviation Offices

Gilliam's Guidepost

Heart Butte, Montana

BRYAN GILLIAM WAS EXHAUSTED. He had been burning the midnight oil the past three weeks managing Fowler-Lemoyne Aviation business. Charters were booked solid for the next month.

Hayden and Nora had been away pursuing their individual interests, and Bryan had been wearing many corporate hats in their absence. Advertising, scheduling, accounting, budgeting, FAA regulatory compliance reporting, fleet maintenance, managing flight operations, leading crew meetings. Nora was gone until mid-September working a paleontology expedition. Hayden was away much of the time, out with state wildlife officials tracking the dinosaur epidemic. Peter Lacroix had jumped in and helped when he wasn't piloting a charter. But Peter was gone now, too, with Hayden granting him a two-week vacation earlier in the week. Well deserved, yes, but untimely.

Hayden had been promising to get Bryan some experienced administrative help, but he had yet to make good on that promise. Bryan wanted to be steamed at the big guy for abandoning his responsibilities and dumping everything on his desk. Nora, too. But he just couldn't bring himself to be angry with them. They had been good to him, so openly generous, and he felt honored they had enough confidence in him to run things while they were away. And Hayden, recognizing Bryan's good work, informed him that he, too, would be getting a couple of weeks off when Peter returned. Bryan had circled that date on the wall calendar and drawn stars around it.

The hour was late, after midnight, and the building was quiet. He sat alone in his office updating spreadsheets on his laptop. He glanced up at the wall calendar, the stars circling next week's date shining like a welcoming galaxy. Just six more days of corporate servitude. And then what? Maybe he and Loretta could vacation in some exotic locale. Hawaii? The Cayman Islands? A romantic couple of weeks in Paris? Sightseeing the ancient ruins of Rome and Greece? They had barely left Montana during their twenty-plus years together at Gilliam's Guidepost and Bryan thought there had never been a better time for a getaway trip.

He looked out the interior window into the hangar, at the two Bell 407s parked nearby, their metallic paint gleaming under the overnight LED lights. The flashy Fowler-Lemoyne Aviation logo—a chopper rising over jagged mountain peaks—adorned their fuselages. Such beautiful rotary aircraft. These helicopters were true aeronautical engineering marvels. Sleek lines. Streamlined aerodynamic perfection. Panoramic tinted windows giving passengers a view of the world from a bird's-eye perspective. These choppers sold themselves. He just had to present them in the best light on the website, in the TV commercials he produced, and the reels he posted on Instagram. And the fact he could boast of having world class pilots made selling charters that much easier. He was proud to be an integral part of this business, even if the hours were long and demanding.

He pushed back from the laptop and rubbed his eyes. So difficult concentrating and digging in tonight. His mind wandered. Too much happening lately. There had been the news from Mike Mathews, shocking and lurid, albeit welcome. Leonard Sheridan had been stabbed to death in Montana State Prison. The man who had led the attack on their ranch and burned it to the ground was dead. Hallelujah! Bryan and Loretta had celebrated with a bottle of champagne. Mathews also told them about the taxidermist, Kyle Birnham, cooperating with authorities, coming clean about his relationship with Sheridan and his part in the severed T-Rex head and Chogan Stimson murder/decapitation. There was also the arrest of a man, Scott Hammond, an AEF member who had been one of

Sheridan's chief assassins. Hammond was caught at the murder scene of a husband-and-wife animal trafficking team. He had also confessed to Chogan's murder and participating in the recent string of hunter murders that were making all the latest newscasts. Mathews told them that Hammond had also been given orders by Sheridan to hit Bryan and Apisi Lyttle for their part in killing several AEF members two summers ago while defending the ranch. Bryan had swallowed hard with that news, but breathed a sigh of relief knowing the guy was now in police custody. He and Loretta could sleep well again. But Mike Mathews cautioned them to not get too comfortable. Hammond had given him the name of another AEF member—Burgess Flood—who was involved in Chogan's murder and had accompanied Hammond in the killings of exotic animal traffickers Mick and Claire Prescott. Flood remained a very real threat to the Gilliam family and Apisi Lyttle. The FBI was still searching for Flood, and he was considered to be armed and extremely dangerous.

Yes indeed, so much going on.

Bryan yawned. Got up and went to the sideboard. Loaded a K-Cup into the Keurig coffee maker and hit the brew button. The machine started to grind. He needed a blast of caffeine to get him through another hour of work.

He watched the coffee stream from the Keurig, thinking about Paul and his girlfriend facing off against the Dromaeosaur three days ago. He'd never understand why the boy elected to go out the back door of the rehearsal space, away from Lou Goolsby's protection. And unarmed, too. He and Sinopa could have been killed. His son knew that Dromes populated the woods on their property. The boy knew the creatures were unpredictable and deadly. That onstage encounter he'd had with two of them a month ago should have been a clear reminder. Common sense seemed to elude his eighteen-year-old at times.

Bryan and Loretta both held much empathy in their hearts for their eldest son, who was much more sensitive and complicated than younger brother Ethan. Paul had spent a couple of weeks in a brooding depression following the Zootown Music Festival disaster.

Refused to even look at his guitar. Loretta convinced him to see the family therapist, Dr. Helen Krickstad. Paul had resisted at first, but after a few sessions, the good doctor persuaded him that playing music was his way out of the depression that bogged him down. She helped him disassociate the music from his horrific onstage near-death experience at the festival. Based on her sage advice, Paul decided to continue on with the band, though Bryan figured Sinopa had a lot to do with that decision.

Bryan and Loretta were relieved to see Paul climb out of his depression. There was music in the Gilliam house once again. Bryan knew his son needed music in his life. Music was the magic elixir that elevated Paul like nothing else could. But the boy had never handled adversity well and now there was a new dark cloud on the horizon. Apparently the search for a new drummer wasn't going well. Hass Oxendine's departure had left the band high and dry. Moonrise wasn't playing out and they weren't recording. The down time was pulling Paul back down. As the band's manager, Bryan wished there was something he could do, but band personnel was something the kids had to work out on their own.

The coffee maker sputtered to a stop, his mug full of steaming hot brew. He added creamer and sugar and took a sip. *Ah, just the right blend.* Went to his desk and sat. Looked at his laptop, but couldn't get back into work mode.

He thought about the Blackfoot boy, Hass Oxendine, who was the source of Paul's current troubles. Ox had taken the drum kit with him when he left the band, the pricey Yamaha Stage Custom set Bryan purchased for him. *That's some kind of gratitude*. Bryan had planned to go talk to the boy's parents and retrieve the drums. But then a guilty wave of shame hit him. Bryan had given Hass the kit as a gift. He couldn't take it back. S*houldn't* take it back. The kid's family was living in poverty on the rez while the Gilliams were wealthy and living on a 1,250-acre ranch. If anything, Bryan thought he should give the Oxendines more. He planned to perform an act of kindness for the Blackfoot family, give them something that would improve their lives, but he had yet to get around to it. He typed a note in all caps to remind himself to pay the Oxendines a visit soon.

But there was something else poking at his brain. Bryan knew Paul well enough to know there was something else going on with him. Something more than the stalled comeback of Moonrise. Something with Paul and his girlfriend. Bryan had been with Paul and Sinopa yesterday, out in the rehearsal barn, and he'd noticed a distinct change in the way they communicated. The way they looked at each other. The way they touched. The comments they made. They weren't as carefree and easy with each other as Bryan had seen in the past. Not as affectionate with each other. He could feel it in the air, something that affected their togetherness. Was it the run-in they'd had with the Dromaeosaur? That would certainly be enough to shake the foundation of any relationship. But Bryan sensed it was more than that. He liked Sinopa. She was a nice, polite girl who possessed a striking dark beauty. She had been a positive influence on Paul. But both she and Paul were so young and inexperienced in the fickle ways of adult relationships. Paul didn't have much experience with girls, and Paul was Sinopa's first serious love interest. They were beginners in romance. Bryan had wanted to press Paul on it but Loretta cooled his jets, telling him to hold back, convincing him it would be best to give it time. That it would all come out eventually. Loretta was much wiser about these things than he would ever be.

He took a slug of coffee and went back to work on the spreadsheet. He'd been working for five minutes when a noise outside made him sit up straight and listen.

A quick series of knocks, like something banging against the exterior wall.

He sighed. *Another goddamned Dromaeosaur lurking about?*

Dromes were still a troubling and dangerous presence on the Gilliam ranch in this third summer of the dinosaur invasion. Bryan knew Hayden and Nora were for protecting the prehistoric species, but he would be just fine if every last one of the dinosaurs expired so they could get back to the normalcy they'd enjoyed before the meteorites struck with their payloads of dino eggs. News reports the past couple of weeks talked of some exotic disease that was killing off large numbers of dinosaurs and domestic animals. Bryan hoped and prayed it didn't infect their horses, but wished it would wipe out all of the invasive prehistoric species. The dinosaurs—especially carnivores like Tyrannosaurs and Dromaeosaurs—had taken too many human lives.

He got up and went to the window. Opened the blinds. A full moon illuminated the grounds, draping the cottonwoods in a shimmery silver blanket. He looked along the fringe of the forest but couldn't see any movement. No familiar predatory scarlet eyes peering out from the trees.

He heard a noise, behind him. Realized the knocking sounds weren't coming from outside.

They were footsteps, padding through the hangar area.

Startled, he turned to see a young guy with short cropped hair standing in the doorway, holding a gun on him. A crooked grin creased his face. A shiver crawled down Bryan's spine as he spied the suppressor extension on the pistol's barrel.

"So we finally meet," the intruder said, calmly poised. "Actually, we've already met in a manner of speaking. I was here two years ago setting free your dinosaurs. I rode in on one of the bulldozers. I witnessed you and your trashy redskin friends kill three of my Animal Emancipation Faction brothers. I've come to make you pay for that."

"Who the hell are you?" Bryan said, fear bubbling up into his throat. He tried to swallow it back.

"Names aren't important. Stand up and get your hands up where I can see 'em."

"How—how'd you get in here?" Bryan said, pushing back his chair and standing, raising his arms, feeling a tremor run through him.

"It wasn't easy," the man said, holding the gun steady. "Came a long way through those woods. You've got more security here than the feds employ at nuclear missile sites."

Too bad one of the Dromaeosaurs didn't get him. Bryan's mind raced in turmoil. *Where did I stash my gun?*

The man gave him a slow smile. "I had to put your guard down outside the hangar."

"You—you *killed* him?" Bryan's bodyguard, Frank Keaton, had been stationed at the hangar entrance all night.

"No, I didn't kill him. He's innocent. Just doin' his job. I jabbed him with a dose of tranq. A mix of xylazine and ketamine. The same shit animal traffickers use. I thought it was a beautiful irony. Your guard will wake up in a couple of hours. He'll be drowsy but okay."

Bryan observed the man. His demeanor and speech were as cool as the cerulean blue of his eyes. Relaxed, composed, obviously educated. But lurking just below the tranquil surface was a stone cold sociopath. Bryan had seen many like him in Afghanistan.

"Let's go, Gilliam," he demanded. "You're coming with me."

"I don't think so," Bryan said, wondering if he could get to the Glock in his desk drawer quick enough. Decided he couldn't. "If you're gonna kill me it will have to be right here. And if you do, you'll never get out of here alive."

"Oh, I don't intend to kill you here. Too messy and risky. I've got a much better spot in mind."

Bryan heard his late brother-in-law, Jimmy Enright, in his ear: *Keep him talking, Gill. It's your only chance.*

He decided to go for broke. "You wouldn't happen to be Burgess Flood, would you?"

The man blinked hard and looked away, his composure gone for a brief second. Bryan knew he'd hit the truth. He was facing one of Leonard Sheridan's hired guns.

"There are a lot of people looking for you, Flood. The FBI put a huge price on your head."

Flood ignored the comment, his calm demeanor slipping further, impatience setting in. "C'mon, Gilliam. Get a move on." He waved the gun at him. "Get out from behind that desk and head to the door."

"You know he's dead, don't you?"

"Who?"

"Leonard Sheridan."

Burgess Flood stared at him for an eternal minute with those unnerving, ice blue eyes. A cold panic settled in Bryan's gut.

Flood said, "Leonard will always be alive in the hearts and

minds of me and my AEF brothers. We will continue to carry on with his work."

In his peripheral vision, through the interior picture window, Bryan saw a flash of movement out in the hangar. He couldn't make out who it was, but he saw a body dash behind one of the choppers.

And then a second body. *Is that Lou Goolsby?* Bryan could only rely on his peripheral vision; he didn't dare take his eyes off of Flood.

Flood moved toward Bryan. One step . . . two.

"You don't start moving I'll shoot you where you stand, Gilliam. Bet your ass I will."

Bryan was losing feeling in his arms, so he lowered them. Stayed behind the desk.

Flood fired two quick shots, *thwitt-thwitt*, the silencer muffling the shots, the slugs splintering the desktop.

Bryan flinched, jumping back, panic clawing at his throat.

"Quit stalling, Gilliam! I warned you! Now get—"

Flood's comment was cut off as he went down hard with a loud gasp, the gun discharging with another suppressor-quieted *thwitt-thwitt* before the weapon clattered across the floor.

Bryan watched Lou Goolsby take a slug in his shoulder and grab at the wound with his left hand while pointing his firearm down at the fallen Flood with his right. Bryan heard sounds of a struggle—lots of huffing and puffing and grunting and straining—but the desk cut off his view. He stepped around the desk to see Paul with Burgess Flood wrapped in a secure headlock clinch, his face beet red as he hung on to the squirming killer.

Holy shit! Paul tackled Flood from behind! What the hell is Paul doing out here?

Lou Goolsby stood over them, training his gun on Flood, his shoulder weeping blood. "Call nine-one-one, Bryan," the bodyguard croaked.

Bryan grabbed his cell phone and called it in, his mind in chaos.

"Let him go, Paul," Goolsby said. To Flood he said, "Get on your knees, asshole. Put your hands behind your head."

"Hang in there, Lou," Bryan said, grabbing his Glock 19 from the desk drawer and covering Burgess Flood, who was sputtering and coughing as he got into a kneeling position. "Help is on the way."

Goolsby plopped down in a chair, his face pale gray, his breathing ragged. The shoulder wound was bad.

Bryan exchanged looks with his winded, red-faced son, a thousand emotions passing silently between them. Paul got to his feet, unsteady. Came to Bryan and hugged him, sniffling, attempting to control his runaway emotions.

After a long, close moment, Bryan separated from him and gave him the Glock. Told him to cover Flood while he tended to Goolsby. Bryan went out into the hangar area and grabbed a few clean work towels, brought them to Goolsby and padded the wound.

As Bryan worked on Goolsby's shoulder, he took it all in.

Paul snuffling, doing his best to subdue his sobbing as he held the Glock on Burgess Flood.

The bullets embedded in the desktop.

The blood staining Goolsby's shirt a dark burgundy.

Bryan felt lightheaded. The small office spun like an out-of-balance merry-go-round.

What the hell just happened here? God bless him but what was Paul doing in the heliport hangar after midnight?

Soon he heard the sirens out on Badger Creek Road, vehicles coming up the drive.

Father and Sons

August 10: Fowler-Lemoyne Aviation Hangar
Gilliam's Guidepost
Heart Butte, Montana

"WHAT WERE YOU TWO DOING IN THE HANGAR at this late hour?" Bryan asked Paul and Lou Goolsby.

Paul deferred to Goolsby, who grimaced in pain as paramedics wrapped his shoulder and attached an IV. "Well, I can't speak for your son, but I was doing my job." He lifted his elbow at Paul. "After this rascal got away from me the other night and ran into that Dromaeosaur, I've been watching him with hawk eyes."

Bryan nodded and turned to Paul. "So why were you out here after midnight? I mean, obviously, I'm quite glad you were there. But why?"

Paul started to answer, but stopped when he noticed his mother enter the hangar with Ethan and Lianne tagging along behind. Ethan's hair was a tangled bedhead mess and Lianne couldn't stop yawning. Loretta spotted Bryan and hurried to him, her movements frantic.

"Oh my god, Bry!" she said, clutching his arm. "Are you okay?"

"I'm fine," he lied. "And so is Paul."

She looked at their son, who looked anything but fine. "Oh, Pauley," she said, pity in her voice. She turned back to Bryan. "What happened? I heard someone got shot. I was so worried, honey."

"Everything's okay, Lor," Bryan reassured her. "We got a visit from one of Sheridan's thugs, but our son proved to be a Johnny on the spot hero." He tilted his head down at Goolsby, laid out on a cot with the medics working on him. "However, Lou took one for the team."

Loretta stared at Goolsby's wound. "Jesus. What happened?"

Goolsby shook his head. In disgust. "Took a hot one in my shoulder. More of a freak accident than anything."

"Are you all right?"

"I've survived worse."

"Lou's a tough hombre," Bryan said. "He'll make it."

Having stanched the bleeding, the paramedics moved Goolsby to a gurney and rolled him out of the hangar to the waiting ambulance. The ambulance left the heliport in a hurry, emergency lights strobing across the quadrangle. Goolsby was on his way to the Blackfeet Community Hospital in Browning, a half hour drive.

Bryan, still shaken, started to give Loretta an explanation but was interrupted by tribal police, who needed to question him and Paul. Bryan apologized to Loretta and hugged Ethan and Lianne before he and Paul followed the Blackfeet officers to a far corner of the hangar. They had already arrested and cuffed Burgess Flood, and were waiting on FBI agents, who were flying in via helicopter from the Billings field office.

More officials arrived. Soon the hangar was lit up and bustling with uniforms. Forensic detectives combed Bryan's office collecting evidence. Guards from the Gilliams' private security staff reviewed camera footage, trying to discern how Flood made it to the heliport without detection. Paramedics had revived Bryan's personal bodyguard, Frank Keaton, and a Blackfeet Law Enforcement officer was questioning him. A pair of detectives threw hardball questions at Bryan and Paul. After twenty minutes of intense grilling, they were released.

They rejoined Loretta. Between yawns, Ethan and Lianne gawked at all the uniforms scurrying around. The hangar buzzed with a beehive-like intensity.

Bryan said to Paul, "You told those detectives the reason you were out here so late was because you needed to talk to me in private. What's that about, son?"

Paul looked at Ethan and Lianne, at his mother sending him disquieting looks. "Uh," he muttered, "something's been on my mind, Pops. Something I wanna talk with you about. I haven't been able to sleep, and . . ." He looked around at all the people milling about and gave another sidelong glance at Ethan and Lianne, who lingered close enough to overhear his words. "Could we go somewhere private? Away from all this? Just you and me?"

Bryan nodded. "Sure. Come on, bud. Peter Lacroix is gone. His office will be quiet." To Loretta he said, "Will you please excuse us again, Lor?"

"Shouldn't I come, too?" she said.

"No, Mom," Paul replied. "No offense, but I need to have a man-to-man talk with Dad."

Loretta slouched, disappointed at being left out. So unusual for Paul to shun his mother like this. He normally confided in her for matters concerning his personal life. But it gave Bryan a pretty good idea of what this was about.

Lianne asked, "Are you okay, Pauley? You look really sad."

Bryan said, "Your brother's had a rough night, Lee."

Ethan chimed in, "Oh, he's all right, Lee-lee. He's just a crybaby wimp."

Ethan's put-downs were the last thing they needed tonight. "Shut it, Ethan," Bryan scolded, his patience worn thin. "Your brother has been through a lot the past month. Paul was a hero tonight. He was brave and courageous and nothing close to a crybaby or a wimp."

"Yeah, whatever," Ethan said, scowling at his big brother. "Nothin' like playin' favorites, Dad."

Bryan had had enough. "Stow it, Eeth. This is not the time or place for your jealousy."

"*Jealousy?*" Ethan protested, incredulous. "You think I'm jealous of Pauley-puke?"

Loretta said, "Quit it, Ethan, just quit. Your father is right. This is not the time or place. You should be glad your brother and dad are okay."

"Yeah, whatever."

It pained Bryan to see his children going through yet another nightmarish ordeal. The Gilliams had been facing one harrowing setback after another the past two years. But he did have to admit, in all fairness, Ethan had a legitimate gripe about parental favoritism. Once the big money from the AEF settlement started hitting their bank account, Bryan and Loretta promised all three kids expensive gifts. For Paul it was new band instruments, studio recording time, and a tour bus. For Lianne, a GoPro camera and a monogrammed riding saddle. They had promised to build Ethan a batting cage on the property in early June, but so far, it hadn't happened. Now, two months later, ground still hadn't been broken for the project. The summer had gotten away from them, what with managing Moonrise and keeping up with Fowler-Lemoyne Aviation business. Ethan had become more resentful and vocal about the snub in recent weeks. Bryan realized his and Loretta's procrastination was creating problems between their two sons, and Ethan's outburst here in the heliport hangar reminded him he'd better get the batting cages done before another frigid Montana winter blew in, making construction impossible.

Bryan and Paul moved into Peter's office, Bryan dreading the talk he knew was coming. He shut the door behind them, deadening the noise from the hangar. He sat behind Peter's desk while Paul pulled up a chair facing him. Gilt framed photos sat on the desktop—Peter's smiling wife Brin and their two kids, Kimi and Jacob. A most attractive family. Bryan was happy for Peter finally being able to spend some quality time with his wife and kids. Colorful aerial photos of western Montana and the wilds of Idaho hung on the walls behind him. The adjoining wall contained photos of a younger Peter in a Toronto Maple Leafs uniform posing with teammates, with another couple of frames showing Peter in action, skating down the ice, hockey stick in hand, handling the puck. Several other frames displayed Peter's pilot's license and commendations from his days flying for the Montana Forest Service. Bryan felt strange inhabiting Peter's personal space, like he was trespassing on private property.

"That was a close call tonight, bud," Bryan said, still rattled. "Are you okay?"

"I guess, yeah. Man, I thought that sonofabitch was gonna . . ." Paul peered down at the floor, unable to finish his thought.

"What you did was either extremely brave or very foolish. If it was foolishness, for once I'm glad you were a fool."

Paul smiled at that.

"You saved my life and I'm grateful."

Paul's face colored. He waved his dad off, like what he'd done was nothing.

Bryan looked at him in earnest. "If you hadn't shown up . . . well, let's talk about something else, shall we?"

"Yeah, for sure," Paul mumbled, tugging on a strand of his hair.

"So what is this private thing you wanted to talk to me about?"

The boy twisted his hands in his lap nervously, staring out the interior window into the hangar. Bryan watched him squinting, thinking, struggling with it.

"I'll make this easier on you, son. Sinopa's pregnant, isn't she?"

Paul's head whipped around, surprised. "You knew?"

Bryan gave him a sad smile. "I do now."

"What the hell? You tricked me!"

Bryan chuckled, amused at how often Paul thought he and Loretta were clueless old geezers who couldn't possibly know what was going on with him. The boy couldn't visualize that they had once been teenagers themselves.

"I didn't need to resort to trickery, Paul. I keep my eyes and ears open. Your old man didn't just fall off the ass end of a hay baler."

"I know that, but—"

"Isn't that what you wanted to talk to me about?"

"Well, um, yeah. But how did you know?"

"I've noticed a change between you and Sinopa the past few days. Something like fear passing between you two. And your mother told me you and Sin are talking about getting married. I put two and two together, and *voila!* An easy deduction."

"Mom *told* you? This was supposed to be between me and her."

"Sorry, Pauley, but your mother and I don't keep secrets from each other. If you're planning on marrying Sin, you'd better learn what makes a successful marriage. It's a partnership. Mutual trust and respect. *Communication.*"

Paul moved his head side to side slowly, disbelieving his mother would double-cross him.

Bryan said, "Your mom and I got married young, just a few years older than you and Sin. When your mother got pregnant with you I was terrified. We both were. Afraid we wouldn't be able to handle being parents. I know that look both of you have exchanged the past few days. I know it very well." Bryan smiled. "Like I said, no trickery. Just paying close attention."

Paul's eyes widened. "*You* were terrified? The big war hero who did a couple of tours in Afghanistan?"

"You'd better believe I was. My military experience didn't prepare me for marriage. I'm not sure anything can. Marriage is a huge commitment. Fatherhood even more so. Have you talked about all this with Sinopa?"

"Yeah, some."

"And what is her take?"

"Sin's scared. So am I."

"Understandable. Does she want to keep the baby?"

"I don't know, Pops."

Bryan sighed. "How do Sin's parents feel about their daughter marrying outside the tribe? I know some Blackfeet are traditional and dead set against their daughters marrying white boys."

Paul seemed to relax. His face brightened. "Oh, Mr. and Mrs. Harwood are both cool. They want me to call them by their first names—Nittai and Makada. They love the band and promote our records on the rez. And Sin's older sister, Freya, married a white dude. They're doing fine."

"That's good. How do Sin's parents feel about the baby?"

Paul looked back out into the hangar area. "I don't know. She hasn't told them yet."

"How far along is she?"

Paul shrugged his shoulders.

"There seems to be a lot of holes in communications, Pauley."

"Look, Pops, I know damn well that I fucked up." Paul's eyes glistened with tears. "You don't have to rub it in."

"I'm *not* rubbing it in, buddy. I'm just trying to get some clarity on where things stand. Do you love this girl?"

"Yeah. And she loves me."

"And Sin is what? Sixteen?"

"She just turned seventeen two weeks ago."

God help them, Bryan thought. "Does Sin plan on keeping the baby?"

"I think so, yeah. But we really haven't talked about that."

Bryan tried to mask his disappointment. "I think that might be of paramount importance right now. Have you thought about where you and Sin are going to live while you're raising this baby?"

"Not really, no. Why the twenty questions?"

Bryan looked across the desk at his oldest son, who slumped in his chair, wiping tears from his cheeks. *Oh, the heartbreaking idiocy of youth.*

"You need to put on your big boy pants and go talk to Sinopa's parents, Paul. You and Sin both. Sooner than later. There's much to discuss. You've got to make sure everybody's on the same page."

"Jesus, that's so hard, admitting this to Nittai and Makada."

Bryan held back a groan. "Of *course* it's hard. Being an adult isn't easy, that's for sure."

"You don't like her, do you, Pops?"

"Where did *that* come from? I like Sinopa just fine. Your mom and I both think the world of her. She's pretty and polite, very sweet and . . ." he almost said smart, "very grown up for her age."

"There it is." Paul pointed at him. "*For her age*. You think she's too young, don't you?"

Bryan tried not to let his exasperation show. "She *is* too young, Paul, and so are you. For marriage. For having a baby. That doesn't mean I don't like her. We'll welcome Sinopa into our family with open arms and give her all of our love. We'll help you out financially and support you however we can. But right now the both of you have a lot of things to work out for what's to come."

"You think I'm a fuckup, don't you, Pops?"

"No, son, I don't think that at all. You're a teenager. You've made mistakes just like all teens do. It comes with the territory. All throughout the history of mankind teens have had to suffer through their mistakes while learning life's lessons. You're not alone with that. And I'll tell you, we'd be here all night if I went into all the mistakes I made when I was your age."

"Really? You?"

"Yes, me. Your mother, too. Everybody goes through it, Paul. Everyone suffers the slings and arrows of the teen years. The awkward years. Trying to figure out who you are and how you fit into this world. We just hope the screwups aren't monumental or catastrophic."

"I know my screwup is monumental. Is it catastrophic?"

How do I handle this delicately? Bryan got up and walked around the desk, stood next to Paul. "Stand up," he said.

"What?" Paul said, remaining seated, looking up uncertainly.

Bryan tugged on his shirtsleeve, trying to get him to move.

"What are you doing, Pops?" Paul reluctantly let himself be pulled out of the chair. He leaned awkwardly into Bryan's grasp.

Bryan hugged him close. "I love you so much, son. We'll get through this."

"I love you, too, Dad. I'm glad you're okay."

"Thanks to my heroic son, we're both gonna be okay."

"I know I don't tell you often—maybe *never*—but I really appreciate all you and Mom have done for me. All you *are* doing for me. For Ethan and Lee, too."

Bryan nearly lost it. It was the most intimate moment he could ever remember sharing with his oldest son.

They remained in the embrace for several long minutes, crying tears of joy, reveling in their togetherness.

IT WAS 4:30 AM WHEN BRYAN got back to the house. Loretta was still awake, propped up in bed, reading a book.

"Hi, honey," she said, seeing him enter the bedroom, worn and bedraggled. "Everybody finally clear out of the hangar?"

"Yeah. I thought we'd never get out of there." He sat on the edge of the bed, untying his shoes. "I didn't expect you to be up."

"Couldn't sleep after what went down tonight." She laid her book aside, reached over and rubbed his back. "Are you okay, Bry?"

"I won't lie to you. The whole thing shook me up good. I mean, we knew we were on Sheridan's hit list and that something like this might be coming. But when it actually happens?" He shook his head. "Sweet Jesus." He turned to look at her. "Are Lee and Ethan okay?"

"Lianne was a little confused and scared about why anyone would want to hurt her daddy, but she finally fell asleep."

"That's good. Ethan was a handful tonight. Did he get over his pity party?"

"He did. I think he was embarrassed about it after he gave it some thought."

"Do you think we give our kids too much, Lor?" he said, unbuttoning his shirt.

"I don't know. Maybe? Probably. But we do it out of love."

Bryan dropped his pants and stepped out of them, laid them across a chair. "I think we are *definitely* giving them too much. We're corrupting them with material things."

"You might be right, honey. Maybe we should cut back."

"We should, yes. But we still need to get Ethan's batting cages built. We promised him that." He spied Loretta's book lying next to her. "What're you reading, babe?"

"*Funny Story* by Emily Henry."

"Is it funny?"

"Yeah. Perfect for tonight. A light romantic comedy. I couldn't take anything too heavy right now."

The bed squeaked as he climbed in under the covers. "Yeah, it was a horror show out there."

She reached for him. "Who was this guy that came after you?"

"Another AEF psycho. Burgess Flood. One of the names the FBI brought up when they were here. Flood claims he was with Sheridan the day they invaded our cookout. Said he rode in on one of the bulldozers and took potshots at me. He's goin' away for a long spell. Good riddance."

Loretta ran her hand through his hair. "Think we can relax?"

"Well, Sheridan's dead. The taxidermist and two of Sheridan's assassins are going to prison. Maybe our path is clear now. I sure hope so. It's been exhausting always looking over our shoulders."

"How'd things go with Pauley?"

"We had a good long talk. Our boy is growing up, learning some tough lessons. We were right. We're gonna be grandparents. That is, if Sinopa keeps the baby. I'm stunned by how little they have talked about it. Then again, maybe I shouldn't be surprised."

"They're *so* young, Bry."

"Tell me about it. Two babes in the woods who don't have a clue about what's ahead of them. So, how do you feel about grandmotherhood?"

Loretta sighed softly. "I think I'm too young. And you're too young to be a grandpappy."

"Agreed," he said, so tired he could barely keep his eyes open.

"This Flood character clipped Lou, but did he shoot at you?"

"He put two slugs in my desktop, trying to scare me."

Loretta nestled closer, kissed his ear. "So scary. Hold me, Bry. *Please* just hold me, honey."

Bryan pulled her close, her body warm and inviting. He smelled the rosemary mint of her hair, the lavender of her body lotion. Her cinnamon mouthwash. Familiar scents that welcomed him. Her breasts, soft and supple, pressed against his chest, her body merging with his as if they were biologically engineered to fit together.

They lay entwined, silent and contemplative. Bryan thought he could never love another woman the way he loved Loretta Enright Gilliam. She gave him his balance, his emotional footing, his *heart*. Every last cell of Loretta was imprinted on his soul like an uplifting message. As he lay with her on this early morning, he thought he might just be the luckiest man on the planet.

Their breaths slowed in unison as they drifted into a deep sleep, holding each other.

This long, distressing day was over and they slept soundly, both lost in peaceful dreams.

Return to Tally Lake

August 21: En Route to Tally Lake
Flathead National Forest, Montana

THEY LIFTED OFF FROM GILLIAM'S GUIDEPOST Heliport at 9:00 A.M. for the 45-minute flight to the wilds of Flathead National Forest. Peter was flying solo today, his third day back from vacation. Hayden sat in the co-pilot's seat. Wildlife biologist Bill Carlton, Hayden's friend, sat in the back passenger area with two Montana Fish, Wildlife and Parks ecologists.

The group was on the way to Tally Lake, where state officials were planning to euthanize a trio of Deinosuchus currently terrorizing the lake. The same creatures that had killed three boaters and four campers in the past two weeks. The same beasts that killed two divers and nearly capsized Hayden and Nora's boat in early June. Montana FWP had closed down all recreational activities on the lake following the camper attacks. Hayden thought Montana wildlife officials were too slow in closing down the lake, that the recent seven deaths could have been prevented if preemptive action had been taken after Hayden's hired divers were killed.

Peter heard Hayden's voice in his communications headset. "The FWP is making a big production of killing these Deinosuchus today. Trying to cover their asses. Typical government CYA."

Peter spoke into his mic. "Aren't you fearful of returning to this place after what you went through with those creatures?"

Hayden emitted a short chuckle. "Are you kidding, Lacroix? I've been jonesing to come back after my last entanglement with them. They're the most amazing of all the dinos I've run across so far. Pure crocodilian efficiency. Perfectly suited for survival in both aquatic and terrestrial environments. Apex predators both on land and in the water. They are zoological marvels, really. I hate that they're going to kill them, but I understand. We do the same for bears who have lost their fear of humans. Rogue mountain lions and coyotes, too."

A chill ran down Peter's spine when he thought about Deinosuchus. He'd seen videos of them. Viewing them on a small screen was terrifying enough. He couldn't imagine what they would be like up close in the wild. He hadn't told Brin about this charter. He and his wife had just enjoyed two wonderful vacation weeks together, and Peter didn't want to jeopardize those loving memories with news that he might be getting close to prehistoric crocodiles. Brin had enough problems dealing with her anxieties as it was.

"I was looking for any excuse to see them again," Hayden continued. "Their astounding power, their primeval beauty. It's really something to behold when you see them in action."

Peter gave Hayden a troubling sidelong glance. "Please tell me we'll be safe."

Hayden grinned. "Why so nervous, Lacroix? We will definitely be safe. We'll be filming them from atop deer stands. The Fish and Wildlife folks will be the ones taking the risk, not us. They'll be out in a boat and patrolling the beach. Of course, you can always stay in the chopper if you're uneasy about it."

"No, no. I wouldn't want to miss out on this," Peter said, wondering if he was speaking his truth. He remained unsettled about the prospect of getting anywhere near the crocodilian monsters.

They flew over rolling grasslands and Blackfeet ranches. To the west, the wall of the Rockies rose above the plains, jagged, shadowy. Dark clouds loomed on the horizon, the sun peeking through in spots. Rain was predicted in the next 24 hours.

They climbed in altitude, Peter's ears popping with the change. "I wonder how Bryan and Loretta are doing in Hawaii," he said.

Hayden smiled. "I'm sure they're loving it. Knowing the Gilliams the way I do, he's lounging on a beach with a cold beer, Loretta next to him sipping a Mai Tai and reading a paperback book. They deserve a vacation like that after what they've been through."

"Yeah, close call for Bryan, eh?"

"Too close," Hayden said. "I swear that family is cursed. Some bad juju chasin' after them the past few years."

He sounds just like Brin, Peter thought.

He said, "So, Hayden, I understand National Geographic is paying for this charter."

Hayden nodded. "They're paying me to film the event, yeah. I wish I didn't have to document these killings. It's been my hope that we could find a way to live in harmony with these animals, but I'm beginning to realize I have to accept that it wasn't meant to be. These diseases hitting the dino population are probably going to wipe them out in a second extinction."

"You think so?"

"Yes. I believe it's inevitable, and it makes me horribly sad. These Cretaceous creatures arrived unprepared for modern diseases. As big and terrifying as they are, their immune systems are weak and unable to ward off viruses and bacteria from our world. It's a shame really. An astronomical quirk of nature gave us these magnificent animals once again, after millions of years—a real gift to science—only to whisk them away after just a couple of short years. I would like to have had more time to study them."

Peter had spent his first two days back from vacation flying Hayden and wildlife scientists around the state monitoring the dinosaur epidemic. The situation had become dire. So many dying and dead animals, both prehistoric and domestic. Scientists had identified the diseases: leptospirosis and brucellosis, both fatal bacterial infections. A large percentage of the animals were also covered with bloated ticks and suffered from Lyme disease. The diseases first took root in dinosaurs and were now showing up in domesticated farm animals. So far there had been no reports of it spreading to the human population, but Hayden told him the infection was highly zoonotic, which meant there was a high probability it could spread to humans if not contained. It messed with Peter's head to see so many suffering and dead animals. He hoped to get back to flying more normal charters soon.

"Do you think these Deinosuchus are infected?" Peter asked.

"We'll find out soon enough. But aquatic animals are more segregated, so there's a good chance they're not."

They crossed over the Rocky Mountain Front, long limestone ridges running north to south with deep, glacial valleys blanketed in snow into late summer.

"It's really breathtaking up here, above it all," Hayden said. "Too bad we're on our way to an execution."

Peter couldn't have agreed more.

Soon the mountains gave way to forestland, a rolling, dark green mosaic of western larch and Douglas fir. Peter looked out over tree-covered ridges pocked with small clearings. Narrow creeks snaked through the landscape.

They cleared a high precipice and Tally Lake came into view, looking like an elongated plate of dark glass. Rugged forested slopes rose from the pebbled shoreline.

"They're set up on the campground beach on the northern end of the lake," Hayden said, pointing through the bubble.

The campground lay straight ahead, a patchwork of cleared campsites and picnic areas. A dock jutted out into the water like a wooden finger, a boat launch next to it. Red buoys bobbed in the light chop, marking off the swimming area.

They flew over a wide stretch of beach where several people stood around a cage containing a couple of small animals.

"Are those goats?" Peter asked, leaning forward, straining to make out details.

"Yeah," Hayden said. "Mountain goats. They're using live prey to attract the Deinosuchus. Much more effective lure than the bait pile Carlton and I used."

Peter frowned. "We're gonna watch goats get eaten?"

"Gotta lure the Deinosuchus out of the water somehow, Lacroix. Live prey is the best way to do that."

"What makes you think they're still here, Hayden. You told me these crocs can move across land as easily as they can swim. They could be miles from here by now," he said hopefully.

"Well, for starters, they killed four campers last week. And wildlife agents found two nests in an inlet on the far side of the lake.

These animals never stray far from their nesting grounds."

"What are those?" Peter asked, pointing at a row of elevated structures set up in the middle of the beach, near the goat cage.

"Tower deer stands. Fifteen feet high with a panoramic view. We'll get some fantastic shots from up there."

Peter saw three people setting up camera equipment atop one of the stands. "I thought deer stands were designed to be in the trees."

"Some are. But visibility gets cut off in the trees. So the wildlife agents opted for the tower stands."

"Jesus," Peter said. "They're treating this like a sporting event."

Hayden nodded. "For the FWG, it *is* a sporting event. Like I said, they want to make a big production out of it. To prove to Montanans that they have public safety in mind, that they're doing something proactive to eliminate the problem."

Peter's nerves returned. "Those towers don't look very sturdy."

"Relax, Pete," Hayden said, reaching over and giving his arm a reassuring light punch. "They're rock solid. Heavy-duty steel and anchored. We'll be fine." Hayden pointed through the windshield. "You can take us down here. The beach is hardened mud and stone, a firm touch down spot. "

Peter radioed in to Dispatch to report their landing coordinates, not sure he was ready to witness defenseless goats being devoured by prehistoric crocodiles from atop a skeletal deer stand tower.

Crocodilians!

August 21: Tally Lake

Flathead National Forest, Montana

PETER BROUGHT THE CHOPPER DOWN GENTLY. Hayden watched Lacroix's hands and feet working in synchronized tandem to bring them in for a smooth touch-down. Sitting in the cockpit, Hayden got an up-close view of the technical complexity of flying a helicopter, and he marveled at Lacroix's proficiency at landing the aircraft on this narrow strip of beach.

They sat facing the row of tower stands. The rotors slowed, then stopped. Peter shut down the engine. Bill Carlton and the two ecologists disembarked from the back with their gear. Hayden heard the bleating of the goats. Crows cawed in the distance.

Hayden grabbed his camera case and strapped it on, opened the door. "You coming, Lacroix?"

"I, um—I think I'll stay here and watch the proceedings from a safe distance."

"Come on, Pete. This is a once in a lifetime opportunity to see prehistoric life. There won't be many more chances."

Peter set the friction locks on the cyclic and collective sticks, basically setting the chopper's parking brake. "I have no desire to see animals getting slaughtered, no matter how vicious and dangerous they are,"

"Okay, it's your loss, Lacroix."

"I've gotta ask, Hayden. Is the chopper gonna be safe here? I mean, it's so close to the action."

"You worry too much, Pete. Last I knew, helicopters weren't part of a Deinosuchus's diet. Might be a little tough to digest, even for them."

Peter ducked his head, trying to hide his grin as he did his post-flight instrument check. He appreciated Hayden Fowler's twisted sense of humor, the way he could keep things light.

Hayden joined Bill Carlton on the walk to the deer stands. He noticed the red flagging tape roping off the swimming area, signaling the beach closure. Signs with crude illustrations of crocodiles overlaid with the word *DANGER!* in bright red were nailed to trees. They passed the boat launch, a large aluminum Munson vessel moored to the dock, the Montana FWP decal and registration number showing on the port side. The thought occurred to him that the boat might not be big enough to contend with the crocodilian beasts.

His legs felt heavy and rubbery, slowing his gait. His lower back hurt like hell. He was exhausted, which he seemed to be often these days no matter how much sleep he got. He feared it was his kidney disease speaking to him.

"You think they'll finally snuff these monsters today?" Carlton said, casting a wary glance out over the lake.

"I don't know. They've proven to be elusive," Hayden replied, trying to keep up with Carlton's brisk pace. "Should be interesting."

They were met at the stands by Oliver Dolan, Deputy Director of the Montana Fish, Wildlife and Parks Department, second in line to Director Christy Clark. Hayden knew him well as they had worked together the past month researching the dinosaur epidemic. Mid-forties with a lanky frame, full head of thick black hair, bushy brows over dark, deep-set eyes. Rigid posture and a serious, no-nonsense expression. Oliver Dolan had the authoritative man-in-charge look.

"Hey, Ollie," Hayden said, shaking his hand, then nodding at Carlton. "This is Bill Carlton, wildlife biologist from Idaho Fish and Game."

The two men shook. The Deputy Director already knew the two ecologists in Hayden's group as they were Montana FWP employees.

"Quite a production you've got set up here," Hayden said,

examining the steel structures, thankful for the canvas awnings that gave the towers ample shade.

"Yes, we assembled it all yesterday," Dolan said. "Took a few hours to construct. Lucky for us, the Deinosuchus didn't make an appearance."

"Impressive," Hayden said, looking around, counting a dozen FWP officials on the beach, some with videocams, others shouldering high powered rifles. "I don't see any media here. How'd you manage that?"

"By design," Dolan said. "We want to control the narrative, so we didn't send out our usual press release. Didn't contact the local TV affiliates. We're keeping it close to the vest. This is going to be difficult enough without the media getting in the way. And we're well aware of the aggressive animal rights groups who oppose this."

Hayden nodded. "Smart thinking." He checked the sky, the dark clouds rolling in over the lake. "You think the weather will hold?"

Dolan looked skyward. "It's not supposed to rain until tomorrow, but it *is* looking threatening. Let's keep our fingers crossed." He pointed to the far end of the tower stands. "Come on, I'll take you to your stand. I've reserved it just for your group."

"Thanks, Ollie. I appreciate you including me in this."

"It's the least I could do after what you've been through with these crocs, Hayden," Dolan said as they walked. "Not to mention all the help you've been with getting our hands around the dinosaur epidemic. We should have done this two months ago, after your altercation with the Deinosuchus." The Deputy Director shook his head in a disconsolate gesture. "Yes, we should have acted sooner. I'm devastated by all the deaths these creatures have brought us. So is Director Clark and everybody at Fish, Wildlife and Parks. We should have done better."

"I really wish we didn't have to destroy these animals," Hayden said.

"Yeah, I don't like these euthanasia programs either, but it has to be done so we can open up the lake again. The public is demanding it."

Dolan led them to their stand and Hayden climbed the steps up the side of the tower. He got to the top and felt faint, winded. *Jesus, old man, it's only fifteen feet,* he scolded himself. He plopped down on one of the stools, bent over and let out a deep, exasperated breath.

"You okay, Hayden?" Carlton asked.

"I think I'll live, Bill" he snapped, irritated by his frailty.

He unpacked his camera gear and set up the tripod. Mounted his videocam and aimed it down at the shoreline, framing the goat pen. The goats' continual bleating gave him a headache. They were so loud he was surprised the Deinosuchus hadn't already stormed the beach. But then he thought, *Is that pair of scrawny goats enough of a meal to entice the crocs out of the deep water?* He wanted to tell the FWP folks they should have brought in larger prey—a bear or a moose or a bull elk—but he remained quiet. This wasn't his rodeo.

The four of them settled in for the wait, sitting on metal stools atop the tower, giving them a panoramic view of Tally Lake, one of the deepest lakes in Montana (Hayden knew there were sections reaching depths of 495 feet). From up here they'd be able to spot the Deinosuchus breaking the surface almost anywhere except in a few coves tucked away on the southern end of the lake.

Hayden checked his camera settings—frame rate, resolution, shutter speed, white balance, focus. Jackson had taught him that initial preparation was vital for getting high quality wildlife footage. God how he missed Jack. Lattimer brought a certain zest to life that had invigorated Hayden, a zest that had been missing since his untimely death. The gonzo photojournalist made life so much more fun and intriguing. *Rest in peace, my brother.*

He swung the camera around and zoomed in on Lacroix, Peter's face visible through the chopper's tinted windshield. Lacroix had the satphone pressed against his ear, more than likely talking to Brin. Hayden really couldn't blame Peter for being cautious. He would be, too, if he had a wife and young children. Hayden was envious of Lacroix's domestic life and the love he shared with his family. He yearned for that kind of familial closeness with Nora.

Nora, oh my hot librarian fantasy.

Hayden had never really known the meaning of love until he hooked up with Nora Lemoyne. She had defined for him what it meant for a woman to be a man's better half. Nora was his partner, his confidant. His *equal.* Someone to share this crazy life journey with. Oh, the things she did to him, the things she made him *feel.* Nora's presence, her aura, was unlike anything he'd ever experienced through his three marriages and many scattershot relationships. Of course, he was disappointed she hadn't accepted his marriage proposal. He had been so certain she would say yes. Sure the humiliation of her public rejection embarrassed him, but that was on him. He's the one who stupidly proposed to her in front of her colleagues. He couldn't really blame her for wanting to pursue her career, wherever that took her. He couldn't be angry about it. He realized now that Fate was playing out in the stubborn, honest way Fate always played out, pulling them apart due to their differing professional paths. Hayden knew their love for each other was still there. Still strong. It was just in a configuration he had difficulty identifying.

He had FaceTimed with her yesterday and she appeared happy. Her entire being lit up in an excitable glow as she talked about the dig team's latest find—a nearly complete 110-million-year-old armored Borealopelta, an ancient relative of the Ankylosaurus from the Late Cretaceous. The specimen boasted extraordinarily well preserved osteoderms, keratin sheaths, skin, scales, and stomach contents. Only the second of its kind ever found in this pristine condition. Of course, the folks at the Smithsonian were ecstatic. Their shining paleontological star Nora had come through for them once again.

Hayden was happy for Nora's success, but visiting with her on a tiny cell phone screen reminded him of just how much he missed her. He had never been more lonely than he had been during this separation, a loneliness that at times overwhelmed him. He never thought he would be involved with a woman he couldn't live without, but meeting Nora Lemoyne two years ago had changed that. He knew when she came to his home in Eden Prairie to recruit him for her first Smithsonian expedition that she was someone special. Little did he know then just *how* special.

Yes, the loneliness was dragging him down, but Nora's

Canadian expedition would be over in three weeks, and she told him she was looking forward to being back home with him again. And their long-delayed second book, *Dragons of the Great Divide: Running with the Beasts,* had finally been issued an official publication date of November 12. A month-long author tour was to follow. So they would be back out on the road together once again where their relationship first blossomed. Maybe then Nora would accept his marriage proposal.

Things to look forward to. It's what kept him going.

The deep rumble of the Munson boat's diesel engines reverberating across the water captured Hayden's attention. The boat pulled out into the lake, the stern drives churning up a spray of backwash. He began filming, capturing the FWP captain manning the wheel in the pilothouse and a pair of deckhands leaning against the railing. They were off in an attempt to lure the Deinosuchuses to the surface.

The hunt was on.

Hayden peered at Carlton and the two ecologists, who had their cameras out and were shooting their own videos. Three other FWP officials were doing the same next to them on the adjacent tower stand. An escalating anticipation hung in the air, quiet but electrified, like the calm preceding a heavy storm. Hayden couldn't wait to get another glimpse at these magnificent creatures. He'd told Nora yesterday of his plans to come here and she had begged him not to do it, reminding him of their disastrous visit, when the beasts of the deep had hooked on to their magnetometer cable like it was a trolling line and nearly sunk their boat. She reminded him of the two divers who had lost their lives and how Hayden and she had come close to dying themselves. He'd responded with, "You've got your Canadian fossil collecting mission and I've got my Tally Lake adventure," immediately regretting how patronizing and juvenile he sounded. Nora had been her usual classy self in responding, "Please just be careful, dearest."

A small flock of white ring-billed gulls flew in over the treetops and circled the lake. Their squawking was loud and raucous. A pair of Quetzalcoatlus followed close behind.

"Well look what the wind blew in, Hayden," Carlton said, pointing at the pterosaurs winging in from the south end of the lake. "It's the evil flying reptiles."

Hayden watched the Quetzals gliding effortlessly over the middle of the lake, their oversized reddish-hued wings extended, lifting them on the air currents.

Seeing the pterosaurs in flight reminded him of Stanley Murchison, a.k.a., Quetzal Whisperer, and his arrest for illegal animal trafficking. To Hayden's dismay, his offense was classified a misdemeanor, and Whisperer got off easy with a small fine and a hundred hours of community service. He was now back at his mountaintop sanctuary working with his hawks and falcons and, as far as Hayden knew, no longer owned any Quetzals.

It pained Hayden that Whisperer had become an overnight internet sensation and a sought-after guest on television talk shows. Last week Hayden had seen him interviewed on *The Tonight Show* with Jimmy Fallon, where Whisperer showed videos of his Quetzals doing their fetch-on-command act. Hayden literally screamed at his TV, "Ask the sonofabitch about his pterosaurs fetching human body parts, Jimmy! Come on, interrogate the bastard!"

And he couldn't very well think about Whisperer without the Prescotts coming to mind. Mick and Claire weren't the most upstanding ethical people in the world, but their crimes weren't any more serious than Whisperer's. Certainly not serious enough to be gunned down in cold blood. While Stanley Murchison was cashing in on his celebrity, the Prescotts were lying six feet under, killed by the same two gunmen who were involved in the murder of the Gilliams' ranch hand, one of whom had attempted a hit on Bryan Gilliam. Hayden well knew the world was an inequitable place, but Mick and Claire Prescott deserved better than what they got.

He heard excited shouts coming from the FWP workboat. He leaned down to look through the viewfinder and trained the camcorder on the boat. A Deinosuchus had surfaced near the stern, its eyes and snout showing as it trailed in the boat's wake. A man stood on the aft deck with a rifle. Hayden knew they didn't want to kill these animals in the water; they would never be able to retrieve the carcasses from the deep depths of Tally Lake. The plan was to lure them onto the beach and shoot them there. They wanted photographic proof of the killings for public relations. They also wanted the bodies for scientific research, which pleased Hayden. The guy with the gun on the boat was just for protection should something go wrong. Everyone here was well aware of the damage these creatures did to Hayden's chartered boat, and the deaths of two divers on that charter.

"Here we go," he said to Carlton. "The fun's about to begin."

"I wouldn't want to be on that boat," Carlton said.

One of the ecologists muttered, "Me either."

The commotion out on the water caused a reaction on the beach. Two men ran to the goat cage and let out the pair of mountain goats, hooking them to heavy duty leashes.

The bleating increased in volume.

More shouts from the other end of the tower stands. Hayden looked and saw wildlife officials pointing at something.

"Jesus Christ, what is *that*?" Carlton exclaimed. "A T-Rex?"

Hayden looked to what had drawn everyone's attention. An eleven-foot-tall beast slowly approached the bleating goats, flexing its massive jaws, opening and closing its deep drooling maw as it lumbered stealthily and warily along the shore. Everyone seemed to be frozen, staring at a beast no one was expecting.

"That's not a Rex," Hayden announced. "It's an Albertosaur. *Albertosaurus Sarcophagus* to be precise. Fascinating! It's the first one I've seen."

Carlton: "Looks like a Rex to me, Hayden. How can you tell?"

"It's in the Tyrannosauridae family, but it's smaller than a Rex, with much more withered forelimbs. Albertosaurus eyes are deep set and positioned more on the side of their heads than T-Rex. And they have larger, more widely spaced teeth."

The Albertosaur ventured closer to the goats, focused on its prey and not the least bit concerned with the humans on the beach. The creature was now directly below Hayden's stand. He was getting some fantastic footage from this close, over-the-top angle.

He heard more shouts and warnings.

"One's coming fast!" and "Take cover!" and "Let him hit the beach before you shoot!"

Hayden pulled back from the camcorder and scanned the shallows. A dark shadow streaked to shore like an incoming torpedo.

The Albertosaur, sensing a predator, stopped and turned.

The Deinosuchus shot out of the water, leaping up as though launched by a catapult, clamping onto the surprised Albertosaur with its formidable jaws.

Bones cracked. Fountains of blood spewed across the rock-strewn beach.

The monumental force of the impact drove the Albertosaur into the base of Hayden's stand.

The tower collapsed, the steel structure coming apart and tumbling, four bodies going down in the debris. Hayden hit the beach hard, landing on his back with a painful thud, the wind knocked out of him.

He gasped for breath. Turned his head to see the croc feasting on the Albertosaur next to where he lay. His hearing was muffled, but he could hear the Deinosuchus slurping and chewing, dim screams and shouts for help.

He tried to scramble away but he couldn't feel anything in his legs. Couldn't breathe, couldn't find the strength to escape.

He heard gunshots: *BOOM-BOOM-BAM!*

The Deinosuchus relaxed his hold on the Albertosaur, letting out a long sigh that sounded like a huge truck tire deflating. Hayden looked directly into the croc's now lifeless eyes, its jaws clamping onto the dead Albertosaur's neck, teeth sunk deep.

A freezing coldness enveloped him and he couldn't stop shivering. He tried to move but couldn't, realizing with mounting horror that the fall had paralyzed him from the waist down. He raised an arm and ran his hand through his beard. Came away with blood. Wondered if it was his own or from the two dead beasts lying next to him.

And then, from out of nowhere, a second Deinosuchus snatched him, its deadly teeth sinking into his upper thighs, powerful jaws gripping tight.

Hayden felt pain like none he'd ever known. A mind-frying *blackout* level of pain.

He screamed until he thought he would throw a lung, shrieked until his voice abandoned him. The ancient croc grunted and snorted as it dragged him into the shallow water.

He used his hands, trying to stop the Deinosuchus from pulling him into the lake, but the croc was too powerful.

He heard more shouts and gunshots as his vision dimmed.

The pain was unbearable.

He could make out bodies moving around him, people talking to him, but couldn't identify anyone.

Two Quetzalcoatlus circled overhead. *Evil birds, evil birds, evil birds,* his mind shouted, even though he knew they weren't birds.

His vision went from dull colors to monochrome to gray.

Then finally faded to black.

Last Call for Love

August 21: Tally Lake

Flathead National Forest, Montana

PETER WATCHED FROM THE COCKPIT, seeing a Tyrannosaur break out of the woods and move toward the mountain goats on the beach. He sat up, grabbed the binoculars, zeroed in on the beast as it walked along the water's edge, drool dripping from its shovel mouth, eyes focused on its prey.

But the creature didn't get far before a Deinosuchus rocketed from the shallows, powerful jaws snapping, taking the Tyrannosaur down in a forceful collision. The big dinosaurs bellowed and snorted as they battled, crashing into the stands, their immense weight crumpling the towers.

Peter saw Hayden fall, recognizing him by his thick beard and long hair, the big man going down hard on the beach amidst the twisted wreckage. Gunshots echoed across the lake as the Fish and Wildlife officials rushed in firing their weapons, killing the croc.

A second big Deinosuchus exploded out of the lake, going after the closest body—Hayden. The croc's enormous jaws clamped down on his legs, its lethal teeth sinking deep.

Peter could hear Hayden's screams, even from this distance.

It all happened in the blink of an eye.

He sat for several long, critical seconds, stunned, not believing what he was seeing.

Then his instincts kicked in.

His friend and colleague was in serious trouble.

He hustled around the chopper to the rear cargo area and retrieved his short-barreled rifle, then took off running.

Chaos reigned all around him. FWP agents shouting. Goats bleating. The wounded crying out for help. Birds and pterosaurs circling overhead, squawking and trilling.

More explosive gunshots.

The bright coppery tang of blood flooded his nasal passages as he got closer. Blood stained the beach, making for slippery footing.

His vision blurred from the smoky cordite in the air, the wild animal stench and putrefying odor of laid-open carnivore entrails.

His mind reeled in confusion. His arms and legs were weak.

Dizziness hit him with a knockout punch.

Somebody called out to him, "Over here, Peter, over here."

Bill Carlton.

"He's hurt really bad, Pete," Carlton said, alarm in his voice. "He's in big trouble."

Peter followed Carlton down to the waterline, noticing he was limping.

"How about you, Bill? You okay?"

"Yeah. Just sprained my ankle. It's minor. But Hayden on the other hand . . ."

They came to where Hayden lay trapped in the mouth of the dead croc. Peter looked down at the Deinosuchus stretched out in the shallow water, its leathery hide pocked with bullet holes, blood oozing from the wounds. The creature had a viselike grip on Hayden's legs with those terrible jaws, its sizeable front teeth sunk deep into his thighs. Peter could clearly see exposed bone and cartilage, and thought he might be sick. The croc had chomped clean through Hayden's legs, mid-thigh. His legs were separated from his torso! He was losing blood fast.

Peter tried to hide his shock while his mind raced. *This can't be happening, this can't be happening . . .*

Hayden, barely conscious and emitting low moaning sounds, peered up at Peter with a glazed expression, his face slate gray, his beard and hair tinted red with blood. Peter exchanged looks with Carlton, the look saying both men knew there was nothing they could do to save him.

"Is—is that you, Lacroix?" they heard Hayden croak.

"Yeah, it's me, Hayden. Hang in there, buddy. We'll get you some help," Peter said, knowing there was no truth in those words.

"My . . . voice," Hayden rasped, grimacing in pain. "It's weak. Come d-down here."

Peter took a knee near Hayden's face, the lake water soaking his pants. "I'm here for you, my friend."

Hayden spoke so low Peter could barely hear him. "Tell Nora I'll . . . lo-love her forever, and . . ." he stopped, writhing in pain, then started again slowly, his words coming with great effort, "th-that I will . . . def-definitely see her again . . . ho-hopefully later than soo-sooner."

His upper body convulsed and he gasped, a look of fear in his glassy eyes. For a static moment, he followed the path of the two Quetzalcoatlus circling overhead. And then his head jerked to the side and he lay still.

There was no doubt Hayden Fowler had left this mortal world.

"No, no, NO!" Peter screamed, grabbing Hayden's arm.

"Come on, Peter," Carlton said, pulling him up and away from Hayden's body. "He's gone."

Peter stood, wet and trembling and angry. He wanted to empty his rifle into this Deinosuchus that had just murdered his friend, but knew that wouldn't bring Hayden back. As much as he didn't want to cry in front of all these men, he couldn't hold back his emotions.

Carlton draped an arm over his shoulders and pulled him close, sniffling, trying to contain his own emotions, but failing, both men letting the tears flow freely.

Behind them Peter heard Deputy Director Oliver Dolan say, "This is a devastating loss, gentlemen, for sure, but we can't linger."

Peter turned to Dolan. "He was my friend. Hayden gave me and my family so much."

"I know," Dolan said. "He was a friend to all of us." The deputy director looked out over the lake. "But right now we need to be hyper aware. There's at least one more of these monsters out there in the depths, and we don't need any more tragedies today."

Peter felt emptied out. An overpowering sadness clouded his soul. The scene here on Tally Lake Beach had an unreal feel to it, like the set of a Hollywood horror movie shoot. He glanced at Hayden lying lifelessly in the jaws of the giant croc.

Peter had been given a directive: *Tell Nora that Hayden loved her and that he would see her again, hopefully later than sooner.*

He wept for his lost friend and business partner.

Final Arrangements

August 22: Smithsonian Expedition
The Puskwaskau Formation
West-Central Alberta, Canada

ON THEIR MOVE WEST THEY UNCOVERED a large bed of marine fossils, which included a paleontological gem: a nearly intact Mosasaur. Mosasaurs were giant aquatic apex predators, dating back to when the Western Interior Seaway fed the Boreal Sea to the north. Back when this entire region was deep underwater. These inland sea creatures died out in the Campanian stage, seven million years prior to the Cretaceous-Paleogene extinction event.

Nora was pleased. The expedition's good luck continued.

She stood at the rim of the quarry along with her lead paleontologist, Clive Driscoll, and chief geologist, Greg Dulowski. They observed the team working in the troughs below as they excavated dozens of small ancient sea creature specimens, and trenched the Mosasaur skeleton. The whine of augers, pounding jackhammers, clinking chisels, and the metallic cracks of rock hammers drifted up to them.

"Hard to believe this was all once an immense ocean," Nora said in awe.

Dulowski nodded. "Just one of the many geologic examples of how our Earth is a living organism," he replied, speaking loudly over the clatter in the quarry. "The transformation was due primarily to the Laramide Orogeny, a massive tectonic event that caused the Farallon oceanic plate to collide with, and subduct, the continental plate. That process pushed up what we now know as the Rocky Mountain ranges. The displacement took millions of years, but it caused a major marine regression, pushing the sea out of western Alberta and transforming this area into the plains, estuarine, and alluvial environments we see here today."

Nora knew some of this from her graduate geology studies. "The area has a low sedimentation rate coupled with a high level of bioerosion, which causes marine reptile fossils to be ultra fragile. Makes it delicate work for our field techs."

"So true, Nora," Dulowski said. "And the heavy composition of shale and claystone out here only adds another layer of difficulty to specimen extraction."

Clive Driscoll pointed down at the exposed Mosasaur sitting on a pedestal of rock, workers trenching the ditch around it. "That Mosasaur skeleton is superb. An exceptional find."

"Yes, it certainly is, Clive," Nora said. "The phosphatic deposits in this region have done a remarkable job of preserving this specimen."

She watched the technicians working around the massive Mosasaur mouth and backward-curving, blade-like teeth, her eyes roaming the 43-foot length of its body.

"The excavation is going to be very difficult," she continued. "A complete, articulated fossil like this Mosasaur will weigh in at eight tons, minimum. Unfortunately, we're going to have to deconstruct the skeleton and remove the specimen from the quarry bone by bone, then reassemble it offsite. It's going to require very precise cataloging. We'll end up with a mounted skeleton rather than a complete articulated specimen, but our sponsors are fine with that. They know the terrain we're dealing with out here. Lots of grueling work ahead of us, gentlemen."

"It will be difficult," Driscoll agreed. "But it'll be so worth it."

"Yes it will," Nora said. "But I do worry about our flatbed truck getting stuck. The ground is saturated and spongy here, and it'll be hell to pay if our transport vehicle sinks in the muck under all that weight. It'll be a lot tougher to get out than that backhoe."

The stuck-in-the-mud backhoe had been just one of many unlucky inconveniences they had faced in their four days here. They'd had to be careful with how they moved their heavy earthmoving equipment in and around the quarry. Their first day here saw them get their backhoe bogged down in the muck. It took three hours and some rudimentary engineering using sheets of plywood and 30-proof coil chains to free it. Then, on day two, an intern, Katy Borrister, walked into a well concealed quicksand bog, getting trapped, the liquefied silty clay slowly sucking her down. Three of the strongest young men on the team exhausted themselves tugging her out using heavily braided ropes. There had been other setbacks as well: a snakebite; high winds kicking up a dust storm; a half day lost due to heavy downpours.

Yes, they had faced a few difficulties in this challenging outback. But the rewards thus far had been great.

Nora, Dulowski, and Driscoll stood together, silently watching the paleontologists going about their business in the quarry below.

Nora turned to Dulowski. "You assembled a blue-chip team, Greg, It certainly makes my job easier having a group of pros like this on the dig."

"Thanks, Nora. Clive here helped a lot with the recruiting. And the Smithsonian spared no expense."

Nora's satellite phone sounded with a series of beeps and clicks. She removed it from her belt pouch and checked the display: Peter Lacroix.

Why is Peter calling me?

"Excuse me, I've got to take this," she said to her colleagues.

She stepped away, turning her back on them, extending the antenna and connecting.

"Hi, Peter. Haven't heard from you in a while. What's up? A company problem I need to know about? You need my approval for a purchase?"

"Hey, Nora," he responded with a slight echo. "I, uh . . . I have really dreaded having to make this call."

Hearing Peter's ominous tone set her alarm bells ringing. *Another helicopter crash? Another attack on the Gilliams?*

"What's going on?" she said, standing rigid, bracing herself.

"You haven't happened to see or hear the news the past twenty-four hours have you?"

"No," she answered. "We don't get much news out here in the badlands of western Canada. Why?"

"I, um, well, this is difficult for me. I, uh . . . well—"

"Just *tell* me, Peter!"

"I would have delivered the news in person if I could, but I felt you should hear it from me before the press runs with it."

"Oh, Jesus," she said, a fluttery panic rising in her throat. "It's Hayden, isn't it?"

"I'm afraid so, Nora. I'm so sorry."

"When?" A sharp pain pierced her chest.

"Yesterday afternoon. I was with him. I flew him solo to Tally Lake. He had a contract from National Geo to film the state's Deinosuchus eradication."

"Yes, I knew about that," she said, trying to keep her wits about her. "What happened, Peter? Did he do something crazy?"

"No. It wasn't like that. It was just an unfortunate accident. He happened to be in the wrong place at the wrong time."

"Tell me about it," she said, beginning to hyperventilate, her heart going into a sprint, skipping beats. A trembling started in her legs making her unsteady on her feet. She moved to a moss-covered boulder and sat.

Peter described what he had witnessed of Hayden's death. She listened, appreciating the way he soft-pedaled it, the way he respected her by avoiding graphic descriptions.

The news was shocking and sudden, but not altogether unexpected. Ever since Hayden's lunatic friend, Jackson Lattimer, was killed, he seemed to have upped the danger level of his work, getting more and more reckless in his dinosaur encounters and disregarding his personal safety. First with the Deinosuchus out on the lake (she knew she should have been smart enough to avoid that outing, but Hayden had been most persuasive), then with the Quetzalcoatlus on Quetzal Whisperer's mountaintop sanctuary. He followed that craziness by throwing caution to the wind and working in the field examining sick and dying dinos that were carrying zoonotic diseases. And now, going back to Tally Lake to film the deadly prehistoric crocs once again.

Hayden's testosterone-fueled misadventures had finally cost him his life.

Nora's pulse was so furious she thought she might be having a heart attack. She was lightheaded. Tears welled in her eyes as she listened to Peter, envisioning her beloved Hayden lying on the beach, stunned and helpless after the fall, the Deinosuchus attacking him, separating him from his legs. She wanted to scream, but could only manage soft whimpering moans. Ceaseless tears wet her face as she tried to catch her runaway breath between sobs.

Peter said, "I was by his side when he passed, and his last words were for you, Nora. He instructed me to give you a message."

"A message?"

"Yeah. He said he would see you again on the other side. Hopefully later than sooner."

"He said that, really? You're not just telling me that to make me feel better?"

"I wouldn't do that to you, Nora. His exact words were: 'Tell Nora I'll love her forever and that I will definitely see her again, hopefully later than sooner.' He was thinking of you at the very end."

It sounded like Hayden, and it absolutely tore her apart.

"I'm so sorry for your loss, Nora. Is there anything I can do for you here in the States?"

"Thank you, but no," she sputtered. "I . . . I'll be returning tomorrow to handle final arrangements. Where, um, where is his body?"

"Hayden's mother Miranda is having it flown to Indianapolis where the funeral will take place. Look, you are understandably distraught, Nora. I'd come and get you myself, but—"

"I understand, Peter," she sniffled, managing somehow to keep it together. "I'll see you late tomorrow. Thank you for your call. I know it couldn't have been easy for you."

Nora disconnected and, hands shaking, collapsed the antenna and returned the satphone to her belt. She sat on the rock, crushed and devastated.

"What's going on, Nora?" Greg Dulowski said, approaching.

She removed her glasses, wiped her eyes, embarrassed by her breakdown. "It's Hayden," she said, tearily.

"Did something happen to him?"

"He's dead."

"He's *what?*"

"He's gone, Greg. Oh my GOD!"

She broke down crying again and Dulowski went to her, helped her off the boulder and embraced her.

"It's going to be okay," he said, rubbing the back of her shoulders consolingly. "We're here for you."

She leaned into him, shaking, crying on his shoulder. Blubbering, she began to tell the geologist what Peter had told her.

Dulowski pulled away from her, looked her in the eyes. "You're in no condition to talk about this right now, Nora."

"I need to leave, Greg," she said, getting frantic. "I've got to get back home and take care of things. I'm leaving you in charge."

He frowned. "Nonsense. You shouldn't be alone right now. I'm coming with you."

"You don't have to do that," she protested.

"Yes, I do. Clive can run things quite capably while we're gone. You need the company and Hayden was a colleague and a friend. I'd like to pay my respects to the man."

As they walked back to the trailers, Nora thought, *I should have said yes to Hayden. I shouldn't have been so goddamned selfish. I'm SO sorry, big guy.*

She glanced up at the big sky and crossed herself, despite being a lapsed Catholic. *If you're listening, Lord, please comfort my love wherever he might be. And for fuck's sake, help me get through this.*

The Romantic Octopus

August 26: Gilliam's Guidepost

Heart Butte, Montana

NEWS OF HAYDEN FOWLER'S SUDDEN AND SHOCKING death swept across international media outlets like a category five hurricane. TV newscasts and social media platforms crackled with different takes on his violent passing. The world grieved for the late renaissance man, celebrated for his paleozoological expertise, his pioneering dinosaur tracking, popular bestselling books, and cutting-edge wildlife videos.

No one grieved harder and deeper than Nora.

She was disconsolate. Devastated.

But she was oh so slowly regaining her emotional footing.

She had spent the last four days at Gilliam's Guidepost in the company of her Cretaceous friends. Nora couldn't face going back to Minnesota and the house she and Hayden had shared for more than a year. Too many memories there. Returning to the house in Eden Prairie would surely have destroyed her. Heart Butte is where she belonged at this vulnerable time. Home base of her company, Fowler-Lemoyne Aviation and home of the people who truly cared about her and Hayden.

The first two days were the most difficult. Nora had cried herself dry. She suffered through periods of distress so deep she wanted to end it all and join Hayden in the afterlife. She vacillated between blaming herself for her selfishness, then blaming him for his recklessness.

She grappled with the nature of grief, how it got under her skin and permeated her internal organs like a metastatic cancer. The way it made her tremble and bring on incapacitating panic attacks. Nora had always been embarrassed by public displays of emotion, and her first two days at the Guidepost had been filled with them. She felt like a burden on the Gilliams and Lacroixes. Her friends seemed to understand, but she still felt like she was imposing, dumping her problems on them. Nora had long prided herself on being strong and independent. She wasn't a mawkish, overly sentimental woman. In her mind, acting out in front of others was taboo. Any personal problems should be dealt with in private.

But Hayden's death had changed that line of thinking.

They had spent just two years together, but the big man with the scruffy beard and brilliant scientific mind had changed her in so many ways.

Feeling loss this deeply proves I loved him, doesn't it?

Nora was well acquainted with personal loss. She lost her father when she was eleven. She had attended three of her grandparents' funerals as a young girl. But Hayden's abrupt vicious death was something else altogether. It was a constant reminder of how quickly a loved one could be snatched away, a startling reminder of the brevity of life.

Would Hayden still be here if I had accepted his hand in marriage?

That question taunted her daily.

After the first two days of gushing tears and raging fears, Nora started settling down with the help of her Cretaceous friends.

Bryan and Loretta had cut their Hawaii vacation short and returned home to welcome her with open arms. Nora apologized to them repeatedly, seeing it as her fault that the Gilliams couldn't finish out their well-deserved Pacific island getaway.

"Nonsense, Nora," Loretta told her. "We can go back to Hawaii anytime. You and Hayden are family. Your loss is our loss. You're welcome to stay with us as long as you want."

Peter and Brin Lacroix stayed in the Guidepost Cellar in the apartment suite next to hers with their children, Kimi and Jacob. Brin's mother, Kachina, had also joined them. Brin and Loretta had been so sweet, tirelessly staying up with Nora through those first two long nights, drinking fresh-brewed coffee and playing endless games of Scrabble, Trivial Pursuit, Blackjack, Gin Rummy, and Spades. The games helped Nora chase her nighttime demons.

The Gilliam children were also a welcome presence. Lianne Gilliam displayed an understanding of death Nora thought to be advanced for a nine-year-old. Lee-lee, as the Gilliams called her, sensed Nora's pain and spent a lot of time with her.

"I know you are sad, Miss Nora," Lianne had told her that first day. "My Uncle Jimmy died two years ago at our cookout and I was sad for a long time. A nasty dinosaur got him. I miss him so much."

Nora didn't know how to respond to that, so she just smiled at the girl.

Lianne also loved to show off her American Girl doll Lila, and Lila's horse Hollyhock, complete with a saddle, bridle, and blanket. Lianne was so cute, doing Lila fashion shows for Nora, first dressing the doll in horseback riding outfits and showing Nora how Lila groomed Hollyhock, even making horsey sounds.

"I'd like to go riding with you sometime, Miss Nora," Lianne told her. "You can never be sad when you're riding a horse."

Nora managed a weary smile. "I'm not sure I'm cut out for horseback riding, Lianne."

"Sure you are," the girl said with confidence. "You could ride Clancy. He's real gentle. Mama rides Clancy all the time."

Lee-lee's optimistic innocence lifted Nora's spirits. Not for the first time, Nora questioned her decision not to have children.

Oldest son Paul Gilliam was also there for Nora, writing a song for her, an up-tempo tune titled "Let the Sun Warm Your Heart," a beautiful melody that unquestionably warmed her heart. Nora loved the song so much she requested he keep playing it for her, and Paul complied, over and over, singing and strumming his acoustic guitar, harmonizing with his girlfriend Sinopa on the choruses. Such a gifted musician and songwriter. And Sinopa was a sweet girl with a lovely voice.

Paul was taking Hayden's death a little more to heart than his two siblings. Hayden had become a huge fan and supporter of Paul's band, Moonrise, and the two had developed a special friendship over the last six months. Paul sent Hayden demo tapes of his songs, which they discussed in frequent phone calls. He told Nora that he was writing a song for Hayden that he would play at Saturday's funeral, and that he would play it for her once he had it all worked out.

The middle child, Ethan, wasn't around much, but when he was, Nora found him to be polite and respectful, if not a bit on the shy side. Looks-wise, Ethan was the polar opposite of his older brother: lithe, athletic, and clean-cut while Paul was heftier with a tangle of hair that fell past his shoulders and a three-day stubble.

Paul and Bryan filled Nora in about the botched murder attempt on Bryan, with Paul and his personal bodyguard Lou Goolsby saving the day. Goolsby, had survived the gunshot wound he'd suffered, and was in Missoula undergoing intensive physical therapy. Lou had reported he would be okay if the therapy didn't kill him first.

On her first day at the Guidepost, Nora received a call from her estranged mother, Grace, who said she would be flying from Chicago to help Nora through her ordeal. Nora was too distraught to argue, and knew her mother would come regardless of how much she pushed back. She and her mother had a long checkered history. Nora blamed Grace for her aloofness and for not standing up for her when her older sisters, Cate and Debra, bullied and tormented her throughout her childhood. Nora hadn't seen or spoken with her in five years.

She had fretted over her mother coming to Heart Butte and wanted so badly to tell her to stay away. But the Grace who arrived at the ranch bore little resemblance to the cold and distant mother Nora thought she knew. Oh, she still had the cotton candy white fluff of hair, chunky large lens eyeglasses, and dressed in her favored soft gray polyester pantsuit and navy turtleneck. But the Grace who greeted her had a whole different aura about her, showering Nora with endearing empathy and uncharacteristic warmth.

"I'm so sorry for your loss, Nora dear," Grace had told her on arrival. "I know what it's like losing the love of your life. I lost your father at a relatively young age, too. He's been gone a long time but I still remember how something like that tears your heart out and slices it into a million little pieces. I know how it feels trying to put all those pieces back together. It seems like an impossible task. I know what you are going through, sweetheart. I'm here for you."

Who is this woman? Nora recalled thinking. *She is cordial and genuine and, dare I say it, loving? Not at all the mother I remember.*

By this morning, Nora had warmed (just a little) to this new version of her mother. They sat in Nora's Cellar suite kitchenette sharing a breakfast of waffles and bacon, and, surprising to Nora, the conversation was mostly civil.

"Did you finally get some sleep last night?" Grace said between bites of waffle.

"Yes, I did. Things are better. I won't say I'm on top of the world, but at least the funeral doesn't feel like an impossible undertaking now."

Tomorrow they would board a flight to Indianapolis for Saturday's funeral service. All Fowler-Lemoyne Aviation charters were canceled for three days in observance of Hayden's passing.

"Are you planning to speak at the funeral?" Grace asked.

"Maybe. I'll be lucky to get through it without breaking down."

"You'll do fine. You're a very strong, articulate woman."

Nora eyed her mother suspiciously. She wanted to say, *How would you know that?* but decided to keep the peace. She said, "I'm not so sure about that right now."

They ate in silence, knives and forks scraping plates.

Grace slid three more waffles onto her plate and drenched them with huckleberry syrup, plopped a spoonful of whipped cream on the stack. A big appetite was one thing Nora remembered about her mother.

Grace took a large bite of waffle and washed it down with a slug of coffee. Looked at Nora. "You know you really make me proud, honey. You have accomplished so much in your young life."

"I'm forty-six, Grace." She hadn't called her *Mom* or *Mother* since she was eight years old. "I'm not exactly a debutante."

"You've done more with your forty-six years than I could do in four lifetimes. I've read your book, you know."

This statement out of the blue shocked Nora. "You have?"

"Yes, along with millions of other readers. My daughter, the famous bestselling author," she said, dreamily, her eyes shining as she peered at Nora across the table.

"I didn't think *Cretaceous Stones* would be your kind of reading material."

"Ordinarily it wouldn't, but it's *your* book, dear. You wrote it and you and Hayden had some really wild adventures together. It reads like an exciting novel. You're a very accomplished writer."

"Thanks, Grace." *Who the hell is this woman?*

"You've earned all the accolades you've been getting. You deserve your fame. Many of your friends here are famous, too. The Gilliams. That handsome Canadian helicopter pilot, Peter, and his Indian wife. They all seem really nice."

"They are. They're great people. They've helped me so much. And I never would have met them if that meteorite hadn't come down in the Gilliams' meadow. Fate has an interesting way of mapping our journeys."

"I know. I read about that in your book," Grace said, lifting her coffee cup and drinking. "I've seen online that your new book is coming out soon and that there's an author tour scheduled. Has that been canceled now?"

"No, not yet."

"Are you going through with it?"

"I don't know. The publisher called me when I first arrived here but I was in no condition to discuss it. It's not until mid-November, so I have some time to decide. In some ways I think it might be cathartic to go out and meet our readers. But then I recall how exhausting the last tour was. And that was with Hayden. I might not be able to handle it solo. I'm not sure I *want* to do it without him."

"That's understandable, hon. You've been under quite a strain."

Nora took a sip of coffee, set her cup down. "Can I ask you something?"

"Sure, you can ask me anything, dear."

Even though things were going well with Grace, Nora decided now might be the time to hit her with the million-dollar question that she's kept close to the vest for years. "Why do you hate me? Is it because I never gave you grandchildren?"

"What? Oh my goodness, Nora!" Grace sat with her mouth open in genuine surprise. "I've *never* hated you," she said, reaching across the table, taking Nora's hand in her own. "I *love* you, darling. I've *always* loved you. You have to believe that."

Nora stared at Grace's hand grasping hers. The moment was too honest and she couldn't look her mother in the eye.

"Are you sure you didn't make this trip just so you could hobnob with us *famous* people," she said, putting air quotes around *famous.*

Grace flinched, like she'd been slapped.

Nora looked up, saw the shocked hurt on Grace's face. "Sorry, that wasn't nice," she said. "But you *have* mentioned the celebrities here at Gilliam's Guidepost several times."

Grace nodded, her eyes brimming with tears. "I know. I guess I've been a little starstruck at meeting people I've read about in your book. People I've seen on the news and on social media."

"I guess I can understand that. I shouldn't have said what I did."

Grace caressed Nora's knuckles. "I came here for *you*, Nora. We have lost so much valuable time, you and me. It's slipping away from us and I didn't want to go on any longer being strangers. I want to believe that you need me right now. I certainly need you, hon."

Nora sighed. "So then why do you always take Cate and Debra's side? You knew they were bullying me when we were kids and you just let it happen. And it continues now that we're adults. You always support them and leave me out in the cold."

"Oh, honey. Surely you must know how insecure your sisters are. Catelyn and Debra are jealous of you. Haven't you picked up on that? Neither of them have your strength or intelligence. Even as a child you were independent and intellectually curious, smart as a whip. Cate and Deb don't have your gifts. I love them both, but they are very different from you. Their idea of happiness differs from yours. They're more domesticated. All they want and need are a husband who can support them, children, and a big house in a gated community with the white picket fence. Education and careers were never their motivation. Your sisters are a lot like me in that regard. You're more like your father, God rest his soul. I guess what I'm saying is Cate and Deb could never measure up to you, Nora, and they know it. That's why I side with them. I've always tried to build them up because they need that kind of support. I always figured they needed my help and that you were strong enough and smart enough to rise above it."

Nora let out a snort, pulled her hand away. "Well, you figured wrong, Grace! They hurt me, and they still piss me off with their passive aggressive bullying. I could certainly use your help on my side once in a while."

"Look, I know I haven't been a candidate for mother of the year honors, Nora. I've made a lot of mistakes as a single mom. That's one thing, with all your smarts and advanced college degrees, you'll never understand just how difficult motherhood can be. You've never had that experience. I am so, so sorry I have let you down and I'm here to make amends. I'd like to start over. I'll do better if you give me the chance."

Nora contemplated what she'd just heard. Her mother did seem changed for the better. She seemed sincerely interested in patching up their frayed relationship. Grace was all alone in Chicago, which made Nora feel a stab of sympathy for her.

"Okay, I'm willing to give it a try, Grace. It pains me to admit this, but I'm a lot more sensitive than I let on. I'm surprised you were never able to see that. Hayden figured that out about me right away. He was the first man to really *know* me. Hayden knew *how* to love me. He was my best friend and confidant, and I treated him terribly."

"Oh? How so?"

"He asked me to marry him and I turned him down. Publicly. Hayden traveled all the way to northern Canada where I was working to propose to me. I turned him down."

"Why? You obviously loved him."

"I did, yes. Still do. He will always fill up my heart. But there were five divorces between us. The odds for a successful marriage were definitely *not* in our favor."

Nora got up from the table and went to the coffee pot, poured herself another cup. "You want some more caffeine, Grace?"

"Sure," she said, sliding her cup across the table. "You know, Nora, your problem was always that you treat love like a line item on a balance sheet. True love isn't a transaction. You were always too businesslike about your relationships."

And there is a bit of the old Grace coming to the surface.

Nora filled Grace's cup then returned the pot to the burner. She stood with her back turned. She tried to keep her voice steady. "You know, Grace, if it's a new beginning you wanted, that's not the way to go about it."

"I'm sorry, dear. I'm being judgmental again, aren't I?"

Nora turned to face her. "Yes, you are."

Grace looked flustered. "Jeez, I don't know what's wrong with me. I haven't learned when to keep my opinions to myself."

Nora returned to the table and took a seat. Took a deep breath. "It's okay, Mother. If we're going to have a fruitful relationship, we need to speak our truths, painful though they may be."

"You called me *Mother*," Grace said, eyes shining.

"I did, yes. When I call you Grace I feel like I'm talking to a stranger. I don't want you to be a stranger anymore."

"Oh, that's so nice, dear," Grace reached across the table and touched Nora's arm. Smiled at her.

Nora said, "We've only been talking about me since you got here. How is life in the Windy City as a seventy-five-year old woman?"

"I'm seventy-seven, but who's counting?"

"Oh, well, you can believe this or not, but I *have* been thinking about you the past few years, a woman your age living all alone in Chicago. I can't imagine—"

"Who says I'm alone? I happen to be dating a very nice man. Arthur is his name. He's a retired banking executive. Artie treats me really well. We have a lot of fun together for a couple of old farts."

"Really? How long has this been going on?"

"Almost three years."

"How did you meet?"

"We met at Ludlow Charlingtons, a wonderful coffee house on the lakefront. They have the best lattes and Danish pastries in all of

Chicago. They sponsor a program that finds good homes for sheltered dogs. Fifty percent of their sales go to that effort. Hanging on their walls are portraits of dogs dressed in Victorian era fashion. It's so cute, Nora. Artie loves dogs. He has three of them. That's what brought us together initially, drinking lattes and discussing dogs. We still go to Ludlow Charlingtons every week."

Nora smiled. "I'm so happy for you, Mother. And here I thought you were a lonely old widower living alone in the big city. Are you and um, Artie, living together?"

"Oh no. We like to keep separate residences." Grace waved her hand nervously. "Let's get back to you. Tell me about Hayden. I wish I could have met him."

Nora took a long drink of her coffee, then set her cup in the saucer. "Hayden was the most exciting man I've ever known. He was six-foot-four, but he had an even larger presence about him. He was always the center of attention when he entered a room. With his untamed long hair and *Duck Dynasty* beard, he looked like a wild mountain man, but his looks were deceiving. He was erudite and intelligent, one of the smartest people I've ever met. I still can't believe I not only met him, but had a two-year relationship with him. I remember being in grad school and discovering his first two books. When I read his writings about the Cretaceous-Paleogene extinction, it felt like he was speaking exclusively to me. I used to gaze at his author photograph and fantasize about being with him. Like a crazed fangirl I searched the internet to learn all I could about him. I'm not proud of that, but there it is. Then, two years ago, I met him when I was recruiting for my first Smithsonian paleontology dig. He was a bit crude and full of himself. He was a womanizer and had problems with alcohol, but I tamed him. And I have to say, he loved me unconditionally from the start. He quit drinking for me and he never wandered on me. He was always kind and loyal to me."

Grace was grinning ear to ear. "That sounds like something out of a romance novel."

Nora laughed. "Yeah, a really *lame* romance novel. Our sex life would make for a *steamy* romance novel, however."

"TMI, dear," Grace said, making a face that was half smile, half grimace.

"Hayden was a very complicated man. He could be irascible and he had a misanthropic streak a mile wide. He preferred animals over people. He rubbed a lot of folks the wrong way, but if he liked you and respected you, he would give you the moon and the stars. You know, I thought I lost him last year after the crash, when he was in the coma. That was hard, but nothing compared to what I'm going through now," she said, her eyes misting up.

"I know, Nora dear, I know. Do you want to stop?"

"No, I need to talk." She shifted to a more tame subject—her and Hayden's week in Paris staying at the beautiful Hôtel San Régis in the Golden Triangle of the Champs Elysées district. The romance of the City of Lights. The restaurants and sidewalk bistros. The historical sights.

Grace hung on every word. "That must have been incredible."

"It was. Truly a dream come true." She paused, emitting a soft snicker.

"What is it, hon? What's so funny?"

"I was just thinking about what he said to me once. Knowing his love of the animal kingdom, I asked him if he could come back as any animal, what would it be, and why. He didn't hesitate, saying he would want to return as an octopus."

"An octopus? Why would anyone want to be an octopus?"

"He said, 'Because then I'd have eight arms to hold you tighter and three hearts to love you more.' Can you believe that?"

"Wow! Hayden the romantic octopus," Grace said, laughing.

And that set Nora off laughing as well. "Yes, and then he went on this long monologue, giving me the zoological history of cephalopods and more specifically, the Octopodidae family. How they had lived in our oceans for more than 330 million years, making them older than the dinosaurs. How their brainpower was unparalleled amongst sea creatures, giving them the ability to solve puzzles and use tools. How they were completely boneless, allowing them to squeeze through tiny, coin-sized spaces and could camouflage themselves to elude predators. That was Hayden: weird, fun, adventurous, sexy, quirky, head full of amazing knowledge. And he had the nerdiest sense of humor. I loved him, Mom, and I miss him so much."

Grace touched her arm again. "You called me *Mom*."

"Yes, I did," Nora said, taking her mother's hand in both of hers.

Grace and Nora Lemoyne sat there smiling at each other.

The healing between mother and daughter had begun.

The Detective and Quetzal Whisperer

August 28: Mathews Investigations

100 North 27th Street

Billings, Montana

MIKE MATHEWS SAT AT HIS DESK LISTENING to the playback of yesterday's recording of his briefing with Bryan and Loretta Gilliam.

Mathews: "Well, guys, I think the law has finally quashed the threats against you for the most part. Flathead County Sheriff's Department detectives traced several large money transfers from Leonard Sheridan to the other three conspirators in his cabal—Kyle Birnham, Scott Hammond, and Burgess Flood. The payments were made more than a month before Sheridan was shanked in the prison yard, and took convoluted paths through a number of offshore accounts in Singapore and the Cayman Islands before reaching the killers' banks. They were well encrypted, which slowed the investigation, but once uncovered, they found something interesting Each payment bore the same reference annotation: 09AEF."

Bryan: "What does the code mean?"

Mathews: "Zero-nine-A is the FBI's National Incident Based Reporting System code for murder. And of course, we know what the AEF is. We think Sheridan tagged his payments to taunt federal authorities. And possibly it was also to throw his hired goons under the bus should everything go south, which it did. The man was arrogant that way. But crafty, too. I'm so happy Burgess Flood didn't get to you, Bryan."

Bryan: "You and me both."

Loretta: "He came close. *Too* close."

Bryan: "I guess the old adage holds true. Follow the money and you'll find the crime."

Mathews: "So true. The payments are the final nails in Hammond's and Flood's coffins. We already had taxidermist Kyle Birnham's key testimony concerning their activities and phone calls between Birnham's burner phones and Sheridan in prison. We also had the blood on the tools used to decapitate the T-Rex and Chogan Stimson. And now these payoffs link all four of them to the hunter killings, Chogan Stimson's murder, and the attempt on your life, Bryan. They're all going away for many moons. Hammond and Flood are bad news. The detectives call Hammond 'Twitchy' and Flood 'Mr. Chill.' "

Bryan: "Mr. Chill is an appropriate descriptor for Flood. I haven't seen eyes that dead since my run-ins with the Taliban in Afghanistan. He's one scary dude. Fortunately for me, Flood's chilled persona gave our son time to take him down."

Mathews: "Yeah. I understand Paul was quite the hero. How is he doing?"

Loretta: "Considering what he's been through, he's okay. Right now we're all trying to deal with Hayden Fowler's death."

Mathews: "Yeah, I heard about that. So tragic. I'm so sorry for your loss, guys."

Bryan: "Thanks, Mike. We're flying to Indianapolis tomorrow for the funeral. Hayden was a visionary and a go-getter. We miss him dearly and . . ."

The rest of Bryan's comment was drowned out by the sound of a helicopter thumping over the Guidepost. After a long minute, the sounds of the rotor blades faded away.

Mathews: "With Sheridan dead and Birnham, Hammond, and Flood locked up, I would say you all can breathe a little easier. The threat is greatly lessened but I would still stay vigilant."

Bryan: "Oh, we are. You should, too, Mike. I'm sure you've got a target on your back a mile wide after all the nasty shit you've stirred up."

Mathews: "I'm well aware."

Bryan: "We've retained two of our personal bodyguards and we still have our ranch security team in place."

Mathews: "Just be careful, Bryan. Remember, Flood got past your security staff."

Loretta: "Yes, we know, Mike. We've taken steps to ensure it won't happen again. Thanks for all your hard work on this case and for keeping us apprised."

Mathews: "We got lucky. A few things went our way early on, especially with the sketchy taxidermist. Wasn't it Hayden Fowler who suggested that line of investigation?"

Bryan: "Yes, it was Hayden's idea."

Mathews: "Dr. Fowler would have made a great detective."

Loretta: "For sure. There wasn't much that man couldn't do."

Mathews shut off the tape recorder and picked up the TV remote, turned on the flat-screen. Time for his daily MTN Afternoon News fix with Amelia Hatcher.

The anchorwoman appeared, standing in a highland meadow, the wind whipping her long blonde hair around her face and shoulders.

> "I'm high in the Bitterroot Mountains of the Selway-Bitterroot Wilderness area in northern Idaho to report on a strange phenomenon. First, let me say the country out here is one million acres of deserted loneliness. It's beautiful but desolate. State wildlife biologists have taken to calling this upland prairie the Graveyard of the Ancient Ones. For some unknown reason, the meteorite dinosaurs are coming here to die. We know *how* they are dying, just not why the Cretaceous creatures are journeying here to this high country meadow to spend their final days. What primal force draws them here? How far have they traveled to get here? And just what are those pterosaurs doing circling overhead?"

Amelia Hatcher pointed skyward and the camera angled up, capturing a half dozen big Quetzalcoatlus orbiting above in a loose circle. Mathews was amazed at the enormous wingspans of the creatures, their impossibly long necks and equally long beaks. He was momentarily hypnotized by the graceful way they soared above the meadow. The camera operator followed their flight for a full minute before returning to Amelia Hatcher, who struggled to keep her hair out of her face.

> "With me today are two people who might have some answers. To my left is Idaho wildlife biologist, Dr. Gunther Reese, and on my right is Stanley Murchison, better known worldwide as the Quetzal Whisperer. But before I continue, gentlemen, I have to tell our viewers that we must keep our distance from the dying fields due to the zoonotic diseases the animals are carrying. I want our viewers to get a bird's eye view of this meadow that has turned into a dinosaur graveyard. Our Channel Three weather chopper did a flyover this morning. Let's take a look."

The broadcast broke away to the prerecorded footage. Mathews watched the flyover, listening to the pilot give a running commentary of the scene below. The helicopter cast a moving shadow over an alarming number of dinosaurs laid out in the trampled wheatgrass. Mathews saw many different species, some still barely alive, most obviously dead. The chopper descended, flying along the crest of the tree line, allowing the camera to zoom in on more creatures lying in the shade of an alpine larch grove. The only signs of vibrant life were the Quetzalcoatlus that circled the chopper, darting at the fuselage, threatening, but staying clear of the rotor blades. He saw a couple of Tyrannosaurs struggling to breathe, a small group of Triceratops pocked with bloated ticks. Other species he couldn't name. The scene was overwhelming. The animals all looked gray and washed-out. Dehydrated and emaciated. The video continued through two sweeping rounds of the meadow, then returned to Amelia Hatcher.

"As you can see, the situation here is dire. The Idaho Fish and Game biologists and zoologists can't get in there to help. I'm told the deadly zoonotic diseases these animals are infected with is highly contagious and that it's dangerous even when wearing full protective suits, masks, and respirators. There is also the danger of being attacked by carnivores made rabid by disease. And then, of course they have these pterosaurs flying overhead to deal with. Dr. Reese, I understand you have some history here with these Quetzalcoatlus."

Dr. Reese: "Indeed I do. I came here five weeks ago with the late great Dr. Hayden Fowler, who was killed earlier this week by a Deinosuchus at Tally Lake in Montana. All of us at Idaho Fish and Game send our thoughts and prayers to him and his family. Hayden had been doing migration studies on Tyrannosaurs and Dromaeosaurs for a year or more, tracking their movements along the Continental Divide. Several of his tagged creatures ended up here, and at least two of them had traveled nearly fifty miles to get here. Hayden told us he suspected that death was a collective ritual with many Cretaceous species. We know from paleontology digs that many Cretaceous species died in communal gravesites. The bone fields in these parts inform us of that. But why this particular mountain meadow? We don't know for sure. We couldn't come to any definite conclusions. But Hayden also informed us that this isn't the only dinosaur graveyard."

Amelia Hatcher: "Really?"

Dr. Reese: "Yes. He said he knew of another one east of here in the Montana Bitterroots."

Amelia Hatcher: "Fascinating. And am I to understand that you were chased away by these Quetzalcoatlus flying above us on your visit here with Dr. Fowler?"

Dr. Reese: "Yes. We were dive-bombed by a couple of Quetzalcoatlus. They came at us making frightening noises. One of them pierced my shoulder as we ran. Their beaks are razor sharp and I lost a lot of blood, picking up a bacterial infection in the process."

Amelia Hatcher: "But you're okay now?"

Dr. Reese: "I am. Thanks for asking. I went through a rough first week, but strong antibiotics knocked out the infection. The wound on my shoulder has pretty much healed, but I've definitely lost some mobility in it. Been going through extensive physical therapy. Those bastards flying above us are trouble. They can be vicious so we must watch our steps out here."

Amelia Hatcher: "Understood. And now to you, Mr. Murchison. I'm sure our viewers are familiar with you from your TV appearances and your amazing work with these pterosaurs."

Murchison: "Please call me Whisperer."

Mathews had never seen the Quetzal Whisperer though he'd heard about him. He was an odd duck. Tall and rail thin with a milky blind eye and a deep scar running down the side of his face. Long, stringy salt-and-pepper hair. Dressed in falconer leathers dotted with small metal studs and a black cape stitched with eagle feathers. Calf-height leather boots with rawhide trim. He looked like a villain from a *Game of Thrones* episode.

Amelia Hatcher: "So *Whisperer*, we have all seen your astounding videos, working with these Quetzalcoatlus. What is your take on why these flying reptiles have remained here, perpetually flying over this dinosaur graveyard?"

Whisperer: "I raised nine Quetzalcoatlus from hatchlings and developed a close bond with them. I understood them from their infancy, communicated with them in ways the normal everyday person couldn't possibly understand. They have an innate, wide ranging intelligence and are quick learners. They don't like humans much—in fact, they consider us their enemies—but they possess a deep empathy for their fellow Cretaceous creatures. I believe that is why they continue to soar over this area. They don't want humans desecrating their cemetery. They also keep vultures, bears, and coyotes away. They want their dino comrades to die in peace. They're very spiritual that way."

Amelia Hatcher: "That's incredible, Whisperer, but I must ask, if these flyers hate us humans, how were you able to work with them?"

Whisperer: "I took them in just after they hatched. I discovered the nest along the banks of Trapper Creek here in Montana and kept watch for four days, waiting for them to break out of their shell casings. They were wet, weak, and exhausted when they emerged, and I took them in, cared for them, fed them. From the moment they came into the world, they never considered me to be human. They saw me more as a paternal figure and from day one, they were subservient to me, eager to learn from me."

Amelia Hatcher: "And you didn't run into the adult Quetzals?"

Whisperer: "They were nowhere to be seen. They were either dead or had abandoned the nest for some reason."

Amelia Hatcher: "Are any of those flying reptiles above us your Quetzals?"

Whisperer: "No! <getting perturbed> The goddamned government raided my property and stole them away from me. Then they locked me up for a few days. All for giving care to my animals. No telling where my children are now. At least two of them were sick when they were taken."

Amelia Hatcher: "Well, with all due respect, Whisperer, you *did* break several wildlife laws. And police reports indicate your pterosaurs brought human body parts back to your mountaintop sanctuary. Do you care to respond to that?"

Whisperer: "What do I have to say about that? <getting more worked up> I say you are trying to pick a fight with me for a ratings boost. Isn't that what you media types hold most dearly?"

Amelia Hatcher: "I'm not trying—"

Whisperer: "Investigators did find a human hand and an arm on my property, I won't deny that. But Quetzalcoatlus are carnivores. They were always bringing me gifts they thought I would appreciate. They are like cats that way. I cannot be held responsible for the actions of wild animals. The police wouldn't have let me go with just a fine if I had been involved with that . . ."

Naomi Newell, Mathews' assistant, entered the office carrying a stack of documents she laid on the corner of his desk.

"Anything interesting on the news today, Mike?"

"Yeah. Dying dinosaurs and yet another celebrity lawbreaker."

"Is that the weird falconer who trained those flying dinosaurs?" she said, pointing at the TV.

"It is, yes. And he might have gotten away with murder."

It disturbed Mike Mathews' well-honed law enforcement sensibilities when someone attempted to get away with murder.

"Naomi, I want you to dig up any and all information you can find on this guy. Legal name is Stanley Murchison. Last known residence was his falconry preserve in the Bitterroot Mountains near Darby. And I want copies of all police reports connected with his arrest for violating the Montana Endangered Species Act."

Naomi gave him a big smile. "I'm on it, Mike. You just made my day."

Turn! Turn! Turn!

August 29: Crown Hill Funeral Home
Indianapolis, Indiana

THE HAYDEN FOWLER FUNERAL WAS A SPECTACLE.

More than 400 people showed up to pay their respects to the celebrated paleontologist/dinosaur tracker. In addition to friends and family, many of Hayden's fellow scientists traveled from all over the U.S. along with Smithsonian and National Geographic brass, and several Random House publishing executives. The large gathering of VIPs had attracted a multitude of reporters from all over the world. The funeral director—a dour man by the name of Puckett—fearing an unmanageable run of press corps, had consigned the media to a large roped-off area in the north section of the cemetery.

The graveyard is the perfect place for those animals, Paul Gilliam thought as he sat in the spacious chapel waiting for the service to begin. He was still peeved after his clash with a reporter on the walk from the parking lot. Many of the journalists refused to stay behind the ropes and had descended on the mourners like a pack of rabid wolves.

Today was the first public gathering of what the media had dubbed The Cretaceous Crew, and this was a golden opportunity for the press to get at them for exclusive interviews. The Gilliams, Nora Lemoyne, and Miranda Fowler were accosted by a mad throng of reporters as they made their way to the chapel. Wildlife biologist Bill Carlton and geologist Greg Dulowski were also waylaid on their way in. The scene had been noisy and chaotic. Reporters blocking their way, shouting questions. Getting in their faces with their microphones. Pushing and shoving. Cameras clicking, videocams whirring. Paul had seen one of the reporters hounding Nora with his hands on her, hassling her, holding her back, and he'd lost it. He charged the man and knocked him to the ground. Stood over him and shouted, "The lady is grieving you goddamned idiot! Show some respect!" The reporter had gotten to his feet, dusted himself off, and threatened Paul with an assault lawsuit. That's when Pops moved in to defend him, and some very angry and ugly words were exchanged.

Paul was still seething fifteen minutes later, sitting in the family section of the chapel. He tried to settle himself by checking out the head shots of a smiling Hayden Fowler that sat on easels up front flanking the closed casket. Deep breaths—in, out, in, out. His acoustic guitar sat in its case on the floor next to him. He had volunteered to play a couple of songs for his "Uncle" Hayden, and knew he had to settle down before he was called on to perform. He hadn't played for a crowd this size in a while and the confrontation with the reporter outside only added to his growing edginess. He was antsy, and started tapping his foot and slapping his knee in time to a song playing in his head. His father, sitting on his right, leaned in and whispered for him to be still. He sighed, and sat on his hands, looked to his left. Nora and her mother, Grace Lemoyne, and Hayden's mother, Miranda Fowler, were all sniffling and dabbing at their faces with Kleenex.

Paul's heart was heavy, too. He was torn up about the death of the big scientist with the wild hair and unkempt beard and loud gravelly voice. His "Uncle Hayden" was a walking encyclopedia of popular music and had taught him so much about the history of rock 'n' roll. He had turned him on to obscure singers and bands that Paul would never have discovered on his own. Swaddled in his grief and trying to cope, Paul had spent the past few days moping around the house, listening to melancholy music—Billie Eilish, Jackson Browne, Radiohead, The Cure, Hank Williams' "I'm So Lonesome I Could Cry" on endless repeat. Yes, he felt sad and hollowed out, just like the women to his left, but he was determined not to let his emotions get the better of him in front of all these people.

The Reverend Thomas Caldwell walked up the three steps to the pulpit and began delivering the eulogy, his voice sonorous and sympathetic:

"I want to thank all of you for coming today to pay your respects to the memory of an exceptional man. I know many of you came from far away, which shows just how special this man was in life, and how special he remains in our memories. We are here to honor the life of Dr. Hayden Fowler, a scientist, a seeker of truth, a colleague, a friend. He was a pioneer and courageous crusader for the health and well-being of the Cretaceous creatures sent to us by God. Hayden was taken from this world far too soon, at the age of forty-nine. His death was sudden and shocking, and the manner of it has left many of us shaken, angry, and searching for words that feel equal to the weight of our grief. Scripture tells us that *'the light shines in the darkness, and the darkness has not overcome it.'* Today, that promise may feel distant. But it is precisely in moments like this, when the darkness feels loud and unjust, that we are reminded why light matters at all . . ."

Paul looked at the closed casket sitting on a wooden stand in front of the dais. He didn't want to think about what was under the lid. Even the most skilled undertaker wouldn't have been able to put Hayden back together to make him presentable. It was godawful what happened to him. Hayden had been a big man, a commanding presence in life, and it scared Paul to think that a man his size could be snuffed out like that.

The preacher carried on:

". . . There is a particular cruelty in losing someone like Dr. Fowler in such a violent and senseless way. It offends our sense of order. It leaves us asking *why*, and sometimes even *how*, a world that can produce such beauty and intelligence can also produce such harm. Faith does not require us to pretend those questions don't exist. Even the psalms cry out in confusion and protest. Even Jesus wept at the tomb of his friend. Grief is not a failure of belief; it is the price we pay for love. Hayden dearly loved the animals that ended his life. He showed monumental courage in leading the way in the study of dangerous prehistoric carnivores . . ."

Paul's mind wandered, zeroing in on the concept of death. The

Grim Reaper had almost snagged his Pops twice, three times if you counted his run-in with the Dromaeosaur in the Guidepost quadrangle last year. And then there was Paul's uncle, Jimmy Enright, who had been taken by a T-Rex. Their ranch hand, Chogan Stimson, had been murdered and decapitated, his body strung up in the trees on the back forty of their property. And now Hayden's life had been taken by a gargantuan prehistoric crocodile. And he could never forget all of their Blackfoot friends who had perished during the AEF raid on their dinosaur habitats during their cookout two Augusts ago.

Paul himself had stared Death in the face twice, the first, during that ill-fated cookout, when a pair of hungry Dromes chased the Gilliams' pickup truck across the east meadow, causing it to roll down a ravine. He'd dislocated his shoulder and was very lucky not to be killed. The second came when two Dromaeosaurs came at him on the stage at the Zootown Music Festival. If his bodyguard, Lou Goolsby, hadn't been there, he would be six feet under. So much death, so many close calls the past two-plus years. He shuddered thinking about it. All of it triggered by the invasion of a prehistoric species that had arrived in a cluster of meteorites.

He tuned back in to the preacher's eulogy:

". . . Dr. Fowler's life reminds us that while we cannot always control how long a light shines, we can honor it by remembering what it illuminated. His work lives on in discoveries made, minds shaped, and curiosity sparked. His influence continues on in the lives of those he mentored, challenged, and encouraged to think more deeply and live more honestly . . ."

Paul drifted again, recalling his and Sinopa's visit with Sin's parents last week. Coming clean with them was one of the toughest things he'd ever had to do. But Nittai and Makada Harwood, good people that they were, had let them down easy. Sort of.

"Pregnant?" Nittai said, his forehead knitting into a frown. He glanced at his wife, Makada, showing her his disappointment. He turned back to Paul. "Do you love our Sinopa?"

"Yes, very much, sir. Sin is my forever girl," he said, smiling.

Sin said, "The baby is proof of our love, Daddy."

Nittai considered his daughter, a tender amusement lighting his eyes. "That's sweet, *nii taan*." To Paul he said, "And you plan to marry Sinopa, young man?"

"Of course. That's why I'm here, sir. To ask for your blessing."

"I will say that marriage rarely succeeds with teenage couples," Nittai said. "And you'd best know we're not in a position to support you."

"I understand that, Nittai. I really do." Sin's parents had encouraged him to call them by their first names from their very first meeting. It had seemed weird and unnatural at first, but he was getting comfortable with it now.

"So how are you going to support our daughter, Paul? Even if you got your band back together it wouldn't be enough to support a wife and baby."

"I'm painfully aware of that. I'm currently applying for a session work at the studios where we've recorded. The pay is good if I can get regular bookings."

"Something will work out, Daddy," Sin said with more hope than conviction. "Paul is really talented and I believe in him."

Makada spoke up. "Yes, he *is* talented, darling. No doubt about that. But talent in the creative arts rarely puts enough bread on the table."

Sin said, "If we get strapped, Paul's parents can help us. The Gilliams are rich."

Paul had cringed hearing Sin utter those words. He recalled the look of hurt on Makada's face as she was reminded of the difference in the financial status of the two families. Paul didn't want to come across to Sin's parents as privileged or elitist. He wanted to do this on his own, without money help from his parents.

Makada said, "Do you promise to be good to Sinopa, Paul? To cherish her through good times and bad?"

"Yes, ma'am," he said, taking Sin's hand. "I will always cherish her and protect her. You can count on that, Makada."

"I don't think you understand how difficult this is going to be for you both."

"Oh, I do. *We* do," Paul said. "My dad and I discussed it, and I understand what I have to do, what's in front of us."

Nittai let out a resigned sigh. "Your parents have been very good to us, Paul. Your father has gone to great lengths to publicize the struggles our people are facing here on the rez. Your family has donated generously to our schools and farming community. To our hospitals and law enforcement. While Blackfoot blood does not run through your veins, you and your family are Blackfoot in spirit, and that's what counts." Nittai looked at Makada, who nodded. "You have our blessing to marry Sinopa. Welcome to the Harwood family, son," Nittai said, shaking his hand.

"You are going to have the baby, then?" Makada asked her daughter.

"Yes, I am, *Na'a*. *We* are."

"How far along are you, sweetie?"

"About ten weeks."

"Have you seen a gynecologist yet?"

"Yes, last week. Mrs. Gilliam took me to the Blackfeet Service Unit in Browning. I've got regular appointments scheduled with Dr. Sandra Vogel. I like her. She says everything looks great so far."

"That's good, *ni taan*," Makada said.

Paul heard the hurt in her voice, saw the disappointment register in her expression, not really happy that her daughter had gone to Paul's mother instead of coming to her. He made a mental note to talk to Sin about it.

Reverend Caldwell finished his eulogy and took a seat in the front row. The tributes began, with various mourners getting up to pay their respects. Representatives from National Geographic and the Smithsonian spoke of Hayden's deep well of Late Cretaceous knowledge, his scientific curiosity, and his professionalism. Geologist Dr. Greg Dulowski talked of the paleontology dig he had worked with Hayden that led to the discovery of the meteorite dinosaurs on the Gilliam ranch. Molly Barnes—Hayden and Nora's editor from Random House—praised his writing skills and ability to work with their editorial staff. Hayden's longtime literary agent, Henry Wycliff, spoke of their twenty-five year friendship and the joys of their intellectual debates. Fowler-Lemoyne Aviation employees followed: head dispatcher Nancy Diehl and pilot Walter Mingus calling Hayden the best boss anyone could hope for. Bryan and Peter Lacroix spoke of their close relationships with Hayden. Hayden's mother Miranda talked about how proud she was of him and delivered a teary-eyed anecdote of Hayden's love of July 4th celebrations, and how he had bonded with his late father designing and producing fireworks shows for their private Independence Day parties in Indiana. Bill Carlton related his days in the field with Hayden, and the way Hayden was always coming up with fascinating facts about the creatures they were tracking. The Idaho wildlife biologist finished his spiel with a funny story about he and Hayden coming upon two Ankylosaurs having heated sex. The way Carlton told the tale got a few snickers from the gathering.

Nora closed out the tributes with a touching reminiscence about their trip to Paris—their romance in the City of Lights; their ritzy accommodations in the Hôtel San Régis; the flea boat cruise down the Seine; dining in impressive Left Bank restaurants; drinking fine wines in Parisian bistros with Hayden falling off the wagon for a few days, because, hey, when in Paris, right?

"Yes, that Paris vacation was the high point of our relationship," Nora told the mourners. "Hayden morphed into European character, wearing a goofy red beret and uttering clumsy French phrases. He actually thought he was blending well with the Parisians," she said with a laugh. "Hayden could come across as snappish and egotistical, but he had a quirky sense of humor that made him all the more lovable. He enjoyed nerdy jokes and bad puns, the bigger the groans they produced the better." She went on to tell the gathering about Hayden's romantic side, and why he wanted to return as an octopus. The reminiscence brought smiles all around. "And that's the kind of man my Hayden was."

It was all she could do to get through her verbal love letter before she rushed off the pulpit in tears, disappearing into one of the family rooms in back to regroup. Brin Lacroix and Grace Lemoyne followed her out, going to console her. The tributes had been a celebration of Hayden's life and work, an uplifting hour of stories told by those who knew him best. Most were short and sweet, but the number of people wanting to share their remembrances ran the tribute portion of the service to more than an hour.

Reverend Caldwell called Paul up front. Time to sing for Uncle Hayden. He felt a fluttering in his chest, his nerves starting up again.

He opened his guitar case and strapped on his acoustic. Moved in front of the closed casket. *This just might be the toughest gig I've ever played,* he thought, turning to face the funeral-goers.

"For those of you who don't know me, I'm Paul Gilliam," he said, addressing the gathering. He began strumming the opening chords of Pete Seeger's "Turn! Turn! Turn!" speaking over the intro. "Hayden Fowler was a close friend of us Gilliams, and my parents were business partners with him. Dr. Fowler took an active interest in my music and supported me and my band, Moonrise, with great enthusiasm. I remember many late hours discussing music and songwriting with him on the phone. He was a great motivating influence for me, and a brilliant and decent human being. The big man was fire. Like all of you here today, I miss him." Paul looked behind him, at the casket. "This one's for you, Uncle Hayden."

He began belting out the first verse:

> "To everything, turn, turn, turn
> There is a season, turn, turn, turn
> And a time to every purpose under heaven
>
> A time to be born, a time to die
> A time to plant, a time to reap
> A time to kill, a time to heal
> A time to laugh, a time to weep . . ."

He regained his confidence with each verse, seeing people in the chapel responding to his musical tribute. Some smiling, others sobbing softly. The song was resonating with them, happy and sad both.

Paul finished the song to dead silence. The quiet response was disappointing. He had to remind himself that this was a funeral service, not a concert hall.

“I wrote this next song for Dr. Fowler last week as my memorial to him. I call it ‘I Listen When You Call.’ I’ll play it loud so Uncle Hayden can hear it up in heaven. Here we go.”

There was a smattering of applause when he finished. Nora had returned from the family room and stood in the wings between Brin Lacroix and her mother. Nora wore a reserved smile and gave Paul an expressive two thumbs-up.

And then it was time to move the proceedings outside for the graveside service. The pallbearers—Bryan and brother Ethan, Peter Lacroix, Bill Carlton, and a man Paul didn’t know—approached the casket and took their positions. Paul put his guitar away and joined them. The six men grabbed the swing bars and lifted, following funeral director Puckett’s instructions as they made their way out of the chapel. Puckett led them to a waiting hearse, which would transport Hayden’s body to the gravesite. The press corps shouted questions at them as they passed, but enhanced security kept the aggressive journalists behind the ropes to prevent any other altercations like what had transpired this morning.

Arriving at the gravesite, Paul noticed Hayden was to be buried next to his father. The epitaph on Hayden’s freshly engraved headstone read:

Here Lies Hayden Thomas Fowler
A Big Man In Stature, Heart & Knowledge

Reverend Caldwell led the gathered in a final prayer and the casket was lowered into the ground. Family and friends took turns throwing handfuls of dirt on the casket. There weren’t many dry eyes in the group.

And then it was over. Now it was on to Miranda Fowler’s house for the funeral reception, where a banquet of catered food awaited. Condolences would be offered and memories shared, and all would hopefully find comfort in each other.

Hayden Fowler was now officially gone.

Paul Gilliam knew his world would never be the same.

A Moonrise Feast

November 25: Gilliam's Guidepost

Heart Butte, Montana

THANKSGIVING DAY. THREE MONTHS AFTER HAYDEN'S funeral. Loretta Gilliam thought it was time to put sadness and grief in the rearview mirror and return to some kind of normalcy. At least as normal as things could be after the passing of a bigger-than-life personality like Hayden Fowler.

They all missed Hayden, there could be no doubt about that. He would never be forgotten around the Guidepost. Loretta still felt his presence, recalling his booming voice and ingratiating smile peeking through his bushy beard. She remembered his take-charge persona and the way he always seemed to be the center of attention. The way his magnetic charisma attracted people. Hayden had done so much for her and Bryan. The kids, too. Especially Paul. They all still missed Hayden, but life for the living continued moving forward as life stubbornly does.

So Loretta had planned this autumnal feast.

And Lianne, the dutiful daughter, had pitched in to help.

Loretta and Lee-lee had gone all out decorating the rehearsal barn to give the room a special Thanksgiving ambiance. Turkey figurines, cornucopias, and miniature pumpkins were on display. Acorns, pinecones, dried flowers, and wheat sheaves adorned one wall, comprising a fall mural. Cinnamon and pumpkin spice scented candles burned brightly on rented banquet tables covered with ginger colored tablecloths. Streamers the color of fall harvest—deep reds, oranges, yellows, browns, and warm golds—were draped from the rafters.

Loretta scanned the crowd of family and friends. The guest list included 42 of their Blackfoot friends and children, plus many others in the Gilliam circle. Sixty-eight people had signed the guest register, and that was not including caterers and bartenders.

The large turnout pleased her.

Paul was with Sinopa, who was showing off her new diamond engagement ring as well as her very noticeable baby bump; Ethan was hanging with two of his high school buddies; Peter and Brin Lacroix watched over their two little ones; Peter's young forest ranger friend George Dantley and his wife Emma; Loretta's sister Olivia Enright and Loretta's niece, Marnie; The Gilliam's lawyer Atlee Pinnaker and his wife Doreen; family therapist, Dr. Helen Krickstad and her husband Marcus; Dispatcher Nancy Diehl and her significant other, Caitlan. The other two members of Paul's band, Kit Reeder and Hass Oxendine. They all made the rounds.

Loretta smiled. Such a beautiful mix of widely disparate cultures and personalities, all coming together for a day of giving communal thanks. Knowing there would be a lot of children attending, she had hired a company to set up an indoor playground along the east wall. She was pleased to see Blackfoot children playing with Lianne and Kimi Lacroix and Marnie Enright. The sight of them laughing together, climbing on the monkey bars, sliding down the corkscrew slide, spinning on the merry-go-round, and hopping and giggling in the Bounce House warmed her heart.

The low hum of conversation filled the roomy barn. Catering assistants served guests from pans set out on folding tables. Enough food to feed a small army—generous helpings of roast turkey and dressing, ham, mashed potatoes and gravy, sweet potato and green bean casseroles, cranberry sauce, corn on the cob, deviled eggs, dinner rolls, a wide variety of salads. And for the Blackfeet in attendance there were dishes that favored their Native palates—bison and elk steaks, pemmican, Indian Bannock bread, corn-bean-and-squash medleys, roasted camas root, wojapi (wild chokecherry and juneberry puddings), huckleberry upside down cake. And for everyone, a wide variety of desserts—pumpkin, pecan, and apple pies. Tubs of ice cream with a dozen toppings. Cups of chocolate, butterscotch, and banana pudding.

In one corner of the barn two hired bartenders served wine, beer, and mixed cocktails. They also served coffee, hot apple cider, and soft drinks to those who preferred nonalcoholic beverages.

A few had declined her invitation, all with good reason. The most noticeable absentee was Nora, who, after great deliberation, had decided to do the monthlong author tour for hers and Hayden's new book, *Dragons of the Great Divide: Running with the Beasts*. She had been on the road a couple of weeks now with what she called her *Litourage* that consisted of her literary agent, Henry Wycliff, her editor Molly Barnes, and her mother Grace. Nora was in New York City preparing for an appearance at the historic Strand Bookstore and Loretta spoke with her yesterday. Nora told her the tour was going well, and that her Strand event was being held offsite at the 900-seat Great Hall at Cooper Union. She had been in the process of signing 1,500 copies of the book when Loretta called.

"The toughest thing for me are all the questions about Hayden," Nora said. "But Henry answers those. He knew Hayden much longer than I did. Henry's been great. He takes a lot of the burden off me. Molly has been wonderful, too. And Mom? Well, I call her my saving Grace. She loves that."

"I'm so glad you patched things up with your mother, Nora."

"Me, too. Now that I'm getting to know her, I'm seeing good sides of her that I was too blind to recognize before. I understand her better now. We've both mellowed in our old age."

"You're not old, Nora."

"No, but she is. If I've learned anything from Hayden's death, it's that I need to appreciate the people in my life while I still have them." A short pause, then, "You're bringing out the sentimentalist in me again, Loretta. You're going to get me crying again."

"Oh, no. Sorry. Not my intention at all."

"So the tour is going much better than expected, mainly thanks to my *Litourage*. I just wish they could sign books for me."

"Oh, yeah? Are you getting writer's cramp?"

"That's putting it mildly. I've signed thousands of copies through the first nine stops, and now I'm sitting here in a back room at the Strand facing another thousand-plus books. And there's another stack of our first book that just came out in paperback. My signature has deteriorated into chicken scratch. Doctors' hand-writing is more legible."

Loretta laughed. "You love it, Nora. You can't deny it, sister."

"You know me all too well, Loretta."

"Sure wish you could be with us for our Thanksgiving party."

"Me, too. Just two more weeks to go on this tour. After that, I'll be back to catch up with you folks. But only after I hide out for a week eating junk food and soaking my hand in ice water."

"You'd better come visit us. We love you, Nora. You take care out there in bookstore land."

Another notable absentee was private investigator Mike Mathews, who responded that he would love to have spent the day with the Gilliams and friends, but that he had turkey carving duties in Billings with his family. Loretta asked him how his investigation of the famous Quetzal Whisperer was going and he'd responded, "As much as I'd like to take that narcissistic bastard down, I haven't been able to pin anything on him. The feds found badly decomposed human body parts on Stanley Murchison's property and identified who they belonged to through DNA testing. But Murchison got himself a top-flight defense attorney and the wizard of flying reptiles skated. So the Quetzal Whisperer continues to cash in on his fame doing the talk show circuit and posting to his huge flock of followers on social media. Sorry to say, I can't win 'em all, Loretta. However, I did enjoy observing him pick up trash in a couple of parks as part of his community service restitution."

Bill Carlton, Hayden's wildlife biologist colleague, also declined the invite, saying his place was with his family in Idaho on Thanksgiving. Three of the Fowler-Lemoyne Aviation pilots also expressed the same family needs in their RSVPs as did mechanic, Carl Lacey.

Loretta strolled, chatting with the guests, thinking about the many things for which she and her family could be thankful. With Nora's blessing, Bryan had stepped into Hayden's role as CEO of Fowler-Lemoyne Aviation. Considering the suddenness of it, the transition had been smooth. Bryan was now interviewing for his replacement as general manager. The GM spot was especially critical now with a second heliport opening next month in Missoula. Another development to be thankful for: the perpetrators behind the threats to her family (and Chogan Stimson's murderers) were all now incarcerated at Montana State Prison. Loretta thought it appropriate that these men were in cages where animals of their ilk belonged. The danger to the Gilliam family appeared to be over, and she was happy to no longer have personal bodyguards shadowing their every move. And perhaps best of all, the dinosaurs were gone. The last official sighting of one was late September in Idaho. State officials continued their roundup of dead animals, carefully transporting the carcasses to veterinary diagnostic labs for pathology and necropsy study. Loretta learned on the news this week that the dinosaur disease had not spread to the human populace as was first feared. *Thank God for that.*

She was looking forward to tonight's big attraction—Moonrise playing their first performance since the tragic Zootown Music Festival. Bryan had coaxed the Oxendine boy back to play drums one last time for this gig, but Moonrise was officially finished after tonight. Hass was playing with his Blackfoot friends in a heavy metal band called Siksika Sonic now, and they were quickly making a name for themselves. Paul hadn't been able to find a replacement for Ox on the drums, but that was a moot point now. A month ago, he had accepted a steady job in Nashville as a songwriter/session guitarist. Sinopa would be moving with him. They had gone to Music City last week and put money down on an apartment. Paul and Sin planned to marry after Sin had their baby in March. Their move was scheduled for next week and Sin had promised her parents she would get her GED high school diploma after they got settled. Loretta and Bryan were excited for Paul's opportunity, but nervous about how the young couple would fare in a strange city trying to raise a child. They both had stars in their eyes, but Loretta knew it wouldn't be easy for them. And the departure of their oldest son wouldn't be easy for her or Bryan either.

She grabbed a plate and moved down the serving line. Catering assistants loaded her up with heaping portions of food. She took a seat at a table next to Bryan, joining Sin's parents, Nittai and Makada Harwood, and Hass's parents, Tyee and Abaki Oxendine. She glanced at Tyee's bolo string tie, flannel shirt, and *Heart Butte Warriors* baseball cap, and thought: *So that's where his son gets his fashion sense.*

"Here she is, our party planner supreme," Sinopa's mother Makada said, smiling. "You've done a wonderful job putting all this together, Loretta. Thank you so much for inviting us."

"You're quite welcome. It wouldn't be right not to have some kind of celebration to see our kids off to Nashville."

Nittai Harwood said, "Are you both as nervous about Paul and Sinopa as we are?"

"Without question," Bryan said. "That said, I admire them for wanting to make their own way."

Makada frowned. "They are *so* young."

"They are, yes." Loretta said. "But they are obviously deeply in love. I think that will carry them through."

"I hope you're right."

Nittai swallowed a bite of food, then changed the subject. "They're saying the dinosaurs are all gone, Bryan. I know you were having problems with Dromaeosaurs. Have you seen any of them around the Guidepost lately?"

"No. Not since Lor spotted one Labor Day. She and our daughter were out on horseback when they were surprised by one."

Loretta said, "Yeah, Lee-lee and I ran into a Drome on the south trail. The thing looked pretty sickly. It turned tail and ran into the woods like it was afraid of us. Not at all normal behavior for them."

Nittai said to Bryan, "Sinopa told us you tangled with one of them last year. Is that true?"

Bryan stopped chewing, a serious look crossing his face. Took a drink of his beer, then said, "Yeah, I did. Two of them as a matter of fact. Right outside the barn here, in the quadrangle where the heliport is now. Lucky I had my gun with me. Lucky, too, that my better half came to my rescue." He leaned over and kissed Loretta's cheek.

"I can't imagine," Makada uttered. "I've seen those things on TV and they're scary."

"They're twice as frightening in person," Loretta said. "I say hallelujah if the news reports are true. Those monsters have been the bane of our existence since that meteorite struck our east meadow three summers ago."

"You folks seen any lately?" Bryan asked Nittai.

Nittai shook his head. "No, we haven't seen any kind of dino activity on the rez since midsummer. Good thing if they're truly gone. We've lost too many of our Native brothers and sisters to those beasts."

"Amen, Nittai," Bryan said.

Tyee Oxendine spoke up. "I haven't had the opportunity to thank you until now, Bryan."

"For what?"

"For being so kind to our son. Hass had no right to take the drums with him when he left the band. You spent a lot of money to get the kids top of the line instruments. You could have gotten mad and demanded that he return the drums, especially knowing the immature and selfish way he left your son in the lurch. But you didn't. You went to Hass, complimented him on his musicianship. Let him keep the drums. Wished him luck. It meant a lot to our boy. It was a classy thing to do and Abaki and I thank you for that."

Bryan smiled. "It was nothing, really, Tyee. Your son is a good kid and a talented percussionist. I'm glad we could help him on his musical journey."

"Well, Hass has always been a little too impulsive for his own good," Abaki said. "He really is grateful for all you've done for him, even if he doesn't show it."

"It's just the age these kids are at," Bryan said.

Loretta said, "We're so glad they could get together as Moonrise and perform for us one last time. Bryan and I have been looking forward to this. I know Paul is pumped up about it."

"So is Sinopa," Makada Harwood intoned.

"Ditto for Hass," Nittai Oxendine said.

They finished their meals, chatting about family matters. Loretta stood. "It was nice visiting with you folks. We're hosting this shindig so we need to circulate. Come on, Bry, let's walk off some of this meal."

They moved to a table where Peter and Brin Lacroix sat visiting with Peter's young friend, Montana DNRC forestry ranger George Dantley, and his new bride, Emma. Three summers ago, a meteorite struck the base of George's fire watchtower, collapsing it and nearly killing him. Peter had flown the medevac rescue mission that day, and despite an age difference of fifteen years, the two were close friends.

"Is everyone enjoying themselves here?" Loretta asked.

"We are," Brin said. "This is a magnificent feast, Loretta. You've outdone yourself this time."

"I don't know about that." She turned to George, trying not to show a reaction to his face. Despite numerous plastic surgeries, the otherwise handsome young man still retained burn scars along one side of his face. "How are you and Emma doing, George?"

"We're livin' the dream," he said, leaning in close to his wife. His beaming smile brought out the joy in his eyes, diminishing his facial disfigurement.

"We haven't seen you in, what's it been? A year?"

"Nine months. At Pete and Brin's housewarming party, the end of February."

"Yeah, that was quite a bash," Bryan said.

Peter chuckled. "If you say so. I don't remember much of it."

George and Emma laughed along with Peter, but Loretta exchanged smirks with Brin, knowing the housewarming party was the height of Peter's opioid addiction.

Brin said, "You look like you're getting around pretty well these days, Bryan."

"I am, yes. As much as I love the cane you made for me, I'm happy to report I don't need it much anymore. Mostly just when I get really tired." To George and Emma he said, "I'll show you the walking stick Brin made for me later. It's a work of art. She's a gifted artiste. Gemstones, metal, wood, meteorite rock? That pretty lady works her magic transforming them into very special objects."

Brin smiled. "You're too kind, Bryan."

Peter said, "Georgie here was just telling us about the big T-Rex he ran into in the Kootenai Forest. It was a pretty harrowing close encounter. Tell 'em, Georgie."

"Okay, if you insist. Well, me and a fellow ranger were in the Yaak Valley, monitoring timber health, when we heard this loud snorting, somethin' huge crashing through the underbrush like an oncoming freight train. At first I thought it might be a grizzly, but the Rex that came at us made grizzlies look like domesticated house pets. Must've been eleven or twelve feet tall. Had to have weighed half a ton. Probably more. This was back at the beginning of summer, late May, and the dino sickness hadn't started spreading yet. This guy was healthy. All fired up and *hungry*. We didn't have time to draw down on him. All we could do was run for our lives. We were taught in our woodland safety classes that we couldn't outrun him. So we climbed trees. I guarantee you've never seen two guys scale trees that fast in your life. My partner lost his gun in the scramble. We were stuck up in that canopy for close to two hours as the demon ogre kept snorting and drooling, circling below us, trying to figure a way to get at us. I got off a few errant shots before I dropped my gun like an idiot. Scariest couple of hours of my life. Freaked me out even more than those meteorites. At one point I thought I wouldn't even make it to our first wedding anniversary."

Emma stared at her husband with a pitying, apprehensive look.

"Wow!" Bryan said. "That's quite a story. *Demon ogre*? That's a perfect description for them."

"George is good with words," Emma said. "He writes stories, you know."

That got Loretta's attention. "Is that so? What kind of stories do you write?"

"Um, science fiction and horror. I only dabble in it. It's just a hobby, a good escape for me. It's therapy, if I'm being truthful."

Emma said, "My husband is just being modest. He's had a couple of short stories published in small press magazines, and he just started writing a novel. George has a deep and vivid imagination. And he writes great stories."

"How cool is that?" Loretta exclaimed. "I'm an avid reader. I'd love to read your work sometime."

George shyly promised to send her a few of his stories, though Loretta doubted she would ever see one.

She and Bryan moved on to visit with their ranch foreman, Apisi Lyttle, and his wife Kanti, who was still a bit gun shy after surviving a frightening kidnapping last year.

"How's it going, Ap?" Bryan said, giving Apisi a playful slap on the back.

"*Oki,* boss, Mrs. boss," Apisi said, doffing his dress Stetson in respect.

Loretta said, "I almost didn't recognize you with your new dental work, Ap. It looks great. Very natural. You look like a whole new person."

Apisi beamed, showing off his new teeth. He had undergone a complex full-mouth rehabilitation with a bridge and dental implants to correct years of living with broken and missing teeth, years when he had been reluctant to smile.

Loretta turned to Kanti. "And I just love your ribbon skirt. It's so bright and colorful."

"Thank you, Mrs. Gilliam. I made it myself. Been saving it for a special occasion. And occasions don't get any more special than this," she said, waving her arms around the barn, at the festive decorations, the tables laden with delicious food, and all the people enjoying themselves.

"How much would you charge to make a ribbon skirt for me?"

Kanti slumped her shoulders. Her face sagged. "Oh, I would *never* take your money for a skirt, Mrs. Gilliam. After all you have done for me and Ap? That wouldn't be right."

"Nonsense, you should be paid for your work. And I would just love to have a ribbon skirt like yours. I'll work with you on the price."

Kanti nodded, an uncertainty to her gesture. "Okay, I guess. But I would feel better if you paid just for the materials. The rest of it is a labor of love for me."

"We'll talk about it, Kanti."

"I must say, Ap and I are looking forward to hearing Paul's band again."

"Yes, one last time," Bryan said. "It should be something special."

Apisi said, "We were happy to hear about Paul's new job in Nashville. It sounds like quite an honor. He must be excited."

"Thanks, Ap," Loretta said. "He is. He's doing what he loves and he's found a girl who makes him happy."

She and Bryan moved on, spending the next hour circulating, catching up, reconnecting with those they hadn't seen in a while. They were in conversation with the late Chogan Stimson's longtime girlfriend, Mika Laurence, when Paul interrupted.

"We're ready to go on, Mom. Do you and Dad want to introduce us?"

Loretta looked at her son, seeing the excitement and anticipation lighting up his face. "Yes, yes I do," she said. "Would you please excuse us, Mika? Come on, Bry, let's get this party into high gear."

They moved through the crowd and stepped up onto the rehearsal stage, in front of a curtain of vibrant handwoven Blackfoot blankets stitched together by several rez women. She could hear the band moving into their places behind the heavy drape. Two thumps on the kick drum. Light taps on the snare. A buzzing amplifier. Muffled voices.

Loretta tapped the mic. "Could I have everyone's attention, please?" The room quieted. "Bryan and I want to thank all of you for joining us today. It's so nice to be able to bring our friends and family together for this holiday feast. Big Sky Catering has done an outstanding job serving us this bountiful feast of food and drink. Thanks, folks," she said with a wave at several of the white jacketed caterers. "I also want to mention our daughter Lianne, who worked very hard helping me organize this party. Thank you, Lee-lee. And our son Ethan helped get the word out. Thanks, Eeth.

"This holiday has traditionally been a day for counting our blessings, and as Bry and I visited with many of you, we were reminded just how much all of us here have to be thankful for. We

Gilliams are blessed that we still have each other. As you all know, it's been quite a wild ride dealing with the dinosaur invasion these past three summers. Most of us in this room have been touched in one way or another by that bizarre twist of nature. Some of you have lost loved ones to the voracious beasts. Quite a few of us in our community have been battered and bruised, but we're a tough breed here on the reservation. We have powered forward. But there is good news finally. If you haven't heard, yesterday the U.S. Fish and Wildlife Service came out with an official declaration that all known Cretaceous species have succumbed to the dino diseases. Dinosaurs on Earth are once again extinct. The threat of prehistoric carnivores along the Continental Divide is over. People can return to their normal outdoor activities without fear."

A raucous cheer and foot stomping shook the walls of the barn.

When the noise died down, Bryan pushed closer to the mic. "Of course, that's only if you believe the federal government," he said. "Rumor has it they're breeding Tyrannosaurs to use as weaponry in their next unnecessary war. The next thing you know they'll be sending cloned Dromaeosaurs to our homes to extort money for a dinosaur restoration fund. They'll be telling us, *Pay up or deal with the Drome!*"

A wave of laughter, then a round of enthusiastic applause amid whistles and shouts of "You know it, Gill!" and "Tell it like it is, Bryan!"

Loretta watched her husband enjoying himself. Normally his government bashing annoyed her, but she knew (as did Bryan) that this was the right crowd for it. The Blackfeet on the rez had zero respect for the powermongers in D.C. There was a long-running, deeply rooted mistrust and hatred of the feds among the tribe, and Bryan played to it often.

Loretta shouldered him aside and took back the mic. "Okay, enough of the Uncle Sam bashing, Bry. This is a party and our friends want to hear some live music. You think you can introduce the band without dissing politicians?"

More laughter.

"Yes, I believe I can handle that, dear." He cleared his throat, beginning to get choked up. "Yes, it's *absolutely* time for some great live music. Many of you have seen Moonrise perform before. Some of you went to Missoula to see them play at the Zootown Music Festival July fourth. Unfortunately their set was cut short with the arrival of some big bad prehistoric beasts. The day that should have been about a joyful celebration of music turned to tragedy. That's the last time Moonrise played together as a band. Four and a half months ago.

"I have had the privilege and honor of managing them from their humble beginnings. They came together two years ago right here in this barn and their collective talent grew quickly. They cut two records of original music and received key college radio airplay. I'm sad to say that tonight will be their swan song. The fickle finger of fate has pushed them in different directions. But we will always have their recorded music. I'm pleased to say that all of you will be leaving here tonight with CDs of both their records, a gift from me and Loretta." He held up the jewel cases. "Their 4-song EP, *Moonrise at Reptile Rock* and their full-length album, *Moonscape Moodies*."

Thunderous applause and more whistles.

Bryan waited for the room to settle before saying to Loretta, "Look at me up here, playin' Oprah Winfrey, givin' away free stuff." He started pointing at people in the audience, giving it his best Oprah impersonation. "You get two CDs, and you get two CDs, and you get—"

"Well, you sure don't look like Oprah," Loretta said with a gleeful laugh. She poked him in the ribs, thinking, *This is wonderful. Everyone's having a good time with this.*

Bryan said, "Okay, since we have a lot of us old fogeys here tonight, Lor and I have requested they play a few ballads so we can get real close with our honeys on the dance floor."

More hoots and hollers.

"So without further delay, it's time to rise and shine with Moonrise. I present to you, Paul Gilliam, Sinopa Harwood, Kit Reeder, and Hass Oxendine—let's hear it for Moonrise."

The barn came alive. The curtain parted slowly and the band

kicked into “Rockin’ Me With Your Vibe.” Young couples moved in front of the stage and began gyrating to the propulsive beat. Moonrise followed it up with a blistering version of “Reptile Rock” which revved the crowd up even more.

Loretta stood at the side of the stage with Bryan as the band played three more high energy tunes. She looked out over the crowd, seeing the joy on friends’ faces, people tapping their feet and bouncing their heads. Onstage, Paul was smiling and making eye contact with Kit and Ox, both of whom grinned back at him. After months of bruised egos and backstabbing snipes, they were getting along and obviously enjoying playing with each other again. The band was tight and ferocious. Kit was laying down a driving bassline and Ox was right in the pocket with him. Paul’s guitarwork was crisp and sharp. The vocals were strong and clear. The sound was mixed well. It’s like the band had never broken up. Loretta was pleased.

And then after a half dozen solid rockers, Paul stepped up to the mic and said, “I promised my mum and pops we would play a few mini-sets of soft, slow music so, quote, the old fogeys in the audience can get close to their honeys on the dance floor, end quote. Dad’s words, not mine,” he said with a husky laugh. “Let’s do it.”

They pulled three stools to the front of the stage and set a mic up in front of each. Paul switched out his electric guitar for his acoustic. Took a seat and adjusted the height of his mic. Kit took the stool to Paul’s left and laid his acoustic bass across his lap, plucked a few strings. Sin sat to Paul’s right, clutching a pair of maracas. She smiled and pointed at someone in the audience. Ox stood behind them holding a tambourine. They started with “You Can’t Take the Heart Out of Heart Butte,” the acoustic arrangement dreamy and mellow. The three-part harmonies were elegant. Older folks streamed onto the dance floor.

“Come on, dance with me, Bryan,” Loretta said, taking hold of his hand and leading him offstage. She fell into his arms down in front and they began swaying to the music. Loretta whispered into Bryan’s ear, “I wish this night could go on forever, Bry.”

“Me, too, hon. It’s so cool, isn’t it?”

“Finally, things seem to be taking a turn for the better.”

Bryan smiled. "You'd better knock on wood when you say that, my lovely. Never forget, we're the hard luck Gilliams."

Moonrise segued into the second song, "Let the Sun Warm Your Heart." The area in front of the stage was packed with older couples holding their significant others close. Romance was in the air.

Paul strummed the final chord. As the applause subsided, he leaned over and put his arm around Sinopa and addressed the audience. "Next week Sin and I will be leaving for Tennessee to begin our next grand adventure. For those who haven't heard, we're headed to Nashville where we'll be doing studio work and having our baby. We'll be back next June for our wedding, but I just wanted to say thank you to everyone who has supported us and that we will miss all of you. There's just no place on Earth like Heart Butte and no better people than those of you we have grown up with. And now, before I get overly emotional, on with the show."

They continued with the acoustic set, doing classic rock love songs: Extreme's "More Than Words," Billy Joel's "Just the Way You Are," the Beatles' "And I Love Her," then closing out with an Eagles medley: an a capella rendering of "Seven Bridges Road" followed by "Best of My Love" and "Love Will Keep Us Alive."

Loretta slow danced with Bryan, her chin up against his shoulder, smiling at the enchanting intimacy of these familiar songs. She knew these selections were Hayden Fowler's influence. He had schooled Paul on 1960's and 1970's music, and Paul had taken to the classic rock era like an obsessed fanatic, learning dozens, if not *hundreds*, of songs from that period. She loved that Paul had taught the band these tunes and that they elected to perform them tonight. Their friends were loving it, too.

"They sound really good," she said into Bryan's ear.

"They do. Turns out, we didn't need to worry. They're nailing it."

"Makes me feel all gooey inside," she purred. "Acoustic ballads do that to me. I want *so* much to make love to you right now, baby."

Bryan leaned back and looked her in the eyes. Gave her a knowing grin. "You're singing my tune, sweet lady."

"I love you so much, Bry."

"I love you more."

"How's your leg?" she asked.

"It's gimpy. Sore and weak. It hasn't gotten this much of a workout in a while."

"I don't want you falling, Bryan. Maybe we should sit down for a while."

"Not a chance. Not when I'm dancing with the hottest woman at this jamboree. Correction, the hottest lady in *all of Montana.* Maybe Idaho and Wyoming, too."

"Aw, after all these years you still know how to turn me on."

The band played for three more hours on this Thanksgiving eve. After seeing their guests off and cleaning up, Loretta and Bryan finally got back to the house around two o'clock. They were exhausted but wired from the success of the party.

Loretta slowly unbuttoned Bryan's shirt. "I've been thinking about this since you kissed me on the dance floor."

"Maybe I should kiss you more often," he murmured.

"Yes, perhaps you should."

His breathing quickened as she helped him out of his shirt. He reached for her, eager to undress her, but she stopped him. "Let's take it nice and slow, Bry. I want to savor this night for as long as we can."

And savor they did, whispering sweet endearments to each other, touching, caressing, teasing, engaging in dreamy, languid sex until daybreak.

It's starting to feel like old times around the Guidepost again, she thought as sunlight streamed through their bedroom window.

That feeling of carefree simplicity they'd enjoyed before the meteorites struck had returned.

Before the dinosaurs.

Before animal rights terrorists and murders.

Before the heliport and choppers flying in and out.

Before helicopter crashes.

Before the severed heads, both animal and human.

Back before fame found them.

Back before they became millionaires.

Back when they ran a 12-room inn and general store and tended to a half-dozen horses.

Back when life was much simpler.

Oh, how Loretta welcomed it. How she *cherished* the simplicity.

She rolled over and reached for Bryan, who was sound asleep, emitting soft snores. Loretta smiled as she snuggled up next to him.

This Thanksgiving had unfolded like a pleasurable dream.

Soon her breaths slowed and she fell into a satisfied deep slumber, her arms around the man she had loved for half of her life.

On the Threshold of a Dream

August 21: Lemoyne Ranch

Belgrade, Montana

One year after Hayden Fowler's death . . .

NORA LOVED HER NEW HOME, this sprawling 160-acre ranch thirty minutes north of Bozeman. Surrounded by a 970-acre wildlife preserve and framed by spectacular mountain ranges, the property gave her the kind of pastoral serenity she desired at this point in her life.

So good to be back home.

She had just returned from a two-week paleontology dig in Kemmerer Wyoming. Her field crew had uncovered two complete 13-foot articulated crocodilian fossils from the Cenozoic Era, estimated to be 52 million years old. They were quality finds that pleased the Smithsonian curators. Nora was happy with the team's success but she couldn't stomach looking at the pair of skeletons as they reminded her of the Deinosuchus that had taken Hayden's life.

She sat in her wicker rocker on the covered porch overlooking the valley, sipping coffee, enjoying the brilliant sunset and watching whitetail deer feed along the banks of Dry Creek. Rolling green meadows spread out before her, the bluebunch wheatgrass and prairie junegrass shimmering in the late afternoon sun. The granite domes of the Tobacco Root Mountains glowed pink in the west. To the north, the dramatic skyline of the Bridger Mountains rose sharply.

The Eagles' "Take It Easy" played through porch speakers. She could listen to the Eagles all day long; their lush harmonies and southwestern folk rock vibe provided the perfect soundtrack for this bucolic Montana backdrop.

She spent a lot of time out here, enchanted by the view that changed throughout the day as light moved across the hollow. This new homeplace brought her an inner peace she had never known. Her eponymous Lemoyne Ranch was idyllic, serene, secluded . . . a place of spiritual awakening.

Hayden would love it here. This place is custom designed for his nature-loving, outdoorsy persona.

He died one year ago today. Nora thought this day might return her to the melancholy lows that had dogged her the past year. But it hadn't.

Changes in latitude, changes in attitude, to quote Jimmy Buffett.

Nora had fallen in love with Montana. Big Sky Country had a vast, untamed beauty she found irresistible. After Hayden's death she couldn't return to Minnesota and the house in Eden Prairie. Too many haunting memories there. She wanted to buy a property in Montana to be closer to the people who had become the best friends she'd ever had—Bryan and Loretta Gilliam in Heart Butte, and Peter and Brin Lacroix in Florence. Both couples were just a three-hour drive away. Loretta and Brin were her Cretaceous Sisters, and Nora loved them both as if they shared the same bloodline.

So, after her book tour in mid-December, Nora rented an apartment in Bozeman and began her search for a plot of Montana real estate she could call her own. On April 15th she closed on the ranch and officially became a proud Montanan. She considered it the best move she'd ever made.

Property in this part of Montana didn't come cheap. Purchasing this ten-million-dollar ranch required a bit of financial maneuvering, even for a newly-minted millionaire like herself. She'd had some unexpected help, however.

From Hayden.

Unbeknownst to her, he'd written her into his will.

Nora had been floored last September after being called to a lawyer's office in Minneapolis for the distribution of assets in Hayden's last will and testament. She'd sat listening in total disbelief as the estate attorney walked her and Hayden's mother,

Miranda, through the probate proceedings. Hayden's will called for his assets to be split evenly between her and Miranda. The will's bequest was staggering in its value. She knew Hayden was wealthy, just not *how* wealthy. He'd bequeathed the Eden Prairie house to her, and Nora immediately sold it for a million and a half. She also inherited half of his investment portfolio, her share totaling in the high six-digit range. He gave her all his present and future royalties on their two bestselling books. And to generate additional buying power, Nora sold her and Hayden's 51% interest in Fowler-Lemoyne Aviation to the Gilliams and Peter Lacroix, along with a new investor, the Gilliams' attorney, Atlee Pinnaker.

Turning over her share of the company didn't bother her. Nora never really had much of an interest in a helicopter charter business. She had gone along with Hayden, wanting to keep him happy. It was his big corporate dream, not hers. Since the formation of the company, she had basically operated as an absentee owner. But the company bore her name and she wanted the best outcome. She felt sure she had made the right decision. The company was now thriving under Bryan and Peter's leadership, with a third heliport opening in Boise a month ago.

Nora's own net worth prior to inheriting additional wealth was close to two million. Put it all together and she had enough to make serious offers on expensive Montana ranchland.

The music changed to "Peaceful Easy Feeling" and she hummed along, looking across the way at the newly-constructed Western barn. To her right was a detached 4-car garage where she kept her canoe, ATV, and pickup truck. To her left sat the 5-bedroom-3-bath guest house, with its weathered timber beams, river rock accents, and deep covered porch—the former residence of the previous owner's ranch crew. Now it was the permanent address for her mother, Grace, her new husband, Art Munson, and their three dogs. They had come for a visit in late April when Nora threw a housewarming party, and decided they loved Montana as much as Nora. They returned to Chicago and promptly sold their two homes, then moved here in June.

It all happened so fast. Nora liked having them here. For the first time since childhood, she had a warm family life and a closeness with her mother she'd once thought impossible. And Nora was overjoyed to have a stepfather like Artie, as he preferred to be called. At seventy-nine, Artie was a happy-go-lucky, younger-than-his-years gentleman with an abundance of energy. He had turned Nora on to the joys of fly fishing and they'd made trout fishing on Dry Creek a regular thing. Nora enjoyed slipping on the waders and stepping into the stream where spring-clear water slipped through a ribbon of willow thickets and cottonwoods. She liked the feel of the rod in her hands as she cast, the whine of the reel and the heft on the drag when a plump rainbow trout hooked on and took her line. Nora relished the time she spent on the creek with her new stepdad. She and Artie had quickly developed a comfortable camaraderie that made Nora feel like he had always been in her life.

Nora attended Grace and Artie's wedding on a blustery January day in Chicago. It was the first time Nora had seen her sisters Cate and Debra in years, maybe a decade or more. They had immediately reverted to their old bullying ways, acting standoffish and treating her like an outcast elitist no matter how Nora tried to mollify them. It made for some awkward moments getting through the ceremony and reception. But her mother's words about her sisters pulled her through, giving her strength and resolve. Grace's voice kept repeating in Nora's head, keeping her calm, allowing her to avoid potentially embarrassing confrontations with her siblings:

"Oh, honey. Surely you must know how insecure your sisters are. Catelyn and Debra are jealous of you. Haven't you picked up on that? Neither of them have your strength or intelligence. Even as a child you were independent and intellectually curious, smart as a whip. Cate and Deb don't have your gifts."

Nora went inside for more coffee as "Desperado" played. She returned to the porch singing along with Don Henley. It made her think about Paul Gilliam and the Eagles cover tunes she had seen him and his band play.

She made the trip to Heart Butte in early June for Paul and Sinopa's wedding. The young couple seemed so happy, showing off their new baby boy, Tyler James Gilliam, a smiling, drooling, happy little guy born March 21. The boy had wisps of black hair, a honeyed complexion, and the plumpest cheeks Nora had ever seen on a baby. And she could tell little Tyler was Paul's son by the way he responded to music, giggling while waving his pudgy little arms, perfectly in sync with the rhythms.

Nora would never forget the way Paul Gilliam had stood up for her at Hayden's funeral. The way he decked that asshole reporter who kept getting in her face. He was a lovely, sensitive young man despite his shaggy-haired, disheveled appearance. And thoughtful, too. At his wedding he presented her with a CD single of the song he'd written for her, "Let the Sun Warm Your Heart" backed with a new Paul Gilliam original she hadn't heard before, "The Moonlight in Her Eyes."

"I spend so much time in the studio playing other people's music, I thought I should record a few of my own," he'd told her.

And Paul had *indeed* been busy in Nashville, working with top artists such as The Black Keys, Jack White, Paramore, and The Kings of Leon. The former leader of Moonrise was quickly making a name for himself as a much-in-demand session guitarist and backup vocalist in Music City. Nora was exceedingly happy for him.

The sun began to creep behind the mountain peaks, casting long shadows across the valley. She went inside to make herself a light dinner: a turkey sandwich and chips. In the kitchen she opened a bottle of Opus One, a Bordeaux-style red wine she had developed a taste for. She poured herself a glass and sat at the table with her sandwich. As Nora ate, she eyed a stack of her and Hayden's newest book, *Dragons of the Great Divide: Running with the Beasts*. The hardcover copies brought back memories of her author tour last November and December, and the subsequent monumental success of the book. Nine months after publication *Dragons* currently sat at number three on the *New York Times* bestseller list and was a top selection in many of the larger book clubs. The trade paperback edition of their first book, *Cretaceous Stones: The Return of Prehistoric Life to Earth,* had been released in June, and was positioned atop most paperback bestseller lists. The hardcover edition was now in its 41st printing. Nora could picture Hayden smiling down from the heavens.

"We did it, Hayden, you and me," she said aloud. "I really missed you on the tour. I think you would have enjoyed it."

She finished her sandwich thinking about her new publishing deal—a memoir of her life, focused on the three summers of the dinosaur invasion. The working title was *The Cretaceous Crew: My Time with the Dinosaur Trackers*. Nora didn't want to do it at first. The writing grind exhausted her and she didn't want to put herself out there so publicly again. She especially didn't want to document her relationship with Hayden for public viewing. And truth be told, she wasn't sure she could write a book without him. Sure, she had done the last book tour without him, but writing a book solo was a whole different thing. There was also the fact that her friends had become publicity shy and Nora knew she would have to tread lightly when writing about them. She didn't want to damage those friendships, and knew she would have to paint them in the best light. That wouldn't be difficult, however, as the Gilliams and Peter and Brin were all fine people.

The advance money was bigger than the first two books combined, but she didn't need the money. She explained all of this to her agent, Henry Wycliff, and the Random House execs who kept pushing her. She kept turning them down and they kept coming back, undaunted. "We'll give you as much time as you need, Nora," they kept repeating. Finally, she relented, convincing herself it would be a welcome intellectual challenge, something to keep her mind occupied through the long Montana winter. It would be a sure bestseller and would give the public starved for dinosaur lore an insider's view of the behind the scenes goings-on. More details than she and Hayden could put in their two books. The project was still in its embryonic stage; Nora had just started putting together a detailed outline. Some days she cursed herself for signing the contract, other days she looked forward to getting started. She had long held a love/hate relationship with writing.

She sighed and stood. Took her dish to the sink and finished her wine. Decided to open her laptop and review the journal entry she had written early this morning, an entry memorializing the day one year ago that Hayden was killed.

Nora had put a good deal of time and thought into it.

It had been extremely difficult to write, but she was happy with the result . . .

August 21, 2027

My Dearest Hayden (a.k.a., my big cuddly teddy bear),
One year ago today I lost you. It was the worst day of my life. I am not going to let sadness take me to dark places on this day of remembrance. Instead, I wish to recall the joy and adventure you brought into my life.

You woke up something deep inside of me that had long been dormant—a zest for living life to the fullest. You brought me out of my shell and made me see a world I had turned a blind eye to. You made me hear music I had been deaf to. You introduced me to flavors I previously could not taste. You helped me grasp for things I thought were out of my reach. The two-plus years we had together were the most exciting years of my life, and I thank you for inviting me to march in your parade.

As you know, I have always been conflicted about the true meaning of love. A shrink I was seeing before I met you informed me I have intimacy issues. I didn't want to believe it, but I guess the way things turned out with us attests to that character flaw in me. I think you'll agree I had no intimacy issues in bed (ha-ha). But you taught me that love is so much more than great sex. You taught me that an emotional investment is also a requirement. You brought a universe of emotion to our relationship while my offering in that area was lacking. You opened up my heart and stormed in while I stood outside yours and refused to enter due to my selfish stubbornness. I used my two failed marriages as a lame excuse. Yes, I was selfish, Hayden. I can confess to that now. But I'm not going to bash myself over the head with my guilt. I'm done with that. I have told you I'm sorry so many times in these pages that those words have lost their meaning. But I will say it one last time on this dark anniversary. I'M SORRY, DARLING. I'm so sorry you had to die the horrific way you did. I'm sorry I turned you away after you made the long trek to northern Canada to ask me to marry you. I'm still embarrassed about the way I humiliated you that day. And I'm mostly sorry I figured it out too late just how much in love I was with you. I would do just about anything to have you back with me here and now.

I should have been with you on Tally Lake. I might have been able to change things, might've been able to save you somehow. Your last words to Peter Lacroix will resonate with me for the rest of my days: "Tell Nora I'll love her forever and that I will definitely see her again, hopefully later than sooner."

Please know that I love you, too, Hayden, and that it's a forever thing with me, as well. You set a precedent no other man will ever be able to live up to. At least in my eyes. I still have a lot of living to do, big guy, but when my dying day arrives, I'll be coming to join you, wherever you are. In the meantime, I trust the angels are taking good care of you.

Nora was tempted to check out one of the TV documentaries about Hayden's dinosaur tracking experiences and his videography work. There were several high-quality streaming channels covering Hayden's fieldwork—Animal Planet's *Extinct or Alive*, PBS's *Nature*, and *Mutual of Omaha's Wild Kingdom* being the top choices. But she didn't want to risk it. She had made the colossal mistake of watching a Hayden Fowler documentary on National Geographic's *Nat Geo Wild*. She became physically ill when the show cut to the videos shot at Tally Lake, showing the Deinosuchus leaping out of the water and attacking the Albertosaurus. She quickly shut it off before she saw something she would forever regret. Nora had learned to be very cautious about what online sites she ventured into as the internet was awash with uncut, pirated video footage of Hayden's work. She had seen enough social media messaging to know that many of those sites had a grotesquely morbid fascination with Hayden's death.

She closed her laptop and stood. She was happy with her journal entry but felt a bit foolish pouring out her thoughts to a man who had been gone for a year. A man who would never read those words.

But only a tiny bit foolish.

From the beginning of their relationship Nora thought she and Hayden were plugged into the same telepathic channel. She had sat by his hospital bed watching over him for four days while he was in a coma, rambling in stream-of-consciousness monologues because the doctors told her verbal stimulation was effective treatment for comatose patients. She was disbelieving at first, but then the weirdest thing happened; she felt him responding. He hadn't responded verbally or given her any indication physically that he'd heard her, but she had felt vibrations coming off of him, and intuitively knew what he was trying to communicate to her. It was a silent but tangible language that only she could decipher. When he came out of the coma he'd told her he *had* heard her voice, and understood most of what she'd said, and to prove it, he'd repeated her passages back to her nearly verbatim. And then there were the vivid and very real dreams where he climbed into bed with her and whispered in her ear while he made love to her with a heated passion. Dreams that left her sweaty and disappointed when she awoke to find him gone, even though she swore she could smell his scent on the sheets.

Am I crazy? Am I a candidate for the loony bin?

Nora didn't think so. Was it really such a stretch? After all, dinosaurs had made a return to the Continental Divide after being gone for 66 million years.

Nothing seemed impossible anymore.

Hayden would definitely pick up on her latest journal entry. She was sure of it. She felt his presence regularly. Here on the ranch. On her shopping trips into Bozeman. It was strongest when she returned to Heart Butte or Missoula. Nora had often heard about people who claimed the spirits of recently lost loved ones were still with them. She had always written that notion off as some kind of New Age mysticism nonsense. But now she knew exactly what they meant. She was a believer. Her experiences since Hayden's passing told her that kind of after-death communication spiritualism existed.

She poured another glass of wine and selected new music to pipe out onto the porch. The Moody Blues *On the Threshold of a Dream*. An album and band that Hayden had turned her on to. Ethereal, mellotron-drenched, space age music perfect for stargazing.

She turned off the porch lights. Took a seat in her rocker and sipped her wine. Looked out at the millions and millions of stars that pierced the wide sky with brilliant pinpricks of light. Nora never tired of the stunning nightscape out here.

She had been rocking and sipping for fifteen minutes, Justin Hayward singing "Are You Sitting Comfortably," when a bright flash of light streaked above the dark peaks of Bridger Mountain.

The northern skies lit up in riotous whirls of color.

A meteor shower!

Spectacular splashes of red and purple and yellow and gold stitched the night sky like a July 4th fireworks show, the colorful streaks fading out on their descent.

Nora stared open-mouthed at the light show, hoping and praying this wasn't another delivery of dinosaur eggs via meteorite strikes.

Luminous tracers of blue and green rocketed across the sky in breathtaking displays.

No, it's too beautiful to be another dinosaur delivery. It has to be Hayden, she thought with a grin. *He was obsessed with fireworks. This is his pyrotechnics show! This is his message to me!*

In a trance, she set her wineglass down and walked out into the courtyard. She looked skyward, mesmerized by the crisscrossing lights.

"I see you, Hayden," she yelled. "I know it's you, my love!"

A lone tear trickled down her cheek, a tear of joy.

Nora watched until the skies darkened, then went back inside the house.

I'll be waiting for you in my dreams, big guy.

Author Notes

*** Warning *** Several critical spoilers are revealed in these notes, so it's best to have read all three books before jumping in here.

Dear Valued Reader: Congratulations. You have arrived at the end of the Cretaceous Chronicles Magical Mystery Tour. Thank you for allowing me to be your literary guide. To quote the Grateful Dead, "What a long, strange trip it's been."

Six years. That's what it took to write the three books. For six years I bounced between prehistoric worlds and modern day Montana and Idaho. At times it was dizzying, shuttling across 66 million years, floating between the Late Cretaceous and present-day Western U.S. I had a blast getting to know the characters and doing deep dives into the wide-ranging fields of paleontology, geology, botany, paleobiology, zoology, astronomy, and astrophysics. As I move on to other writing projects, I will miss my fictional friends, both human and dino. I will also miss my studies of Dinosauria. I thought I knew a lot about dinosaurs before I began, but I soon realized my knowledge barely scratched the surface. On every research dive, I uncovered some new amazing fact about the creatures that survived on our planet for 180 million years, through the Triassic, Jurassic, and Cretaceous periods. And then a single cataclysmic happening—an asteroid strike known as the Cretaceous-Paleogene extinction event—wiped them out 66 million years ago. Dinosaurs were (and still are) fascinating creatures, perfectly adapted to their environs, allowing them to grow to gargantuan sizes.

The idea for Book 1, *Cretaceous Stones* began percolating in my mind 35 years ago, after Michael Crichton published *Jurassic Park.* For years I thought about Crichton's inventive device for bringing dinos into our contemporary world—extracting ancient dinosaur blood from mosquitos frozen in amber, filling out the missing DNA sequence with frog DNA, and then inserting the reconstructed DNA into ostrich eggs to hatch out dinosaurs. Far-fetched? Yes. Possible? Doubtful. Exciting dramatic science fiction? You bet.

With this trilogy, I wanted to steer clear of the tired, worn out dinosaur tropes that had gone before. I didn't want to put the dinos on another planet. Too easy and clichéd. I didn't want to use traditional time travel schemes where humans go back in time to prehistory. Too common. I wanted to come up with a fresh and innovative method of returning dinosaurs to modern-day Earth. Something completely outrageous. Something *earthshattering*.

Since you have read this far, Valued Reader, you know how I went about it. I employed *reverse* time travel, bringing Late Cretaceous dinos from the distant past to Earth as eggs packed in large meteorites striking Montana and Idaho. The resulting hatchout brings the dinosaurs full circle, returning them to the same geographic area from whence they vanished 66 million years ago. I thought it would be a wonderful irony to have them return in meteorites, delivering them encased in the same physical objects that wiped them out. Yes, my idea is equally as far-fetched as Crichton's. But we're talking science fiction here, the key word being *fiction*. And speculative fiction at that.

I must confess that plausibility was a big concern of mine before *Cretaceous Stones* was published. I worried whether I would be able to pull it off. Would I be able to make readers believe it? Lots of anxiety in those early days. But then I started comforting myself with the knowledge that nobody questions vampires, zombies, werewolves, or winged fire-breathing dragons. Nobody thinks twice about sorcerers who conjure incredible feats of magic. Nobody bats an eye over demons or ghosts or alien close encounters. Speculative fiction readers want fantasy and escapism in their stories. They love tales that spark imaginations. So why should they question meteorites packed with dinosaur eggs? I finally convinced myself that my narrative device would be okay. The real challenge was convincing readers where those meteorites came from. Book 1 tells that part of the tale in all its scientific glory.

I knew I didn't want to pen just another tried-and-true sci-fi trilogy—all action with very little character development or emotional impact. I wanted to examine the human condition and give readers something that would tug at their heartstrings. How would my characters deal with an invasive prehistoric species? How would their lives and relationships change? My reading tastes and interests have always run deep and wide. I love well-told literary family sagas and noirish crime stories. So, I weaved those two subgenres into the trilogy, with the Gilliam and Lacroix families, and a horrific crime that ends the first book and carries through Books 2 and 3. These elements gave the narrative more emotional punch, making the characters resonate with readers. I also like romance in my stories, so the relationship between my two celebrity paleontologists, Hayden Fowler and Nora Lemoyne, is front and center through all three books.

Dinosaur Fact vs. Fiction: When it comes to dinosaurs, all we have to lean on are paleontology findings. We can only glean so much from 66-million-year-old fossils, and much of what is considered to be fact about these amazing prehistoric marvels comes down to conjecture grounded in scientific postulation. That said, I tried to remain true to what is known about these Cretaceous creatures. For the most part, I kept to the broadly accepted "facts" about these animals—the way they looked and moved, their behaviors, biological features, feeding habits, migratory practices, etc. It's true that all of the dinos mentioned in the trilogy originally roamed what is now the Wyoming-Montana-Idaho Continental Divide corridor and up north into Alberta, Canada. Hayden Fowler's natal homing theory is also perceived to be accurate, with most paleontologists agreeing that many dinosaurs returned to their places of birth (the meteorite sites in the trilogy) to lay eggs, similar to the site fidelity exhibited by modern birds. I did, however, invent a few things to dovetail more closely with the narrative and to give the human-dinosaur encounters more dramatic suspense. My biggest fabrication was the dinos' growth rates, which I greatly accelerated. A fully mature T-Rex reached lengths of forty feet and weighed in at 10 metric tons, but at two years old (the age of my Rexes), paleontological studies suggest they weighed only 150 pounds. I had them at 800-900 pounds and standing twelve feet tall. I figured I could get away with that fantasy because everyone is aware of how big these creatures grew to be. It is also not known whether dinosaurs would hibernate over the long, harsh winters of Montana and Idaho the way I presented it. The climate in what is now the northwest United States was subtropical 66 million years ago, so they would have had no need to hibernate. One thing I've been criticized for is that I have dinos mating and laying eggs at one year old. This is a gray area for paleontological scholars as the sex lives of dinosaurs cannot be gleaned from ancient fossils. What is known is that a great many species of present-day reptiles reach sexual maturity in one to two years. So my early-life dinosaur reproduction leans closer to fact than fiction.

Scientific Fact vs. Fiction: In all things science, to the best of my ability, I tried to stay close to facts derived from my research. I presented a realistic view of the way paleontology digs are run. Same with geology. Everything about meteorites—where they come from, how they're formed, their geologic composition—is all true, including their high content of the rare and extremely valuable heavy metal, iridium. Ditto the astronomy: the descriptions of interstellar space, wormholes, galaxies, universes, the space-time continuum based on Einstein's theory of relativity . . . all based on known fact. The only thing I invented was how the dinosaur eggs ended up packed inside meteorites, and even that is modeled on possibilities presented by a few top astronomers and astrophysicists. Also, the diseases that kill off the dinosaurs—leptospirosis and brucellosis—are bacterial infections that an alien species would most likely pick up due to having no natural biological immunity. Nor would the dinos have much internal protection to ward off diseases carried by parasites such as ticks, fleas, and mosquitoes.

Geographical Places Fact vs. Fiction: Most of the locales in the Cretaceous Chronicles exist. Heart Butte, Montana is located on the southern border of the Blackfeet Indian Reservation. The Camels Hump Lookout Tower in Montana's Lolo National Forest exists to this day, and was never brought down by a meteorite. The River of No Return Wilderness in Idaho is real, as are the Roundup Rodeo at the Park County Fairgrounds in Livingston, Montana and the Zootown Music Festival in Missoula. Tally Lake is real and accurately described as one of the deepest lakes in Montana, reaching depths of 495 feet. Mount Bennett Air Force Base is fiction modeled on Mountain Home Air Force Base in southwestern Idaho. Gilliam's Guidepost Ranch is also an invention, based on other ranches in the area. Vista Hills Custom Taxidermy is a fabrication, a blend of two other taxidermy shops in the Columbia Falls, Montana area.

Odds and Ends: Helicopters are fascinating but complex flying machines. They were a critical mode of transportation in the Cretaceous Chronicles, as they were in three of my early novels (*King of the Hobos, Hobo Jingo,* and *To Touch Infinity*). Former Vietnam pilot Mike Jimison schooled me in helicopter flight and operations, lending me his expertise for those early novels. I carried Mike's informative helicopter tutelage over into this trilogy. Also, I did a lot of research on Blackfeet spirituality and customs, which lent credibility to the traditional Blackfoot funeral and Native American foods enjoyed at the Gilliams' Thanksgiving feast.

So there you have it, Valued Reader. I want to thank you for taking the time to read the trilogy. I had fun taking you on this journey.

Acknowledgments

It takes a village to produce a science fiction trilogy. I have many villagers to thank.

First and foremost, my most heartfelt thanks go my lovely wife, Cheryl, without whom the Cretaceous Chronicles trilogy would not exist. She believed in the concept from the beginning, back when the narrative was but an unformed embryo of scattered scientific ideas. An award-winning technical writer, Cheryl is a very skilled developmental editor who kept the technology honest, and my female and child characters true. Her efforts greatly improved all three books.

Next I want to thank graphic designer, Carole Maugé-Lewis, for another exceptional cover design, the sixth outstanding cover she has produced for me. Also, adding fantastic flair to the *Endangered Species* cover is internationally celebrated paleoartist Raúl Martin's striking illustration, "Deinosuchus vs. Albertosaurus." The first time I saw the painting, I knew I had to have it for my front cover. It perfectly captures the excitement and danger of the critical scene at Tally Lake. Thank you, Raúl for trusting me with your beautiful artwork.

Moving on, so many others to thank for their support of the Cretaceous Chronicles. The following folks helped make the trilogy a success in a million-and-one different ways. My apologies if I forgot anyone . . . Beth Ahola, Lisa Barker, Debbie Bassett, Jessie Bradford, Sally Brazelton, Ina Castillo, Katherine Crowe, Jan Fredrickson, Victoria Fulenwider, Teresa Gale, Jim Garrison, Robyn Hercey, Jade, Jessica Joel, Jos, Lisa Klemens, Jo Lee, Ronnie Lee, Mark Leinweber, Michael M, Carlos and Alecia Markyna, Crystal McLanahan, Scott Meredith, Len Myers, Mike Neimeyer, Nathaniel Orsburn, Melanie Pendleton, Nero Phillips, Quinten Pierce, Barbara R., Jacob Ray, Tracy Rud, Ashley

Schleicher, David and Julie Shockley, Cass Spooner, Robert Stevens, Jeffrey Thomas, Bonnie Turner, Cale Turnipseed, David Vorster, Mary W.S., Alba Wolfgang, Ashley Yeager, Kahri Yeager.

Thank you, one and all. And now I must move on to explore new storybook frontiers. I hope you will join me again on future literary journeys.

Jeff Dennis

Loganville, Georgia

April 16, 2026

About the Author

Jeff Dennis is the former editor-in-chief/publisher of the award-winning speculative fiction magazine, *Random Realities.* He is the author of seven novels and a short story collection.

jeffdennisauthor.com

jeff@jeffdennisauthor.com

www.ingramcontent.com/pod-product-compliance
Lightning Source LLC
LaVergne TN
LVHW050912080826
845145LV00001B/66

* 9 7 8 0 9 9 1 1 8 7 1 9 5 *